I0726360

NOTHING PERSONAL

Carol A. Strickland

Copyright © 2018 by **Carol A. Strickland**

All rights reserved. No part of this publication may be reproduced, distributed or transmitted in any form or by any means, without prior written permission.

Published by Carol A. Strickland
www.CarolAStrickland.com

Publisher's Note: This is a work of fiction. Names, characters, places, and incidents are a product of the author's imagination. Locales and public names are sometimes used for atmospheric purposes. Any resemblance to actual people, living or dead, or to businesses, companies, events, institutions, or locales is completely coincidental.

Book Layout © 2017 BookDesignTemplates.com
Cover illustration by Travis Hanson. Cover design and interior illustration by Strick.

Nothing Personal/ Carol A. Strickland. -- 1st ed.
ISBN Print edition 978-1-941318-22-5
ISBN Print Ingramspark edition 978-1-941318-24-9
ISBN Digital edition 978-1-941318-23-2
ISBN Digital Ingramspark edition 978-1-941318-25-6

1

The glare outside made silhouettes of the three strangers until the tavern door closed behind them. Here were new faces for me to add to my growing list of those to learn: two guys and one woman. All were late twenties, early thirties, and thus not the usual student clientele.

They gave the room a good look-over as if they'd never been there before, then chose one of the back booths. The shorter guy steered the woman with a hand low on her back, not quite cradling her rump–but it was close.

The mini-skirted brunette wrinkled her nose at him in cute flirt mode. I heard a shrill giggle that was decidedly inconsistent with her age. To judge from his expression, Shorty ate up the little-girl act.

I nabbed some menus and strolled over to distribute them as the three settled laptops on their table. "Afternoon," I said. "I'm Tam. First time here? What can I get y'all to start off?"

Shorty wore leather pants so tight he couldn't sit straight. Instead he balanced on one hip. He lifted an expensive-looking set of sunglasses by the corner so he could actually see me, and gave one of those wide smiles that don't reveal any teeth. "Tam," he said. "Short for?"

"Tamara." Customers didn't need the last name. I clicked the top of my pen, let it hover over my order pad, and waited with a pleasant, professional expression as Giggler gave Shorty a pouty kind of frown that might have looked adorable on someone ten years younger.

"Eat, drink and be merry," Shorty said, the demi-smile still in place, "for Tamara we die."

"Clever." I tried to sound like I meant it as Giggler made like that had been the most hie-larious joke in the history of the world. Shorty gave her an approving squeeze.

"You might like today's specials." I pointed the pen at the entry wall, which had been painted to be a giant blackboard. My boss, Greene, not only made hearty sandwiches but also drew cartoons to liven up the listing.

Shorty took the hint and ordered for himself and the Giggler, plus sandwiches from the menu. Then his phone sang at him and he paid attention to that. Giggler squinted at it a moment before busying herself by looking around the dim room. I got the feeling she did that so she wouldn't need to squint and thus create wrinkles. Time was her enemy.

I'd almost forgotten the taller guy. He had curly dark hair and a turtle-ish air about him, probably because of his thick turtleneck sweater. Over it he wore one of those tweedy jackets with professorial elbow patches that you only see in old movies. There were also tan cords involved, and boots that were a little pointier than I was used to seeing, like he'd been cloistered in some library since the Sixties. His shoulders hunched as he tucked his chin into his turtleneck. Maybe he wanted to be invisible. He was doing a good job.

In my short time here I'd found Greene's Tavern tended to attract a homogeneous crowd. No, I don't mean they were gay; they were just pretty much all the same. Undergrads and graduate students. The university's west edge was just eight blocks of industrial brick buildings away. They came here to learn about adulthood by drinking themselves stupid during the day and getting throwing-up sick at night, with a side of cheese fries and jalapeños. They usually abided by the uniform: too-large jeans and tees–usually emblazoned with some profanity and/or sexual innuendo–with maybe a baggy sweatshirt if it were as cool as it was today. They were walking piles of dirty laundry.

But professor-guy's pants looked as if an iron had actually touched them. Maybe his maid did his laundry, or a dutiful wife. More likely it was his mom, in whose basement he lived.

The professor had produced a very used paperback from his laptop bag and proceeded to open it. This was also a usual activity, but one of which I approved. It proved that somewhere in that male head lurked something beside just a lizard brain. Or maybe it's a reptile brain. That part way down at the back of the head, you know?

Of course there's that other male brain, the one waaay down but in the front that guys usually think with too. Most of the guys who came by here only used that part for thinking and thus thought by doing so they were more attractive to the females in the bar, in which group they always included me though I was a couple years older than the usual college-gal crowd.

But only a couple. Maybe one.

In a few years these same guys would be making a dollar for every eighty cents I did. Someday I must sit down and figure out how to acquire just enough testosterone-brain so I could bring in the big bucks, too. I hoped that wouldn't require growing a penis. Penises are dandy, but I didn't want one of my own.

By the time I reminded myself of the professor's presence, he'd clipped a small light to the book so he could read it in the corner's relative gloom. The most his male companion read was the laminated beer list. I mentally checked him off as typical college ape of the older variety. I doubted the Giggler could read at all.

So I turned to the Professor. He looked up at me and blinked as if I'd materialized from another dimension. Maybe he was one of those geniuses who think so hard they get lost in their own worlds and don't notice the one on the atmospheric side of their eyeballs. "Ah," he said, and something just in that "ah" sounded British. The rest of the sentence confirmed it. "Right. Some ale, if you please."

"You have a preferred brand?"

His forehead creased as if the problem were something Einstein had missed. "Yes, well." He thought some more and finally a light dawned. "Why don't you choose for me?"

"You trust me?"

"I always trust beautiful women," he purred, and damned if it didn't sound like a pickup line. BritSpeak puts such a classy twist to things, doesn't it? I mean, when you can understand them at all.

"You three with the university?" I asked conversationally. Shorty and Giggler didn't really hit me as academic types.

"Just checking out things here," he replied.

"Student or faculty?"

He gave a little British hiccup that I interpreted as a chuckle. "I'm always a student of human nature."

They must teach those lines in British schools. I figured him for a nerd's nerd. He had that kind of blank look around the eyes, like he didn't quite get the world. Nerds have that new rep of being the Go-To Guys when you want an electronics genius who makes seven figures but still adores tinkering on your little home setup for free. Yeah, right.

He needed a haircut, though. That mop of curls looked like a bad wig. Still, the rest of him was as cute as a bug.

I shifted sideways so he could see the blackboard better since he hadn't discovered his own menu. "Anything to eat from our specials, or do you want a few minutes? I can recommend the ham and cheese on sunflower bread. It's all local."

He just blinked again at me and I could tell when he saw the board. "Food, too? Ah…" And this time there was yearning in that "ah." "I haven't had a ham and cheese sammie in ages."

"We also have wheat, rye, pumpernickel…" I went through the mantra. When he'd decided on everything, which included two pickles and french fries (with mayo, ick), I trotted off to transfer the order into the POS and then repeat it all verbally to Greene, who never paid attention to the POS. Evie saw to the drinks, and by the time I returned with the sandwiches, Shorty and the Giggler were involved with each other. The Professor was almost too engrossed in his novel to notice his "sammie."

The last wave of the lunch gang finally arrived. I had a chance to chat with regulars like Jim the Accounting TA–talk about your nerds–and Ronnie and

Brady, the jocks who were too good on the field to flunk out. They flirted with me even though they'd already learned it wouldn't get them anywhere. Hey, I've got my standards, though I'd had to lower them lately due to having had to start over in a new town. Since they weren't going to get any other kind of thrill from me, I regaled them with a story about one of my mother's more heroic exploits.

I enjoy telling those as much as people get a kick out of hearing them. Their eyes widen and their mouths gape when I tell of her and her partner and the big drug bust in Durham, and they always say, "You must be proud of her."

I sure am. She'll always be my hero.

Karen stopped by just to give me the latest on what she'd heard Evie was up to with Greene. It was nice that we were getting to be friends.

Over time my circle of support had disappeared. Dad had died five years ago, and the people who were friends with our family because of him gradually drifted away. Then Mom died just last year, and none of her friends were really that attached to me other than in the theoretical "one of our own" kind of way that the police department has. I sold the house, paid off the last of Dad's medical bills, and had a trickle left to finish a degree while I rented a two-by-four apartment that seemed so far from home, though it was only in the next town. My BFFs had dispersed to adult lives in different states.

Let me tell you: Twitter is a lousy way to keep up real relationships.

Professor Britguy was beginning to look pretty good to me. He and his friends stayed a long time while I tried to figure how to sound him out alone. Eventually they got out the laptop and huddled over what must have been an enthralling game of Dungeons and Dragons. Giggler cheered on her man. Shorty kept looking up from the screen to glance around the room as if he were expecting someone else. Then again, maybe he was waiting for the place to clear out so Giggler could duck under the table to give him a little, ah, personal service.

After his own more vague perusals of the room, Prof. Britguy would give a quick nod and keep doing whatever one does in those dungeons. Knowing guys, it probably involved innocent virgins. Or maybe not-so-innocent working chicks in chain mail bikinis. My skin chafed just imagining it.

Eventually Shorty and the Giggler left, leaving the Professor with the bill and laptop. He reached into his pocket a while later and plunked a small stack of green paper on top of the ticket. It included a nice tip. As I came by to pick it up, he jerked to full consciousness, unobtrusively hiding the screen from me. Now I wondered: porn?

"Pardon me?" he asked, and I admit his little accent was too adorable for words.

"I said it's a shame you didn't try one of our local brews."

Those weak eyes sparked and he gave me a real smile. Somewhere there was a girlfriend in his life, I was sure. It turned out he wasn't through. He stayed in his booth and indeed sampled a couple of the county's brands. There was also another sammie to be eaten over the next hour or so, more pickles, a slice of Sherry's pecan pie so he never got drunk, and zero personal info, no matter how I tried to wheedle. Maybe he just didn't understand my subtle hints. Men can be so obtuse.

Eventually he closed his laptop, plunked another pile of bills on the table (earning him the booth for a while more), and settled back to make real headway in his book while I gave up the chase.

With the long afternoon, the customers thinned out. I opened my own book. I was taking the Firefighter II course nights, and my busy life only allowed me this time for focused study. From a favorite side booth I kept one eye on my customers and the other on my text.

Once he knew that was My Spot, Greene had let me hang a couple framed news clippings at the booth detailing my mom's more spectacular police cases. He said it celebrated local people, which customers appreciated. I'd thumb-tacked her obit next to them, not because I wanted to be depressed but because it was a damn fine obituary and said everything about my mom that I wanted to remember her by. Plus it gave customers someone to toast to. She would have liked that.

Dad had died a hero too when I was in high school. He was a firefighter, and he suffered complications from an injury incurred in the line of duty. For two years he never left his hospital room. He came home just long enough to pass away in his own bed.

Eventually Prof. Britguy was the only customer left. Greene and Evie took their late lunch break, leaving me in charge of the place. The background music settled into a muted drone.

With a sudden exclamation and a curse, Britguy slapped his book shut and jumped up from his table. Must have been a helluva plot point. I stretched my shoulders and then disengaged from my text to check his tab for that last drink. He trotted over as I assumed the position at the cash register.

"Terribly sorry about this. Nothing personal," he said as he reached into his jacket for his wallet. For a moment I wondered why he was sorry before I saw the hand emerge with a shiny plastic oval.

It was flat on the bottom with a curve to the top, and was less than the size of a drink coaster. He pointed it at me, delicately held between thumb and crooked index finger.

"I'm supposed to be afraid of your mouse?" I asked drily though my insides clenched almost unbearably tight. My mother wouldn't have been afraid, not of Britguy, so I wasn't going to be either.

My question put him off. He double-taked on his whatever-it-was he held. "Does this look like a mouse?"

Brits! "Computer mouse."

He blinked twice. "Mouse. For a computer. I must have missed something."

His eyes moved as if he were trying to figure it out and I stretched my foot to the right to trigger the silent alarm Greene had installed after a robbery last year. Got it.

"Oh, computer mouse. Right. It's been a while," he apologized and then brandished the thing in my face. "Get to the back. You do have an exit there, don't you? Your coworkers disappeared so I'm assuming that's how they went."

"You'll have to do better than a mouse." I stalled for time. The closest police station wasn't that far away, but who knew where the nearest police car was? I didn't see any kind of barrel in the thing. It wasn't big enough for a combustion chamber or batteries to power a taser mechanism.

Britguy took a moment to point the thing to my right. Following his aim, a line of bottles and glasses exploded. The shrapnel melted into nothingness before it could reach us.

When my brain started functioning again I was three feet to the left of where I'd been. Thank god for reflexes. But they weren't fast enough to deliver me from this crazy Mad Scientist Britguy.

He waved the weapon at me. "This is for your own safety," he said. "My… computer… signaled an imminent disaster. Please proceed to the rear. I believe we must make haste."

The brick warehouse across the street exploded.

When people say "exploded," you don't usually think of things going pop-pop-pop-KAPOW!!!! with KAPOW being the biggest noise you're ever going to hear in your life, even louder than that THX notice they used to play at the beginnings of movies. I had to grab onto the bar to stand upright, though it wobbled on its own from the roar.

The smoked glass tavern windows shattered inward. A few of the front ceiling lights followed suit. Something big hit the car parked just outside at the curb, and its security system went off. It honked almost mutely against the noise that was the explosion.

Apparently just one explosion wasn't enough. The warehouse kept exploding. A fireball cannoned out of one of the remaining windows across the street, followed quickly by another and another. They landed on the sidewalk outside the tavern.

I huddled under the back of the bar alongside Britguy. The lights went out, although the inferno outside kept everything lit all too well. Another fireball threw a missile of some kind through the tavern's largest, now-empty window. Britguy shoved me to the side, heaving himself after me as it landed in what was– but never would be again– his booth.

"Follow me!" I scrambled to the exit doors, Britguy cursing behind me. Bricks began to pelt the bar. I heard tables and chairs splintering as the fire alarm squalled.

Back in the storeroom we stood up, though Britguy kept his hand on the back of my head. Sounds of destruction from the front didn't cease.

And then the real thunder began.

It had been loud before, but now came Armageddon. Deep, rolling blasts followed each other, punctuated by a primal din that announced the end of the world.

The connecting door to the front room blasted open behind us even as we reached the back exit.

"Run!" Britguy shouted, like I was an idiot. I grabbed my coat and purse on the way out– it didn't take a nanosecond– as I fumbled for my cell.

911 got their call as we burst through the back door. We were joined by people from the businesses to either side. Yelling, cursing, crying… with a little blood here and there. The air whiffed of sulfur and industrial solvents, just enough to be a hint that there might be more coming, which would not be good for human lungs.

A wave of heat rolled through the alley like someone had opened a pizza oven, then closed it quickly. A section of air visibly distorted by heat waves passed us. At the north end of the alleyway a less intense field of distortion lay lazily close to the ground.

Britguy said something that sounded like an expletive. A Russian one? German? Then he said, "It must be koritzo."

Chorizo? I decided to take my leave of Britguy right after I snapped a pic on my phone in case the cops wanted an ID later. The cooler end of the alley seemed my best route. Everyone else came to the same conclusion and we all ran off.

Except Britguy.

Damn him anyway. "Hey!" I yelled at him. "This way!"

He spared me a glance but went back to eying the hot end of the alley as if he were planning to peek at the fire.

Jesus, I just have too many ethics. I went back, grabbed him by the sleeve and pulled. "What are you, some kind of fire bug?"

He pulled back and damn it all, just because he was male he had more strength than I. I kicked him hard in the shin to show my determination and pulled again. My firefighter dad had had a slew of horror stories of gawkers who got in the way. We didn't need one here.

"They'll have to rescue enough victims as it is without an extra idiot," I shouted kindly and manhandled him out of the alley toward safety. He didn't fight me, but he didn't exactly go peaceably even though he was limping.

We were the only ones left back here. At the cool end of the alley we saw that a constant bombardment of bricks and debris now fell like a waterfall onto what remained of the street pavement. The bricks were beginning to pelt our alleyway as well, due to the rapidly-diminishing shelter of buildings crumbling between us and the conflagration. Now it looked as if the other end was the safer one even if it was Death Valley hot. We might get a little burnt but at least we wouldn't be pancaked. That is, if we could make it there without getting killed along the way.

We had a couple close calls. Ethics be damned, my duty to him was over. I deposited him on Lloyd Street and made my way as fast as I could– hot! hot!– down all the way to the intersection of Weaver and Main, where I could get a good view without being in danger. I arrived just as two police cars screamed to a stop a half-block from me. A fire truck slammed their brakes farther down.

I was going to ask the cops if they needed any semi-trained help, but the scene was mesmerizing.

I mean, the line of brick warehouses that had faced the tavern was now an actual volcano, a rising cone of debris that spewed streams of glowing lava and building materials through the air and out into the street. Odd spots of cool purple dotted the air above the inferno. The ground shook under our feet. The storm drain ten feet from us glowed orange from within. Even from my position three long blocks away from the main event, I could feel the heat, especially through my shoes' soles.

Had anyone been in the warehouses? There must have been. I prayed that all the people around the blast had been able to get out.

What the hell had happened? That was just some warehouse, not a hazardous waste disposal site. Or a nuclear reactor.

I remembered hearing of that volcano in Mexico that had sprung up overnight. But volcanoes give warning: earthquakes and such. We were in an earthquake-free zone. The closest major fault was way down in Charleston.

I jumped when Britguy appeared beside me. He whistled low and said, "Fracken die wizzult," or something like that and, "That's new."

I turned. "What, you know what it is?"

And did a double-take. Now he was dressed in some kind of white hazmat suit, a protective hood with face shield hanging over the back of his shoulders. When had he–?

Despite the imminent volcano, I considered calling a cop over to check him out, but the cops were busy rescuing a huddle of three people trying to escape. I started to get antsy about not helping out. Mom would have if she were here.

But what could I do? This was not a fire that could be fought. The volcano was building in size. Smoke had blackened the sky. The cops were handling the only refugees. I stood paralyzed and asked myself if the cops would truly welcome an amateur's bumbling efforts. Instead of helping I'd just get in the way.

Three blocks down the firefighters were assuming their standby positions, taking measure of the inferno. They looked as if they'd sized it up the same as me, a lost cause. The only plan was to keep surrounding structures from going up as well.

As a rank amateur, my considered opinion was: run for the hills.

I paced with frantic energy from side to side of our sidewalk. If I ran I'd be a coward. If I stayed I'd be in the way. The only real thing I could do was get some information out of Britguy.

He spared me a glance but went back to his observations.

He seemed fascinated by the inferno. It occurred to me that firebugs often liked to watch their work, but here I was, too. Then again, I was a firefighter in training. I'd never seen anything like this.

Britguy and I decided at the same time to retreat another block. He didn't leer at the fire or watch it with wide eyes or a smile like I imagined firebugs to do. Instead he seemed to be studying it, taking in the entire environment.

"You some kind of chemistry whiz?" I shouted at him above the din. "You know what that stuff is?" Another street grate showed a glowing river making its way through the sewers. Again with the weird purple sparks. I shuffled away from the extra heat.

Britguy grunted.

"Not good enough." I pulled on his white sleeve. "If you have an idea of the hazardous materials, you need to talk to the fire department."

He shook his head. "It's beyond anything they can handle," he said. "They'll just have to wait until it burns itself out." Then he scratched his chin. "I think."

Another explosion rocked the air, making us bounce in place and duck as small debris rocketed toward us out of the next closer block of buildings. A window across the street shattered. I was surprised there'd been an intact one remaining.

Mount St. Helens let loose another fireball from wherever she had enough structure to form one. Despite the smoke-darkened street, I could see that every building within two blocks around the conflagration was now a mass of rubble. The crumbling was slowly heading our way.

And yet a tiny part of my head was functioning on different problems. Poor Greene. He'd rebuild somewhere. In the meantime, I was out of work.

I programmed that mental section to setting a reminder to check the internet and local classifieds in the morning, and to make sure my go-on-interview outfit was presentable. I was also firming up my description of Britguy for the cops just in case he decided to run. And planning my own route out of here. Multitasker supreme, that's me.

"Britguy, what's beyond what they can handle?" I asked behind the neckline of my shirt, which I'd pulled up to form a makeshift mask. I'd draped my coat over my head and shoulders as spark protection. I didn't think we both could stick around here much longer. Buildings were starting to disintegrate down our block and the air was getting really putrid within the fog of glowing ashes. From the hazy look of things down the road, the fire department was coming to the same conclusion and quickly packing up from where they'd just unpacked.

"Britguy?" He had the nerve to look insulted.

"Sorry. Hey, Mister, what's beyond what they can handle?"

He thought a moment. "Max," he finally said.

Damn it, evading my question.

"Okay, Max. What's beyond what they can handle?" Wait– was the street pavement melting? Closer to the volcano its texture became smooth and shiny, and then rivulets formed into black pools. The surface slumped. Part of the sidewalk tumbled into a morass of a trench.

"Nothing you'd understand."

Despite what my senses told me, that made me mad. Did he think that just because I was female my little brain couldn't fathom big-boy matters? I must have growled, because he glanced at me sharply.

"Try me," I said. "In English. As we get out of here."

That brought the ghost of a smile to his Britguy face. He started off at a brisk pace and I matched him, scrambling through the shifting, steaming landscape. "There's no English term for what's going on." He didn't look nerdy any more. There was a sharpness about him, an awareness of a larger situation that nerds don't possess. He reached behind his neck to untangle his hood and facemask. "Let's just say that it's completely illegal on all worlds."

Britguy– Max– crossed above the melting block to Roberson and began to elbow his way through a small gathering of idiot gawkers, away from the encroaching destruction.

"Hey!" I called, and pushed to catch up. "If you know what's happening, you have to talk to the authorities. What do you know about this? Did you have something to do with it?"

He harumphed. "If I had done this, it would have been a bloody f– more subtle."

"So you do know something. What was it? Some kind of super-crack house?"

For that he paused and granted me a withering stare. I shut up… for a moment.

"Okay, Mr. Bigshot," I said, "you tell me. I'll tell the authorities so they know what they're getting into. Don't want your name mentioned? Okay, I won't." Couldn't tell what I didn't know.

With the rapidly– very rapidly!– dispersing gawkers we made good time heading in the opposite direction of where everyone was looking. I badgered Max as much as I could, but he kept on at a brisk trot. If he really was a nerd, he was one of those spooky ones. But I was beginning to think that maybe he wasn't. I didn't know what he *was*, but I was working on it.

At our distance, we heard the next explosion and the answering shouts of the spectators simultaneously. Max muttered angrily.

"Didn't catch that," I said.

"I was merely commenting on the operational safety of the organization behind this," he answered. "Even with minimal equipment they should have been able to avoid this. They're stockpiling something new, for it to have broken through the shields like this."

"Shields?"

He turned to give the far-off scene a final assessment. A pit the size of a football field had swallowed my former place of employment. "Obviously they're not working," he said. "Good thing my sensors spotted the danger in time, or else we'd both be dead. I wonder why their fail-safes didn't trigger. They must have had some for all the weaponry."

"Weaponry?" I'm afraid I squeaked.

"Mm. Contraband type, but this–" He squinted. "This the system couldn't handle. It must be new. It's got to be stopped at the source of supply."

"Are you a cop?" He didn't have cop vibes. That accent– "A spy?"

"Oh yes, I'm a spy and I'm telling you all this," he snapped as we rounded a corner onto Prince Street. It was deserted, a distribution center already closed for the coming weekend. Thank goodness.

Another blast boomed down the street we'd just left, and a tremendous gust of wind came with it.

Max's hair slid to the left. He gave it an angry tug and the entire thing came off: a wig, over short blond hair that stuck close to his head like hat hair all over. He pulled up his hood, its face mask flapping above, unsecured.

A little stupid bug in my brain finally began to scream, "Danger, Will Robinson!" at the situation. Strange man, empty neighborhood, volcano, wig, hazmat suit. Final straw time. I slowed down. Maybe I could just call 911 again from home and give them Max's picture, let the cops pick him up for questioning. On the sly I angled to take a full-on cell pic of him.

But as I did that, something appeared in the air. Not high above the town, but just below the three-story height of the building in front of us, poof, it was there.

Blazing brick projectiles trailed across the sky behind as it hovered over the street. It was long as two railroad cars, narrow as a street lane and a half, and I could only really see it because of the reflections on its metallic exterior, which was overlaid with things that caused those reflections to distort this way and that.

Suddenly a bank of lights ringed the bottom of it and it settled to a landing.

"Holy shit, it's a UFO!"

Max the unwigged Britguy turned to me, his look of disdain punctuated by pursed lips and one tweaked eyebrow. "It is not," he declared. "It is a Nucleon 350-B model Brane-rider with multi-generational gravity drive. It has Z-44 prangles and a five-star hemiquad. Extended luxury interior with custom passenger comfort stations and emblet-quality climate-control ecosystem."

No, it was a UFO.

The air turned yellow-green– some damned exhaust system that thing had! Or did the color come from behind us, from the destruction? I choked. Choked bad. It was as if I'd dunked my head in a vat of industrial solvent with a pure acid chaser. I couldn't catch my breath. It felt like my lungs were melting, but my eyes were doing the same thing.

"Bloody hell," I heard Max say behind his face shield just before everything went black.

2

It was a slow day at the tavern. Most of the regulars hadn't come in yet, but they would. As it was, I had some free time to study. I was taking night courses to get my first-level accreditation as a Station Safeties Systems technician. On top of those I was still struggling through Conversational Lingua, and devoted most of my weekends to EMT Basics.

It was tough learning all the different emergency treatments for aliens.

I looked up just in time to see Kreeger crook several phalanges at me as s/he settled into her/his favorite spot next to the window that looks out onto the street. Hers/his was a booth with a wide, encircling bench and pillows so almost any species could sit in comfort. I said "almost." Being a bolink, Kreeger set up on the bare floor, after positioning her/his lower body into a triangular seat. It gave her/him a great view of the traffic. I smiled not just because s/he was a good customer. Kreeger's a good ol' gal. Or guy. I made my way to her/him.

"What's on the menu today?" s/he asked in that quavery voice that reminded me of Vincent Price in drag. Of course Vincent wasn't a bolink: eight feet of solid, carapaced rolly-bug stature. If you rolled her out flat I guessed s/he'd look like a huge, quilted tongue depressor that was thick for its size. S/he had dozens of short arms and legs lining her/his sides that tended to work together but could, at times, work separately. A few were larger and longer than the others and used independently more often. S/he usually "walked" in an undulating wave that quickly got her/him where s/he wanted to go.

I'd seen a bolink in a bar fight once. He (or she) heaved him/herself about, sometimes curling him/herself into a hoop, and saurs rebounded from his (or her) armored back as if s/he'd been a bulldozer.

But Kreeger didn't have a violent bolink bone left in her/his leathery, violet-tinged body. It was just odd s/he'd ask for the menu offerings today because s/he almost never ordered anything but her/his regular meal with her/his drinks. It must be that time of season for her. Or him.

Kreeger went way back with the space station. S/he had helped weld the final spokes in place even as the first starter spores arrived for her (I give up) farm down on Level 24. Nowadays she had three kids and handfuls of grandkids and great-grandkids who helped her. I couldn't figure out if they were boys or girls either. They tended to wobble back and forth as the year progressed, or at least their coloring changed. And I couldn't find if there was any Mr. Kreeger. Maybe that would be a Mrs. Kreeger. Maybe Kreeg spat out kids all by herself.

She could sure spit out a story about the Old Days before things got all civilized here and often a woman had to protect her fungi with her own gun, since the local sheriff was often too busy with hooligans and pirates.

Sometimes I got the impression that Kreeger spun her tales a little too crazy to be true. If I sniffed at some of 'em, she'd rattle off a deep Vincent Price chuckle and spin something else that just might have, maybe, really happened to someone on some station somewhere, sometime, though she placed herself in the role of the rugged leading man. Or woman.

And she always carried a valise. It was made of some kind of leather or faux version, and it carried her seeds or spores or whatever. She'd worked long years to develop her crops, cross-pollinating and whatever it is really sharp farmers do. This was her family's future: next year's crop and the one after that and after that. I guess the years of having to defend her land made her a bit possessive of it. No one touched that valise but her.

I reeled off the day's choices and recommended Sonny's open-faced curd sandwich with grilled moss that just happened to come from the Kreeger farm. Smart girl; Kreeger took it. Sonny grilled one helluva moss. Tasted like steak. Plus Sonny said he cooked love into his food, or at least a laugh or two. He was always joking around and his boisterous laughter often rang through the place, when he wasn't singing.

Kreeger complimented me on getting the "th's" right on my adverbs. They're tricky. Sometimes you use the hard "th" and sometimes the soft, depending on the sentence's emphasis. I felt a little ping of triumph that was even better than a tip (though I took the tip, too).

That's another reason I liked Sonny's Brewery and Grill. Besides all the fascinating folk who came through, it allowed me to practice my conversational Lingua with people who were usually too mellow to take offense for any linguistic insult I might accidentally offer. Plus Sonny had a sign next to the front door that asked people to be patient with us. It assured them that we were all undergoing rigorous linguistic training. It implied that extra tipping was encouraged.

The place employed a lot of new immigrants. We were cheap labor. Immigrants were an important source of manpower for the station. It provided minimum wages for everyone, but even those went only so far. You needed shelter, air, water, furniture, a basic spacesuit or at least emergency wear, dishes… None of it was frills. Most people understood; most people tipped.

Though I had my basics by now, I saved every credit I could get my hands on. If I ever figured out where I was– in relation to Earth, I mean– I'd need to buy a ticket home. Who knew how much that would cost?

Britguy hadn't left me with any info on that front, but at least he hadn't left me completely helpless. I'd awakened in hospital with only the underwear that I'd had on and a half-dissolved set of outer clothing, plus my earrings, Mom's necklace that I'd been wearing, and a few items from my purse and coat pockets that had made it through with me, all packed in a little box. From the state of the clothing everyone knew that something very caustic had breezed in on us that day. Judging from the state of my skin, lungs and eyes, and the fact that I was suddenly bald all over, that caustic had been damned fast-acting.

But I'd also been left an audio player with English-to-Lingua lessons, and a short note from Max the doctors couldn't decipher.

It had been long weeks before I'd been able to see so much as a blur, longer months before I'd drawn a deep breath. Most of the time I had only confusion and the audio lessons to keep me company. Using my halting vocabulary, I lied my way into getting a set of blue eyes– crystal blue, you should see 'em, even though they took an extra two months to grow in– to replace my melted brown ones. And my hair finally grew back, thick and black as it ever was, widow's peak and all, including two eyebrows that really wanted to intermingle, just like they had before those laser treatments back home. I now worked daily to keep them apart.

The note? It was in English. "You're on Port Malabar. Have a nice life." It was signed merely "Max." And you'll recall that it was several months before I could read it. Thanks sooo much for the detailed explanation, Max, you slime.

I wondered how I'd arrived here. Wherever I was. Out in the middle of nowhere, in a galaxy that was a spiral but not necessarily the Milky Way. I'd seen star maps, but no point of reference labeled "Earth."

Max Britguy was nowhere to be found.

He'd disappeared. He'd dropped me off in a stasis box– that's a coffin-like gizmo that freezes time (instead of the actual body. You freeze that, and you cause cell-deep damage) until medics can work on a grievous injury. These particular medics worked at the hospital here on Port Malabar up on High Spokes. Max had informed them that the lump of flesh in the box was human. Then he took off.

Apparently none the worse for wear.

Thank god the station has a few hundred humans so the hospital staff had some idea of what they were working with. Out here humans are called "malac."

Most of that medical stuff had been two-plus years ago if my timekeeping was right. It was hard to tell. My sense of day length was cockeyed after spending months in hospital with nothing more to do than nap, listen to my lingua lectures, not freak out from all the big lizardy-birdish-bug types– the malac called them "saurs" to differentiate them from us (well, "saurs" is actually my translation of it, but close enough.)– and heal. The days seemed in the general area of a day in length, and the gravity of the station seemed right, depending on what level you were on. To tell you the truth, sometime early on I lost count completely and had to check in with the local malac to catch up.

The malac didn't know what to make of me. My skin was a shade or two too light and oh, how some of them were spooked by my glorious blue eyes! They all looked to be South Pacific types with maybe some Chinese and India-Indian thrown in. If I absolutely had to point a finger at a single place to name where they'd originated, I'd say Indonesia. Not that I was an expert or anything. None of 'em spoke English, but rather used a language I assumed was some kind of

Earth-speak. All spoke Lingua. They kindly kept tabs on me and tried little by little to bring me into their community. I was touched and grateful.

None of them claimed to know anything about Max Britguy.

And they had no idea where Earth was.

Port Malabar was a space station, but in my opinion it was too big to be called that. It was actually the area of a good-sized county or two. It was stuck in mid-nowhere, which it seemed was just where you wanted to be when you were launching for major distance, galactically speaking. We were a fair piece from the nearest star system. Call it a light-year, though I really didn't have any idea.

Anyway, ships came to our station and either launched for some equally remote port on the far side of eternity, or passengers and cargo transferred to local transport to get over to Bar-Tok, a cosmic cosmopolis that aforementioned light-year away. Bar-Tok was the capital of our local region and part of a larger political unit, the Confederation, whose capital, Nik-a-Dell, was, well, not that far away from us but not that near either.

How I wished I could have laid my hands on a map I could decipher!

For the nonce Port Malabar was big enough for me. The station's one of those wheel things, like in *2001: A Space Odyssey,* except that it stretches out along the axis maybe fifteen, twenty miles. Don't make me try to translate that into kilometers; I'm American. More than a dozen different levels expanded out from the core, with a few spaces between left for future construction. Plus those levels aren't fully complete. It's a here-and-there thing, with some agricultural sectors in full running condition, as are a lot of housing and business sectors. But it's still a lot of swiss cheese with room to expand.

The big city is spread among a good handful-plus of levels. We have parks and lakes and even some four-star bogs that the saurs love to luxuriate in. Temps are on the warm side, complicated by high humidity. Think of it as Florida without the bugs. Think of my hair as in a constant state of frizz.

There's about a zillion acres of farmland from fields to swamps, plus barer sections that service all the coming and going cargoes. Small shuttles dock within the hollow core where it's zero-gravity. Most of the inhabitants live around Level 21, give or take a level or two, where our spin gives us a comfy approximation of gravity.

The farther you are out from the core, the greater the grav– or centrifugal force– is. I can't get around on the farthest ring without mechanical help, but that level is just used for the more outré self-servicing kind of stuff the station needs.

Take Sonny's Brewery and Grill, where I worked. Level 21 was the main entrance to it, and the gravity was fine. It extended to Level 22 and when I went down there (half my shift), I noticed that things were a little heavier, though not uncomfortably so. I couldn't tell you which one was nearer to Earth normal.

I had a nice little place on Level 20. I figured that lighter gravity during sleep period could only help for longevity and fewer sags, right? But I made sure that I exercised on Level 22 so I didn't get lazy.

And I didn't get homesick much either. Of course, getting home was top on my "to do" list! I was pretty much obsessed with scheming how to do that, though after a few thousand dead ends, you go kind of numb, you know? Otherwise I went into deep dark depression less than once a month any more, and lately I'd been forgetting to do that.

Luckily I didn't leave anyone who depended on me back on Mama Earth. At least I happened to be wearing Mom's necklace the Day It Happened. That necklace was the most important thing I had left of her, the only luxury she'd allowed herself after Dad had died and the hospital had left us with all the bills insurance didn't want to handle. She never went out that she wasn't wearing it under her uniform. When she died I kept it. I didn't want her buried in it. It kept her alive for me as long as it was lying against my sternum.

When not studying, I spent my days plotting what I'd do when I got home. I missed reading the occasional romance novel, and wondered who the latest mega-moviestar was, and where I could find a good cheesecake– chocolate, please. Chocolate! Chocolate!– and mainly I wondered if there was a normal male human left in this sector who wouldn't mind an occasional but satisfying roll in the hay with someone like me.

Apart from that, Port Malabar was a fairly interesting place. Exploring it and taking all my courses were enough to keep me from freaking out about when I'd ever find my way home again.

Almost.

So I sat enthralled as Kreeger regaled me with yet another tale of frontier justice in space. She had big, bulgy eyes that looked like she had a bad thyroid. For emphasis she'd widen them so they stood out on her face like bubbles, then in a calmer place in her story, they'd withdraw to be flush with her other features. Such drama!

She downed three sandwiches that would have fed a small school class back in North Carolina. Other patrons had to be on guard as she flailed her arms and legs, her supple phalanges and their unique wave rhythm providing even more of a show. She'd bare all rows of pointy teeth during the fight scenes, and when someone back home might have punctuated punchlines with a rimshot on the drums, four larger legs would thump the floor, ba-DUM-bump!

When she slowed down from her recollections, she looked a little pained and I recalled how old she must be. Instead of complaining, she turned her saucer-sized eyes toward me and asked, "Found a way home yet?"

"Nope."

"Ah. Hss. Someday, someday. So what are you doing in the meantime?"

"Got that job interview tomorrow," I told her.

"Station Safeties?" She nodded. "Good for you. You study hard; they should hire you. You'll learn to like it around here."

"It's tough work. They might look at me–"

Kreeger shrugged, which involved the top of her patterned carapace rising and falling. That patterning was a lovely abstract painting that had been refreshed recently with bright colors. "Tiny malac. So you can't handle the heavy things. You'll take care of the little ones that we can't, no?"

No, I wasn't sure about that at all. I only knew that while I was stuck here, this was the job I wanted. What would I do if I wasn't hired? Sonny was great, but I didn't want to wait tables my entire life… or until I found a way home.

"They ask for a reference, you give them my name," she said. "Everyone knows me."

"Thanks, Kreeger."

I tried to display confidence as I sat down– or rather, climbed up– into a chair in a Station Safeties Systems HQ cubicle. I gave a full-toothed grimace and hissed, a friendly saur-type greeting, to Lt. Bree Grumble-Burp-Wheeze (close enough), my interviewer.

You don't have to remember the Grumble-Burp-Wheeze part. That's just formal stuff saurs include in a first meeting's introduction. I doubt if others even remember it much afterward. It has to do with which revered egg the family clan claims to be descended from a few hundred generations before, like a tribe of Israel. If you're impressed, or a cousin, maybe it would stick in your mind. Otherwise such information ordinarily isn't mentioned.

I had more a pressing matter to concentrate on: getting the job. This Bree saur lady didn't seem to be on my side from the get-go.

"As a malac…" Here she included the tiniest trace of a groan after the race name. I could see the Affirmative Action notice on my file in front of her. "How much can you lift?"

I showed her my latest gym results and didn't reveal that I'd strained myself in achieving those numbers. She looked at them and stuck out her thick saur lips about three inches. They undulated back and forth on her face in waves, demonstrating her unhappiness at the result.

Lt. Bree was a gimigol, which was the primary species hereabouts, all heft especially in their lower section, which is compounded by their large, dragging tails. Watch out for those; an angry gimigol can use it like a battering ram. They may look like lumbering, bow-legged louts on their short legs but their hands have six long fingers (one is opposable) which would do any piano proud, and they can bellow a song out to that piano with the best of 'em.

Gimigols are more a– Let me figure a scientific comparison. Oh, the heck with it. Picture Dino from the *Flintstones* only taller, say one and one-half Fred Flintstones high. Make the tail longer, less dog-like so it falls to the floor, and the entire body more Kong-ish. Sturdy stuff. Able to leap tall– no, they weren't any good at jumping, but boy, could they stop a locomotive if they wanted! Well, maybe a bus. And Lt. Bree wasn't pink or purple or whatever Dino was. She was a roasted brussel sprout green dressed in the natty SSS silver uniform that could take all kinds of damage.

I told her about my training on Earth for work that was comparable to beginning Station Safeties Systems. She looked doubtful. I showed her my Port

Malabar grades, explained the schedule I adhered to in order to up my skills since I'd arrived on the station.

Lt. Bree bobbed her fuchsia cranial carapace (it had to be dyed; nothing is naturally that color) to indicate speed it up, and I tried to fit as many words into the remainder of my appointment time as I could. Though the same info had been included on my application, I flashed certificates, showed her my citizenship application, gave her reports from my teachers and doctors.

"Your accent is terrible," was all she said to that.

"I'm putting in extra time on Lingua lessons. I'll have full certification soon." Time to pull out all the stops. "Kreeger said I could use her as a reference if that was needed. She and my neighbor help me with Lingua."

"Kreeger." Again the pursed lips. Lt. Bree's eyes darted to that Affirmative Action note a few more times. "I need to discuss this with my supervisor." She gave me a slow blink. I still hadn't figured what that meant. "A malac. Now, if I ran things…" Then she stood up.

"We'll be in contact one way or the other within a week," she said stonily.

I assumed I'd been dismissed and tried not to slide off the seat on my own sweat.

I shouldn't even hope that I'd get the job. I dragged myself home from the interview, trying not to obsess. There was so much other stuff I could obsess about, like Lingua school. If you wanted a good job anywhere here, you needed to speak well. My final proficiency tests were less than a year off. I knew how fast time could fly, especially when you were trying to get too many things done at once.

One of the things I'd have to do as a Station Safeties Systems Tech was to communicate crystal-clearly over the comm lines. My accent was still hard to understand in places, and there were lots of basic words that I stumbled over.

"Evening, Nuke," I said as I made my way up the walk to my door. That much of the language I had zero problem with.

"Evening." The sidewalk may have shaken a little at the low, booming register of his voice. Then again, it could have been my imagination.

Nuke was my neighbor, and yes, that name was not a translation. "Nuke." It fit him so well. We lived in a subsidized duplex on Level 20, just off the edges of the business district in a surprisingly homey neighborhood. Most of our neighbors were gimigols or doils, the two saur species that make up the vast majority of the station's population.

But Nuke was in a class all his own.

Where a gimigol will stand, oh, eight feet tall or so, Nuke stood at twelve-plus, the height of your average doil. Unlike a doil, Nuke didn't look like a Big Bird reject at the toy factory. He had been based on the Dino-like gimigol physiology, but genetically restructured. Half as wide as he was tall, he had longer legs than your average gimigol, and was packed with solid muscle. He also had an extra set of arms.

Nuke didn't like to discuss his past, but I'd heard he had been bred and raised to be a super soldier. He was deep blue, bulky as a pro wrestler on ultra steroids. Armored somewhat like a bollink, taloned like a doil, with a tail and heft of a gimigol, he could swear fluently in thirty languages– or so he claimed.

He terrified the other saurs on the station. He certainly did me, the first time I saw him. I'd walked up to my new apartment with my knapsack of mostly nothing on my back, and he had emerged onto the porch from his door. I came to a stop, looking up. And up. Homina homina…

For lack of anything else to do and since there was no way in hell I was going to give up this place, I bared my teeth and hissed at him in a friendly manner.

He'd been looking me over like his mere gaze could scour my flesh. Slowly he bared his mighty fangs and gave a roar of a hiss.

So he didn't like me, huh? I grimaced and did my best roaring hiss back.

"That's better," he growled. "You have a terrible accent."

Sometimes I think he scared himself, because every now and then he'd take a day off work just to meditate for hours in a remote section of the station, calm himself down. Then he would emerge again to repair whatever damage he'd done to his walls and then lounge in his chair on the porch, watching the world go by. Everyone else gave him a wide berth. A very wide berth.

Though I still couldn't tell most saurs from each other, except by general species and sub-species, Nuke was unique on the station. Maybe in the universe, I didn't know. But back in hospital when my new eyes started functioning, I'd found myself surrounded by scary saur creatures that had my regrowing hair constantly standing on end. I couldn't truthfully say that Nuke was particularly more frightening, except for his incredible bulk.

Because I was an immigrant, I was pretty far down on the ladder of importance in securing glam living quarters. Having a low-paying job for so long hadn't endeared me to the system. Nuke couldn't get a higher-level job, so he had to settle for subsidized housing, too. They found him this place, which had not been good news for the neighborhood. Who wanted to be a monster's neighbor?

I volunteered for the remaining space since it was conveniently located next to something I desperately wanted. More on that later. The place was modest only by saur standards. I found it spacious, airy and comfortable. Maybe a little empty, as I couldn't afford much furniture. I'd have paid a fortune for the same square footage back home.

Nuke and I got along fairly well. I didn't come with any preconceptions and never threw loud parties. We were both outsiders.

My neighbors to the east of the side path by my place were terrified of Nuke. They would hurry past our walk, not even looking up at the porch. They didn't mind me. They were a kind of gimigol, a smaller than normal type like Sonny. A married couple, Burdt and Shkarb. I met them when I'd admired the flowers in their little garden. A while after that Shkarb met me on the street with a pot of what I'll call begonias in her hand, and gifted them to me. I asked her over, tried to tell her she had nothing to fear from Nuke, but she shook her head vigorously.

"He's dangerous," she warned me.

I put the begonias in a pot on the deck railing. I loved those flowers.

Nuke worked in construction. Currently he had a job up on Level 16, where the new ring was going in. Every morning I knew to keep quiet because on the other side of the wall he'd be meditating before putting on his construction helmet, picking up a very large lunch box, and heading off to work.

This evening he was sitting in the rocking chair on the porch, drinking a beer and watching the foot traffic pass by beyond our front hedge. Vehicle roadways lay beyond the intersection down the block, but here it was pedestrians only. He had his huge feet up on the railing and the kind of dazed look that you get after a hard day.

"You had supper yet?" I asked. Nuke always seemed calmer if he had a full stomach. "I got some extra groceries."

"I'm fine."

After I'd put my own groceries away and managed a supper of my own, I sat on the porch in silence next to Nuke. He'd made a small version of his chair for me, and I'd shown him how to put on rockers. After that he'd altered his own quadruple-armed chair to rock as well.

It was peaceful out here. We had a great view of the neighbors as they made their way home. Our view was mainly to the north, up the station's axis. Our landscape curved upward away from us if you looked east or west, then was cut off by the level's ceiling. Because that ceiling was fairly high even by saur standards, and because of the humid atmosphere, things fuzzed up at a distance and thus didn't impart any claustrophobia. If you ever did get a cramped feeling, all you had to do was look either north or south, where it seemed like things went on forever. There were actually mammoth section breaks that divided the station, but those were maybe two miles from our place.

The level's light was dimming for our artificial version of dusk. Passersby gave Nuke a quick, nervous glance. Some newbies would squint to see Benny and then give a start before hurrying off.

Benny was Nuke's. He was a four-armed skeleton of either some vanquished enemy or beloved pet that Nuke had had back on whatever planet he was from. He kept it on a pedestal in the corner of the porch. Even when I tried to imagine that Benny was a mere Halloween decoration, it was disgusting.

To keep the heebie-jeebies away, I found or made different hats for those bones and rotated them depending on my mood. Some children's toys I'd found contributed eyes that could light up and blink in different colors on command. After that, Nuke had rigged a system that moved one of the skeleton's arms in three different rude configurations.

I'd named the thing "Benny," and Nuke had grunted but allowed it. Today Benny wore a cheery toboggan cap with a red pom-pom topper, though our climate was on the tropical side. His eyes weren't flashing; they only did so when Nuke was in a mood. An empty beer container was grasped in his lower left paw. I hadn't put it there.

We watched the saurs, Nuke and Benny and I, saw the jolts of fear as they spotted Nuke. They didn't even know him. Why, he wouldn't be the type to yell at kids if they played on our shared property. Of course, no kids ever did.

It was their loss. Over the past couple months, Nuke had helped me adjust some of the saur plumbing in my place to accommodate human physiology. Just the last week I'd gone over to his place to repair some Safeties Systems equipment that had futzed up on him. Studying for that job I'd hoped to get had come in handy.

"What's that?" I asked as a new species ambled by.

"That's a kalid. They like to keep to the upper levels, eighteen and fifteen in particular. They're jumpers." He mimed a kangaroo-like leap with his fingers in the palm of his same-side hand.

I tried to recall first aid techniques specific to kalids and didn't come up with anything. I'd have to ask at the next class. It was great that I had Nuke to explain the everyday to me. He didn't mind if I were completely ignorant of things the people out here grew up knowing through sheer osmosis of their familiar environment.

Of all the people, human or saur, on the station who could have been my neighbor, I think I lucked out getting Nuke.

I was so comfortable that I jumped when my timer beeped at me. I said something vile I'd heard my friend Derra say once. I'd been meaning to look it up.

"Class?" he asked me. Nuke was a saur of few words.

"Conversational Lingua," I told him, as if I didn't do this three times a week. He grunted and I trotted off.

I missed the cross-town tram by a hair, so I decided to take a shortcut through the secluded red-light district to catch up to it again once it hit Bog Street. By now it was full "night," but crime is rare on the station and I felt safe enough.

It was a lot easier making time here on Level 20 than it would have been on Level 22. My steps had a bound to them. That tram was going to be a cinch to catch.

As I hit the second block on Fi-Age Street, right in the midst of the steamier, species-specific clubs, I heard a giggle.

I'd heard that giggle before. Two years before, to be exact. Then I saw them.

Malac. Humans. Like I said, there were a few hundred hereabouts. But these were a male and female, her the first light-skinned woman I'd seen in two years, but without the guy in shades to hang onto. I focused on the male. Light-skinned as well, lighter than me, he was tallish even though he hunched in on himself and shuffled alongside two brawny gimigols, their heavy tails rolling left and right behind themselves. He wore a plaid jumpsuit with black boots, a common fashion for the saurs but less so for malac. He topped the outfit off with what I could see from a block away and behind was a mass of dark, curly hair piled on his head like a furry dessert topping.

They all ambled to a dark loofa bar.

I let out a wordless yell and galloped toward him.

3

Britguy looked up at the second whoop. He gave a start at the sight of his imminent doom charging toward him, and urged his companions inside while I was still five businesses away.

I could have flown, the adrenaline flushed through me so hard. Every breath gave me more righteous energy. I crashed through the double doors of the bar.

"Members and invited guests only," the gimigol bouncer there told me.

I ducked under his grab, thankful for being a member of a small species. The interior of the place was very dark. On scattered individual stages, spotlights followed female lampeys whose antennae were oddly engorged and whose mouths hung open. Not in shock– from TV I knew enough about the skinny species of lampeys to know that this was some kind of sexual come-on for their kind. Did all male saurs find this arousing? Even the non-lampeys? With the wormy skinniness and open mouths, I thought it just made them look hungry. You know: *braaains.*

Female gimigols worked the floor, dressed in far less material than one usually saw on the street. They swished their tails at their customers and occasionally jiggled their jaws and shoulders suggestively. Three male gimigols worked a corner across the room, letting out the occasional sexy bellow. Hubba-hubba!

Through all the various other species I spotted him: sitting down with the Giggler, his gimigol friends and some doils in a corner, watching me with a sick grimace on his face. Shorty wasn't with them.

I hoped I looked like Hell Incarnate.

I launched myself at him. Yes, I actually jumped over a hunching male lampey sitting at the next table and landed right on top of Britguy. "Goddam bastard!" I screamed at him. "Effing sicko prelathie bifurb!" I dished him a lot more vocabulary I'd learned from Derra.

He didn't seem impressed with my language skills as I pounded his head and shoulders, but the blows found their mark. He squawked and tried to block me with his hands. But he was a dork, a goddam freaking jerk, and I was Wonder Woma—

One of his doil companions grabbed me with his talons.

Sharp talons. I let out a shriek and tried to dislodge his hand, to no avail.

So instead I kept up the onslaught on Britguy with my free hand. Somewhere I noted that his faithful giggling companion had disappeared.

The bar crowd's attention had switched from lampeys to me and Britguy as we both fell to the floor. They closed into a cheering circle around us. Through the sudden din I heard a couple of 'em start a pool behind me. I think I was favored to win.

Great gluts of booze and snacks pelted us all as the crowd sought to join in without actually daring injury. Someone belted the doil who had me, and the talons released long enough for me to snap free.

I clambered on top of Britguy and pummeled his head with my fists. He made a cage around his cranium with his arms. Unfortunately only they caught the brunt of my fury. So I switched positions and kneed him where it would hurt. He howled but never broke the cage of arms, instead bringing up his knees to protect his nether regions. Such a wuss.

"Is there a problem?" one of his gimigol buddies asked in an amused voice through the yells and taunts from all around.

"No, actually." Britguy sucked in hard breaths between slugs. He had the gall to have a British accent on top of the Lingua as he attended to the task of defending himself from my Fists Of Fury. He tried grabbing my wrists but I was too fast for the slug. "I believe this is a horrid misunder—ruddy Nora! [I got in a good one, right on his jaw]—misunderstanding."

The friend hooked one of my arms. The right. I'm not a good lefty.

"Misunderstanding?" he inquired.

"Misunderstanding, my ass!" I bellowed. "Let me at him!"

Britguy finally got a firm grip on my remaining hand and held it away from himself. "The young lady is obviously in heat, sir," he told his friend.

"Heat?! You bastard!" I couldn't move my arms so I kicked as I could, though I only punished the floor.

"Sink me, yes," Britguy continued, now seeming quite unflummoxed. He raised up on one arm, taking a deep breath–with some effort, I was pleased to note. "They get like this every month. We have to lock them inside. They go–" He aimed a freezing gaze at me. "Nutters."

"You… kidnapper! Somebody call the cops!"

"Goodness, my my goodness," Britguy clucked as he shook his head sadly at his friend. "She'll be all right in another day or so. It's the mating drive. Uncontrollable in the female malac." He turned to me. Past a drip of blood, the corner of his mouth showed the tight grimace underneath. His nostrils were flared, his eyes slits. "Someone needs to *fuck* her until she's quiet."

Around us the crowd roared their disapproval that the fight had stopped. Three more fountains of beer arced through the air to splatter across us all.

"What is this 'fuck'?" His friend asked as he regarded me at an angle.

"Part of the sexual ritual, sir," Britguy assured him. "Her mate must be somewhere nearby. They don't usually leave when the female is in this embarrassing a condition."

I assured him of several things. Things concerning vulnerable parts of his anatomy that had nothing to do with places above the neck. I reared back to place the kick and he managed to shimmy to his left so he took it on his thigh instead. Though the room was dark, I believe he went pale. He managed to sit up on his knees, while his partner and himself had my hands imprisoned. The crowd let out a disappointed groan.

"Too much commotion," one of the gimigols said so quietly only we in the inner circle could hear. "Too much attention."

"Don't worry, sir." From his jumpsuit Britguy produced a few small skin patches displaying medical symbols. He considered and chose one.

"No you don't! Kidnapping bastard! You aren't putting that on–"

But as soon as the patch touched my skin I blacked out. This was the second time I'd done that with Britguy.

Deja vu: He wasn't around when I woke in daylight in the gutter a block away from the bar, next to a saur puking his drunken brains out.

When the pavement stopped spinning I was too angry to be thankful that I hadn't been dragged off by the cops. That would have been an end to my Safeties Systems aspirations. Luckily there'd been trouble along the axis yesterday, smugglers or something. Good cops who normally kept our streets clear of the small amount of derelicts and other such problems we had were busy elsewhere. My record remained spotless, unlike my tunic.

I dragged myself home, hardly taking note of the impromptu concert some of the neighbors had started in the park that forms the wide median in our street. Relaxing in their yards for the weekend, others along our block could enjoy the sweet if froggy harmony from the group.

Nuke wasn't home. It was past his meditation hour and I couldn't hear him yodeling in the shower (don't ask) (I never did), so he must have gone for the day to pull some overtime or whatever. That meant I couldn't grouse to him about my night.

I scowled at the cheery pot of red sorta-begonias that decorated the railing on my side of the porch. I was so not feeling cheery. I pressed my hand to my door latch for the lock to read me. As the door shooshed open, a piece of paper fell out.

Paper. I hadn't seen paper in a long time. I bent down and unfolded the tiny packet.

It said, "My mum was right. Don't ever trust an American girl. Nice uppercut." It was signed "M.F.B."

My heart jumped into my throat and quivered. I was being stalked. My kidnapper–the guy who'd dumped me out here with nothing but a language tape– knew where I lived. I didn't have a clue where he was.

He was my only hope for how to get home.

Remembering detective shows on TV, I scanned the note for further clues. A distinctive watermark? A line that said "Property of USS Intrepid"? A crumb from a food that was only prepared at one place on the station?

Nothing. Just handwriting that was a slight shock to read since it was in English. It took me a second for the words to register. The handwriting wasn't too illegible, too guy-like, but it wasn't flowery, either. It was straight and to the point.

Britguy had a last name: B. Maybe it stood for Britguy. And maybe the entire thing was a joke and just stood for Mother-eFfing Bastard.

The note flummoxed me for so long that I couldn't figure out why I was missing something.

Uppercut.

I ran into my place and pulled out my office. It, like much of my furniture basics, was kept stored in the floor but popped up easily enough if you knew where to gesture. Even large rooms seemed so much bigger if you stored the non-essentials out of sight. During the days I kept two chairs and a table up, but now I needed my desk.

I held my breath as I searched emergency rooms for humans who'd come in with minor injuries. I told the system that I was looking for my cousin.

Bingo. Friendly Outpatient Services up on Green Terrace ("Serving all known sentient species") had registered a malac last night. I couldn't get access to his medical record, but the screen did give me his name– it wasn't anything MFB-ish– and stated address.

I hurried to the Malabar Breeze Hotel on Level 19. He was gone; checked out three hours before.

Damn.

The concierge was quite accommodating as I faked being a Safeties officer. Britguy had been staying with a small group who left at the same time. I cross-checked ships' manifests. They'd all taken the *Bundolo-La*, which had gravitied out just before 0200, heading toward galactic center along a route that held three ports of call, none of them labeled "Earth."

Damn, damn and damn!

I'd lost Mother eFfing Bastard. Again.

Okay, he was gone. Maybe I'd see him in another two years. Maybe I'd never see him again and I'd never get home.

No.

I realized that at some point I'd given up hope. Now that hope burst forth again. I *would* get home. I would!

I made a copy of the *Bundolo-La's* route and then spent all my free hours checking every bar I could find on the gravity-friendly levels of the station, just in case. All it got me was sore feet and the tiniest bit of a buzz. I finally rested the swollen tootsies on the stool next to me as I swigged iced boady at Derra's Diner. It's a fair-sized deli with a buffet and tables inside and out, only two blocks from my place. If I'm too tired to make my own meals, I eat at Derra's.

Since she lives upstairs from her shop, that also makes Derra my near neighbor. I met her when she was cussing out some weeds in the plot she has in the community garden. A little help from me, for which she taught me some interesting words, and we became friends.

She's a doil, which is a common species on the station, though not as numerous as the gimigols. Doils look like a cross between Big Bird and a small, wingless dragon, with colors usually in the goldish-green range except for those I'd seen in Derra's kitchen. Derra and her cousins were red-bronzes.

As a doil, she stood about eleven feet tall, a few heads higher than gimigols, who had them on breadth. You always see doils peering about from the back of crowds since they have the best views. They were covered with scales that looked like feathers, right up until you accidentally brushed one. They were like thick fingernails. Doils had perky little tail stubs instead of the great things gimigols dragged around. A doil's flat, triangular tail was attached a hand's width under the waistline and bent in an upward slant at rest.

If you saw that tail lying flat, you'd best get out of the way. I've seen doils attack each other for almost no reason. They're hyper things. And Derra was a hyper doil. A few minutes with Derra's mood swings could tire a person out worse than a ten-hour bar shift on Level 22.

Derra had an odd shade of Lucy Ricardo red running across many of her scales. On her cheeks was what seemed like a spot of rouge, though that looked quite natural and the cousins had it as well. She had a mirror behind the counter in which she'd admire herself several times a day, prompting her to perfect her look by preening. This involved using her stubby, malleable beak to fluff the scales on her shoulders and upper chest, and do other things that the health department wouldn't think highly of. Though I don't think it would be enough to get her closed down.

The rest of her time was spent ordering her employees about. As far as I could tell, they were all her cousins (earning a "-zio" suffix), all coming in varying, more natural-looking hues of rust, yet they took her abuse with only the most hidden of eye rolls and chirps.

Once I'd considered asking her for a job, since my primary skills seemed to be restaurant service-related. However, I'm not a masochist.

I didn't know how long Derra'd been on-station. It was many years more than me, though her Lingua was far worse. "Who workin' on the bakka back there?" she'd shriek at the swinging doors that separated the kitchen from the deli. "You better be getting that out now! We got plenty customers!"

She might acknowledge us customers but she never did anything to make a more congenial atmosphere. Unlike Sonny's homey, cave-like tavern, the diner had a comparatively antiseptic decor. Its spotless checkerboard floor and stainless steel counter edgings had caught my eye in the first place. If I squinted hard, it could be a mint-condition 1950s-style diner. It was always hectic, with the entertainment of at least one cousin getting blessed out for not living up to Derra's standards.

But she gave me a break on prices. That buffet bar charged by the plate, no matter how full. Me being a pitiful little malac, she let me fill up the saurian equivalent of a saucer for a reduced price.

The first few times I went to her place she watched me closely as I walked the buffet line. I tried to sample a spoonful of everything. She waddled over. "Yep." She bobbed her head with its long neck at me. "We do good food here. Good some people knows it." Me, I was just trying to find things in the saurian cuisine that would agree with both my stomach and my taste buds.

Sometimes she'd peer at me and turn her head from side to side, clacking her short beak to herself. It took me a while to learn that this meant she'd set out a food new to the place and was waiting for customer opinion. Her daughter, Liv, was training to be the head chef back there in the kitchen. She was a sweet young saur and liked to experiment.

Usually I could fake approval. Once or twice I dug in for more, and she clucked approvingly. "We keep dat on menu," she told me. "You tell your malac friends." I did indeed bring in new customers, which also endeared me to her, but hadn't been able to get any malac to stop by yet.

Once I actually got up the nerve to tell her that her greetie was awful. I tried to hedge a bit and explain that malac were different from saurs, but she still let out an awful squawk and demanded that the cousin who had made it come out to apologize to me.

"It's just me," I explained as the cousin cowered under Derra's disapproval. "I'm sure that saurs would think this was great. You all probably would hate the food I ate back home."

"Well. Mebbe," Derra admitted. "Malac strange folk. You–" She poked a claw into her cousin's chest. "You go back and do better."

I liked Derra because for the most part she did made good food and because her mind ran in often devious directions. That could be murder when she was playing opposite you in a game of ar-tsinlad, or if you were one of the cousins back in the kitchen and she heard something clang that shouldn't be clanging. Bless her, today she noticed that I was in awful shape. Between bouts of yelling at her cousins she listened to my story and clucked sympathetically.

"Good shot," she commented when I got to the part about attacking Britguy's family jewels. "Now tell me: why malac wear genitalia on the outside?" She eyed me and my loose tent of a jumpsuit. "Where yours?"

"Just the males do. You'll have to ask the guy who's in charge of evolution about that."

She tapped her beak thoughtfully. Perhaps her people's medics had tweaked their own genetic code and perfected practical doil body structure centuries ago. "Next time," she told me, "you reach into his pockets and grab some ID. Or maybe personal possession he want back. Maybe hotel key."

"Sure, next time."

"But only if he's with others," she cautioned. "If he alone–go for it. Give him what he deserve. People only respect what they fear. And revenge is good eating." She smacked her rubbery beak-lips.

I took a swig of my boady. It was better than beer in that in mass quantities it gave a bit of a buzz minus the less appetizing aspects of a morning after. Plus it had a lot of healthy nutrients so after-guilt was never a factor. Not as good as Sonny's Best, which he brewed himself, but it was up there.

"How do I ensure that I have a next time?" I asked.

"He be back."

"And then?"

The bottom of her beak worked back and forth as she considered. "Mebbe you be nicer to him. Sometimes people respond better to Good Cop than Bad Cop."

"I *was* nice. I didn't aim for his 'nads except the once. Well, twice." Okay, a few times more than that.

"No kill. Even lowlifes don't like someone trying to kill them," Derra said. "Maybe he mad because you question his honor in public. Maybe he thought you interfere in something he had going. You say he wear disguise?" She chirped at my nod and then shook her head at me. "People don't like interference. Not if they playing game. That why referees invented. Honest ones, that is."

Now that was a thought. Britguy'd been in that wig again. I'd noticed that this time it was glued securely on. Who were those gimigols he was with? I tried to remember distinguishing marks, but I was still new to this alien stuff. Gimigols were the most common species on the station. I could tell male from female, and maybe distinguish three or four distinctive features other than clothing, but that was all.

They all looked alike to me. I snarled at my own ignorance.

I'd tried at the loofa bar earlier and they wouldn't let me through the front door. They certainly remembered malac me. Not a member, and a troublemaker at that. Two strikes. And no, they didn't give out the list of their members, much less their guests.

Derra said she'd tell her boyfriend to ask there. "He convince them to show surveillance records," she said. "He pretty persua–"

"Henk?" I tipped my head at her with skepticism. Henk was whipped. I couldn't see him whipping others.

She shrugged. "I'll get him to bring Moezu-zio along," she decided. "He talk anyone into anything. But don't know if he'll–"

"I'll give them a ten-pak of Sonny's Best for their trouble," I volunteered. Sonny's own label was legendary to those who knew about it. It tasted just as good coming back up as it did going down. Barter was cheaper than hiring a detective, wasn't it? I mean, since I had an employee discount.

"Sonny's Best." Derra actually purred. "They do it for Sonny's. No sweat."

Something hit the floor in the kitchen, followed by a round of distant squawks.

"What you doing back there?" Derra shrilled. My ears rang from the volume as she bolted to the kitchen. "You make shit mess! Cousins or no, I fire you this time, I swear!"

It was a start.

4

I reported to Station Safeties so excited I could have bounced off the walls. Got the job! Got the job!! Unfortunately, Lt. Bree was not as enthused. Nor was she pleased to be assigned as my training officer.

Sonny and I had negotiated a flexible part-time schedule at the bar to accommodate the new job. I was cheap, non-citizen labor who worked hard for him. He liked me, it was vice versa, I wanted that extra money for my savings account, and he didn't mind getting tax points for helping to support an SSS trainee.

I was exuberant. Even if I'd let that Max Britguy slip away, I felt the possibilities increase of having that return ticket to Earth in my pocket some day. He'd be back. I'd catch him. I'd find out where Earth was. Anything was possible.

Lt. Bree told me this first day was a routine one as far as Station Safeties went. Part of my required duties as a Safeties Systems apprentice was to check the emergency lockers on Levels 20 through 24, which was actually only four levels since there wasn't a 23 yet. You'd be surprised how many lockers there were, and yet I wondered: what would happen if something really bad happened? This place wouldn't suffer any sudden volcanos, but my textbooks gleefully mentioned any number of possible apocalypses an SSS officer might have to handle.

Every half-mile or so you had the lockers with three spacesuits (different sizes to fit most species, which would be good if you had only three victims, one each of each size), but was that really enough? Sometimes I'd find myself humming the tune to *Titanic* as I made my rounds. Not enough lifeboats there; not enough suits here. Everyone had suits in their closets at home, but no one carried one around with them.

But realistically, what kind of extreme crisis was there likely to be? Kreeger would talk about the dangerous Old Days, but those times were behind us. The station's rings rotated slowly behind a stationary outer protective hull designed to guard against breaching due to interstellar debris. Even my gloom 'n' doom textbooks agreed that this solved 98.5 percent of externally produced emergency situations.

What was important about the safety lockers was that they stored a good number of gas masks. Most environmental accidents would affect atmosphere content, not air pressure. The masks came in a variety of configurations that would protect faces, snouts, and various proboscii, even gills. That and the various sealing body-blankets would be enough to evacuate large crowds to safety.

Inspecting emergency lockers might be tedious, but it made me feel as if I had a real duty here. After a week, Lt. Bree– now just Bree– let me do inspections on my own, though she assured me that my every move was being monitored and she was double-checking.

Locker inspections weren't all I did. SSS inventories were brutal. Bree claimed that if she ran things, we'd be inventorying in a way that made more sense. She often said she had better ideas than did the regs. What did I know? I was just a newbie.

By the non-Bree rules you had to dig out massive equipment from storage and check that all systems were still in top working order. Bree would hand me what seemed like a half-ton of stuff and I'd buckle from it. That always produced a derisive snort.

It was tough that Bree didn't think too much of me, because she was well-liked in the department and on the station in general. Her record was spotless. She'd received a couple medals along the way. Even her husband, who was a police officer, was respected in the community. Port Malabar Power Couple #1, that was them.

Me, I had no rep. And I couldn't help it if I was from such a small species. I tried to make up for it with energy. I often volunteered for duty on the lower levels, where the gravity got to be intensely uncomfortable for gimigols. Bree saw that I was trying, and very occasionally she'd give me a grunting gimigol half-smile, which revealed her right-side incisors. If I'd done particularly well, she might nod.

But I was still early in the training process, making more mistakes than getting things right. It wasn't easy adjusting to an entirely new culture, much less concept of the cosmos, while learning a new job.

It could be frustrating but I liked being so useful. In protecting the station I felt as though I was continuing my firefighting courses from back home. Once I got back, I could apply what I'd learned out here. I wouldn't have that much to catch up with, right?

Already I was allowed to do so much more than I had been back on Earth. SSS had been very excited that I was able to add basic human first aid techniques to our first response data bank. It all made me proud. I liked to think that my mom and dad would be proud of me, too, as they looked down from Heaven.

I was a child of heroes. How could I do any less than they?

One day I finished up Level 21 to find Bree waiting at the lift. It was a bright day today on all the levels. I quickened my pace and waved. She bobbed that fuchsia headpiece of hers to indicate *speed it up,* and I hustled.

We arrived on Level 20 just in time. A group of elementary-level kids were ambling toward us from their school, paired off so they made a column of two following their teacher. First or second-graders, I supposed, though some towered over others because of species difference and one crawled on tubefeet, like a gargantuan starfish. The crawl had a definite skip to it of excitement. Kids– they're great whatever species they might be.

"Good morning, children," Bree said as the group made a semicircle around us and the locker we stood next to.

"Hiya, kids," I said. Many of them stared at the strange malac alien. Most were already my height. Still, my silver uniform matched Bree's and was the universal symbol of Safeties Systems, and thus meant friend. The kids warmed up to me quickly as I helped Bree go through what all was stored in the lockers and how to use it.

We even had a little skit to improvise. I played the kid because I was so much shorter than Bree. I got to spot an "emergency" and then showed them how I called it in to SSS HQ. I went to the locker, chose a mask and secured it. Then I wrapped a safety blanket around myself, which sealed to me though I could still use my feet and hands to aid my friends and get to the nearest airlock.

Of course the kids wanted to know why they saved themselves first instead of helping their friends. This time I got to play the friend who hadn't noticed the emergency, and Bree the one who had. I went down the block to play my part, and she spent extra time to collect me. By the time we both got back to the locker, we were gasping from inhaling god-knows-what. I really hammed it up, crawling along the pavement, unable quite to make it. I reached out to the kids for "help" as I theatrically flopped about, managing some quick final words before I clutched my chest and "died."

One of the kids started to cry. Then another. Then another. I hopped to my feet to assure them that we were just playacting. I even did a little dance to show them how well I was. They regarded me uncertainly.

Bree took charge and reiterated that I was fine, that it had just been pretend to teach a lesson. There'd be enough crying if people didn't suit up first and save later, right? She quizzed various members of the group, getting them to repeat their locker lesson to her. That straightened them up quick enough.

We got them all to swear that they'd attend to themselves first, and then we let them try on the masks and blankets and play around with the funny feel of those. Then we passed out shiny decorative stickers and safety list apps for their homes. They bowed to us and we did the same back to them, and then they all took off for either an amusement park or some confectionery that would top off their field trip.

Nice kids. I hoped they'd never have to use our lecture.

As soon as they were out of earshot, Bree hissed in that way only truly angry saurs can, "What the hell was all that? Were you deliberately trying to scare them so badly they'd freeze up in a real emergency? Were you trying to traumatize them?"

"Honest, Bree, if I'd done that before some malac kids, they would have been laughing their butts off. I was totally overplaying it. Cultural differences, okay?"

She darkly eyeballed me, muttering deep in her belly without using any consonants for me to figure out what she was saying. She let me hear the final word: "Malac."

"Next time," she decided, "we will rehearse. We will have no cultural misunderstandings. And you will stick to the script."

"Absolutely. Great idea."

So Bree checked off the duty from my job list and I continued solo on my rounds of Level 20, mindful of the time. I had Lingua class in two hours. After that it would be hit the sack, another honest day's work completed, if not necessarily perfectly.

I loved my SSS uniform, even though it fit me as if I were half-gimigol. Every time I changed out of my waitress overalls into my Safeties suit in the back of the bar, I pictured my mom getting ready for work. She usually took me to school on her way in, all dressed in police black with her heavy belt and visored cap. She kept her gun in its case until I'd gotten out of the car.

It wasn't just her; the suit was also a reminder of my father, who'd died when I was twelve. I had few memories of him when he hadn't been confined to his hospital bed. One of those was vivid: him lifting me up to his shoulder while he was wearing his bulky brown fireman's jumpsuit with the neon yellow stripes. That was the best of what I had of him, that memory of the uniform and his strong hands.

He'd been terribly injured saving a fellow firefighter from a three-alarmer. He'd lingered for years, a shadow of his former self. Sometimes I hated to visit him, his condition scared me so. He was like a stranger there, though it seemed he lit up whenever he saw me. I should have visited him more. I should have gotten to know him better as I got older.

His name had been on a memorial plaque at City Hall.

Mom also wore a uniform, though hers was snugger. Her badge and gun were shiny and impressive. And though she was a few inches shorter than how I turned out, I thought she stood ten feet high.

"There's nothing more important than protecting your family, your community," she'd always told me. She'd been protecting a neighborhood from some doped-up burglars when she'd been shot. Police Headquarters' marble memorial to fallen comrades included her name on it, freshly incised the last time I'd seen it.

And now the family duty fell to me. I was the protector. This station was mine, the citizens here under my watch. As long as I was here, I'd see to it that they stayed safe.

There are all too many ways for a frail bubble of air and steel in space to come to harm. I was determined to learn them so I could make sure they never happened. Not on my watch.

I haven't really talked about the other malac yet. One of them was Randi, a guy around my age, maybe a few years older. He had nut-brown skin that showed off tattoos from his forehead right down to his toes. If it weren't for them he'd have been a real looker. For him those tattoos were a source of pride. Apparently no one had used an anesthetic when applying them, and the process took a long, long time. The tats, especially the long one across his forehead, showed him to be a man of high reputation and respect in the malac community. I thought they interfered with what had been a fine face.

Then again, his butt tats were… intriguing.

Many of the malac had tattoos, primarily the men. Those few women who had them told me they were to show their equality to the men of the malac. Though we were out here in the middle of galactic nowhere, and the saurs didn't seem to have many sexism problems, the malac did. Ah, humanity.

A malac with tattoos on his forehead ranked high in society. Tattoos on the hands signaled someone who excelled in creativity. I wondered if the process of getting those tats might impede the manual dexterity needed for that creativity, but Randi's hands were tattooed and he had no problems with that, if you know what I mean. That's not to say he was perfect in bed, but I'm willing to admit that neither was I.

He was nice but Randi had occasional 'tude probs. Put him in a group of other guys and they went all uber-macho. Women might as well be a lower species. Was that the reason he didn't go for foreplay? Oh, he was all gung-ho about me doing it on him, but turn the tables? Forget about it!

People say there are millions of fish in the sea, but in this particular one there were less than a thousand. That's a small pond. So unbeknownst to him, I had Randi in a training program. At first he'd refused but when I made it clear to him that no foreplay equaled no nookie… Well, he was coming along. Reluctantly.

Men are a real project, aren't they?

But Randi often made me laugh. He was a funny guy, a people person. He knew every human on the station. I could see that he was really moving up in the malac community. There was no reason why I shouldn't be thoroughly charmed by him.

One night Randi waited for me in the service alley behind Sonny's as we closed up. The tip jar had been full, thanks to a party of Kreeger's family celebrating harvest, so I was in a party mood as well. Sonny, bless his heart, saw Randi and "discreetly" put his index finger to his left nostril. He wiggled his giant gimigol hips at me as he rolled his eyes at Randi. I stuck out my tongue at him even as Randi put an arm around my waist.

Randi gave me a quick kiss as I turned. "Yo, Tam," he said in his endearing way, or at least he thought it was.

I chided myself for that afterthought. What was so wrong with Randi? Nothing. Okay, so he was covered with tattoos. It was better than scales, though sometimes it made me think I was in the middle of a maximum security gang prison.

So he came from a different culture than mine. They often did things that left me clueless, and none could understand why I, a fellow malac, didn't know their ways. Shouldn't I mesh well with my kind? I had infinitely more in common with them than I did with the saurs.

Randi wore a skirt. He called it a "maro." Almost all the guys wore maros, and the women mostly wore sarongs. It was impossible to find fitted human clothing. The saurs didn't understand human anatomy and the way our bodies need to move. My first basic work jumpsuit cost me a fortune to get it even halfway right, and since then I'd given it to various tailors to make civilian-style knock-offs. They hadn't turned out as well as I'd hoped. I just needed to put on about three hundred pounds and they'd be fine. I did what I could with them, but I'm no seamstress. Everything I owned had a saggy bottom and low crotch.

So on a date I usually did the sarong thing as well. They were fine as long as you didn't have to be too active. And they were great if you wanted to look good for a guy.

Randi looked great to me tonight. He kept his long, straight hair pulled back in a ponytail. Randi was a big guy, proud of his muscles and willing to spend a significant amount of off-time perfecting them. He did have a devilish smile, so contrasting to his darkish skin. I think it was what attracted me to him in the first place.

Plus he was human. You couldn't get a bigger plus than that!

Naked, he was a god. Have I mentioned that butt?

Unfortunately he went for skanky maros that never seemed like they were draped right. Those Hawaiians on tourism shows wear their breechclouts neatly and they're hot. Randi's looked like he'd thrown on something in the dark. They were always bunched up, hooked onto his waist like he was trying for the loincloth look. It was less Tarzan than an overgrown, swollen diaper mode. I suppose he couldn't help it if he wasn't the skirt type. Maybe I could introduce him to kilts?

Maros were often worn with shawls that wrapped around the upper arms, creating a bit of a mini-cape effect. At least those were hard to mess up.

I could learn to love him if I stayed here long enough. All relationships were compromise, right? He was coming along with his lessons, if slowly. I was hopeful, and looked forward to the evening.

"Hey, Randi."

Before I could say anything more he pulled me down the alley toward public trans. "Dian's having a party," he said. He didn't stop to look back, and I stumbled to keep up with his long lope. "Malac only, and there'll be dancing. How long since you been dancing?"

I assured him that it sounded heavenly.

"We'll have malac food, too. Not this alien stuff."

"Soylent green is people," I joked, but he didn't respond. He'd never seen the movie. Maybe he wasn't listening.

I insisted that we make a stop at my place even though it was a good bit of the way around the station, because there was no way that I was going to show up in overalls.

"It's informal," Randi protested. "Some of the people will be in their work clothes, too."

He wasn't, thank goodness, or he'd have deposited splotches of black slimy gunk left over from his workplace on my chairs. I managed to calm him down by telling him how much better an impression he'd make if I was at least a little dressed, and he let me change.

I went through my closet. Sarongs, pareos, tunics– they were basically draped and secured cloth rectangles, of which I had many. My best rectangle was boldly patterned in blues and cream with vaguely organic shapes. Mom's necklace matched it nicely. The girls in the malac community had given me lessons on the 101 ways to drape a pareo. I added several secure pins to the outfit just to be sure and wrapped a shawl around my shoulders– also a long cloth rectangle.

I would have killed for a ratty pair of jeans.

They wouldn't have fit in at the party. For some reason the human populace here was Polynesian, Indonesian, that area. They'd been here for many generations, and tended to wring the latest news from back home out of the rare newcomer. They weren't interested that much in Earth; just in human/malac matters.

While I'd been recovering from my kidnapping injuries, the malac who had discovered the station's newest arrival told my doctor that he'd gotten my skin too light. It had taken a lot of effort with my practically nonexistent Lingua to reassure them that a medium tan was my proper pigmentation. My new blue eyes (so sue me; it was my one indulgence) spooked more than a few folks.

Just how long ago had it had been that these malac families had traveled to the stars? Every now and then I thought of Easter Island and those huge stone heads looking outward, and I wondered…

The ride over to High Spokes on Level 21, where most of the malac population lived, consisted of Randi complimenting me on my outfit despite the wait, alternating with complaints about his work day. He's in transportation, making sure all our public moving parts are well-lubed. And yes, I've heard all the jokes about it from him.

"Don't know why you have to live so far from here." The old argument came up as we exited the tram to hoof our way to the apartment in question.

"If I wasn't subsidized," I began but let it drop. He'd heard the logical argument before. Because I was a Safeties Systems trainee, I was encouraged to live within quick running distance of a Safeties Tunnel personal transport entrance. The Tunnels were part of the network that crisscrossed the station behind the scenes, just like Disneyland. Emergency trans within that was much faster than the normal stuff, so fast you had to be trained how to ride it, much less drive. The Tunnels also held electrics, water, magnos, atmospherics, you name it, all ready to be patched or utilized in case of emergency.

My duplex was right next to such an entrance. That's why I'd lusted after the place so badly. It would complement my resume when I applied for the SSS. I couldn't help it if other malac didn't live in my neighborhood. I could stand living among the interesting alien species well enough; don't know why they didn't.

The party was a big one. Our hosts had taken down the walls between three apartments so there was a great room that could fit everyone comfortably. I wasn't used to such low surroundings. My place had fifteen-foot ceilings, which were fairly standard for the station, but here they were only about nine feet high. The sound system played a mix of non-English world music, but occasionally an American country song from not that long ago would pop up. I wondered who had gotten it, how they'd gotten it, and if the music was stored on CD, MP3 or maglines.

Everyone greeted me politely, but many didn't want to talk to someone who couldn't speak their native language. Lingua wasn't an option with them, so I palled around with those who didn't mind my Lingua. Randi stayed by my side most of the time unless I was speaking with a group of women.

It was so wonderfully strange to talk to my own kind. I sat on a cloud of contentment as excited plans were laid for a ladies walking group, every week-day at noon–which managed to coincide with too many shifts at both my jobs, darn it. I had to beg off the next few days and hoped the others didn't take it as a dis.

The local gamelan set up with drums, a flute and several stringed instruments. Half the place started dancing. During one of the more raucous numbers Randi joined a line of men who shook and shimmied and stomped their feet. The walls vibrated to the beat. Then some women danced to a gentler set, swaying and sensuously moving their arms while part of the crowd nodded. I didn't know if they were following the story the women silently told, or the general tradition that was being upheld. One of the guests explained the dance to me in heavily accented Lingua. It was sweet, about a god who'd fallen in love with a human woman and eventually took her to live in the sky with him.

When the dancers changed again, Randi came up to me with a drink refill and steered me into a corner. There was a coed group of Lingua-speakers lounging on low couches with their multicolored drinks in hand. I noticed that one of them had a Sonny's Best, which pleased me. If I had known about this party's tastes in advance, I would have brought some myself.

I knew a few of the women there. Zara was on a first date and let her guy participate in most of the conversation though she nodded a lot. I didn't think that boded well of the relationship.

As it often did, the fact that I had come in from Earth came up. I asked a few of them if they would go back if they knew the way. "What for?" one of the younger men asked. "We didn't even know what the world was called until you came. We wouldn't fit in there. We have a good life here. Plenty of jobs. Plenty of money if you've got the right skills. Plenty of women. Plus this port has malac-friendly doctors."

Everyone gave a grateful murmur about that. It hadn't been until about twelve years before, when the word had gotten out that Port Malabar was a hub for humans, that many others had drifted in and the local medical facilities had been required to know how to deal with the population.

"Plus we've got brite now," one of the guys, Dian, said as he lifted his glass. It held a liquid of a peculiar teal color.

"What's that?"

He gave me a knowing nod. "It's the latest out of the nebula," he said as if that meant something. "For aliens it's illegal."

"But for malac it's not?" an acquaintance of mine, Irdina, asked.

Dian handed her the glass. She tilted it back and forth as she peered at it.

"Just gives us a good buzz," Dian said. "Aliens go hallucinogenic. Lose their free will. Sometimes it gets so bad their systems come to a complete stop."

"But it is legal for malac? Safe?" I asked as the passed-around glass got to me. It smelled of potent limeade. I let Randi take it.

Dian shrugged. "It might be a little illegal," he said, "but since the reason it's banned doesn't affect us, I don't see why we shouldn't be able to get it."

The group generally agreed so I tried to stay out of it. Randi took a swig and pronounced it good. He insisted that I do the same. I sipped as small a sip as I could. Definitely ultra-concentrated limeade with a chemical rinse. Ick.

"It's never going to replace Sonny's Best," I said, and a few people laughed in agreement. At least it broke up the "illegal" conversation and we returned to party-type talk: which team was going to win in the coming tournament (there was always a coming tournament), what was that construction up on Level 16 all about, who was sleeping with whom, where was the best restaurant.

"Did you hear about that mess on Rom-i-yon?"

I passed a bowl of pita bread to the woman next to me, Mawar. "What's Rom-i-yon?" I asked.

"It's a world," Randi told me. "A couple of sectors over." He shrugged. "Saurs."

I turned back to Mawar. "Rom-i-yon?" I prompted.

"They just had a coup there," she was good enough to explain. "They've been fighting for generations, some kind of civil war. You know how saurs are. I don't know what it was about, but about four, five years ago the one side finally won."

"I take it peace didn't follow?"

Mawar made a face. "Tell my supervisor that. He's got to go there on business and wants to drag me along. Luckily, we just got a new hire at the office, so there's someone with even less seniority than me who gets the shit duty."

"Congratulations."

"Anyway, the civil war was over but apparently a bunch of saurs on the losing side didn't agree with the peace treaty. They call themselves Lingus or something–"

"Limbus," her husband, Zikri, corrected from her other side and Randi nodded.

Mawar continued, "Limbus. They bucked every ethics pact on the books, assassinated thousands who had put away their weapons. And they took back their world."

"So now there's peace."

"If you can call it that. My supervisor says it's a government of terror. Saurs are dragged from their homes and families in the middle of the night, never to be seen again. If anyone dares to question anything, they're charged with treason and executed."

"Remind me to stay away from there," Randi said.

"Which is my number-one intention," Mawar sniffed. "I hope Roggurd– that's my supervisor– gets back okay. He's a good ol' saur. For a saur," she amended with a wink to the group.

I turned to Randi. "This all is two sectors away, you said?"

"Even farther." He gave me a squeeze. "Nothing to worry about here."

This was a very liberal civilization. I approved. In addition to having about a zillion kinds of recreation– some of which humans could actually participate in– there was universal health care, a welfare system that helped people down on their luck to get back on their feet, maybe even better than before, and also a "too much work is bad for you" state of mind.

Meals were long, lingering affairs like I'd always imagined Europeans enjoyed. Musicians roamed everywhere and played for the joy of their muse.

Work weeks? Three days on, two off; three on, two off; repeat. The station's computers had everyone's schedules interlocking smoothly, and a last-minute emergency or vacation whim was easily accommodated. For the most part. The new guys were expected to work harder to fill in for the seniors, and I was the newest of the new guys.

Plus I was in Station Safeties Systems, and we were expected to drop whatever we were doing whenever our section's alarms went off. Even so, I managed a lot of money-making time at Sonny's, as well as working on my education and questioning every visiting crew I could about Earth.

There was an ease of life here on Port Malabar, a sense of security that I'd never experienced before. Once I got my first-level certification my salary would go up as well and I could indulge in a few of the comforts that I had only heard about.

Bree was a fourth level officer, going on five, and married to another high four (whom she assured me was a solid ten in her book). She had a zillion days more of vacation than I did, plus they had a sleek home on Level 21 in an Open Rec community. Not only were there swimming pools and jogging paths through pretty woods there, but there were (so she said) both public and very private mud pits. During a day of dull inventory that she had to help me with, she regaled me with torrid tales of one particular pit located in a leafy glen. Its mud was heated to five degrees above her normal body temp. Her eyes practically rolled out of their sockets as she let out a soft howl of pleasure at the recollection.

Yeah, I wanted some of that. Not the mud so much, but the success in life. Though really, I had it pretty darned cushy. I could stand it very easily here until I found a way home. I didn't have to buy anywhere near the amount of groceries that doils and gimigols could plow through, so my food allowance stretched nicely. I loved the square footage in my apartment. I had dated a couple guys from the malac community, enough to be pleased with Randi. We'd see how it went. I liked the neighbors I'd met and the way I spent my days.

Except for school.

I've never been that bad a student. It's just that now I'd had to learn everything all at once, and big blocks of it refused to catch up with others. Language, for one.

Oh, I spoke better than Derra, but to be in Safeties you had to speak perfect. Perfectly. When communications suffered technical problems, and you'd be surprised at how often that happened but then we could get into strange situations the rest of the station didn't suffer, the other end had to be able to understand you through the worst static.

The human mouth just wasn't built like that of the gimigol, and a gimigol-centric language was the lingua we used. It involved too much grimacing and forcing sounds from the back of the throat. Forward consonants didn't work the same way since our lips and teeth are built differently from gimigols.

Dannko, a doil in my department, often commiserated with me, but assured me that diligent work would bring results… in a few years.

I didn't have years. Finals were looming in my future. If I flunked them I'd have to repeat an entire cycle of Lingua, which meant that I couldn't take Levels exams for my job for another year.

Sometimes I wondered: what would happen when I finally got home? Would I be happy to give up all this? Of course the answer was yes, absolutely! But more and more I felt like maybe I'd miss parts of Port Malabar. Sure, I was an alien, a malac and thus weird. But I was pleasantly weird. Some saurs thought we were a cute little species, and that was fun.

It was true that I couldn't pull the literal weight of my coworkers, but every now and then I could do things they couldn't. I could get into tighter spots. When we were left with only hands instead of machinery to manipulate things, I could do far more delicate work than they. And lord, I was faster! I could leave just about any of the saurs in the dust when I felt the need to run.

Okay, some of the smaller saurs were faster but they were rare. And so far the ones I'd met didn't have much staying power. One short burst and they were done.

So there was a potential place for me here if only I could seize it. Buckle down and study. Work my face into grimaces that a human wasn't meant to make, just so I could pronounce my words correctly.

I just hoped my face wouldn't freeze that way.

5

Wahoo! I'd just finished my first meteor deflection simulation. My first real, big-time duty. Well, sort of real. Even so, it was so cool!

The set-up for the exercise was that a meteoroid was on track to hit the station, or come close enough to endanger one of the docked ships around it. The port's hull could handle space dust and small debris, but anything larger than that SSS liked to take care of, if only to keep in practice.

In a zero-grav room at the core that would make every Hollywood special effects crew blush with shame, I strapped on my spacesuit (which, after ten alterations, didn't fit so awfully badly) and climbed into a fake spaceship with a fake captain at the helm. I stuck my arms into sleeves that would mirror my actions using huge robotic arms on the outside of the ship. The size difference in what SSS used for its saur officers versus me took a while to get used to, but the instructors let me play with the setup a lot longer than I'd have during a real emergency.

At last the "captain" maneuvered us to the meteoroid, about the size of a city block, and hovered just over its rotating surface. I used the robot arms to set a bucket of explosives on the thing. We "zoomed" away, turned and waited, and I got to see a lovely explosion on my monitor. Success! All it needed was a dramatic symphony in the background and some movie-spectacular booms. Which weren't simulated because, as you know, in space no one can hear you scream because sound doesn't travel through a vacuum.

Just as I was gloating at my moviestar efforts, the intercom announced that placement had been off so some of the debris was headed to the station. That meant I had to man the lasers, bzap! Bzap! Except that they also don't make a sound. But you can feel the ship go "unh" with each blast, so something was doing something. I got all three rocks with ten shots.

"Good for your first try," the training commander told me as he checked off the duty on my records. "You'll need nine more before you get your grade on this."

I might be nine tries away, but I felt I was one step closer. I exulted. Fire Fighting 101 didn't have anything like this back home!

So I was still on Cloud 9 later, even though I was actually on Level 20, where Derra's daughter, Liv, was conferring behind the deli counter with her. Liv was a spectacular shade of red, like the last tinges of sunset. I had the idea that Derra's own Lucy Ricardo coloring was an artificial attempt to mimic that, L'Oréal for scales.

Their conference involved a lot of quiet chirps in their native language. Liv was usually reserved, almost shy, but here she stood her ground. Finally Derra noticed me loading up a sandwich at the buffet. "Tam!" she barked.

I snapped to attention.

"Come!"

I couldn't see the state of Derra's tail from here to provide early warning of her mood, and besides it was covered by her smock and apron. I obeyed.

"We need malac opinion." Derra stiff-armed a small bowl at me. "You eat."

The bowl contained grooved brown cylinders about the size of medium eggrolls. Likely they weren't poisonous. "Oookay," I said and reached to take the bowl.

"Just one!" Derra squawked. "What, you think I made of money?"

Liv cocked her head at me, whether in sympathy or suspicion of gluttony, I couldn't tell. I eased one of the cylinders out of the bowl and turned it around for a thorough examination. "What is it?"

"Pickle. You eat pickle. Give opinion."

Derra stared at me in an intense way that on any other person would be a glare. Her long neck snaked her head around so it was practically in my face. "Eat," she repeated.

I spared Liv a glance. Her claws drummed against the tough material of her apron. She nodded at me, I hoped in encouragement. Maybe it was to tell me that they'd call an ambulance if I started to die.

I sniffed at it. The interior of Derra's pickles were usually edible, kind of chewy with a slight snap of crisp on the outside and a taste of, I don't know, something green. I didn't particularly like them.

This smelled different. Familiar. I didn't place it until I bit down.

Mom had been home from work, "Trying to be a real mom," she told me but I wasn't old enough yet to fully understand. I knew my mom was different from lots of others, but that was okay. She was important. She did important things. She protected the people of the town.

But this day must have been in spring when the final cool breeze of that season stirred the short drapes above the kitchen sink. I was sitting at the table, having raptly watched Mom not only roll out a pie crust from scratch– "real" moms didn't use that refrigerated stuff, she told me– but trying and sometimes failing to hold back the string of curses for that dough, which persisted in sticking to the rolling pin.

She'd let me pour in the filling, gooey and rich, made with real cherries and not from a can, and I helped her wash the dishes as we waited for the pie to bake. We talked and talked like we'd never done before as that warm cherry and almond extract smell filled my nose. The afternoon light caught the back of Mom's hair to illuminate it like a halo.

It took forever for the pie to cool. As we waited Mom told me every joke she knew that was suitable for a young girl, and a couple that weren't. Then she explained those to me.

We couldn't wait any longer. With the utmost care, she set a knife into the crust and eased the first cut through. The crust crunched prettily, and we both smacked our lips. The second cut went much faster and then we couldn't hold back. We both grabbed a fork and ate off the same slice.

It was sour– tongue-twistingly sour against the sugar-sprinkled crust. Mom was appalled and started to apologize but I told her it was the gods-truth best pie in the entire world. And it was. She smiled at me and managed to finish her portion.

Later I saw she'd thrown the remains away. She must have bought a store pie and taken out a piece before we had it for dinner the next day. She tried to fool me, tried to put on a considering face and say, "I guess it was okay after all. Maybe it just had to age a while. Get the flavors to mellow," but I knew about the cherries in the garbage. I told her that the first slice had been the best of all, and her cheeks pinked and she hugged me hard.

"Well?"

Derra's grating squawk brought me out of the vision. "Say something. Bad? Good?"

It took a moment to find my voice. "May I have another, please?" I asked. I had awakened from that startling vision, rubbing the necklace from my mother that I always wore under my shirt like a security blanket. "May I have the bowl?"

Liv let out a quick shriek and clapped her hands while Derra cackled. "You like? You like, Tam?"

"It tastes like cherry pie. Like a pie my mother made for me once."

"You like this tcherriepi?"

"It was wonderful. This is wonderful. Can you make it often? Please?"

The two doils congratulated each other in a frenzy of barnyard yelps and general jumping calisthenics. The cousins all came out from the kitchen to add to the celebration.

When a gimigol got up from his chair to volunteer to try the pickle, he also announced it as excellent. Upon which commenced more raucous celebrations. I was surprised the station didn't shake from all the commotion.

Derra pushed Liv forward. "Is her recipe. She come up with it from scratch!"

"I got an idea from–"

"From scratch!" Derra insisted. "My daughter is genius. Will be genius when I finish training her to be chef. You watch!" She shook an index claw at me and the other customer. "Five years from now, everyone will know Liv. She have restaurant in best part of station."

We all congratulated Liv once again.

Finally Liv turned to Derra. She shifted from spindly leg to spindly leg. "Mama," she began.

"Yes? Darling Liv, best daughter I have!" Derra leaned over to me and whispered in her loudspeaker of a voice, "Only daughter I have!"

"Mama. I'm, uh, I'm, ah."

"Yes?"

"Pregnant!"

Utter silence blanked the deli. Then Derra let out a full-frequency whoop and squashed Liv within her arms. "Baby! I gets grandbaby!"

The deli resounded with renewed celebration. For my own safety, I backed far out of the way.

"Why you not tell?" Derra demanded of Liv.

"Oh, Mama. I know how you feel about Dibi."

"You the one has to live with him. Baby have your genes; baby be fine."

Liv laughed. "Baby will have Dibi's genes as well."

As far as I knew, Liv's boyfriend was a student who was taking the slow route through school. As in January molasses slow. If he had a supporting job, I hadn't heard of it. The government here was generous toward students– like me. But I had a job. I had two jobs.

Now and then Dibi would come into the deli when I was there. He wore the same outrageous cap and kind of slouched around the place. Liv would come out of the kitchen and then he'd perk up, puff out his chest and chin scales, and they'd rub necks for a few minutes in a corner if the deli wasn't too crowded.

Derra sighed like a walrus' belch. "We live with what we get. Grandbaby will be family. Dibi," she sighed again, "Dibi family too. Family is the important thing." She hopped, Liv trapped in her arms, in an up-and-down dance of joy. "Grandbaby! Grandbaby!"

When Derra left Liv to hug every one of her cousins, Liv offered me the bowl of pickles. "You take what you want," she told me. "Mama hates Dibi. I didn't think she'd take it this well. Whenever we have tcherriepi, you get a free one."

She added in a whisper, "Just don't tell Mama."

6

Along with the pickles, I got enough from the buffet for a takeout dinner for two. Randi came over to my place after his shift and we had dinner together. He made a sour face at the pickle, but I forgave him. In fact, I had sex with him.

Sometimes I felt as if anyone would do in my romantic situation, but I was glad that Randi wasn't just anyone. I hoped he felt the same way but we never got around to discussing emotions. It was good enough for me. My life was too busy for more than that.

He stayed all night because he was too tired to go home. I wasn't used to that. He slept like the dead, spooning me. I'd left a night light on because, you know, a guest and needing to know the way to the bathroom in the dark. Around midnight or so I turned over–

The dim light caught his face:

Darth Maul in a death mask!

I couldn't catch my breath. My heart pounded as I scrambled out of the sheets with enough force to bring the house down, but the monster in my bed merely groaned and turned over without waking.

Oh, it was Randi. Just Randi and his all-over tats.

Someday I'd get used to this. Unless I got home. Then I could forget about scary skin decorations. Until then it was all I had. I shuddered and reluctantly returned to bed, where Randi was sleeping as soundly as ever.

In the morning he hauled himself to the breakfast table, tying last night's maro into place (his grimy overalls would be in his locker at work). "Tam, do me a favor."

In my lifetime I've learned not to immediately say okay to statements like this. "What?"

He reached into his short cloak (Thao's Tailors, over on East Broad 20) that he'd left thrown on the floor, and pulled out a mylar packet that pulsed with liquid inside.

"What's that?" I asked.

"Brite."

"You brought brite into my apartment?" I tried not to shriek, but it came out loud. Not loudly enough so that Nuke next door had heard, I hoped.

Randi shushed me and glanced at the wall that divided the duplex, apparently thinking the same thing. "Do you want the cops to hear, too?"

"Sheesh. Brite." I stared at the package.

"Just store it. Temporarily," he said as he handed it to me. I made no move to take it.

"What's the penalty for possession?"

"Let me do the worrying. Remember, it's perfectly harmless to malac."

"Which I'm sure any court will appreciate."

"Look, all we're asking–"

"'We'?"

He shrugged and set the package down on the table before he pulled on the cloak. "Me and some of the guys. Look, Tam, you've got access to the Tunnels. Just hide it in one, someplace that no one, malac or saur, will ever find it. No one will get hurt. We just want to get a good buzz going next month at the twins' birthday party."

"I don't think so. No."

He knocked himself on the forehead with his fist. "Damn, and I convinced them, too."

"Convinced–?"

"They said you wouldn't do it. They said you wouldn't because you weren't one of us."

For a moment I was so shocked I couldn't say anything. "But–" I sputtered. "Don't they have eyes? Do they think I'm a saur?"

"It's not that. You're still new. Different. They don't trust you."

I pushed my chair back to stand. "I'm probably friends with them, whoever they are. I'm friends with their girlfriends. And their families."

He shook his head. "You don't know our language. You pall around with the saurs."

"I also work with the saurs. They're my neighbors. Is that not permitted?"

"Now, don't get all hysterical about this. I told them. I said you'd been here for a while now. Like you said, you know just about everyone, and the girls all seem to like you well enough for a… They like you well enough."

"Oh great, you guys think I'm some kind of alien."

Randi shrugged and then held the pack of brite at my eye level. "I told them you'd do this," he said. "It'll prove to them about where you stand. They won't be able to deny it."

I stared at it.

"You'll be one of us."

One of them.

It sat there, quivering at each small movement he made. It wasn't harmful to malac. No saur would ever be harmed by it. And I did know some very good hidey-holes in the Tunnel next to my place.

"Well," I said out loud. It was like an out of body experience. Someone else was operating my mouth. "I suppose I could do it. Just for a day or two. But I don't transport it across station. I get it into the Tunnels, I get it out, and someone takes it from there." Already I was considering options of concealing every trace of identifying DNA from the package. Yeah, I could do that. I sank back onto the chair as the import of it all bore down on me.

"This only happens this once." To make it crystal clear, I added, "Never again."

"Yeah, sure." Randi bent down to give me a kiss on the forehead even as he reached for a porta-breakfast. "Just this once. You're a princess."

"Right," I said to the package. It sat there on my table looking as un-innocent as a silver package could.

As soon as Randi left I fumbled through my household Safeties Systems emergency kit and retrieved its cleaning supplies. Though I hadn't finished dressing, I padded out the back in my bare feet, went around to the side of my place and keyed the Tunnel opening that was just off a semi-public footpath providing the boundary between my property and the neighbors'.

This had been why I was so keen to live in this apartment. Quick access to the Tunnels: a requirement for Safeties Systems personnel, and here was one at my back door.

I had to flip up a circle of lawn to enter. With the package tied into a sling I'd rigged in my robe, I slipped down the ladder inside. The opening was wide enough for a larger saur to utilize, so no claustrophobia probs here.

At the bottom was the dock for my SSS vehicle, which looked like an overgrown ladybug. It was even red. Okay, it wasn't mine; anyone in emergency services could use it, but it was under my back door and it would recognize me if needed. It could seat two adult saurs and had emergency supplies already packed in the back. Part of my job was to make sure Bugs across the station were up on their supplies.

A dark tunnel led forward and back, with the first intersections only a block away. They went up, down, left and right, angled here and there. The Tunnels themselves weren't fancy and finished. Wiring and tubes ran all over them, adding to their structure. There was no track; the Bugs moved within an electromagnetic field in the tunnels.

You did NOT go into the Tunnels themselves. You never knew when a Bug might whiz past and flatten you into jelly. There was only room for a Bug to move with maybe four inches on a side to spare. There was an occasional emergency wall indentation just large enough for a single saur to plaster themself into, or one large enough for a dock like this. On occasion a tech would have to walk around, but an alarm would sound in time for them to scramble for cover as a Safeties officer zipped by at mind-numbing speed, or traffic would be diverted until the job was done.

There were hidey holes between the pipes along my dock. I found a dark spot that was in a zone where security sensors wouldn't quite reach. My supplies wiped all evidence that I'd ever been around this package, and I used them to do the final securing so I didn't have to touch it. There was only the obviousness of the location for anyone to pin this on me, unless someone checked a video record. What were the chances of that?

Enough. This was dangerous. I was sweating just thinking about the consequences.

But it wasn't that awful, was it? A minor thing. Not like I was intending to use the brite against anyone. This was for Randi, just once. I'd be one of the malac. I set my jaw, turned around and climbed back up to the surface.

Randi didn't come by for the brite the next day. He wasn't answering his comm. I doubt he was blocking me. Overnight we'd had a slight what they call a tsunami. I hadn't even felt it; it only showed up on morning reports when I checked in for duty at SSS. Public trams up on Level 9 had taken a bit of damage due to the event and Randi was probably neck-deep in finishing the repairs for his department.

After I finished with the day's business, I reported back to Bree, who explained that this happened maybe every ten months or so. Hot-shot pilots gravitied in too close to the station. Interstellar travel is accomplished by a ship creating a gravity bubble around itself that effectively boots it out of regular space, so it can break any or all of Einstein's laws and for all intents, travel faster than light. I don't think it's hyperspace or warp drive or anything like that. It's just…different. People call it "riding the brane," as the brane is the outer side of the skin of our universe? I didn't know for sure. Something akin to absolutely nothing was out there beyond normal space, and it was easy enough to travel through if you had the right vehicle and a good map. Which I didn't.

A ship's gravity bubble wasn't a perfect circle. Instead a ship's captain shaped it to be lopsided. "That's how you get direction to it," Bree explained in the break room. "It's like eating an artie." With that, she'd spat out part of the snack she'd been eating. Ahead of the fountain of green-brown sauce she'd had with her fruit bowl was a black artie seed. It was about the size of an peach pit, tiny for her. It arced across the room to ricochet off a wall with impressive velocity.

When people gravitied in too close, their gravity bubble came with them. The bubble could hit the station, usually amplifying through the station's hollow core, which caused structural vibrations. It was against every law on the books to be such a bad navigator that your ship posed harm to a station and its inhabitants.

"Could be an idiot; could be smugglers," Bree surmised. Her head carapace rocked left and right as she fumed. Its tiny bubbles of texture caught the light. "We haven't seen any of those in a long time." She noticed my curious look. "I'll talk to Brindle tonight, find out what he knows."

Brindle was Bree's husband, the cop. They made an impressive couple in their uniforms.

But this tsunami had been a minor one. "Probably some idiot pilot off his mark," Bree admitted, and so we dismissed worrying about it so she could finish my evening tutorial. She was walking me through the lo-grav hazmat instruction manual at the central desk when a sniffer alarm turned red and beeped five times. Bree snapped her middle non-opposable fingertip against it, as if a connection somewhere were on the fritz that she could fix with a sharp vibration.

It kept blinking. Again it beeped. Sensors had noted a sudden difference in atmosphere. Not pressure; composition. Something somewhere was stinking up the air enough to trigger a non-evacuation alert. We didn't know yet if this was a collected cloud of farts or a bottle of hydrochloric acid leaking into inhabited territory.

I synched the alarm with the port map. It centered on Level 26, section 3-42. Bree let out a groan of dismay. I could handle the heavy gravity there better than Bree could, but I wasn't looking forward to it. It didn't take long to convince her I could take this job on my own. "I'm three-quarters through my hazmat grade," I reminded her.

She tossed me an extra sniffer as I grabbed mask and gloves and slung them over my left shoulder. "I want a complete record of whatever this is," she told me. "And anyone in the area previous to this, I want their pictures and ID," she instructed. "Do that after you lock it down."

"Got it," I replied. I checked out a Bug, strapped myself in, and peeled out of the station through the Tunnels.

I travelled laterally first, taking the shorter route across Level 21, before shifting down-level. Higher centrifugal gravity kicked in with a vengeance. I sank deeper into my seat as the Bug rolled out of the accessway at the much slower street speed it was programmed to maintain outside the Tunnels. My siren kicked on and civilians, shorter, stouter and more heavily scaled than their upstairs neighbors, shuffled out of my way.

I made sure mask and gloves were handy before I heaved myself out of the Bug. I secured the exit wing– didn't want to tempt any thieves, a habit left over from my Earth days– and dispatched an area sensor. It rolled in a quick zigzag pattern through the street, sniffing the air, taking photos of bystanders.

There weren't many. It was evening and this was a business district. I tossed an extra sensor into an alley that would run around the back of the block. Most people had gone home or off to after-work entertainments. A storefront advertised various exotic imports, its alert light signaling that this was the source of the problem. Judging from the window displays the business trafficked a little bit of everything, from soup and small electronics to stringed music instruments.

The door opened to my security code and I stepped inside, gloves and mask in place. It was dark; sensors didn't recognize me. I had to manually switch on the lights; how odd. Maybe a malac was too small for them to notice.

It was all I could do not to gawk at the merchandise as I dragged my protesting legs through the place. I didn't know what most of it was, much less had any idea what it was used for. It sure looked interesting.

I wasn't after *interesting*. I was after toxic. I could come back later to shop. I loosed my own localizing sensor and it nervously skittered around for a few seconds before making a bee-line for the back.

I knocked my right shoulder with my jaw, and the inside of my wide mask lit with a translucent data stream that would transmit back to the station. It showed a respiratory irritant. Low concentration. It wouldn't harm anyone out on the street or even come to their attention, but it shouldn't be here in the first place.

"Seal outer doors," I instructed the security systems of the store and heard the responding *shush* of a secure seal. When I got to the rear of the store I instructed another seal around the entry to the back storeroom to do the same as I went through.

"Here we go," I said.

"What is it? Can you stand up a little higher?" Bree's voice came over my comm system. She was wired into my mask; she could see the same things I did, though being here made the context clearer.

To the side of the storeroom was an incongruous cache of plastic barrels. They were separated from what was obviously the regular stock by a foot of empty space. There were no labels, though the rest of the stockroom was scrupulously inventoried. On top of each was a sealed opening.

Except my sensor hopped around one seal, beeping like crazy. Here was a seal that had slipped.

I ran my gloved finger around it. Standard haz chem seal. "Heat damaged," I surmised.

"What kind of chemical is it?"

"I dunno." I'd been kind of proud I recognized the signs of heat damage.

"Don't just look at the top. Investigate, trainee!"

Ouch. I was getting lazy. I examined the sides and found a couple numbers, then tilted the container to check the bottom rim. Sure enough, there was a small, typed label. Bree translated the chemical-ese.

"That's listed as an cold vacuum-use explosive. Who would subject that to heat?" Bree asked incredulously.

"It's not going to explode now?" I quickly asked.

"No. No problem. Unless there's an open flame nearby."

"Nope." Thank goodness for small favors. I opened my utility bag, glad I kept it in orderly fashion, and found its sealing kit. It was the work of only a few minutes to cover the defective seal and test it.

"Secure," I reported.

I walked around the storeroom and sure enough, found a few live imports sitting quietly in cages. I lifted them up and dragged them forward to the main store. Then I checked more thoroughly to see I hadn't overlooked some life forms I wasn't familiar with. You can never tell just by appearance.

When all bio-labelled items were dealt with, I sealed the door to the storeroom again– with me on the outer side– signaled Bree, and through the seal heard the air system in the storeroom hesitate. It's something you don't register until it becomes different. Now it stopped for a second and then inhaled quietly.

Nothing like a little vacuum to clear out a joint quickly. I was glad I wasn't in there. Without a spacesuit in a vacuum they say your blood boils right in your body. If you ball yourself up tight you can stave it off for a few minutes. (I didn't learn that out here; I watched the interesting parts of *2001: A Space Odyssey* a few times. The guy did it there, and somebody somewhere told me it was a real thing. Neat trick.)

A few air tests in the shop reaffirmed that with just a little recirculation with controlled airflow through special SSS filters the store would clear out just as well. I installed them. In another hour, much less by morning, no one would know the difference.

I stuck around until I got the all-clear, then opened the outer seal long enough for the cops to troop through. One of them was Brindle. I could tell it was him from the name on his badge. Me he could recognize because I was malac and SSS.

He wasn't happy due to both the explosives and the gravity. He must weigh a hundred-plus pounds more than normal. I showed him the contraband chemicals. They'd already arrested the shop owner and employees, plus researched recent purchase orders to try to trace the stuff. Brindle lingered in the front of the store to copy surveillance records and allowed me to copy for SSS.

I glanced around his burly arm as recent customer images flashed by on his palm unit.

One of those customers was Max Britguy and his ugly wig.

He'd been through about eleven hours before. I'd been sleeping, missing the night's tsunami. The tsunami that had probably been triggered by sloppy smugglers.

Don't know why, but I didn't immediately chime in with, "Hey, I know him!" My mouth stayed firmly closed even while my brain was screaming.

Max was my ticket home. Shove him in jail for the rest of his miserable life, and where did that leave me? Here.

Then again, maybe my hesitation was because Max the Britguy Bastard was human.

Was that why I'd gone along with Randi's scheme? Damn it, yes. Humans had to stick together. There weren't that many of us out here. As long as I was here, I wanted those humans to include me in their number.

But Max was bad news.

I didn't want the saurs to think that humans were evil. Right now we lived under everyone's radar. No one had had a chance to form an opinion one way or the other about us as a species. I wasn't sure how much I could trust Brindle not to make broad assumptions and then go ballistic, start rounding up every malac on the station because of one bad seed. I certainly didn't want Bree to think less of me.

Lately she'd been showing less disapproval about having to train a puny malac, and I didn't want to set her back. She saw that I was trying. Very occasionally she'd give me a small gimigol smile: incisors bared, crinkling eyes above barely flared nostrils.

So I kept my mouth shut and checked ship manifests later. No one recorded any malac arriving on the station. I managed to find video feed of three Customs entry points for the past day, but never saw Max come through.

I hated thinking of a human involved with interstellar smugglers. I hated thinking of that pulsing silver bag I'd hidden in the Tunnels. I wanted one of Derra's pickles to soothe me. Instead I rubbed my mom's necklace through my uniform top. She would have known what to do.

7

Bree and I were just finishing installing new thermostats on the Hatching Grounds when an alarm came through: trouble two levels up, Level 16. Construction accident. My heart immediately rose to my throat. I couldn't breathe. In addition to the tram problems on Level 9, Randi had been working there yesterday as part of the tsunami cleanup. Was he hurt? We were the nearest team to a lift in that sector, so we took the call.

It wasn't Randi. The quake had not been kind to the construction on 16. A two-saur crew had been repairing a slumped stretch of unfinished roadway using a truck-mounted crane to prop things up, when the truck partially collapsed. These things happen. But when one of the saurs crawled under it to reset the leveling equipment (I suspected he'd used the "hit it until it fixes it" method), the entire vehicle keeled over on him, bringing down a mess of the roadway as well.

Bree took only five seconds to assess the scene, her mouth set with a wide frown. The victim's partner was having hysterics. His bounding up and down in the low grav, swishing his huge tail side to side, was not helping the situation. The level was only a quarter finished in this section, hardly solid at all, so the vibrations were making everything sway back and forth. Upright pieces of modular roadway stacked next to the accident visibly vibrated. They could fall any second.

Bree shook the partner hard. "Call another crane," she ordered. "Now. Get a couple in here."

I didn't know if that was a real plan or just to get him out of there, for she turned to consider the situation some more, hands on her hips, her head swinging from side to side to get a good view.

She crouched next to the wreckage. "Hello in there!" she called. It looked like a stack of concrete pancakes. "Can you hear us? Safeties Systems. We'll get you out in a few minutes!"

We were silent as we awaited an answer. None came.

"What's that?" I asked.

"What?"

"Can't you hear it?"

"Is it–"

I shook my head. "Very high pitched. Soft. Like air escaping."

Bree rumbled deep in her chest. "You sure? Safeties hasn't–"

Suddenly an alarm went off and red lights began to flash throughout the area.

"Air leak," Bree groaned. "Can you tell where it is?"

I pointed dead ahead, toward where the victim must be.

Bree added to my vocabulary as I tried digging some smaller stuff out. I reached for a flashlight and trained it into the darkness. More debris up ahead, but I might be able to shift it around. "I think I can get through this," I told her.

She peered in the same direction. "You sure? He won't be able to get out the same way."

"I can assess and administer first aid."

Bree made a sound low in her throat, but then said, "Very good. Proceed. Don't give us another casualty."

Using a hydraulic crowbar, I crept into the hole even as Bree called for medics and another Safeties supervisor. When she was done she told me she was on her way out into vacuum to see what was going on there. "Double-think before you do anything!" she called after me. "No, triple-think!'

I crawled and heaved and propped up the overhanging debris as best I could. I passed the tip of a tail sticking out from under a slab and thus was able to aim roughly for the guy's head. Sure enough, I found it. His eyes weren't open. The sticky liquid on the ground was saur blood.

Back in here the slight hiss had grown to irritating levels. I grabbed an oxygen mask out of my kit and put it on.

Then I pried some more debris so I could get his pulse. He had one. Erratic. I had to shove and brace more things around, so difficult when in tight quarters and when you're only a human and trying to move concrete slabs. But I made a space to better reach his head and shoulders, and managed to unpack my medi-pak. First thing, he got an oxygen mask just in case we lost more atmosphere.

By then the medics had arrived. I shouted readings at them before they tied into my equipment. This guy's temperature was very, very low. The air in the compartment was getting cooler by the moment. Saurs don't like cold. It screws them up like anything.

I snapped some resuscitant onto the victim's mask and fed it in. His eyes blinked three times before I could see them focus.

His partner had told me his name. "Feldon, I'm from Station Safeties Systems," I told him, my voice hollow from the tiny space and my own mask. "My name's Tam. You're going to be fine. We have a crew here. We're going to free you and get you to a hospital."

"Cold," he managed.

"Let's fix that first. Be right back."

I crawled backward to get out and sure enough, the medics had hot paks waiting for me. "I'll need more," I told them. "Maybe some more oxygen if we lose enough air."

Behind their own masks they looked nervous. I didn't blame them. Vacuum was encroaching. Already floor-to-ceiling safety doors had come down to seal off this sub-section with us inside.

I dragged the heat paks back with me and surrounded the guy with them as I asked him questions about his name, did he know what day it was, what had happened, all that. I used my comm to communicate with the outside world so the guy wouldn't have me shouting in this echo chamber. He was feeling bad enough and moaned.

"You're doing great, Feldon," I told him as I stanched his wounds as I found them. Mini-sensors placed along his body would transmit more precise info to the medics. "Warming up?"

He gave a small nod. I unpacked my comm-phone and showed him. "How about you talking to someone while I go back and tell them what's what here?" He told me who to call and I propped the phone so he could talk to his wife. After her first scream I grabbed the phone. "Keep him calm," I ordered her, and she nodded in quick jerks.

I loaded more heat paks into the space until it was downright stuffy in spots, though you could fill up an ice machine near my feet from the cold I was getting there. Poor Feldon shivered as I strung situation sensors along the route I'd taken.

Without warning, the continual, high-pitched hiss I'd been hearing went up in tone and then stopped. It was replaced with a rhythmic *ping ping ping* from the wall. "That's my partner, Bree," I told Feldon. "We'll have this air thing fixed in a jiffy."

"How ab-about…t-temperature?"

"We'll have you out of here before you can freeze all the way through," I assured him, and hoped I was telling the truth.

The three pings had come from just to his right. I managed to shift some of the smaller debris around and saw what had happened: a deep hole had gouged through to the outer layers of the station and a support had slammed into what remained of the wall like a spear. Being in such beginning stages of construction, Level 16's thick, final layer of outer shell was missing. A bead of caulking began to appear around the tiny open gash. As I watched, it expanded and solidified. Bree's work. Tiny ice crystals began to form along the wall and in the debris, sparkling in the light of my flash.

I covered Feldon's head with a wrap over his air mask as I worked my kit around and fished some insulating sealant out of it. Clicking my own protective face mask into place, I gave the wall as heavy a coating as I dared, as the spraying process was messy and might clog our breathing equipment. It would do as a temp until we got Feldon out of here.

As I removed the wrap, now as covered with goo as I was, the wreckage around us groaned hellishly. They were lifting it with equipment Feldon's partner had hustled in. I relayed the news to Feldon. "How good is he?" I asked him.

He managed a tiny smile. "Trained him myself."

"I take it that's good. How're you doing, Ms. Feldon?"

The wife gulped courageously onscreen at her husband. "We'll be waiting at the hospital for you, dear. I've called everyone. The children are anxious to see you."

"Kids should be in school," Feldon croaked.

"Maybe not today."

Then I had to secure some grapples on my end of the tiny tunnel. More frightening sounds came from above us. "It'll be all right," I said as I held Feldon. I sure hoped I was telling the truth.

"You're warm," he accused me. "Thanks."

I was out of hot paks and not about to emerge into who-knew-what kind of anti-construction chaos to retrieve more. "I'm a mammal. Warm-blooded. Let's try this." I wrapped myself around him as best I could, careful of the injuries I'd found.

Bree was standing there when they lifted enough that we both could see out of the mess. "Stand back!" she bellowed as a dozen saurs began to rush forward. "I want a safe way in. No casualties for the rescuers!"

They obeyed her, perched on the tips of their brawny steel-toed boots, ready to swoop in when she gave the signal. Nuke was one of them, flexing all four of his arms in anticipation. As more parts of Feldon were uncovered I could pack heat more efficiently around him. He had a couple nasty lacerations that started to bleed fiercely when the weights were removed. I managed to close them, and I administered anti-shock meds and pain killers. There were some broken bones in there, but no compound fractures that I could see from this angle. The sensors I'd attached all over him would give the medics outside a much better view of him than I had. "Easy," I told him. "Not long now."

But it sure seemed a long time before two saurs and Nuke in helmeted construction outfits barreled in, picking their way as quickly as they could. Picture baby elephants trying to stampede along a tightrope. A medic followed them, and together the four wrestled Feldon onto a gurney. Vacuum doors had been lifted, and an ambulance awaited.

I let Ms. Feldon see he was in good hands and then clicked off. It was a relief to stand again. I'm not particularly claustrophobic, but thought maybe I could become so if I tried. A remaining medic quickly checked both Bree and me. I was the one who got a few minor bandages for some of my scrapes.

At my side, Bree watched the ambulance leave. "If I were in charge here," she muttered, "we'd fine people for looking the other way when it comes to safety regs." Without looking at me, she knocked me on the shoulder. "Good job."

"You too," I said.

8

Ali and Arti were malac fraternal twins whom I palled around with when I could. Ali worked at an agricultural supply warehouse and Arti scheduled atmospheric maintenance crews up at Central Station Command. Arti was the boisterous one while Ali was more introverted and often let Arti do her talking for her. They were both shorter than I, darker skinned, and tended to wear their hair alike, in double braids that wrapped tightly around their heads, as if they wanted to be identicals.

I think they thought of me as their project. Here I was, the new human, I mean *malac,* in a town that held very few malac. Despite my being too pale, even with olive skin, and my new eyes a peculiar shade in their view (though I loved, loved, loved them!), they looked past all that, saw me floundering my way around their world, and wanted to help.

They didn't know what to make of me. They could see I was human, but I didn't speak their native tongue, whatever that was. I'd read somewhere that the most common word on Earth was "okay," but they'd never heard of it. I thought whenever their ancestors first came to Port Malabar, it must have been from a time before "okay."

Learning their language wasn't as huge a priority for me as was perfecting my Lingua. I knew a few phrases here and there. They were teaching me, though not with the scientific approach or persistence that most language education comes with. Their enthusiasm touched me but also often made the lessons confusing.

Their people had come from the South Pacific/southeastern Asia region, that much I was sure of. Their skin settled in the brown range. They were well acquainted with Islam, though my father and his side of the family would certainly be stumped at the way they practiced it. Apparently no one of the malac had come away from the home planet with a copy of the *Qur'an*. Their practice had taken a side step or three over the centuries. Maybe they'd gone through a Reformation, same as Christianity; I didn't know.

Most of it was familiar enough. I'd grown up with just the highlights, as I had with my mother's Judaism on the other side, added to the modern secular society all around me. I got the gist and out here the gist was enough to be another tie from me to these malac.

So Ali and Arti had taken me under their twin wings, determined to make a respectable malac out of me. At least I was a respectable female malac, in that we shared the joy of shopping. Correction: the frustration of shopping. This was a world in which most inhabitants were at least twice our size and no shopkeepers had ever seen an issue of *Vogue*.

Today we shopped for shoes. The search for proper footwear was the worst and therefore needed a support group to accomplish without losing one's mind. Where there were a zillion saur styles in both fashionable and orthopedic forms, shopkeepers tended to take one look at us and try to pawn off saur toddler crap.

What it came down to was having to have foot molds made for soles, upon which shoemakers plastered wraps that formed into flexible boots. For my first pair I had managed to get a crude arch support built in, and Ali and Arti were intrigued enough to order some too. The result so delighted them that now the entire malac community enjoyed supported arches.

Since I was also an SSS trainee, I needed boots that could withstand toxic chemicals and hard living, with occasional vacuum work. Well, I hadn't actually done any of that last stuff yet, but I was looking forward to it soon. It would be a great story to tell when I got back to Earth!

Right now the theory was that we were picking up two pairs of industrial boots for me that I fervently hoped would match my uniform the way I'd asked. Two hours into shopping for the twin's apartment, we finally got to the shoe store. I unwrapped my new boots to try them on.

I heard a giggle.

It was high-pitched. Simpering and yet a bit desperate, followed by a feminine human stream of Lingua. Familiar.

Instead of bobbing up to look around, I remained hunched in my oversized saur chair before squirming down out of it. Barefoot, I duck walked to the aisle, hidden behind the store's seating arrangement, and peeked around a counter.

"What the–" Arti began, but I shushed her with a hand signal.

Just outside the open doorway to the store I saw her: the Giggler. Talking with some gimigol.

Arti and Ali stared after me, but I got them to understand that I was hiding. So they quite subtly craned their necks, Arti actually half-standing to see who I was hiding from.

"Leslie!" Arti shrieked and waved at the Giggler. Arti wasn't nearly as smart as her twin.

With an afterthought she glanced guiltily at me, but I waved her off– don't look at me!– and she resumed her smile in the Giggler's direction. "Ali, it's Leslie," she announced, leaving me out of the conversation. "Over here!" She managed to look abashed, though not quite directly at me. "Where have you been?"

Hurriedly I changed my listening post so that Giggling Leslie didn't catch sight. The girls practically threw themselves on her, everyone screeching in rapture at the reacquaintance.

"I just got in," Leslie/Giggler told them.

She would also know the way home.

"What did you bring?"

"Oh, please have brought some decent shoes! We're absolutely desperate," Arti told her.

"I might have some back on the ship," Leslie said. To my friends' delight she reeled off some other merchandise: shampoo, coffee, movies subtitled in Lingua that she'd brought for sale to the malac on the station. They all made plans for her to meet with the stuff and then Leslie left.

Quickly I made my own goodbyes and followed, boots tucked under my arm, untried. Where the Giggler was, so would be Max the eFfing Bastard. Bet? Either one would do for a ride home, but I wanted to land a few hard knocks on Britguy first.

You might think it would be difficult for a lone human to fade into the background on a station full of aliens, but when the vast majority of those aliens are Godzilla's cousins, it's easy enough to disappear behind a row of fat bottoms and tails. But getting found is not impossible. Especially when the searcher is desperate.

I was desperate.

Leslie didn't giggle again until she met up with some doils. When one of them squawked, I wondered if it was trying to come close to the sound with her giggle. It was every bit as grating.

They were a female and a male doil, the former youngish and the latter on the old side, with brittle-looking scales and taloned hands that had emaciated to the point where you could clearly see the bones under the tight skin. His voice was high and tended to squeak in places.

Yet his polite arm-punch still had enough power behind it to make Leslie stumble. I wanted to applaud.

The three talked for a while as they strolled the edges of the shopping district and then the elder went his own way. The female and Leslie watched him until he boarded a tram. Then they took off at a good pace on foot, heading east.

At times it was difficult to keep up since we were heading into less crowded streets. I had to stop and pretend to examine windows or peruse my phone-comm until the moment came when I could sprint to make up distance.

After a while they joined up with a small group: two gimigols, a doil…and another human. He looked familiar and I racked my memory.

It was Dian, Randi's friend. For some reason I immediately recalled him as being the one who'd produced the brite at the party the other night.

Crouching in the shadows, I tricked my comm into tying into the surveillance cams I could see near the group. I got about six good pics before the group broke up. For a moment I felt as if I should follow Dian. Brite was bad business, something I didn't want on my station.

But Leslie would lead me to the Bastard. I followed her.

Our tour introduced me to parts of the station I'd never been to before, most of them rather uninteresting and industrial. I waited outside while she went into one elegant office building in the financial district and came out on the arm of a nattily attired gimigol who carried a larger than average phone-comm on his belt that signaled his importance in the business world. I grabbed shots of them as I could.

After that it was two lampeys– female, I think, but maybe the males have antenna as well– who escorted Leslie down to Level 22 and then to 25. Leslie's heavy walk showed her discomfort with 25's gravity that didn't seem to bother the two bony aliens much. You didn't see many of the larger species like gimigol or doil down there, but small, squat folks seemed to get along just fine. They made keeping track of the tall lampeys easy–but hiding difficult.

From there it was up to Level 16. I wondered what business Leslie could have among the construction–or was it the construction crews? Finally she took the lift alone up to the core. Busy gal. I kept track of her over security monitors, long enough to see her transfer to a shuttle, where I couldn't follow. Then I quickly caught the lift back to Level 21, heading for SSS Central.

I was looking at my comm while jogging down First Street, trying to tie the ship's name into Systems Info. I didn't want to wait to get to HQ to ask Bree how that was done, so most of my attention was focused on programs I'd rarely used. I bumped into someone.

"Sorry," I said automatically and registered: human.

Male.

Not just male– Bastard!

By his quick intake of breath I could see he was every bit as surprised as me. His features quickly twisted into annoyance. I realized that I'd already made a fist and drawn it back, ready to let loose.

He grabbed it with one hand, hooked my arm behind my back, and manhandled me into an alley. Being the station, of course, it wasn't dark or dank and was really quite cozy. But empty except for us.

I thought of any number of questions I needed to demand answers for. Where was Earth? How could I get back? Why did he kidnap me? But what came out of my mouth was, "Where the hell do you get those cheesy fright wigs?"

For indeed he was wearing another one. This was a twelve-inch black 'fro, straight out of disco times of yore. He didn't have the complexion to carry it off.

His mouth worked a moment as he blinked. "Cheesy?" he said as if I'd just insulted his mother.

I freed my non-fist arm to poke him in the chest. "And where do you get off doing this schizo thing? 'Oh, rawthuh, let's have a cuppa tea, guv'nor,' one minute and then you're John Wayne the next. Well, not John Wayne. Jack Nicholson. Somebody. You know what–"

He secured my arm again. "We need to talk. Privately."

"Private enough here. Where's Earth? And how do I catch a ride there? On your dime."

A small voice in the back of my mind asked why I would want to go back. I ignored it. He'd destroyed my life. Principle was involved, among a great many other things.

"You have no principles," I told him.

"I– What?" Again the blinks like he couldn't understand my train of thought. Loser.

I tried to poke him again because it was obvious he didn't like that. He deflected it. Instead I managed to twitch my elbow into his side. "What are you up to?" I demanded. "You caused that… that… volcano thing back on Earth. And then you kidnap me and then you leave me to–"

"What is it with you and kidnapping?" he cried out, and then looked behind him to see if we'd caught anyone's attention on the street. "I never kidnapped you," he hissed. "Stop accusing me of that. And I didn't have a thing to do with that volcano. Bloody hell, I saved your effing life!"

"And kidnapped me out here without a clue to where I was. Without anything."

"I left you with a Lingua tape."

"How bloody lovely," I drawled. "Not even a longer note: 'Sorry to have stranded you in the middle of nowhere without any eyeballs or anything. Do have a nice life. Ta ta.'"

He scowled at me. Finally he said, "I do not talk like that."

"What the hell is going on? Wait– I should be calling a cop." Idiot me, I said it out loud. The thought must have occurred to him as well, because he snatched my comm to stuff into his pocket.

"You'll do no such thing."

"That's mine! It's official departmental issue! And I deserve an explanation at the very least. Preferably while you're behind bars."

"You deserve nothing. I deserve a thanks. I saved your worthless life. Isn't that enough?"

He dragged me with him to the other end of the alleyway.

"Where are we going? Are you kidnapping me again?"

At that he turned abruptly to me and pressed his nose against mine. "I. Did. NOT. Kidnap you!" He cursed under his breath and added something about people who had no gratitude.

"So why weren't you hurt?" I asked as we stumbled down the street. Some people looked at us but the sight of two malac doing something strange didn't seem to bother them. After all, we were strange creatures.

I didn't fight too much because we were stumbling toward my house. Right now I wanted explanations more than I wanted to see the Bastard hang in a public square. Maybe Nuke would be there to help out.

"I suffered minor injuries," MFB told me. "But I was wearing a protecto suit."

A protecto suit. I knew what those were. Now. Oh, right. Yeah, that's what he'd worn. Nicely tailored for malac.

"You couldn't have gotten an extra for me?"

"I had to protect myself first. You weren't in the program."

I made quite a few sounds of protest at that, even though the Safeties trainee in me reminded myself that that's the first rule of an emergency: see to yourself first, others second. Survive to save.

But I wanted to make him feel guilty so I protested at that, called him ungentlemanly things– well, maybe I used a few stronger terms than that. I included a few insults about his ship as well.

That made him mad. "It is a Nucleon 350-B model Brane-rider with multi-generational gravity drive. It has Z-44 prangles and a five-star hemiquad. Extended luxury interior with custom passenger comfort stations and emblet-quality climate-control ecosystem."

Lord help me, I'd heard the same spiel from ads since I'd been here. I mostly understood what it meant. Those were its primary selling points, but he proceeded to tell me details about it, enough to fill blocks and blocks of travel. Finally we stood on my porch and he pushed me toward the lock.

I rolled my shoulders at him to demonstrate that I was doing this of my own free will. "I never had a chance to admire its interior," I said. Once inside, he looked around.

"Small."

"It is not. Look at that ceiling height. It's fine."

"Small for saurs. It's not in the Terran sector. Why aren't you over there with them?"

"I'm a Safeties officer-in-training. And poor, thanks to you."

He made a dismissing noise.

"I need subsidized housing. Where did you get your ship? How did you know all this was out here?"

He ignored me and continued to look around, though there wasn't much to see. I'd made as close a copy as I could remember of my mother's obituary and had it framed on the wall, next to a picture I'd drawn that showed an American flag folded into a triangle, like the one that had been on my father's coffin and had hung in my mother's house. I'd tried my best to depict a brass label on a frame, engraved with my father's name.

Heroes.

"I come from a family of heroes," I told him so he'd know. "Not kidnappers."

"I didn't–" He sighed and shook his head at himself. Then he turned to me. "I come from one as well. Generations."

"Coulda fooled me."

"We cover a bit more territr'y than your family. We protect Earth."

What could I say to that? Besides: "Kinda messed up there two years ago, didn't you?" The look he gave me was suitably pissed, so I added, "What the hell is your name?"

The anger erased, covered with smugness. "You don't need to know. I want you to stop following me."

"So I'll follow Leslie instead."

"Who is Leslie?"

"Oh, you're smooth." I meant it. His face hadn't revealed any kind of emotion at hearing me know her name. "Leslie. The Giggler."

"Never heard–"

"Yeah, yeah." I grabbed his arm and pulled him toward the door. "She was down around the end of the block last I saw her," I lied. There was a police substation at that intersection. "Let's see if she's still there, if she recognizes you."

With the merest show of effort, he shook me off. "I mean it," he threatened and backed me against the wall, his hands on my upper arms. "You stop following me. I did not kidnap you. I saved your worthless life. You should be falling on your knees thanking me."

"On my knees, sure. Wouldn't you love that. Should I thank you for blowing up Earth?"

That took him back. His face showed astonishment that I'd accuse him. Maybe he wasn't behind it? "Earth wasn't blown up. Just a…"

"Small chunk?"

"Volcano. They caused a volcano."

I chewed this over. It had certainly seemed volcano-like. Right in the middle of town. "How many casualties? Who are 'they'?"

"It's not going to happen again. Not on my watch."

"Just kill everyone here? Is that your plan?"

"What?"

"You came crashing in on a gravity wave, didn't you? You're the one who caused the tsunami the other day."

"That was–"

"Do you realize how much damage you caused? You could have hurt people!"

"It was just a–"

"Was it just to cover up something else? So we'd all be looking the other way and wouldn't notice you? Those chemicals on Level 26." A sudden thought occurred to me. "You're running brite."

Ah! Shock registered all over him: tightening of his hands, drawing back from me, his jaw dropping.

"Brite," I repeated, just to see the results. "Brite, brite, brite! You bastard, you do have something to do with it!" I slugged him. I'm not the slugging type. Maybe I was mad with myself about the brite hidden in my Tunnel, I dunno. But all I could really see were my saur friends being hurt by the stuff someday. Stuff he supplied.

I must have taken him by surprise, but he bounced back quickly enough. He grabbed me again and this time he shook me. "Good god, you're violent. American. What I do is none of your business," he snapped. "Thus you will stay out of it."

"It?"

"My business."

"Your *brite* business."

His words came out as a hiss. His nose poked precariously next to my own. "My business is *not* brite," he declared. "My business is not your business. I'm warning you–"

"Ooh, he warns me."

He snarled at me. "I don't care if you're Terran. You come near me, come near–" I could have sworn he was about to say "Leslie"–"any of my people, any of my business, and I swear, you'll pay."

"Are you a killer?" I asked. Through the cloud of my anger, it seemed a prudent question. If he was, maybe I didn't want to make him too angry.

"I have killed in my time."

Damned if I couldn't see the truth in his face. He'd never killed a human, but he had killed. Yeah, noted.

He released me suddenly, sending me sprawling backward. "I warn you!" He pointed an accusing finger at me. Then he reached into his pocket, threw my comm on the floor and left, getting in a dramatic slam that, if it had been me, I would have messed up and had to come back for a re-do. Britguy was not one for redos.

I stood there for a moment recovering from the incident before my brain began to scream: *You're letting him get away!*

Effing Bastard! Distracting me from my primary mission! I pushed the door full open. It couldn't have been more than a half-minute after he'd left. He was gone.

Unless he was the Flash, he couldn't move that fast. I trotted out onto the porch and down, then circled the house, taking precious time to peer behind the bushes. When I'd made my circuit, I stood on the front walkway, hands on hips, and saw his rear end disappear around the corner at the end of the block.

Damn.

I knew I couldn't catch him. I knew I'd be unable to find him on station monitors. He was a slippery thing.

Like Randi. All that talk about brite reminded me that Randi had been talking his way around my demands that he pick up his little package so I could be rid of it forever, amen. It had been days. Almost a week.

Was it still there? Had someone discovered it?

Were Randi and Britguy business partners?

I tried to make it look like I was just moseying around the house. I checked the soil on my geraniums, studied the side supports of the porch… Then past the screen of bushes at the side of the property, I cracked open the hatch to the Tunnel. Once inside, I shot down the ladder like the hounds of Hades were behind me. At the bottom I forced myself to calm down. I held my breath, tried to stop my heart for a moment as I listened.

Nothing. No one was here.

The package was just a few feet from the ladder. Too close. Maybe I should move it. But there it was, still hidden in the shadows. Whew.

Randi would have to take it. Tonight. No excuses. I'd had enough of his procrastination, especially where my career, my honor, my possible criminal record was concerned. I was also going to check those station monitors. Britguy was not 007. He'd slip up somewhere. I'd get him eventually. I climbed back up the ladder with new determination.

9

Nuke was sitting in his rocking chair on the porch, drinking a beer, when Randi arrived for our date. I was waiting for him with a small, brown wrapped package. I wore gloves so as not to leave any incriminating evidence, and shoved it toward him.

"Take it," I ordered. "It goes back now."

He eyed it. Nuke took a sip of his beer, watching. My hands shook as I held out the box.

"You keep it for a while more. I'm not ready for it," Randi decided.

"Too bad. You're taking it."

Randi looked to Nuke. "Let's take this inside," Randi said.

"No."

Randi took the box, placed it at the side of my front door, and opened the door. He grabbed my arm and dragged me through.

"Tam?" Nuke asked.

"I can handle this," I told him and shut the door behind us.

"You're being–"

I pointed my finger at Randi. "If you don't take it now, I'll put it on your doorstep tonight– and then call the cops."

"You wouldn't!"

"I warned you. I've asked you for how many days now to take it back?"

"But– It's difficult to get rid of. You should know that."

"It's more difficult if I get caught with it! That would cost me my job. More than that; they'd toss me in jail!"

He stuck his hands into the back of his maro and lowered his chin at me, frowning. "And what do you think would happen to me?"

I couldn't believe the audacity of the man. "So you'd rather they throw the book at me than get in trouble yourself?" I opened the door and gestured. "Out! Get out! And take it with you!" I gave him a full-out Lingua hiss, and not the one that meant "hello."

Nuke was still watching but now his eyes were sharp. He'd set down his beer and stopped rocking. His lower right hand grasped his chair arm, ready to lever himself up.

"We're fine," Randi hastily assured him. "Just a little difference of opinion. Let me straighten it out. No problem."

He shut the door. I was too angry to stop him. Apparently I didn't mean enough to him that he'd shield me from the danger he'd exposed me to? What kind of man would do that? What kind of person?

"We are through," I announced. "Over. Get out of my house."

"You're making a big thing out of nothing. This is nothing. Nothing."

"So take yourself and that nothing away. Now. I mean it."

Randi paced the living room, pulling at his hair. By the second lap he was muttering. Then he stopped, stared at me like that would make me give in, and resumed.

"Is this accomplishing anything?" I asked as I crossed my arms.

"You're supposed to obey."

"Obey whom? You? You must be kidding."

"Look, Tam. I'm a man. I've been here all my life, practically. You've only been here a little while. You don't understand how things go."

"I understand the law. I understand what that stuff can do to saurs. I understand that you think I'm some kind of patsy." I used the word that meant menial, a servant… worthless low-life.

"I never said that."

"That's how you acted. Now take that brite and get out!"

He rushed to me, putting his palm over my mouth. "Quiet! That thing out there might hear!"

"He's not a thing. He's my friend."

"You hang around the saurs too much. What you need is to move to the malac sector. It's not right that you don't spend your time with us."

"I need this place for my job." It was difficult to talk around clenched teeth. "I like working with the saurs. I like my neighbors. Why can't the malac mingle with saurs?"

"Let the saurs deal with their own kind."

"Then why bother living here at all? Why not just take yourselves off and establish your own colony somewhere?"

He flung himself into a chair and stared defiantly at me. "We get medical care here. And we don't have the techs to support our own colony."

"So enjoy everything you've got on Port Malabar," I said. "You all should get out and about. Learn from the saurs. See what the saurs can learn from you. They make good friends."

"Friends?" He choked and recovered. "Who can trust a saur?"

"I'm sure they ask 'Who can trust a malac?' We set examples, let them know that they can count on us to be part of their society."

He snorted and gave me a patronizing look that involved the touch of a sneer. "Malac stay with malac."

"At least respect them enough not to deal with drugs that can harm them."

"They're just saurs."

I stomped my foot hard; flung the door open again. "Out!" I demanded.

He muttered and fussed and tried to change the subject again, but eventually ambled out. I shoved the package into the crook in his arm. He didn't bother resisting.

Nuke looked at me thoughtfully when Randi had gone. I just gave him a non-committal huff and went inside.

A million pounds had been lifted from my shoulders. I locked the door behind me.

And then collapsed onto the floor to bawl my eyes out.

I hadn't felt like this in a long time. No one else to understand me. No one to really talk to. Stuck out here in the middle of nowhere– alone.

I wanted my mother for real, not by way of some stupid pickle. I wanted her to hug me and take me to the shabby sofa in the living room and sit next to me and dry my eyes. I wanted my friends from school to come over for a laugh and share some secrets– in English. I wanted an old boyfriend or two, who didn't have tattoos and who dressed in jeans and tee shirts, to hold my hand and make out. I wanted to watch the stupidest TV show, as long as it was one from Earth.

I wanted to go home!

But there was still life to be lived, and eventually a new day dawned.

I reported to work and learned my job. I went to school. On the days off from Safeties Systems I went to Sonny's to work.

One day I showed up to SSS and Bree surprised me with a new duty: checking Safeties systems on the ships docked in port. I got to ride out on a shuttle and see real space ships– big ones– and make sure they followed all our regulations. Sure, it was usually a matter of taking their computers through a Safeties check, but I also got to walk the actual decks. The ships weren't like the *Enterprise* at all, but they still held that exotic edge.

I made sure all pressure suits were in good condition, and that airlocks were stocked with collapsible stasis boxes, the things that apparently I'd been brought in with. Once closed, they cut off the flow of time. They were like portable and quick suspended animation capsules. You didn't have to go through all the medical and rather lethal rigmarole of cooling a person down, etc. (and I had no idea what "etcetera" entailed) to use them.

Very handy for bad accidents in space, which was why the things, as well as pressure suits, were stored in air locks. Most bad accidents in space happened outside the ship while someone was working on a problem in vacuum. This way they could bring the guy inside, pop him in the capsule, and not worry about him until they could find good medical facilities.

I never did see any malac on those ships, but I did meet some friendly saurs. Most of them liked to talk. A lot. They were really curious about my species, too. I guess riding the branes of physical space doesn't make for the most entertaining of cruises.

But that was an addition to my job, what I got to do every two weeks or so, in rotation with other trainees. When I got back, Bree would check my records.

There was another guy doing the same work who always had to have his supervisor go out and attend to something he left out, but I never had that problem.

"You're thorough enough, I suppose," Bree said to me one day. High praise!

That afternoon swept by on a cloud of exultation. After my shift I had plenty of time to change to civvies and go for a walk before dinner and class. Up ahead as the wheel of the station rose in the haze of distance I could see that twilight had already settled in.

Our light did not come from any kind of electronic lighting. It was all done by mirrors. I didn't know how they worked those things outside the station–and I didn't know what it was they actually mirrored. There was no nearby star to focus on unless you counted the one by Bar-Tok, which didn't seem much brighter than Venus or Jupiter when I'd seen it and besides, was on the other side of the station's shield.

However it happened, we got a simulation of day and night inside Port Malabar and some days were brighter than others. Sometimes they were cooler or warmer, though never extreme. The saurs liked warm climates. It was like living in Florida without the hurricanes, I suppose. I've never lived in Florida. Here on the station you never knew what you were getting when you got up. I'd never seen a weather report on the local news; never saw a mention of a meteorologist. Each day was a surprise, the weeks ever-changing.

So was the city. It had its suburbs, but I was finding I preferred the heart of the city with all its ethnic or species-ic (is that a word?) neighborhoods. So many new kinds of aliens to see, so many new ways of looking at things in so many ways. Most of 'em were good folk, too. Guess I'm a people person.

Derra's Deli was on the way to class so I stopped for a quick supper and take-along drink.

I was always fascinated by her buffet. There were deep, rich soups and wrap sandwiches that had more heft to their filling than Earth-standard. And now there were the tcherriepi pickles. Derra always got a kick out of me eating them as dessert instead of a side item. I bought several and carefully packed them away for later.

Kreeger had literally rolled in a few moments before. Yes, rolled. When they're in a hurry, her kind gathers themselves up like roly-poly bugs and scoots around like hoops with good speed. The young grandkids make like they have no control over their direction and will bump into you for kicks if they think they can get away with it. As I've listened to their elders chew them out for doing such, I've discovered that the bollink language is a very musical one.

Kreeger wanted to know what the tcherriepi were, so I treated her to one. She chewed it thoughtfully before placing three on her plate. Derra would have liked that. I looked around to see where she was, but she was in the farthest reaches of her kitchen, not paying attention to her customers.

Today she was in a dither. "Dibi!" she was babbling. "Dibi!"

I pulled one of the Cousins, Moezu-zio, aside. "Liv is pregnant," he told me.

"Yes, I know."

"Dibi is the father."

I nodded.

"Dibi has decided he doesn't want to *be* a father."

Derra let out a squealing bark of a shriek back there. Then came a bunch of jabber flavored with the four-letter words I'd worked so diligently to learn.

Kreeger moved closer to listen in with us. She kept her valise tucked next to her, yet managed to handle several plates with her many other tiny arms. A few customers leaned in our direction to catch the conversation.

"Not want to be a father?" Kreeger exclaimed, then hummed with excitement. "This is a problem."

"A disaster," Moezu-zio declared. He wrung the towel that hung at his waist. "The shame! And the baby! How will this affect it?"

"On my world, lots of babies are raised without their fathers," I said.

Both Moezu-zio and Kreeger stared at me. Finally, Kreeger reminded Moezu, "She's malac. She doesn't know." She put her primary hand on my shoulder.

Moezu-zio asked, "Doesn't know?"

"Is there something wrong with this? Really, I don't know anything about doil customs." Something occurred to me. "Or is it something physical? Will the baby be all right? Will Liv?" I ran to the door to the kitchen. "What's wrong?" I asked. "Can I help?"

I could, by joining the circle of Cousins surrounding Derra and Liv. Derra let out siren-pitched caterwauls that I assumed meant great distress. Her fin of a tail stood straight out in back, vibrating like a pneumatic drill. A woman who tended to drama, Derra could fire up a hissy fit in nothing flat, but today she had something legitimate to hiss at. Her cheeks and jaw flushed red in rhythm to what must have been an agitated heartbeat.

Liv just drooped like she was melting. Great tears fell from her eyes as she sobbed.

I helped lead them out to the diner so they could sit down. Other customers cleared a table for them. Cousins brought them soothing broths and supplied Liv with tissue after tissue. Kreeger set down her dinner so she could encompass Liv in a hundred-armed hug. "There, there," she cooed.

Slowly even Derra's squawks petered out. Her head hung down as she grasped her broth bowl with both hands. I hugged her as hard as I could, and she finally let out a grunt.

"What can I do?" I asked her. "Tell me what's wrong. Why it's wrong. I don't understand."

"Dibi has taken off," she told me. "He's hiding."

I had to ask, "Will this affect the baby?"

"Of course it affects baby!" Derra raised up, flapping her arms. All the Cousins patted her, giving me what I classified as the Evil Eye for riling her.

"I'm sorry. I don't understand."

"Dibi. He's the father."

"Yes."

"He has to be here. He has to!"

Derra rose from her chair in a fury and stomped around the diner, into the kitchen, then back again, screaming in short spurts. I thought her tail might pop off.

I looked over at Liv. "I'm sorry. Can you explain?"

Slowly I got it out of her: doil biology 101. Males of Derra's people had an internal pouch that babies were popped into for after-birth development. Then again, it sounded like pre-birth development, as at that point the baby was still very much a fetus. Only the males could handle that phase. Now Liv's mate was nowhere to be found.

"He told me he w-wasn't ready to b-be a father," Liv's crying jag was down to spent sniffles. Her eyes were swollen to twice their normal size. "He n-needs to go off and think about it."

"Sounds like how some malac males react. He should have done his thinking before he created a baby."

Liv let out a whoop of a sniff.

"He'll be back," I assured her. "He'll realize he needs you and wants the baby. He loves you both."

The Cousins all agreed and offered more supportive words. Liv nodded but I didn't think she meant it.

Derra's squawks had wound down as she circled back to us. "I kill him."

"No!" Liv exclaimed, clasping her hands to her chest.

"He'll be back before you know it," I assured Derra.

Kreeger agreed. "It's not that big a station. If nothing else, someone will find him soon. Everything will be all right."

Derra kept letting out angry squeaks and trotting around the premises. She alternated between cussing over minor kitchen staff snafus and weeping about the baby's prospects.

Out of Liv's hearing, I asked Derra, "How about Rilf?" Rilf was Liv's ex-boyfriend. "Would he do it?"

She inhaled sharply and thought a moment. "He not primed. A baby need a primed father with good parenting attitude. Otherwise they turn out… like Dibi!" Derra actually spat on her immaculate diner floor. "That lout!" She used a few adjectives in there that I wasn't sure of. I'd never run into them in Lingua class.

She stomped off to the kitchen. I didn't like the way her flushes got faster and deeper as she cursed. According to my first aid classes, that was not a good sign. She upset the staff back there and the snafus became more frequent, punctuated with tinny clangs and bonks of kitchen equipment. Which precipitated more curses.

Were doils prone to heart problems? Back to the kitchen I went, and in as soothing a tone as I could manage, I told Derra, "Get Rilf primed. Send him to the hospital and they'll pump him as full of hormones as you want, will that work? Or just pretend that he's done it. Then let Dibi find out." I tried to steer us out of the kitchen, away from the nervous Cousins.

"Rilf," Derra squeaked and one of her scales slid down the edge of her ear to fall on the floor with a tiny *tink.* "Do you think Rilf would do it? I told Liv that Dibi was a coward, but would she listen to me? I swear, that child–"

"Why don't you see if Rilf will cooperate and then get him primed. If he refuses, fake it. Then you'll have time to find Dibi and, uh, talk with him." Right now I couldn't imagine Derra doing much talking. Hitting, yes. Strangling, sure. "How much time do we have?"

"Time?"

"Until the baby…" What? Uh… "Until you need Dibi for…the process."

Derra blinked at me. "Five months."

"Months? Dibi will come to his senses by then."

"You don't know Dibi. Dibi doesn't have senses."

"You should see to Liv. I bet she's even more upset than you are right now, and that's bad for the baby, isn't it?"

"Rilf must do it. Absolutely!" She nodded at me like a bobblehead on speed. Another scale fell, this time off Derra's chin to ricochet off the buffet's drool guard over steaming pots of roasted grains. "I see that he does. I always like him. He brought me present one New Year's. Such a nice present. I don't remember what it was."

Someone back in the kitchen said something and Derra's head whipped around. "Back to work! I don't pay you to listen in. Just because your mother is my second-cousin thrice removed–"

"Four times!" came the reply.

"Four? Then I pay you too much!" Derra and her help eyed each other the way cats do when they meet unexpectedly, sidling around each other and sizing up the coming fight. Then with a signal I couldn't detect, they both broke eye contact and puffed out their cheeks. The cousin returned to work. Derra clucked once. Her colorful pulses dimmed in intensity.

I just don't get alien politics or intrafamily body talk. Instead I filled a glass with boady and handed it to Derra. "If Rilf doesn't want to do it, try calling the cops. Maybe they can drag Dibi's butt in and threaten him with child endanger-ment."

"Dibi doesn't like cops." Derra tapped a talon to her teeth. The front ones were more than slightly pointed. Her tail began to flip up and down like a slow Southern fan. Again came that cluck, but this one she drew out like a chuckle. A shiver ran down my back. "I bet he not like my cousin Noon even worse."

It turned out that Cousin Noon was a rather unsavory type who also didn't like cops but for more concrete reasons. To hear Derra quietly brag about him, he probably wore pinstripe suits when on business and left horse heads in peo-ple's beds.

"I can get him here in a few weeks, maybe a little more," Derra declared. "That give us time." Her scales weren't flaking any more, and her eyes held a sparkle they hadn't had before. To my protests, she said, "Oh, Noon-zio is scary, but he all bluff. Those two men on Vanero? All a mistake. He told me so. Still…" She took a moment before returning her attention to the temperature controls on the buffet. "I explain very carefully that I want live son-in-law out of this."

"Uh, good idea."

"Yes. Cousin Noon, Cousin Noon. Now, where did I store his contact infor-mation?" She clucked confidentially at me. "You can't keep that kind of data on your home drive." She began to poke around the many nooks of the store and I drew a take-out drink. After a while I heard a "Bu-kaw!" of triumph. Derra emerged from the back to wink in what I'm sure she thought was a surreptitious manner, though some of the other customers looked at her as if she'd lost her mind.

I left with a cautiously lighter heart and ran off to Lingua class.

Men. Dibi was a class-A jerk for doing this to Liv and his kid-to-be. Max the Bastard… Well, the name said it all. Randi? Number one, the brite. Number two: brite. Number three: he was always telling me I should be more malac-like, like him.

Okay, Randi might be right on that tiny point: I needed to interact more with the humans on the station, seek the company of my own kind. With my schedule

I didn't have much time, but this was something I had to make a priority. Otherwise I might go mad.

A couple weeks before, Randi's mother, Eliane, had invited me to help with Eid al-Adha preparations. Here they called it Eid Peru. Though I'd told Randi where he could go, there was no reason for me to cancel on his mother. Randi hadn't been going to help us. He left the hard work to the women folk. The chances were practically nil that I'd see him.

The malac might drink alcohol and not observe all the prayers faithfully, but this Islamic holiday they remembered, even if it had a different name. It takes place after Hajj, but the station's malac had no way to go to Mecca. They recalled Abraham's almost-sacrifice of his son, and they took a day of feasting and prayer to observe it.

Back home, a third of the feast is consumed by the family, a third is given to friends and relatives, and the final third is distributed to the poor. My dad's sister used to come over and supervise the rituals, as Dad was kind of lax about such things before he landed in the hospital. Here on Port Malabar everyone in the malac community went house to house to share food. There were no poor so there was no one to give the final third to.

The day called for halal food prep. Out here this meant that they had to make everything themselves. Since there were no animal products on the station, there were no worries about halal– or kosher, for that matter. One of the things I enjoyed about Port Malabar was never having a pang of residual religious guilt when I ate. Our station provided a wide range of vegetables, grains and fruits that, when prepared correctly, produced a very acceptable meat substitute.

Once again I wondered just how long it had been since the malac had left Earth. Over time their Islamic faith had re-formed into something I hardly recognized. They knew the old stories but in a vague way, not like they reread them often. They prayed up to five times a day, but didn't mind if they skipped a prayer or three or even a day or two. They had no call to prayer. Out here where there were no Earth calendars, someone had placed Eid al-Adha, or Peru, at the beginning of the year, and Eid al-Fitre midway through.

I bet Allah didn't mind.

When I arrived in early morning, Ali and Arti were at their aunt Dwi's house up on the edge of Green Terrace. That was the section of the station where almost all the other malac lived. The row house looked upon a park across a spacious pedestrian thoroughfare where saur children shouted and ran around a playground. No human children played with them.

The twins were full of questions for me about The Breakup. I didn't want to talk about it. They didn't take my subtle hints until I laid down the law to them. I tried to be nice, but might have been a little more abrupt than was necessary. I was raw.

But since my old girlfriends had deserted me well before Earth had, these were the most logical available replacements. They were silly but nice, kind of like my BFFs back home. Come to think of it, I hadn't been very silly myself for some time. Maybe I should change that. These girls were curious about me and had helped me a lot during my time here. I tried to cool my temper for the sake of our budding friendship.

The girls looked at each other and then finally changed subjects. Thank you. "Aunt Dwi's kaboba is better than Eliane's," Arti confided, "but everything else, you choose Eliane's cooking if you want the best. She'll show you how to make it if you ask. She'd like that, if you helped."

Kebabs becoming kababa: it was only a tiny change. I felt more at home hearing something familiar.

"Your last name is Yussuf? You are Muslim, Tam?" Aunt Dwi asked as she prepared a basket piled high with fresh produce. Her kitchen was of modest size; its ceiling was much lower than mine. It was proportioned to humans.

"Only on my father's side," I told her. "My mom was…" I didn't want to broach my Jewish mother because I didn't know how these people felt about Jews. "A different faith. We didn't practice much of any religion," I could sum up truthfully.

"You'll convert, of course," she declared and before I could offer an opinion about that, she was piling my arms with foodstuffs.

"What do you substitute for the lamb?" I asked as we packed things onto a large trolley.

It took a while to explain what "lamb" was. Dwi, Ali and Arti were all horrified at the thought. "Kill an animal? To eat it?"

"I'm glad it's not done here. I always felt sorry for those lambs."

Ali and Arti made faces at each other. Arti tried to wipe the idea of meat off her tongue by scraping it with her teeth. We wound up having to stop, we were laughing so hard at her expressions.

Silly was good.

When we got all the food to Eliane's place, Dwi and Eliane descended upon it like crows out to grab what they could of roadkill before a car could mow them down. One moment the food was in baskets on the trolley, piled like a mountain; the next, it was lined up on kitchen counters– twenty-foot-long counters.

We took a minute to catch our breaths before starting on food prep. "Are you and Randi…?" Aunt Dwi sidled next to me to bump me with her hip. She giggled in her husky voice.

"Randi says they're on a hiatus," Eliane declared. Gone was any trace of the Silly. Randi's mother gave me an icy stare that my grandmother would have called the Evil Eye.

The two older sisters chattered for a moment in their native language, perused me, then reached for more food. Eliane was short and slender to the point of angularity. Her dark hair was piled into a smooth dome on her head, except for a pouf at the very front that highlighted the narrow, patterned tattoo across her forehead. The tat indicated that she held power in the community– though never as much as a man would, of course.

I couldn't help but notice that no one of the male persuasion was helping with all this work.

It was difficult to accept that I felt less in common with her than with Derra, who wasn't even my species. How we humans do manage to mess up the simplest things! I determined to correct this. I gave Eliane a smile warm enough– I hoped– to thaw her.

"You have such a lovely home," I said.

Was that obvious enough? I didn't want to talk about Randi. All it did was encourage Dwi to interrogate me. I tried to deflect her, but when would I let

Randi back into my good graces? What had I done to drive him away? It couldn't have been anything he did, could it? Wasn't he the most handsome single man around?

I didn't think things could get worse. As Eliane remained stonily silent, chopping vegetables, the twins joined in the teasing. The older women sometimes took a break to talk between themselves in their language before Dwi started in on me again. Ali made a double-entendre. Arti upped it to a triple that referred to saur reproductive jokes. Dwi slapped her nieces.

"Don't get dirty," she warned.

"Have you set a date?" Arti actually asked out loud.

"A date for what?" I asked around pounding some spices.

All three women who were speaking to me giggled in a horrifying way. I stepped back from my work, unnerved. "Uh, we were just dating," I told them. "Past tense. It was nothing serious."

"But you are planning on marrying him?"

"I hadn't really pl–"

Eliane slapped her spoon against Arti's arm. "Of course she is. After all, there aren't that many good men here to choose from. It's just her good luck that my boy shows interest in her. She'll come running back soon enough."

Arti rubbed her arm and then poured some wine into the marinade.

"Is that halal?" I asked. I guess I could understand everyday drinking– but on a holy day?

"It burns off in the baking," she assured me.

Even so I was startled when, at the dinner itself, everyone from the block sat down with a glass of wine by their plate. Maybe Dad's family had been orthodox or something. I'd never been around them that much. Maybe just being away from the flock for so long had caused these people to stray.

At any rate, I slugged down the wine along with them. Good Jewish girls have nothing against a fine alien wine.

10

Since there were lots of leftovers, I had to borrow a trolley to take what was given me home. First I stopped at Derra's, where business was slowing as evening wore down. I chose from my stash what I thought she'd like. She sniffed everything carefully. Then she tasted– and insisted that I get her the recipes for sambal and raff randang.

SSS HQ was almost empty as the skeleton night shift was out on their rounds. Safeties standby systems weren't left wholly to electronics. I thought that was a voluntary decision and not because computers couldn't do a lot of the work. At some point people had to draw a line, show the machines that we liked to stay busy as well. Too much leisure time causes stagnation.

That didn't mean people turned up their noses at leisure. Bree was working overtime tonight covering for a vacationing officer, and was out and about. I stored a large bag of goodies in the lunchroom, with instructions that people should leave at least a little for Bree. Just to make sure, I bagged a portion and labelled it with her name and a dire note for trespassers. It might have seemed ironic because I also wrote, "May you be inscribed and sealed in the Book of Life."

Down a level, I found Sonny stirring his not-as-famous-as-it-should-have-been mash in the back of his tavern. His hours were over for the day and now he was killing time waiting for a date to arrive.

"She's a hot one," he confided in that bear-like purr of his.

All of Sonny's dates were hot. Or so he said.

Sonny was a gimigol but shorter than average. He was of a subset of the gimigol race, so his size was normal for his people. He had big, wedge-shaped teeth that displayed fully when he produced one of his frequent boisterous laughs. When he worked on his beer he wore his lucky apron, a garish green and purple affair with stay-put glitter trim. Tonight he wore it over a spiffy blue jumpsuit that left a provocative length of his tail uncovered.

"Don't take this the wrong way," I told him as I set down his Eid plate, "but how do you tell a not-hot female from a babe?"

The affable Sonny always gave me practical info that my classes didn't cover. He showed me how babe gimigols moved that was different from other females. He pointed out facial and body features that he looked for. I told him that they sounded like what most saurs had.

After a long thought during which he handed over the stirring of the mash to me so he could use sufficiently broad gestures to make his points, Sonny went through the general inventory of saur qualities, including those of species besides his own gimigol one: Scales. Feather-like scales. Bumpy areas. Big bellies. If they had claws or talons, were they sheathed? Did they wear them long? Carapaces: painted, decorated, or plain? Different tails and ways of holding them. Chins were important, imagine that. Teeth: sharp or wedge-shaped? Big eyes. Squinty eyes. Almond-shaped eyes. And different kinds of pupils– saurs could control them enough to show emotion, though that also involved the muscles around the eyes.

The emotion he was interested in in babe saurs was, of course, carnal interest.

"You think I'm addicted to sex," he accused me.

I shrugged. "I think you've got a lot of women in your life."

His laugh filled the brewery and then he danced around the vats. Spreading his arms out, he clicked his talons as his butt rocked back and forth. His neck and tail coordinated in a sinuous wave. "*La la, forenda yaffa,* I am their hearts' desire!" he sang and I couldn't help laughing.

"I give them happiness!" he proclaimed to the cosmos. Really, Sonny had missed a theatrical calling. "I give them joy. And they give me–" He rolled his eyes at me, clanked his carapace, and wiggled his hips.

I made a very rude noise. "Just like a man."

"Men make you very happy?"

"Men are only interested in–" I wiggled my hips at him. He laughed. "They don't listen. I can't talk to them. At least the ones around here."

"I thought there were lots of malac on Port Malabar."

I stirred his brew with frustrated vigor. "Maybe not enough."

His hand settled on mine. "Too hard, Tam. An easy touch makes a better beer. And you're too picky. Even for a malac, I suspect."

"Oh, you don't put any thought into your relationships. It's hard, dealing with other people."

"Think too much and the world passes by without you noticing. Get out of your head. Get into life!"

With that he went into another dance, this time involving a lot more shaking of his booty as he made large figure-eights across the storeroom floor. I couldn't help myself; I locked down the kettle and then joined in. He showed me to add almost hula dancer-ish arm movements that were echoed by the chin, and then I showed him how to do the Robot. Sonny was astonished when I snapped my fingers to imitate his talon-clacking. Try as he could, he couldn't mimic it without his nails.

His date's arrival interrupted us. Sonny wasn't embarrassed a bit to be discovered dancing, and after giving my malac self a long, curious look, she joined us for a final dance. Now I could see the bits of babe-oscity she had. Her carapace was quite dainty, and her makeup underneath it dark and sultry. And man, could she wiggle her butt! It was amazing how well all that mass could gyrate.

I gave the formal blessing: "May you be inscribed and sealed in the Book of Life," and together they sampled the Eid plate as I explained the holy day. Sonny nodded over the plate. "Very interesting. Tasty. It's good that malac believe in food for celebration, as we do." He tilted his head. "Celebrating the new year with food and good wishes and remembrance– that's a very good thing. We should start that tradition here, more widely than just the malac."

Sonny locked the back door as we left. "Have a great evening," I said. I slugged him hard on his upper arm– a friendly gimigol gesture– then braced myself as he slugged me back as gently as he could, which still staggered me, and we laughed. "And thanks for the lessons."

"You are a good friend, Tam."

Saurs weren't so bad. Maybe humans could learn from them.

When I arrived home Nuke was still up, rocking on the front porch next to Benny, who was wearing a sporting helmet with a sprig of my geraniums over the earpiece. I pulled a small, round table over. On it I set up a large platter for Nuke. I explained the holiday and its prescribed tradition of food for friends.

"May you be inscribed and sealed in the Book of Life," I told him.

His eyes were wide as he watched me. When the platter was complete, he rose from his chair. He actually bowed to me. I think I saw a little moisture gathering in his eyes. Before I could break out into a full-blown bawl I bowed back, and then went inside to bed so he could eat in peace.

It was a couple days later that I survived another Lingua class. I was pretty jazzed. I finally got my "drfz's" perfect enough that the teacher nodded and added a few bonus points to my day's grade. That loser Nekrof, who always sits in the back of the class, snicked his narrow tongue at me darkly, but I just gave him a bright smile in return and tweaked my necklace at him.

As I swung up to take the tram home, I noticed the somewhat rare sight of hair peeking over the top of the middle seat ahead. Bad hair. Great, gawping curls piled on top of a familiar head. Apparently Maui was in town…or someone trying to look like him. My heart began to thud and I fought against a surge of dizziness. Mustn't screw this up!

As I sidled close, his entire body gave a twitch. "Get away from me," he muttered when I blocked his way to the aisle. "I'm not up for any injuries today."

That hurt. I spread my palm across my chest. "Moi? Hurt someone?"

He looked up to glare at me. "Vanish," he instructed through clenched teeth.

In the short time he'd disappeared, he'd either grown a cheesy goatee or stuck one on. It just added to his nightmarish appearance.

"I do not take orders from kidnappers. Here's another idea," I told him. "You come with me to visit the police. There are a few charges I want to level against you." Bree's husband worked downtown, and the tram went right by there. I eyed Max's bulk appraisingly as he continued to utter vile suggestions of what I could do with myself, just as long as I did them away from his person.

"And I am not going to sleep with you," he finished.

I shrank back from him in horror of the very suggestion. "What gave you that idea?"

"You're looking at me like I was a roast beef dinner."

"You're such a doof."

He blinked. "Doof?"

"Idiot. Here we go."

Speed was my only ally. Before he could react I grabbed him and almost threw him off the tram. The columned plexiglas entrance to police HQ was a mere two doors down.

I'd counted on a few officers hanging around whom I could flag for assistance. None were in sight. Still, I managed to push the creep a few paces before the surprise wore off and he whirled around.

"What the bloody eff do you think you're doing?" It was plain that he'd wanted to shout that, but he kept his voice down, as unobtrusive as his wig. Passersby glanced at us.

From here I took to trying to drag him, pulling him along with me as I inched my way toward HQ. "Tell it to the judge!"

Unfortunately it was easy for him to halt our progress. "What are you thinking? Oh wait– the harpy from Earth doesn't *know* how to think, do you?" He tried to shake me off.

But I kept catching him and holding on, pulling with all my might. He broke away. Damn testosterone muscles! My estrogen-charged ones didn't stand a chance. Max took off at a trot. Though I had a female's endurance to beat his, he got a strong, manly start. Damn all men!

I tried to keep him in sight. Bad disguise or no, he was still a human on a station of non-humans. If I lost him I discovered I could generally look around and, between the stocky legs of the gimigols and doilish stilts, there would be a familiar human form walking at a brisk pace. I suppose he didn't want to stand out from the crowd more than he did by running.

Maybe he got tired after a while. I know I did. We were both strolling hard along the streets of the city, him managing to keep a maddeningly consistent distance from me. Then I saw a couple of gimigols approach from the opposite direction.

A flash of familiarity almost knocked me over, obliterating my need to grab Max.

These guys were both wearing copies of Mom's necklace!

Mom's. Necklace.

What an incredible coincidence! I gave a thought to changing priorities during my chase. All I knew was that I had to see them up close, to check if it really was true. Mom's unique necklace, out here in the middle of eternity?

"Hey!" I shouted at them and waved. One glanced my way and I opened up the neckline of my jumpsuit so they could see that I wore the same necklace. I hoped they made the connection.

Instead the one nudged the other and they both stared at me. Their gimigol mouths rippled in agitation. From a dead halt, suddenly they lunged in my direction.

It didn't seem like a friendly "let's compare jewelry" thing to me. I yanked the neckline back into place as if that might stop them. But maybe they just didn't like humans yelling at them. Maybe they thought I was hostile?

I ducked behind a pair of passing doils and made a beeline for whatever narrow space I could lose them in. It was kind of funny. When I was chasing Max I thought I'd used up all my adrenaline, but now I ran like Usain Bolt on speed. Not one but two devils were behind me. I could hear the heavy *thump-thump-thump* of their feet and tails– elephants charging– and the startled shouts of the crowd as they barreled their way through. They were pretty fast for gimigols.

Oh, why hadn't I aimed for police HQ? Too late for that. I wanted to scream, but didn't have the breath. I didn't see anyone I knew in this strange side of town. No one in familiar uniforms stood around to help.

My heart definitely rose in my throat, pounding its beat through me like gunshots. My vision narrowed to what was right in front of me, targeting, targeting… Where would be safe?

Even superhuman adrenaline can run out. My legs began to feel like sticks. My ankles burned all the way up my spine. I couldn't get enough oxygen into my lungs.

Thump-thump-thump!

Someone from behind grabbed my sleeve.

11

I didn't even have the strength to look around. The only thing I could think of was to drop to the ground, just to get out of the grip.

As I went limp a voice said, "For god's sake, don't fight me now!"

It was Max.

I used every iota of strength to straighten my knees and force my feet to move. Luckily Max had all those testosterone-fueled muscles. He steered me, pulling me along in a crouch until I could half-catch my breath.

"Why– are they after– you?" he said between gasps of his own.

"Who are–?" was all I could manage in return.

We hid under a stand and watched them go by. Someone arguing nearby covered up our attempts to breathe.

Max pointed to another gimigol down the road. He wore a copy of my mother's necklace. Another gimigol– I didn't think it was one of the original two– joined him and they began to peer into the nooks and crannies of the street and its crowd.

"Who the hell are they?" I whispered to Max.

"Limbus operatives." He studied them, his eyes almost slits. His nose wrinkled as if he smelled something foul.

This time it was a doil, wearing that necklace, who joined the others.

"An entire nest," he muttered as I saw the originals? coming back from the opposite direction. We were between the two. Max cursed. The two groups made some signals to each other and then began to walk the street in a search pattern.

Where were we? I checked for familiar shops and buildings. If that was a charging station over there, then there would be a– There was. A Safeties sub-station, where gear was stored. Which meant–

"Come on!" This time it was me grabbing Max and running for it.

"What the f–"

We were out in the open. Instead of arguing with me, Max kept pace. I ran for all I was worth as shouts roared behind us.

I found the almost-invisible service door behind the substation. It took me only a moment to use my passchip to get us inside.

"Where does this go?" Max asked as he took in the ramp before us. Toward this end were some computer panels, fire suppressants, hazmat supplies, and two emergency one-size-fits-all vacuum suits. A confusing web of supports and Safeties materiel lined the walls.

"Safeties Systems Tunnels honeycomb the station," I replied and then looked behind us. "Who were they, really?"

He glared at me as if our pursuers were *my* fault.

The door vibrated. Someone was pounding on the other side.

"Do you know your way around here?" Max asked.

"Sure." As we descended below the level's main decking I signaled for a Bug. Within a minute one screamed to a stop at the dock front of us. Max jumped back so hard he hit the Tunnel wall.

I slid into the Bug. "Get in." I indicated the seat next to me.

He made decent time fitting into the saur-molded seat. I showed him how to strap himself in and then I sat there. Where to go?

"My place," I decided, and punched in the coordinates.

Max let out a yelp at the sudden acceleration, another at the 90-degree turn we made. "I rode something like this when I was a kid," he squeaked. "They called it the Corkscrew."

"State fair?"

"Something like that. Afraid I threw up in it."

He did look pale, though that might have been because I wasn't used to seeing his particular pasty skin tone. His eyes might be bugging out just a touch more than they were supposed to. Miles away now, I slowed the Bug down to street inspection speed.

"Thanks," he breathed.

We de-Bugged at my house port. I cracked the hatch and looked around before we climbed up out of the Tunnel. Only neighbors strolled here, friendly faces all. Still, we crept forward across the porch– no Nuke, unfortunately. I'd have liked to ask his opinion– and went inside.

"Do I call the cops?" I asked. "Do you have proof these guys are Limbus? They're the drug runners, right? Limbus."

"No." I didn't know which question he was answering. Max reached for his comm and sent a non-voice zip to someone.

"Let me guess," I said. "For Shorty? Or the Giggler?"

"Giggler?" Max looked at me.

"I believe her name is Leslie."

He rolled his eyes just a trifle, maybe ninety degrees worth. At least this time he didn't deny it. "That damned giggle drives me crazy."

"Crazy with lust?"

He made a face. "She's my cousin."

"Right, cousin," I said. "Ew. There are laws."

"No, really." He glared at me as if how could I think such things? "She's my partner. Business partner. And second cousin."

I gave him a doubtful stare.

"On my father's side."

"Okay, whatever. How about Shorty?"

He gave me a puzzled look so I mimed: short guy. I imitated his smirky laugh. "Wears his pants too tight to move. Liked to feel up that 'cousin' of yours."

His eyes moved left to right, as if he were trying to remember. "Oh. Oh. Yeah, I think his name was Sam or Travis or something. A Terran in league with the group responsible for the volcano. I haven't seen him since. We're beyond that."

That gave me something to chew on. "So. I should call the cops? My partner's husband is a cop. He'd be interested in nabbing these Limbus guys."

"No. This is bigger than Port Malabar." Max took my upper arm in a grip and steered me toward the front door. "Let's meet Leslie downlevel."

As I triggered the outer lock I started to say, "Not too far," as I was afraid he'd be the type who liked to lurk on the really heavy levels, when I noticed two unfamiliar gimigols hoofing down the street in our direction.

I didn't like their speed or the path they took.

Max saw them as well. "Let's get out of here," he told me, again with the hand on my upper arm. "Leslie needs time to get to the rendezvous point. She doesn't have Tunnel access." I could have sworn he added, "Lucky her."

We were back in the Bug in a trice. I set it to Sonny's sector but after leaving the Tunnels there we didn't get much more than halfway down the block before Max spotted some likely thugs coming our way. How were they–?

By the time I got us secure inside the Tunnels again Max was breathing so hard he had to support himself by putting his fists on his knees. I used his inattention to slip off my necklace and shove it into a pneumotube. I punched in delivery coordinates with my birthday as security seal, and hoped that the thugs wouldn't be able to access it.

It had to be the necklace, didn't it? There was too much coincidence involved. They had to be following something and since they were all wearing copies…

So I was hoping that when we got out to kill time on Level 16 we'd be in the clear. It seemed that way for ten, twenty minutes as we wandered around, peering into every dark recess of the construction site. There were a lot of dark corners up there!

This time the guy Max spotted didn't wear a necklace. Max hid me behind some big saur butts almost before I could register it.

"What–?"

"I know this one personally," he said. "Limbus."

It took a few zigzags before it hit me: He knows them well enough to recognize them.

"Is there a wanted poster for these guys?" I whispered. "Something I could signal Central Command for?"

He shook his head. "There are only a handful of known operatives."

We tried to get lost in a group of construction workers going off-shift. We got on a lift and Max hit the button for Level 22.

I cancelled that and made it Level 27.

"We won't be able to move fast."

"They probably won't be able to move at all."

My logic was rewarded with an affirmative grunt, and we enjoyed the restful minutes it took to offload passengers at their various stops on the way down.

"This is no good," Max muttered to me. "Two humans together. Can't get much more conspicuous than that."

"Green Terrace," I suggested. "That's where all the humans live. Well, except me."

"No."

"We'd just be faces in a crowd. Aliens can't tell us apart."

"I know that. But we don't endanger humans."

"Who's 'we'?" I asked. He didn't answer.

My legs were already shaky enough from all the running, but at Level 27 they gave out yelps that I thought Max could hear.

He buzzed Leslie. "Find a map," he told her. "We need to rendezvous fast. You're getting closer but the port's crawling with Limbuses. I think they might recognize me."

I couldn't hear Leslie's response as we stumbled through the streets. We grabbed a tram, got off, and then took one traveling perpendicular to the first.

Still on his phone, Max asked me, "Dobie Farms raftin fields?"

I checked my own equipment. "Level 24, section 9-55, east side."

He parroted that into the phone, clicked it shut, and then told me, "Let's keep to this level to get over there."

I led the way while he scanned what crowd there was. These were the smaller species for the most part, with a lower center of gravity and less bulk to move around. We didn't see any suspicious gimigols. We found a cart stand quickly and were able to ride north to the ag sectors without unduly torturing our suffering arches. Once we reached the right section we sent the cart back and then took the lift up to Level 24. My arches began to feel alive again, though they were still angry.

This ag sector was a marsh. Non-blooming lilypads grew thick in mud with only raised walkways between patches. The walks were slick with condensation from the humid air.

Now was the test: was it the necklace they were following, or was it Max? And how did they get a lock on either of those?

It took us a long while to get across the farm. No Limbuses showed up. Ahead of me on the pathway, Max slipped and tumbled into the muck. He emerged covered with dark mud. It clung to his wig like clots of cottage cheese.

I squatted down to give him a hand out but I couldn't help it; despite goons chasing us with who-knew-what on their mind, I had to laugh. This I could understand. I could see where the mud had gotten inside his jumpsuit because it pooched out in pockets. Must not be very comfortable! I'm afraid I was laughing so hard I snorted.

So he pulled me in, too.

"Not so funny, eh?" he sneered at me as I emerged, furiously swiping the gunk out of my eyes and ears.

I pushed him back. He must not have been expecting it because he made a very satisfying "sploink!" sound as he submerged, flailing his arms. While he straightened himself I struggled to heave myself and my extra mud poundage out of the swamp.

The mud squelched inside my jumpsuit as I got my feet under me and managed to lever my too-heavy self to a stand. Max glared at me.

"Well?" I asked him. "Are you going to stay in there all day? Don't we have places to be? People to meet?"

He tried to get out. He jumped and fell back. He tried pulling himself out but could never get beyond chest-above-swamp. I could hear very soft curses coming from him, but they were never directed at me. Finally he put his elbows on the walkway, crossed his wrists, and stared up at me.

"Magic word," I prompted.

He gritted his teeth. "Please," his voice came out like gravel in a cement mixer.

But I waited. "You won't pull me in?"

"No."

"Swear."

Oh, he swore a bit, and unfortunately those words concerned me. When he saw I wasn't moving, he finally said, "On my honor as a Guardian. I. Will not. Pull you in."

What was a Guardian? Could be a fake word to fool me; could be something to keep in mind for later.

So I nodded and pulled him out– not a thing I'd recommend anyone else doing in that condition. Slick pavement, mud everywhere, heavy grav– I had to sit on the path and pull his arms before we made any progress.

"A little out of condition, are we?" I smirked when it was all over.

His eyes sent fury beams in my direction that I could almost see. "I'm not used to all this… activity."

"Tsk, tsk. Healthy body, healthy mind. That fancy ship of yours needs a treadmill."

He said a few words as he pulled himself up to stand, and some mud oozed out above the waistband of his jumpsuit. "Eyuch," he muttered.

"East side," I reminded him.

"East side." He bowed and motioned me ahead. "You first."

I hate to say it, but I soon got used to the warm ooze sharing clothing with me. What can I say? If I were picky about such things I'd never be in Safeties. But prissy Brit behind me kept muttering about his unkempt state and mad Americans.

"I doubt Leslie's been able to make our time. She's not a farm girl," Max said as we passed through the airlock from this section into the eastern one. There was no marsh here, just hanging vegetable plants, red on our right, greenish gold on our left. They made a slow mechanical circuit of their beds, run by a belt placed about five feet over our heads. Vines cascaded everywhere, obscuring our view.

"You got a more precise location?" I asked just as blue light flashed by me. What?

"Run!" Max grabbed my hand and pulled.

We ran away from the direction those blue pulses came from. Around us vines dropped to the ground as the blue cut them in pieces.

I steered us diagonally, across the vine beds. We ducked into the thickest of it, then trotted at slow speed (damned difficult in the grav!) so as not to rustle anything. I think our mud-covered condition added to our camouflage.

"Exit ahead," Max hissed at me.

I could see it too: an emergency manual exit. It would have a ladder inside. Maybe a lock, though I doubted that; this was a new section of the port, manufactured after the "no lock on exits" laws went into effect. But we ran for it anyway. The word "exit" was just too tempting.

It was only the last three strides that brought the blue pulses zapping in our direction again. I screwed the air lock latch clockwise (righty loosey, lefty tighty) and Max pulled the door open. He waited for me to get in. A blue pulse missed his wig by inches.

Once inside I secured the latch. "Hurry, dammit!" Max urged.

"You go ahead. This will slow 'em down."

"Not by much."

"Big gimigol butts on a ladder in heavy grav will slow 'em down even more," I said. "Get going!"

By the time he was five rungs up I'd joined him on the ladder. Ever try a ladder in heavy grav? Where the rungs are farther apart than they should be, because they weren't built for humans? With about fifty pounds of mud and lily vines oscillating within your pants?

Still, we got up to the next viable level before we heard the door below us open. Max grabbed and lifted me before I was level with this floor, and we took off to find a quicker route.

We got halfway across this section before a new array of blue pulses appeared. The plants they hit sizzled. I didn't want to know what my flesh would sound like if I got targeted.

Finally– "There!" I yelled, and we both stumbled as fast as we could to a sub-Tunnel entrance. Sub-Tunnels were just up-down non-public lifts, connected in spots to the actual Tunnel network. Fine with me. I slapped my passchip against it and the door took an interminable time to squee open. No one must have used this in some time. We slipped inside and then the door had to slooowly close.

"Hang on to your stomach," I said and hit the button for Level 16.

Max reached over me, cancelled that, and signaled the Core.

I added the "quick rise" function.

The rapid acceleration hit first, driving down to our ankles, but then gravity loosed its hold, a sensation that gulped me in a big wave from those ankles up and then bobbed down to settle in my stomach. *Easy, fella,* I told it and gritted my teeth.

"Good– lord!" Max gasped as he turned green underneath the mud. He grabbed for the steady handle on the side of the lift, and clutched his gut with the other hand.

Through the changes in gravity I could definitely feel the station's rotation. I hung on to the left of the lift. It came to a sudden halt. I had also taken hold of a handle, but Max had lost his grip and now bumped hard against the top of the lift.

"Do not throw up in here!" I ordered. Zero-G barf was disgusting. It got into everything. Bree had cussed me out good the first three times I'd done it.

Max desperately looked about for something. Finally he took his sleeve cuff and yakked into it. Afterward he tugged the adjusting strap so whatever was inside there stayed inside.

"Color's better," I approved of his face as I triggered the door. "Now where?"

Again with the steel grip. "This way," he said, and we took off at a fast, well, swarm since we couldn't walk. We had to swim, grabbing what handholds we could find. As a rule, in-station zero-G areas weren't meant for fast travel.

I'd never been this far into the civilian zero-G parts of the station. The panicked rush must have made me clumsy. I noticed that Max also missed the occasional handhold, but he was good about checking his movement with a touch on the wall here and there, which righted himself.

He reached out to wrap his arm around my waist just as I overshot my landing spot. I was just about to land on top of some blinking lights that didn't look like they should be touched except by an expert. He yanked me back.

"Thanks."

He didn't say anything, but he looked lost. It's one thing to have a general direction and another thing when you get to that vague place. We both poked our heads around a corner for a moment before withdrawing like turtles into their shells.

"I know where we are," he said.

"Great. Where?"

"You stay here." His eyebrows came together in an inward frown. "No," he said, "you stay behind me but make yourself small where you can while I take care of some business."

12

"Small?" What, did he think I was fat? The cad!

We emerged into a major corridor, a world of hand- and toe-holds, magnetic strips, and the occasional rope railing. There was no floor, no ceiling, just a passage going north-south. Max grabbed my wrist again–that was getting old–and pushed off against the wall from a squat.

I think he did it harder than he wanted, for we zipped through the air and he grabbed a landing with an "Oof." I landed fairly lightly behind him.

About a dozen more such trajectories in this less-travelled area of the station, and he pointed to a projection in the wall. "Small," he ordered.

I managed to nail the position exactly on my own jump. He flew past me, arms outstretched like Superman. His speed carried him to a storefront– no, a hotel front– a hundred feet from my position.

He chatted with the screen there for a few minutes and dug into a pocket. Ident check. I wondered what kind of fake ID he had.

That wasn't ID; that was a credit chip. Whoever was on that screen was getting a bribe. Good boy. With that fancy spaceship of his I knew he had the money; he could spread it around.

A glance over his shoulder was my signal to push off toward him. I kept it low, below the view level from the screen, and crouched by Max's knees as he affirmed our rooms.

"With laundry and shower," Max insisted.

"Laundry?"

Max made a show of his filthy sleeve, which matched his generally filthy condition. Mostly mud, a little yak, and a whole lotta ugh.

The female voice onscreen said, "If you want cleaning facilities, you should try a gravity-fed area."

Max waved his credit chip at the screen. "Three showers. I'm pretty dirty."

I guessed I could force myself to use Max's shower if my own room didn't have one. I scratched under my chin. The mud was drying and beginning to flake. It itched like crazy and left clouds in the air behind me.

"Three showers worth of water, plus laundry. Chemical," the screen finally decided.

"Done."

The screen dispensed a room card. I waited for the second one to appear.

"C'mon," Max told me as the screen blanked.

"One room?"

"Why would I want two? We're keeping you secret, kid. Let's get going. Eyes are everywhere."

His pocket beeped and he retrieved his comm. I could hear someone whispering in his ear, though I didn't see an earpiece. He told it, "Going dark. I'll contact you tomorrow."

I had to learn more about what the hell he was involved with, which side he was on. For now, though, a shower was my priority. I swam inside the hotel, curious to see what a zero-G hotel room with shower would entail.

Actually, I don't think I should really give it as grand a name as "hotel." The center of the place was starkly utilitarian and built like a beehive: entry holes stacked upon each other. There must be hundreds of holes in the place.

A few unfamiliar alien types swarmed up ropes, oozing into the tinier of the doorways. Two of them could constrict like snakes, puffing up the parts of their bodies that weren't currently trying to make it through the hole.

"Kind of like pulling on jeans that are a size too small," I decided, and prayed that the interior was a lot larger than the exterior. Perhaps these were tunnels that linked to large rooms further on.

"There we are." Max pointed midway up from the spot designated as "floor." Was that hole even smaller than the ones closer to us?

He gave me a boost via my behind. It surprised me, so I flailed and began to spin clockwise. I wound up against the wall, looking down at him. I gave him a sour face for his efforts. "Hands off," I said, and proceeded to squeeze into the doorway. I wanted to be far enough inside so I could watch him and his larger self try it.

Wriggling in zero-G is difficult, but I made it. I could feel the heat from Max's hands approaching my butt again to push, and there was no way I was going to allow that humiliation! So I pulled myself through and… in.

The size of the room so surprised me I forgot to turn to watch Max's entrance, punctuated by three grunts and a curse.

"We need another room," I told him.

There wasn't enough space to breathe, practically. It was shaped like a hot dog bun with fully half the "room" allotted to a sleep sack. That's right; it was two bodies wide and only enough more for elbows. Good thing I never suffered from claustrophobia.

"It'll do," Max said, but he couldn't mask his grimace. "We'll just have to get cozy."

The cloud of dirt and grime was still drifting off both of us and seemed to take up an inordinate amount of space. "Where's the shower?" I asked. "I'll go first. Is it down the hall? Where's the door?"

Max looked around and found a screen. "Where's the shower?" he asked it. Instead, room instructions came up. We both studied it. I think the low sound of surrender came from both of us.

The shower was part of the room's mechanics. It would take care not only of our own grime but that stuff that was now floating all around.

"Laundry," Max told the screen. Hidden in the wall was a chute for deposit and a separate one for return.

"You go first," I volunteered. I prepared to squeeze out of the joint again. I wanted to track down a robe or blanket for modesty. Heck, I'd even let him wear it while he hung out in the lobby and I took my shower. I was a generous person.

Max pointed at the room charges. "Damn it, we're just allotted one shower per eight-hour period."

I let a beat pass. "I am not going to sleep in this filth."

"And I'm not going to sleep next to your filth," Max agreed. He snapped his fingers. "Come on."

"Come on, what?"

"Strip." He began to pry open his shirt. Right there in front of me. He pulled it off, trying to keep the section around the worst of his yak closed, reached for his pants, and paused. "Well?"

"What? You don't… I'm not…"

"We will if we want to get clean."

In this small space, my own fumes were starting to get to me. They were a heady blend of benzene and BO, combined with something that reminded me of fresh cow droppings. Must be fertilizer from the mud.

There was nothing to be done about it.

"Turn around," I insisted. I did the same, bumping up against him as I disrobed. I did it fast, as if that would make it less revealing. Fast doesn't work in zero-G, especially when two people are bending over.

"I think we should undo each other."

I clamped my mouth onto a shriek. The nerve!

"These chambers are built for taller species," Max said as he tried to work his jeans off his lower legs. "If you could grab the ends of my pants, I could do the same for yours."

Rather than squishing my face against his butt so I could reach my feet, I reluctantly agreed. We didn't say anything as we peeled each other.

"Watch the barf," I reminded him, and he made sure to keep that sleeve as closed as possible as we maneuvered.

He wore red briefs with a little black stripe.

Max partially jackknifed to get back to head-to-head position, and we gathered up our things to stuff into the chute.

"Thank you," it said. "Your laundry will be delivered in seven hours. Alarm?"

"Yes." I told it a half-hour before my normal wake time. I was exhausted and wanting to forget this entire day, but I did have a job to go to tomorrow.

Max stowed his nasty wig in a net drawer tethered to the wall. Underneath it, his hair had matted. The blond had turned into literal dirty blond. He peeled off his goatee. I squeaked; I had begun to think it was real! But it came off in one piece, goatee and matching mustache, giving a little ripping sound as he grimaced. He stuffed it into the waste chute.

"We need a shower mask," Max told the room screen as he handed me the one that had been fastened to the wall.

"Rooms are provided with–"

"There's nothing here," Max lied. "Your last customer must have stolen it."

After a few minutes, another mask popped out of the clean laundry chute.

We hadn't looked at each other during those minutes. Max made a show of securing his mask around eyes, nose, mouth and ears so he wouldn't have to look at me.

Me, I had to watch how he did it because I'd never showered in zero-G. He reached to flatten the seal around the bottom of my ear.

"Commence shower," he instructed the room.

The sleep sack rolled up upon itself and tucked with a snap behind a cabinet door. Protective covers rolled over the various room screens.

Then a jet of soapy water hit my shoulder, ricocheting off to smack Max in the face. Nine more jets hit us at various angles. We rearranged ourselves to get the most out of the scouring. I tried to scrub the suds into my filthy hair, only to have Max's face slide across my boobs.

"Sorry." His voice echoed from within his mask.

There was no helping it. Space was at a premium, we were weightless, and the very force of the water kept propelling us against each other's wet, soapy bodies.

I saw something with nubbies on the wall. It came off in my hand, and I used it like a washcloth.

"Me, too," Max said, so without thinking I began to scrub his back.

The water went into pause mode, giving us a chance to attack that dirt. Max obliged my back as well. Because neither one of us could bend over far, he took it all the way down. I decided that the least I could do was to return the favor.

I mean, I didn't want to sleep with someone who reeked.

And he did have a nice butt. No tats, though. It gleamed with soap, and when I touched it, it tweaked a bit.

I couldn't help myself. I wondered how much more it would tweak and dimple if doing something else.

No, we didn't handle privates. Those we could reach on our own.

Max twiddled my toes as he washed them. From behind, thank you.

When he replaced the nubbie thing, we got a three-second countdown before the rinse cycle began. That soap was slick. As the water blasted me against him, I slid down his body as much as the room allowed.

I think he found the experience interesting.

"Nothing personal," he assured me and turned to rinse some other parts.

A powerful fan drained the room and sent us crashing against the wall and each other. For a moment the strength of the vacuum made me wonder if it would strip all our natural body moisture from us, but when it stopped my hair was still slightly damp. No beads stood on my skin, but that skin was moist and healthy.

We disentangled ourselves from each other.

Max was eying me in a most disconcerting way. The right corner of his mouth kept twitching until he noticed my frown. Then he'd look at something else and that twitch came back.

"I didn't pay for vid," he said. "Not much to do now, I suppose. You have any ideas?"

"Comb," I said, and held out my hand to the laundry pick-up chute. A comb appeared there and I went to work on my hair.

It wasn't my hair he ogled. "Zero-G has its… points, doesn't it?"

I was darned if I was going to clutch my bosom just because he couldn't be professional about this. So I kept combing. I might have added a little more energy to the job than usual.

"Yeah," he said.

"No," I said. "We're going to need at least a newscast, to see what's going on out there."

"Maybe later."

"So they can grab us right now in our altogether, while news crews film the action."

That made him rub his chin. Which had sprouted the merest shadow by now, damn him anyway. I always liked the wilderness guy look.

With a sigh he turned and gestured. The screen nearest the top part of the sleep bag compartment– about nine inches wide– blinked on, showing local network feed. Max switched to the news.

We watched for a full round of stories before they began to repeat themselves. Max used my comb on his own head thoughtfully.

"Not a word about any gunfire on the station," I remarked, and he nodded.

"Odd."

I resisted the urge to call Bree and ask her what was going on. This was her day off. She could wait until tomorrow, but I'd have a lot of questions for her then.

Even without the water we kept bumping into each other. He turned me away from himself even as he triggered the sleep bag to release. "This means the station's sensors didn't register us, the sensors have been edited by someone, either friend or foe, or Central Command authorities aren't announcing because they don't want us, whom they've pegged as 'foe,' to know that they're actually waiting just outside, about to take us down."

"What if," I said, "someone at Central is trying to cover this up from the authorities? Someone working with these goons. We're off scot-free that way."

"Unless they use us as a pay-off. They present us to Limbus for a nice, quiet reward, and those are their people waiting for us outside."

We pondered. "I prefer the 'we got away scot-free' scenario," I decided.

"Hem," was all he said.

"Why don't you stick your head out and see if anyone's there?" I looked at the sleep sack. It wasn't much; just limp red material strapped to the wall with a bump of a pillow sewn on. A few more straps floated half-heartedly from its side-seams and what might be the bottom if it was unrolled all the way.

Surprisingly enough, Max rolled himself into a ball, flipped over, and did indeed peek through the room's aperture. "All clear," he said, followed by a low mutter I couldn't make out. I could guess; he'd want to have access to a view of the hotel entry as well. Maybe the entire level and the level below us.

Who knew if an entire team was poised nearby?

Our room screen reminded me when I checked that our clothing wouldn't be returned for a few hours yet. Maybe the bedsack could be draped into some kind of tunic?

I tried it on for size, though it was still secured to the wall. It covered all the important areas.

"What will you wear to jail?" I asked him coquettishly as he unwound back into a feet-toward-the-door position. I gave his lower area an eyebrow-wiggle.

He actually blushed. Good. Then he grabbed the sack from me.

"Hey," I said, "dibs on the bed." I mean, what was the difference between a sack and air in zero-G? It was the principle of the thing.

"Service, I need another bedsack."

"One has been provided."

"I like double-sized. More comfortable."

So after the screen displayed a surcharge and Max okayed it, we got another sack. We tried them side-by-side. No matter how still we were in them, we still bumped.

Max growled to himself. Then he yanked the sides of his sack open and did the same to my sack.

"Hey!"

"Shut up." He held his one sack side to mine, and the seams reached out to each other to close. He did the same to the other side, and now we were in one large sack. Face to face. And other parts next to each other as well.

It wasn't as embarrassing as you might think. In fact, the room seemed to be getting a little warm.

"Turn around," he said.

"Yeah, right."

"Okay." Max turned around, and our sack went every which-way. I reached out to steady us, same as Max was doing. He used one of the extra straps to secure that side to the opposite wall. It barely reached, despite the close space.

I must have made a noise, for he said, "Go to sleep. I need to think this thing through. We might be able to– separately– grab a ship to the Nowall system. You could go to Bar-Tok, that would keep you away from the action–"

"Think quietly," I said. "I'm trying to sleep, remember?"

He shut up, and I pretended to settle down.

Zero-G was quite comfy once you got used to it, despite being smashed up against a man. A naked man. A naked man from home.

Sure, he might not be the most pleasant of men. He might have been the one who kidnapped me and plopped me into this predicament. Well, even if he had saved my life doing so.

Why, he had saved my life again today. I smiled at the back of his neck. He had a nice neck, a nice hair line. It was good human hair, too, not that mangy wig.

Good shoulders. There was not one tattoo on them. Those shoulder blades reminded me of happier, more innocent times back home with similar shoulder blades in front of me, on a bed, full gravity.

My breasts pressed against a rather ripply back. I used the slight movements of the bag to bump against his butt. He did have a solid one. I wondered again about that dimple as the bag shifted to press me against him.

"Oh, hell," he said, and before I knew it, he'd turned around. Which sent me turning as well, except that the bag stopped me. And his hand on my arm.

He de-rotated me so that we were nose to nose. And then–

Mouth to mouth.

I don't know if the arm around me was an embrace or a clamp, but what the heck. I added a little more stability of my own and slid my arms around his neck and shoulders. His tongue was rather insistent, but I was coy. I waited. Okay, a microsecond before I opened to him. We did a hot tongue twist. Oh yeah, this was going somewhere I might not particularly want to go, but I could enjoy the journey getting there. His chin scratched my cheek as I nipped his ear.

The Bastard could kiss. I dug in for some more. Hot. Not too moist.

Thorough.

"You'd better not have any diseases," I growled, and he gave a growl back.

He pulled my butt toward himself, which involved even more interesting sensations.

But then my head bumped hard against a projection on the wall, snapping me back to reality. I rubbed it with a grimace. "I don't think this is going to work."

That glint came into his eyes, the one that meant that all neurons in that male brain– the one above his waist– were firing. "Don't be so sure," he said.

He commenced to putting all those extra bed straps to use. He tore one off to attach it to the wall. Next he fastened my arms with it, comfortably apart.

"S&M," I remarked, and he licked his way up from the strap to my shoulder, then kissed me again. No bump. A lot of tongue, which petered out as Max floated away from me.

"Whoops," he said. He looked at the straps and then tied the two of us together loosely at the waist.

For a moment I had a mental image of the authorities coming upon us in that position. A major section of my brain pushed that out of sight and I returned my attention and skills to the gentleman in the room.

It was like swimming with both people caught up in different currents. The straps helped, but not enough. I didn't want to wrap my legs around his waist because damn it, I wasn't ready yet. So I ripped the one strap off the wall and grabbed his shoulder while he took hold of my butt and began to work his way down me.

Soon his shoulder was out of grab-reach, but I didn't mind. I steadied myself with my feet and hands, bobbing there in mid-air, while Max attached like a leech to some very sensitive spots.

No begging involved. No threats. He did it voluntarily.

I chided myself for my selfishness, but if I let go to attend to my partner's needs, I'd just– there. There! *There!*

I forgot about his needs for the blessed moment. Good Max. Dutiful Max. He kept at it and followed my instructions.

I've been to a lot of places in my life, but I hadn't been to that particular one in a long, long time.

After a while when my brain began to function again, I hoped that the room was sound-proofed.

And that Max couldn't back far enough to see the ridiculous position I was in.

He did back off, but only to tether his knees. "Grab on to something," he instructed me tenderly, and went for the gold.

What a piece of work is man! How noble in reason, how infinite in faculties, in form and moving…

Lord, I was melting in poetry and porn. I wrapped my legs around his manly waist and held onto his shoulders, potential skull injuries be damned.

This was worth it. (And on occasion my head did find the little pillow.) Spheres of sweat rolled off us to collide again in tiny exploding sprinkles. He heaved and we missed true juncture, heaved again and *whammo,* it was exactly right.

"Change," he said and though I had been thoroughly enjoying the experience, I was open– way open– for a permutation.

Our next two tries were utter failures, but when we strapped his shoulders to a toggle and I braced myself with two wall handles, he took hold of either side of my hips and went to town.

"That's the ticket!" he grunted to me while wearing a grin that would have done a Viking berserker proud. I'm afraid his backside got a little pummeled during that position, but he didn't seem to mind.

At that point I wasn't minding anything. No outside thoughts dawdled; no sudden reminders of things to be done.

All there was was Max, and particularly Max's body. All man, so much muscle, and working it so very, very well.

Every time I voiced my approval he grinned again and went at it with renewed vigor.

Finally it was time for him to let loose with a few yodels of his own. Manly ones, ones that came from his gut. He was magnificent even in that.

A small cloud of sweat beads exploded across both of us at The Moment. I don't think he noticed, but it seemed the perfect capper to me.

Of course, right then everything was pretty perfect. The room. The world. The history of the universe. Us.

His gaze followed the mechanics of pulling out, then came slowly up my body as I straightened out. Finally his eyes met mine.

Such eyes. Dark teal, glinting and deep. Primal and penetrating. yet so intelligent.

For a moment I couldn't breathe. His being filled the room so that there wasn't space for me unless I burrowed inside his self.

"Who *are* you?" I asked from out of nowhere.

That brought him out of it, as if I'd struck him or dashed him with a bucketful of cold water. His body went from relaxed to attention, the warmth in his eyes washed away to cool gray.

"You don't need to know that."

Men! I huffed, "I just want to know– You play at being such a dork. Or sometimes an ordinary joe. Then–"

He busied himself with readjusting the bedsack for sleeping double. "Discharge fan," he instructed tersely. Our sweat-globules and other liquids were quickly sucked out of the room.

A final snap of a line and he secured us for sleep.

"Jeez," I said. "You can't even talk. Not even a little bit."

"Don't make this something it wasn't. We need to sleep. Tomorrow will come soon enough."

What a jerk. Still, my body must have realized that what he said was true enough, for after the various excitements and exercise of the day– and with our backs to each other– I dozed off quickly.

And awakened to his hands moving on me. Then his lips. I arched to him and was rewarded with a knock on the brain by the wall.

We managed to do it a little more efficiently this time, and this time I gave him some personal attention. It was only polite. And besides, it might make him friendlier afterward.

But no, the rat bastard. When I was ready to hum, perhaps break into song and then talk, he made like a clam and pretended to sleep.

The arrival of our clothing in the morning was as good a wake-up call as any. Wearing an air mask while taking a zero-G shower might seem a deterrent to sex, but we managed it in fairly good form. Hell, in excellent form!

I couldn't stop smiling. Even when he frowned at me, I just half-closed my eyes and smiled a little bigger to make up for him. I didn't mind. Didn't mind at all.

"Nothing personal," I assured him cockily as I secured my jumpsuit fastenings. I was a lady who took what I wanted, that was all.

"Right-o."

Now I finally had a chance to ask him questions. I began again with, "Who are you?"

"I told you, my name is Max."

"Gee, most guys would at least buy me dinner for what I just did. Full name. Or shall I continue to call you Max Effing Bastard?"

His lips kind of flapped at that before a troubling look passed over his face. Finally he set his jaw and ground out, "Maximilian Fitzhubert Blakeney."

"Oh my god."

He made a face at me. "'Max' will do."

"Well." I considered the information. It was just a beginning. "Good enough. Not your fault. Now who the heck are you? What's going on? Are you a smuggler? Who were those guys?"

He fiddled with some of the ties from our bed. "Members of Limbus."

"Limbus. Drug runners."

"A terrorist organization."

I blinked. Okay. "You a member? Or just working for them?"

The look he gave me could have soured an entire grocery display of milk. "I work against them. Against them spreading."

"So… You're a cop? An undercover cop? A spy?"

"You don't need to know any more. It's for your own protection."

I wheedled. I urged. I nagged, but he didn't open his mouth. Finally I asked, "Where's Earth? How do I get off this joint?"

"What, you don't– No, you wouldn't. Not many do. We're trying to keep it secret. There are too many people, organizations, that would use that information and invade… or worse."

"Invade Earth? For real?" Now it was my turn to think about things. "But I'm me. I'm not going to invade. I'm just going to go home. Tell me. Tell me now!"

Again he turned into the Great Stony Face.

I may have slugged him a few times. Maybe hard. He still didn't say a word.

Bastard!

Good thing I hadn't felt the need for pillow talk last night. I would have blabbed, blabbed, blabbed and he wouldn't have returned an iota of the favor. Jerkface.

He made a show of adjusting his clothing and pushed himself toward the exit. After he stuck his head out to check for prowlers, he paused for a second to look back at me. Did he want a farewell kiss?

"Were your eyes always that blue?" he asked.

I batted them at him. "They are now."

Bless the boy, his face clouded as he must have begun to realize what I'd been through. He let me swim out of the room before he checked out.

"Bastard!" I called sweetly over my shoulder.

And that was the last I saw of him for quite some time.

13

Two weeks later Bree and I were going down to Level 27 and entered the lift at 19 along with a lot of other folks to various levels. Level 27 was two levels lower than Bree ever wanted to go, so she was in a bad mood. I just hoped that my new insoles could help my feet. I wasn't sure those feet had recovered from my last trip down there.

Bree had been able to confirm that Limbus was indeed a terrorist organization. She'd been intrigued that a malac named Max the Bastard had shown up on the station, fresh in from my home planet, but I didn't really go far into our story. I wasn't sure what it was yet. When I had things figured out, I'd discuss it with her.

We had to check on methane emissions from heavy-grav swamp farms, which was one of Bree's least-favorite duties. This added to her disgruntlement.

Inside the elevator we moved to the side only to discover Nuke taking up most of the back corner.

"Good morning, Nuke!" I told him brightly. I didn't run into him much away from home.

He was dressed for a hard day's work, clad in rough overalls, a utility belt that would have supplied a dozen Batmans, and had lunch bucket in hand.

"Tam," he said quietly and cocked his head at me.

Right. He didn't want to attract too much attention. As if that were possible, him with all his bulk and extra arms and everything.

Bree took one look at him and turned her back with a snuffled mutter. I could hear a couple syllables of it, and they weren't pretty.

"Nuke's my neighbor," I told her in low tones. "Cut it out. He's nice."

She muttered again, and this time I could swear I heard the word "freak" in there.

I shook my head at Nuke in apology and he twitched his two left shoulders. It was an odd movement but I instantly translated it as "It happens. Nothing you can do about it."

He got off on our level and slogged heavily to a public tram as Bree held back. Apparently we were catching the next one.

"What was that all about?" I demanded.

"War-mongering mutant monster," Bree told me. "Never understood why the station let him come here, much less made him a citizen. If I were in charge, things would change. You should move."

"He's a great neighbor."

"He's mutie scum." The next tram appeared in the distance and we shuffled along with the rest of the crowd to form a queue. "Made for war and killing."

"Then the sin falls on those who created him," I protested. "He's peaceful as far as I've seen. I think he's lonely."

"He'd better not invite more mutie filth here," Bree snapped.

"What has gotten into you?"

"I've seen too many of 'em."

"Not of him. He's Nuke. You don't know him."

"We don't want trouble on this station. He's the first sign. Others will see him and figure they can come, they can bring their war and crime and perversions here. I want my children brought up on a safe station."

"Nuke's not going to harm your children," I said. "They'll see what a good friend he can be as well."

But she just gave a drawn-out gimigol grunt.

We were still waiting for the next tram when both our shoulder comms buzzed. "Meteor deflection run," HQ told us. "This is not a drill." We were conveniently close to a sub-Tunnel lift, it being grouped with the civilian ones. Bree gleefully signaled that we were on our way. Anything to get out of heavy-grav duty.

My first real deflection! Of course Bree would handle most of it since I hadn't received full accreditation, but I'd be there helping out.

We grabbed vacuum suits– I knew how to cinch a generic one so I wouldn't be swimming in the material– and then took the ascent to the axis at a quicker rate than civilian lifts. If a difference of three levels is noticeable down where I usually hang out, a difference of ten or fifteen (they tend to space out as they come in to the center) makes your stomach sit up and take notice with a squawk. The first few times I'd been to the axis I'd thrown up the big breakfast I'd previously been served by Safeties staff. Would've felt real stupid if three other newbies hadn't done the same thing. The seniors got their jollies out of seeing us upchuck. I'd certainly gotten a kick out of seeing Max do it.

But you get used to it, even when it came rarely. Zero G? Even without sex it's every bit as fun as those astronauts back home would have you think. It's controlled freedom– controlled, that is, if you're inside a station. I wouldn't want to be outside it, especially without a tether or nav system. Float off forever into that big blackness out there? It wouldn't take me five minutes to go crazy.

But Bree and me, we had a job to do outside Port Malabar. SSS has a small dock inside the hub, and we half-pulled, half-swam our way on the vacuum side of the wall that led to it. That's not as cool as it sounds, as we had to keep attaching and detaching roped anchors along the way. Regulations. Still, it was something I'd practiced on my own a few times– just not in vacuum– since That Night and I managed well enough. Our pilot was just swimming in from the opposite direction as we pulled up to the designated ship's airlock. We nodded to him and he began the process of opening the thing.

While he was doing that I looked around curiously. The hollow axis stretched into what seemed like eternity, though we were at a point close to the bay entrance. Shuttles were tethered here and there to the Core walls, next to airlocks. Compared to them, our Service ship seemed largish only because of the pseudopods that hugged it all over. If you took those away, it wasn't much bigger than three SUVs strapped together. Betcha its mileage was better than anything back on Earth.

Bree required the two of us to go over a checklist while our doil pilot, Captain Arcus, went over one of his own. Some idiot on a previous mission had shortchanged us, and Bree made a note to reprimand whoever that had been. That meant that we had to blip over to a storage hangar, grab a small bomb or "juice bucket," and wait while Bree took it out into vacuum where she secured it on the ship to bring us up to full armament. All our buckets were stored outside, as was most of the equipment. That way it didn't take up precious room inside.

The interior of the place wasn't as roomy as the simulators made it seem, though the lack of gravity helped. A person could hang upside down next to the other crewmember instead of spreading out on the same plane. Still, with her bulky spacesuit on, Bree had to wriggle carefully between jutting station boards before she strapped herself into her seat. I did the same above her. Or maybe that was below her. We checked our displays and coordinated back with HQ and Central as Captain Arcus eased us out of the core.

I held my breath. I'd never been outside Port Malabar, not with time to rubberneck. We swung out and our route allowed me a decent view of the station I'd been living in the past two-plus years. It didn't look all that elegant. It was pretty much a cylinder because all we could see was the hull that protected the real goods. It was mostly black against the darkness, interrupting a sky full of stars, but where various ships shone their lights on it, it showed white as snow. There were some splotches: airlocks and hatches and tie-to's, as well as bright sparks that were navigation lights. The most important thing you could say about it: it was big. Damned big.

We cruised over the surface, our floodlights illuminating nooks and crannies. Then I checked the general neighborhood. It was startling to see just how large cruisers were compared to the more usual frigates that came around. A few cruisers parked nearby like moons though there was no gravity holding them to us. They stayed where they were while the shield rotated ever so slowly below us. Frigates hung around them looking like tugboats though the frigates operated within their own rights. Only tiny ships like ours were allowed in the station's core. With my sense of proportion all screwed up out here with space and no really great source of light and everything, I had to wonder just how big everything really was.

For a moment I wondered: Could you stick large enough engines on Port Malabar and move her like a gigantor spaceship?

"Wake up over there," Bree chided as the station shrank behind us until it was just a dim, dark dot with a couple of red sparkles here and there.

I blinked back to my monitors. There it was, dead ahead: a block of space rock heading toward the Port. It was maybe quarter of a mile across, too big for us to chance it hitting the Port's hull. I began to think that maybe this had been chosen to be part of my training. Central and Safeties had probably had the rock under surveillance for a long time, unlike those that sometimes sneak in under the radar for one reason or another. Still, it was dangerous, and up to us to shove it out of the way.

My monitor suggested various trajectories we could apply to it. We'd try to get it at the farthest point from the station so we could use the least amount of force.

Luckily I didn't have to learn any combination of buttons to move the giant pincers that lined the outside of our ship. I just stuck my arms into some long gloves, same as Bree was doing, and pincers rose on the shell of our runabout, mimicking our movements but in super giant size.

Capt. Arcus got us to hover just off the surface of the tiny moon that could wipe out a few tens of thousands with one punch through the hull. The surface looked ordinary enough, rocky ridges that ran willy-nilly.

Bree and I used our pincers to worry at strapping. I got a juice bucket loosened before Bree, so I got the glory of the first plant. Just like in simulation, I picked the thing up between my dainty little twenty-foot mechanical fingers– and missed my grip. The bucket floated out of my reach.

I let out a very fluent curse in both English and Lingua and Bree laughed behind me. "Butterfingers," she accused. "We'll get it on the way back. I always pack twenty percent more than I need."

But if she did, she didn't do it for her own clumsiness. She picked up her bucket and gingerly placed it right on the button, right where our computers told her.

I took extra time on my next try and got Bucket #2 adhered within five feet of where it should be.

Again Bree placed hers right on, and I tried to mirror her precision with my next one. Only missed it by six inches.

"That'll do," she told me. "We might make a Safeties Engineer out of you yet."

I could have burst with pride. Instead, I took just as much time on the next one and got it perfect.

We got all the remaining allotment of juice buckets in place and Arcus didn't even take a minute to hang there to admire the job. Instead he spun us around and we retreated a safe distance, picking up my lost bucket along the way.

Our headsets buzzed with Central chatter. Were we really far enough? I started sweating even though my suit was already damp from my efforts. In five minutes of waiting I was soaked through.

"Two… One… Fire!" came the signal from Central.

Arcus had dialed the windows down to almost total polarization but still the inside of our SUV lit up like the Fourth of July. Did I just imagine a dull boom as a zillion tons of explosive knocked that rock off its path? In space no one can hear, you know.

The flash didn't last long. It was formulated for power, not light.

Our craft provided a handy long-range set of "eyes" that Central could use to plot the rock's new course in milliseconds. I saw the new path overlay the old on my monitors, with projected course measured against Port Malabar's position.

"It's good," Bree said about two seconds before Central's confirmation arrived. She looked at me and her wide mouth gave me that sideways, toothy opening that I knew was a grin. I bonked knuckles with her and then we both nodded to the captain.

That left us to set a satellite rock next to the largest remnant, to utilize subtle gravitational pull to set it on a course that would never threaten the Bar-Tok system either.

We returned home, mission accomplished. Safe for another day.

Mom would have been proud.

I was basking in the glow of accomplishment when Capt. Arcus bellowed something so loudly I couldn't make it out. He was pointing out the fore windows. I could see a white flash in front of us.

The flash coalesced into a dot heading toward Port Malabar at tremendous speed but visibly braking hard. It couldn't be a meteoroid.

"Smugglers!" Bree yelled.

We were out too far, going too slowly, to do anything. On my screens I could magnify it: a ship, a small one. It came to a sudden stop next to the station's pole, next to the opening to the Core.

I could see the station's walls shuddering behind it.

Did a handful of specks catch the light outside the ship, shooting into the Core?

Was one of them Max?

"Hang on!" Arcus warned us, and we did.

A vibration hit our ship, rattling my teeth almost out of my mouth. Bree and Arcus both cursed fluently. I joined in.

By the time the cabin stopped quaking the ship was gone.

"Let's go!" Bree ordered Arcus, but he'd already upped our speed.

We'd be needed.

CHAPTER

14

We strapped ourselves into the Bug in the Tunnel nearest the Core's pole. Its main screen blinked red. Two of the Tunnels were unusable. It must have been a bad quake if that happened. On the other hand, it was only two Tunnels among hundreds. Bree avoided them as she plotted a route to HQ.

Once there we ran in tandem to our section's supplies room. There she began to toss various equipment we'd be needing at me. Most of it was saur sized. After a few yelps I got her to stop long enough for me to find a cart, and then I loaded it up.

She led the way to the Tunnel with a cart of her own and never bothered to ask if I needed help. In a way that was a mark of respect, that Bree could trust me to handle what needed to be handled while she checked in with HQ and got our assignment.

Level 27. I heard it called even as I saw Bree's face go sour. She hadn't missed out on working down there after all. Level 27 was the lowest habitable one we had. Lower ones than that are all mechanics. Robots would be handling repairs there. But the grav down on 27 was murder for me. Imagine what it'd be like for big, bulky Bree.

"Why don't you handle 24?" I asked her. "Send me with someone else to get 27."

"No. No one else is used to working with you," she rumbled. "Besides, that's where they sent us. We go where we're sent."

She had guts, Bree did.

There were places on 27 where underlying girders had begun to twist, but that's not where we aimed ourselves. Instead, we went straight to the gaps in the outer skin of the level. You could hear the worst by the gawd-awful sucking sound they made, even over the clanging of alarms. In our pressure suits we double-checked the now-blocked areas to see to the evacuation of stranded citizens before we locked the smaller access doors that sealed entire sections of street off from the rest of the level. Thank god for the station's safety lockers; most of the folks we found had availed themselves of the seal blankets and masks there. They might be awkward in them, but they were alive. I'd checked most of the lockers within the past month.

Once we got all the major leaks isolated and secured, we went after the small ones. These we had to rely on station computers to find as they sniffed out the slightest changes in atmospheric pressure. The immediate mission was to keep people safe from the damage. We'd come back for repair later.

"That's weird," I muttered as we were taking a breather. I'd been checking for more anomalies and now one of the swamp farms out in Level 27's boonies was showing a slight temperature drop.

Bree came over to check my comm. "They probably lost some insulation," she said.

Then the temperature shot up. Within moments it was way over normals.

Despite the grav, we ran for our Bug.

It took fifteen minutes to go that far along the axis. We used the time checking monitors and sensor readings. Fire suppressants weren't controlling things, and someone was down there. They were screaming on the emergency lines. They'd panicked when the farm's temperature had begun to drop. Instead of realizing that minor, easily fixed damage to the Level wall insulation was the problem and calling for that, they decided to fix the problem themselves. They lit homemade emergency heaters.

Yes, illegal heaters. Heaters that used flame. In a methane-rich environment.

The gases in the section had ignited. Luckily, the idiot had been wearing some kind of safety gear and escaped with a good bit of singeing. She must have been born under a lucky star.

HQ, Central Station Command and we went over our options as our Bug raced across the station. HQ gave us final instructions. Central yelled at the farmer even as they sent medics down to collect her. It was the farmer's fault; she should be glad she'd still have the land afterward. Well, maybe, if she ever got out of jail for having illegal equipment onboard– and using it. As it was, her crops had been incinerated by now.

Bree and I pumped what clean gases we could out of the section. As far as I could tell, there were about ten acres within the safety doors that had sprung up at the first hint of uncontrolled fire. After that, we opened an airlock– remotely, so we wouldn't get caught in the tornado of escaping air.

It took about three, four minutes to empty out the place. Temp sensors showed the place cooling down, even starting to freeze, before we closed the airlock. Space is harsh, man. We sent robots into the inter-Level void to pick up loose items that had been propelled out as well.

"There should be a screen or something to catch things," I observed as we walked into the section. My voice echoed ever so slightly within my helmet.

"This doesn't happen often enough to install those," Bree told me.

The flash inferno left the acreage decimated. Walls, floors and ceiling were covered with thick black soot. At least this hadn't happened in one of the habitation sections. I caught Bree checking out Level 18 on her monitor. That was where the Hatching Grounds were. She had friends with eggs up there.

"All secure," she breathed. She snapped the view off to check more on Level 27. "Let's get back to work," she snapped. "This is over and done. Repairing the mess here is now low priority."

After that, we sealed off some more ag sections, then returned to the metropolitan ones, where we opened up SSS storage sheds for bulky supplies.

"Need any help down there, Bree?" HQ asked us.

They were reminding her that Bree's partner was a puny malac. I looked at Bree. She returned my gaze thoughtfully. "Nope," she decided. "We've got things under control. If things cool off up there, feel free to send down some extra hands. No emergencies here."

It took herculean effort just to load things onto motor carts. We hitched a ride along with the hoses and then set about applying temporary sealant to interior hull damage. If you think wearing a pressure suit is fun, try it when you weigh about three times what you're supposed to, and are carrying around almost unmanageable hoses that weigh a ton and refuse to point in the direction you want them to.

Toward the end of the run down there on 27 I turned around to see Bree looking like a ghost through her suit's visor. I pointed to a paved step in front of a store. "Sit," I ordered.

"Still got—"

"Sit, you stupid saur!" I bellowed. "After you catch your breath, then you can help out. But if you don't take five right now I'm going to report you to the Chief myself. See what she has to say about it all tomorrow, why don't we?"

Sullenly she sat, splayed on the pavement. The sight of the mighty Bree there perked me up. Here I'd been about to give out myself, but I'd outlasted her! I tried not to strut as I positioned myself for the final round of sprays.

Strutting's hard when you weigh far too much. Still, I managed it on the way back, and lent Bree a hand to haul herself up so we could get back to lighter climes.

"I might buy me a place down here," I told her as we entered a service lift.

I got a grumble in return.

By Level 24 some color had returned to her. By level 22 she made a saur face at me. "Trying to outshine your superior," she accused.

"We'll keep you around for the gruntwork," I sunnily said, relieved that I was back to normal weight.

She let out a small laugh at that.

Even after the emergencies were dealt with and contained, there was the business of rebuilding to attend to. I didn't report in to Sonny's for almost a week during the worst, and after that he graciously allowed me as much personal time off as if I'd been a full-time employee. Sonny was a great guy.

For the preliminary work, the neighborhoods of the station saw to their own. Ours gathered to see to the Khundays' and Ranzzes' damaged homes in particular, as well as Pen-Hik's Steamery. The Steamery we had to tear down almost to the foundation and rebuild, but everyone pitched in and it went back up in amazingly short time. Those with pertinent tech skills worked side by side with others who just did what they were told, like me.

Derra and other merchants provided the food for everyone. Various musicians who were working the entire station came around to lighten spirits. The single people of the neighborhood were drafted to make room for some of the displaced families.

Nuke didn't have anyone assigned to him. I think that might have hurt his feelings. Anyway, I volunteered (with his permission) to shack up with him while the Ranzzes squeezed into my place, all four of them. I hadn't imagined that my apartment could be called small until I saw four gimigols try to live there.

Nuke went out a lot for his meditations for the duration. We awkwardly did our best not to get in each other's way and spent more time away from home than usual– which meant that we had an excuse to do more repair work– but otherwise we made it through okay. We never actually tried to kill each– well, maybe that once– No. We made it through okay.

After we got our neighborhood up and running again, we spread out to other ones to pick up the final pieces. It was an efficient way to handle the situation.

Kreeger was farming out sandwiches over on South Point one day when I was there, and told us of a time when a meteoroid had smashed all the way through to Level 21, section 45E. Sure, that caused overall damages but the entire population flocked to the destroyed section first to secure it and see to the safety and well-being of its inhabitants before they dealt with their own homes.

That had been a long time ago. Now, with me and the rest of the SSS on the job, people could rest easy that no meteoroid was getting through the outer shell.

It all made me proud to be a Malabarian.

Now if only we could stop those damn smugglers. Did I count Max as one of them? I didn't know.

Our kitchen was warm, but not too warm. Bright. Not humid. I breathed in the comforting aura of home. I said, "Mom, I met a guy."

Her smile brightened as she paused in rolling out the pie dough. "Really?"

"Not that way. There's this… His name is Max. I don't know anything much more than that. He kidnapped me."

She looked doubtful at that.

"Okay," I admitted. "He might have saved my life instead of kidnapping. But he just left me here. With nothing!"

She took that in. "And?"

"And I think he's into something illegal. Smuggling maybe. Drugs or explosives or something."

Mom's eyes flashed as she laid both her hands flat on the tablecloth. "We can't have that. No, Tam."

"But he doesn't act like– I'm not sure what side of the law he's on with this. He might be some kind of undercover cop. Or a rival gang member. Can I trust him, really?"

"Criminals can be tricky, honey."

"Yeah. He's definitely in league with these guys who are making all these earthquakes. Probably the same guys who blew up the town I moved to after you… After you…"

"Society needs order. Without law we fall into chaos."

"I didn't tell on him."

She put up a hand, stopping me from speaking. "It's laws, official and common sense, that keep everyone working together for the greater good. And come to think of it, for the individual good. This is why I became a cop, remember? We achieve with laws. A secure environment allows us the freedom to reach for what we want to be. We abide by laws. Does that work differently on your station?"

"But Max is my way home, Mom. If he is doing something wrong– and I'm not sure of that– I can't let him get caught, at least until I find how I can get back. But I'm not sure I'm seeing the whole picture yet. I don't want to bring down the wrath of authority until I can figure out what's what with him."

"You're taking the law into your own hands."

"Isn't this an exception? A small hiccup in the law that can be overlooked? I'm checking it out. When I find out for sure, I'll do the right thing."

Slowly she nodded, but also let out a disapproving grumble. "You're a big girl now. I'll have to trust you on this, but be careful. Don't be getting yourself into trouble over a troublemaker– or worse."

I was on the tram heading downtown to meet up with Arti for some shopping, general chatter and food. My tram was heading north. We passed another going in the opposite direction. I don't know what it was that had me not only look at it, but notice.

Dibi! No one had seen him in over a month.

Well, it could have been him. He looked the right age and shade of rusty brown, and he wore those orange striped coveralls with the metallic threads that I thought I'd seen Dibi wear. I vaguely recalled Liv boasting about how Dibi had tried to dye himself red like she was, and he'd turned out brown. The other doils with him had the more doil-standard greenish-gold scales.

Plus this Dibi wore a garish green toboggan cap. All his buds did the few times I'd seen them. I'd registered it because I mean, who needs a ski cap on a space station? It wasn't a gang kind of branding; it was just a "we're young and free males on the prowl" kind of thing that drove Liv crazy because single males wore flashy accessories and Dibi was not supposed to be all that single. Still, his hat was always the identifying mark to me, as well as his slumpy attitude when Liv wasn't in the room. There were a couple other mated males in his bud group who also wore the hats. I bet their mates didn't like it, either.

Men. What ya gonna do?

With a baby on the way there was something *I* could do. I swung off the tram at the first stop and hot-footed it after the other tram. Really, you can make good headway by running if you don't have far to go. Auto-traffic runs a leisurely pace here on Port Malabar.

Still, I was huffing by the time I caught up to the tram. I swung on and waved my passchip at the sensor, then made my way up the aisle to stand next to where Dibi was seated.

"Dibi?" I asked. Okay, I was only 95% sure it was him. But he looked up at me.

"I'm Tam. We've met, remember?"

A slight shrug indicated that perhaps he might. "I'm a friend of Liv's."

His right eyelid twitched. He eased back from me ever so slightly.

"She really wants to talk to you. You should call her. She's out of her mind with worry."

"It ain't none of your business."

"Of course it's not. I'm just passing on the message, okay? They're saying something like if they can't find you they're going to ask Rilf if he'd get primed."

He stiffened all over. "Rilf!" Then, "Primed?"

I looked out the front of the tram like I was interested in the landscape. "Yeah. Isn't he Liv's ex? I'm confused. I thought you were the father of Liv's baby, not Rilf."

He muttered something dark under his breath.

"Well," I said, "they think that he'll do it, so if you're not interested you shouldn't worry." I clucked as close to a doil-cluck as I could. "Derra says that Rilf just got some kind of promotion at work and he's moving into an apartment big enough for a growing family." My mouth moved; these words came out.

Now the mutter became a growl.

I gave Dibi a smile and that slamming knock on the shoulder that means, "Have a good day," and got up out of my seat.

From under the dark cloud that roiled over his head, Dibi muttered, "What does Liv say?"

I paused. "Liv? Oh, I haven't really talked to her about this. Just Derra. Derra only wants what's best for Liv and the baby, you know her."

The tram pulled to a stop and I began to move forward to the exit. Over my shoulder I called, "Derra's called her cousin Noon to come, did you know? He wants to be here for Liv."

If Dibi had been a cartoon, he would have exploded in panic-sweat. His scales stood on end, his beak flexed quite unnaturally, and his color… well, it went through several bright hues of alarm.

I waved merrily at him and hopped to the street. Perhaps he'd do the smart thing and go voluntarily. I was sure that if this Noon-zio tough guy got his hands on Dibi there might not be much left for Liv to appreciate.

Like I said, I had time off that day. Instead of putting in more hours at Sonny's or hitting the books, I decided to, you know… relax. With friends. So it really was with haste that I ran off to relax.

Hours of vigorous shopping achieved a reasonable facsimile of a flip-flop I could wear. Arti (sans Ali) and I swung by Derra's after we'd bought enough tchotchkes to completely furnish Arti's new place, plus maybe Ali's as well. We'd picked up Arti's brand-new IS tech husband, Kefli– nikkah mubarak and mazel tov!– along the way because they were going to eat for free, courtesy of me. Sort of.

Derra had promised free dinners for my malac friends if they'd give their opinion on different dishes. Six freeloading malac was her limit. She told me it was up to me to keep track of who'd gotten their freebie, as she couldn't tell any of us apart.

It took fast talking to get malac to venture this far into saur gastronomic territory, but now Arti and Kefli– malac #2 and 3, after Randi had gotten his back when we were dating– were both making their way through a khoutor casserole with a side of sam as we discussed what remained of the Randi situation, mostly with Arti. Kefli would put in a word or two, but he was more interested in the food.

"He misses you," Arti assured me. "Doesn't he?" She nudged Kefli and he grunted.

I must have done the same because Arti said, "He wants to get back with you. He said to tell you he's sorry for whatever he did."

"Is he?" I tried to sound uninterested.

"He says he's sent you lots of messages. You don't answer them."

"I must not have seen them."

"Good grief, Tam, what the heck did he do? He didn't cheat on you. I would have heard."

I considered telling her. Would she be as shocked as I? Brite wasn't a problem with humans.

"Forget it," I insisted, and changed the conversation to telling her the situation with Dibi– and then very quietly mentioned that I'd just seen him. Her eyes got wide. They swiveled back and forth between Derra across the room and me.

"Does she know?" Arti hissed.

I waved her down in volume and shook my head. I was never sure of the various saurs' hearing capabilities.

"So what are you going to do about it?"

"It's not really my problem. I just did it because Derra and Liv are my friends. And this Cousin Noon guy sounds like trouble."

Derra had the TV covering the west wall playing quietly so those who wanted to be deluged with news could, and those who didn't, could ignore it. As I worked my way contentedly through some of Derra's chopped-veuwy salad with mushroom gravy (think: pot roast and mashed potatoes, minus all the cholesterol), the word "Limbus" caught my ear.

It sounded familiar before it registered. The drug people. But Max had said "terrorists." So I turned to the TV. The picture they showed was a too-familiar scene.

An urban setting. A volcano rising from the ground, blasting all around it into rubble.

It didn't look like Earth.

If I looked hard I could see little purple sparks rising above the lava.

"The terrorists call their weapon the *cinderu'um*," a voice-over informed us. The word had "revenge" and "weapon" Lingua roots, I thought. I'd look it up later maybe. Right now I was having flashbacks as well as terror for the present. "Limbus claimed this was a minor attack, that they can blow away the entire crust of a world if they want."

Arti let out a squeak. Derra sidled up next to me, with two cousins behind her. "What is it?" she asked in horror.

One of the cousins enhanced the viewscreen with smaller info screens that blossomed next to the main picture.

"That's Vereu," Derra whispered, her squawk quieted to an eerie rustle.

"What's Vereu?" I asked.

"World two systems away from home."

The announcer went on, "This footage came with a list of Limbus demands. They want five worlds ceded to them or next time, according to them, a gimigol world will be targeted."

"This Vereu," I asked Derra. "It's a doil world?"

She nodded tightly, her feathers standing on end. "My uncle-in-law, he lives there. That's family. Terrorists practice on doil worlds. Like we were nothing."

"They'll get 'em," I assured her. "The Confederacy won't stand for it."

"Yes."

We watched until Derra finally ordered Moezu-zio to change to an entertainment channel. Still, we were spooked. Arti and Kefli made their food reviews to Derra, and she had Kefli try something he hadn't eaten yet to get his reaction. Moezu-zio made some jokes about appetites and Kefli actually joked back– I was so proud of him– and then we made our way back to our own homes, pondering the state of things in this corner of the cosmos.

Limbus might be threatening the rest of the Confederation, but here on Port Malabar life went on as usual. Bree and I had just come from a minor chemical spill down on the dreaded Level 27.

"Gawd, I hate 27." Bree's tail switched as she limped alongside me. "Why do they have all the problems?"

"It's not all that bad." I could say that now that we were back on Level 21 and my ankles had decided they'd work again.

"Says the tiny malac," she drawled. Then her tail took to a different rhythm, pulsing along the pavement.

"Bree?"

Her face bloomed into an enormous saur grin. Another gimigol was approaching us, wearing a cop's uniform. A captain.

"This must be…"

"Brindle!" Bree and the newcomer slammed into each other, a gimigol embrace. They gnawed at each other's cheeks and noses.

Brindle was the husband Bree always spoke about. He stood about six inches taller than she, though he was more slender. As I looked at the two of them, I saw his face had a more chiseled look compared to Bree's. His lips were puffier; his shoulders and upper arms broad. He wore his uniform to crisp perfection, though it was late in the work day.

Bree introduced us. "What are you doing here?" she asked her husband.

"Just got through delivering some dealers to the local station," he said. His voice held a touch of Barry White.

"More drugs? On Port Malabar? That's the third time this month."

Brindle's mouth curved so his center teeth showed. "The chief said we got it all this time. Brite."

I hoped they didn't see me freeze.

"Brite!" Bree hissed.

"Yeah, it's hit here. We've seen it mostly up on Level 16, you know, with all the temporary workers brought in from anywhere they could find someone to do scut work."

"But here–"

"Here's not that far from Level 16, honey."

I managed to get my mouth to work. "I thought brite was rare."

"Not rare enough. Pretty soon it's going to be nonexistent. Here, at least. We can make this station brite-free," Brindle assured me.

"These… They were dealers? How will they be punished?"

"I hope they space them," Bree rumbled. "I had a cousin, almost died from brite a year ago."

"I didn't think you liked her." Brindle cocked his head at his wife.

"I don't. She's stupid. Hell, she took brite; how smart could she be? These days she's even stupider. The stuff ate most of her brain. But still, I don't want brite around my family– or friends."

We made our way slowly down the block. Brindle would probably have to turn at the next intersection to police HQ, while we'd be going on straight to our station.

"So we scare the hell out of these monsters," Brindle assured Bree. "Spacing's the thing for a brite runner. They'll probably get twenty years hard labor instead."

"Too soft. We need to change the laws."

"So you run for Station Manager next election."

Bree replied by blowing snot out of her nose. Brindle obviously thought that was cute because he laughed. "One of these days," he said, "you're going to realize that all the times you've said you know better on how to run things, that you were telling the truth. You're going to be Manager one day."

"Right."

He laid his hand over his heart. "And I will be the Manager's Spouse, lounging in deep mud baths all day and eating fried giant cockroaches with beer." He narrowed his eyes at her. "Sure I can't sign you up for office?"

She gave a half-snort. "Maybe next round. Right now I'm deep in training my protégée."

The comm unit on my shoulder dinged and I bipped it. "Tam Yussuf," the dispatcher addressed me. "You know any malac from off-station?"

"Not to my... Wait, I know a couple. Why?"

"One just docked in a fancy private ship. Sent an emergency medical beacon. He's in High Spokes Hospital and when he woke up, he mentioned your name."

"On my way."

Grabbing a lift and then a tram, I called High Spokes Hospital and told myself that they had great malac specialists there. I clicked through an annoying set of levels in the hospital directory and finally found a friendly looking lampey receptionist, if you find mucus-drippers friendly looking.

"I'm trying to find my friend," I told her. "I was told he was hurt, and asking for me. Just got in to the port."

"Name?"

"His name is Max." Good lord, I forgot his last name. It wasn't "Bastard." "Blakeney. Yeah, Max Blakeney."

"Right. Are you sure?" She chuckled in that sucking, clucking way they have. She searched through records and then suddenly brightened. Surprisingly, she broke a few hundred privacy rules and began telling me Max's medical information. All I'd thought to get was a room number.

But she gave me a doctor's name and even flashed me copies of those 3-D X-rays they have, as well as prescriptions given. I tried to hide my astonishment at the impropriety. Some hospital security. Or was it just the way lampeys worked?

But shock rolled through me like a lightning bolt when I got off the tram at the hospital and paused a moment, still on the comm, to read the doctor's own report as well as a full inpatient ID report of Max Britguy. Blakeney.

"I see the doctor agreed that the patient was prone to underestimate the extent of his injuries, including the older ones," she told me. "You will make sure your husband takes his meds?"

I nodded mutely. Stunned to silence.

Max Blakeney Yussuf, they listed him. Married. To Tamara Yussuf.

"He can be very cantankerous about things," I managed to croak, "but I'll get the meds in him, if I have to tie him down."

The nurse chippered at me. "Males," she said, and I nodded as I tried to work up a knowing smile. I signed off as quickly as I could.

So I had a husband. At least on paper. Funny thing, this hadn't shown up on any of my official paperwork before.

"What the hell have you done to yourself?" I bellowed as soon as the nurse closed the door behind me.

"Where are my clothes?" Max demanded. He was sitting on the edge of his bed, the sheet still drawn up around his waist, as he gave the place a visual search. There were fair-sized bandages on his face, one on the side of his head, and another on his lower right shoulder. Other than that, he was naked, missing even his miserable wig. "Try over there." He pointed to some built-in drawers.

"Do I look like your servant?" But I still checked them. Empty.

The nightstand held his ident card as well as a wallet. Both had been half-eaten by something. Max turned it over sourly. "So much for family pictures and my car keys," he said.

The sight of the holes made my stomach churn. "Where were you stowing that on your jumpsuit?" I asked. "Not over your heart… or toward the nether regions, I hope?"

"Everything down there's working properly, I can assure you." From his perusal of the wallet's remnants he looked up at me with a crooked grin. "Or shall I arrange a personal demonstration for you? Just for your personal reassurance?"

"Not interested," I said. The guy was injured so I added, "Maybe later if I need a laugh."

"I shall make a note in my calendar," he said and turned the wallet over again. "Which is also missing. Dammit, that info padd had better not have gotten into enemy hands."

"Do you take notes in Lingua?" I asked.

He gave a heartfelt sigh. "Right. No, I keep them in the queen's English. I doubt if many of these blighters will be able to read that. Or find a program to translate."

"So there's a perk to being a member of such a rare minority out here," I said. "Give me a moment."

I went to the nurses' station and returned with a couple of saur-sized towels, smaller towels like washcloths, and adhesive bandages. "Wrap this," I instructed Max, and he soon wore one white towel like a maro, the malac version of a kiltish loincloth. Washcloths secured at the ankle with tape became slippers. Max stood up and looked down at himself.

"Holy–" I won't repeat the rest of it. Be assured that he wasn't pleased. I told him that we could return the towels now or the next day. He sulked all the way to the tram and then the passenger lift to the core.

As we floated to the shuttle that would take us to his ship, he admonished me, "Don't you go looking up my skirt!" What a control freak.

It took a while for his ship to recognize him without his full ident, but eventually it let us in. I hadn't been able to appreciate the interior on my first trip in it, but now I certainly could. Max must not only be rich, but big, freaking rich. There was luxury this, luxury that, and genuine leather seats, probably from genuine leather Earth cows, poor things.

Max gathered some clothing and stepped into another compartment to change. He kept the door open.

"Sure you don't want to come help me?" he asked.

"As if," I hedged as I poked around. He wouldn't have any chocolate bars, would he?

He emerged a few minutes later in standard jumpsuit and with that awful dark clown wig, the curly-fries one.

"Can't say that's any improvement," I told him.

He made a face at me. "Let's get out of here. Go out somewhere to eat. They haven't fed me."

We found ourselves at The Lazy Mosquito, maybe not the swankest spot on the station, but the swankiest for people wearing jumpsuits. He was paying. The yeast and mushroom roast was fabulous! Even the salad was very nice (don't tell Derra!), especially since we washed it down with a deep red wine that left me feeling a bit dizzy.

Or maybe it was Max, damn his kidnapper hide anyway.

I turned down dessert. There's no reason to stuff oneself if one is expecting hearty exercise soon. Which, judging from the glint in Max's eyes, he certainly was. From under the tablecloth he produced a small package, wrapped in real gift paper with a little, slightly sad, bow on it. He gave it to me.

"What's this?"

He shrugged, so I read the attached card: "Sorry for kidnapping you."

I drew out tiny slivers of black lace, and realized it was a thong and the smallest bra I'd ever seen in person. Everything was elasticized thoroughly so it could fit anyone from a supermodel to Free Willy.

I held up the thong to examine it. There were only aliens around us; they wouldn't have a clue as to what the things were.

"A little personal, isn't it?"

"I figured we got a little personal a while back. I saw what you were wearing then. It's a crime for a beautiful woman to have to wear that."

I discovered that I didn't mind being called a "beautiful woman" by Max. Then I tried to remember when– and if– Randi had ever brought me anything approaching all this.

"I take it you want me to model it for you."

"I don't demand it. Though you do owe me your life, if I recall. But if I could put in a request…"

Gravity and a few healing wounds didn't seem to affect the energy we two produced in my bed. It was still frenzied at points. Definitely concentrated at others. The boy had focus! And a surprising amount of finesse. I wished I could have filmed it to give Randi some pointers, except that I decided that I really didn't want Randi to watch, not even in a kinky daydream.

Max didn't seem to mind that I hadn't seen a decent razor in years; he was European after all. He didn't mind that my hair wasn't professionally styled or that I usually wore baggy jumpsuits or even that I shot passing meteoroids for a living.

As for me, I thought I could get used to that awful wig sitting on my nightstand. Sure, the boy might be super-secretive, but I could bring him out of his shell.

Just as I was completing the sentence in my mind of, "I can change him," it hit me that I was beginning to look at this thing long-term. Sure, he and I had known each other for over two years, but how long actually face-to-face? He was the wind. Did I have a guarantee I'd ever see him again?

15

Okay, so I was giving Randi another chance. A week-plus had gone by since I'd last seen Max, with no word from him. Randi kept sending me message after message about how it had all been a youthful mistake and he'd given up… *you know* (he was probably afraid his message would be read by some enforcement agency) and would never, ever do it again and wouldn't I *please* give him another chance?

Arti and Ali had also been on my case, as had more than a few other malac. People I didn't know I'd met stopped to remind me what a great guy Randi was, such a pillar of the malac community with a great future ahead of him. A woman was just what he needed to set his roots down and start making a real name for himself.

Oh goodie, like I was some kind of required accessory.

Then Randi's mother, Eliane, had practically run into me the other day. We stood there in the middle of Ridge Road, nose to upturned nose, her disapproving gaze trying to freeze me dead.

I didn't need this. At the very least maybe I could let Randi down slowly, get the malac community used to the idea and on my side again. "Divorcing" Randi shouldn't have to mean that I divorced myself from my own kind.

So I found myself walking with him through evening streets past the more interesting windows and clubs in mid-Vinetown on Level 21. "We should go there," he pointed at one. "Maybe next week, eh? Awang and Katya said it was a lot of fun. Good music."

He kept up his side of the conversation and didn't seem to notice that I had little to say. I tried to smile when he made a joke, but my heart wasn't in it. This was a big hole I was digging for myself. Every time I started to climb out he dragged me back down. But I kept walking.

At one point we changed levels up and began to drift westerly, in the general direction of my place, though we were still quite a distance from there. I tried to keep my eyes focused straight ahead, so my funk wouldn't permanently be associated with these neighborhoods that I was learning to love.

We stopped to have dinner at Duki-Ya, another place I wouldn't have been able to afford on my own. It was a shame that I couldn't enjoy the food. If I were on my own or with, well, somebody else, I'd probably have thought it terrific. Randi actually began to notice my mood.

"Something wrong?"

I evaded the question, claiming butterflies about upcoming finals. If I passed I'd no longer be student grade and my income level would rise considerably. I asked if he'd talked to Zara or Irdina lately? Weren't they just the nicest girls?

It wasn't quite a candlelight dinner– open flames are forbidden on station– but every culture I can think of has some kind of memory of a prehistoric communal fire. Our restaurant had a lovely false-fire pit in its center so all tables could view the realistic hologram and hear the crackle.

Randi talked about his own job and the rungs he was targeting. "Sure, I'm comfortable," he said proudly, "but I could be even more comfortable, you know?" He poked at the noodles on his plate. "I've bought a few things lately that need paying off."

"Your vid system," I guessed. He'd been talking about his friends coming over to enjoy it. I reminded him that Irdina loved to watch vid sports.

He ignored the attempt to funnel his energy elsewhere. "It's great. And I found someone who sells me the latest movies from Earth." He gave me a crooked smile. "Or at least that's what they claim."

He must know Leslie, who brought knickknacks for Arti and Alli. I considered asking him about her and if she had a regular schedule, but decided I didn't have the energy.

After that he started to ask me about how work was going. "I don't see how you can stand to hang out with those saurs after hours," he told me around a bite of fried polenta. "Why not come over to the Terrace more often?"

"And I don't see why you're so stand-offish of them," I replied. "We're the minority here. They're the people we work with, live with."

"Not if you moved up with us."

I was not going to waste my time arguing this conversation again.

I perked up when he added, "Or not. I suppose you have your reasons."

"Yeah. I do." Imagine, Randi showing consideration for my personal business! Had my haranguing paid off? Was he beginning to… change?

I was quietly astounded when he began asking about Bree and what kind of officer I thought she was. What did we talk about off-duty? He seemed interested about my classes. While we waited for a soup course he even complimented me on my apartment. It might not be up on Green Level, but it was a nice place and certainly convenient to my needs.

The food began to taste better. I noticed the music the restaurant played in the background. Randi's tattoos seemed to fade ever so slightly, or at least not seem to be staring at me. We concentrated on the food and conversation about what everyone was up to, as well as the new homesites going up just north of Green Level.

Randi excused himself to talk with Gedder Sam, the malac community rep who was seated across the firepit from us. They glad-handed as I figured they talked about the need for water system repairs and whether they should hire Randi's friend Zikri for the job.

You couldn't pay me to be a community rep. Too many people want to bug you on your private time.

For some reason in my mind I kept comparing Randi to Max. Randi was the one here. He'd be here tomorrow and the day after that as well. Was that a good thing? I was going through mental lists of Port Malabar's single male malac as we talked.

Then he told me how much he liked being with me. He fed me some farmick pudding: warm and rich and melting on my tongue, and I began to melt as well. Color came back to my world. Randi was his charming best. He had a smile that just wouldn't quit: bright, wide teeth set against warm brown skin. His tunic shirt was open in front, and I enjoyed watching the slight flex of his muscles throughout dinner.

My brain kept saying no, no, no, but for some reason my mouth never did. I blamed every bit of it on hormones. Still, I found the strength of will to return to those mental lists.

Afterward Randi let me pick a small bistro so I could hear the band that Bree had told me about. Randi liked them, as did I, and I downloaded some of their songs to my personal system.

In spite of our past, as we walked to my home from the tram I was thinking I could get to like this. I could name someone it would be nicer with. I wasn't stupid. I wanted to check Randi out a few more times, see if he truly was maturing into a responsible adult. My expectations weren't high, but if a certain person was going to make me wait so long between his visits, Randi might suit for the occasional date. Very occasional. With other possibles filling in the spaces on my calendar.

His hand was warm in mine as we climbed the front steps. He wasn't going to stay. We both knew that, except he thought we had a future. The goodbye kiss he gave me was long if a bit wet.

As I opened the door he caught it and held it open. "One little thing," he told me.

Oh hell.

I must have frowned at him because he quickly said, "It's not that big a thing."

"All right, what is it?"

From the inside of his draped tunic he produced a metallic bag.

I took a step back. It had to be brite. "Did you have that on you all night?"

"Well, yeah. Tam–"

"Under your clothes? The whole time?" And then before he could say anything else, I said, "No. I can't believe you'd do this to me again."

"It's not my fault. Dian brought it in last night, and he said the authorities were sniffing around the port for it. He just needs it hidden for a couple days."

"No."

"Just a couple days, Tam. Do it as a favor to me."

"Thought I'd already done that once."

"Then do it as a favor to Dian." At the roll of my eyes, he added, "For Kem, then. She's his wife, you know."

Yes, I knew Kem. A nice woman. She and Dian had two kids. It wouldn't do for Daddy to be in jail or worse.

A million arguments went through my brain but all I could see was the kids sitting at their birthday parties and Daddy wasn't there. I'd missed a lot of birthdays without my daddy.

"Oh shit," I mumbled, and Randi brightened.

So I found myself tucking the stinking bag far into the tunnels again, hating myself for lacking balls. After all, I didn't want to be in jail for any birthdays, either. I reminded myself that I wasn't doing this for Randi. I was doing this for innocent Kem and her kids.

Nuke sat on the porch, watching a game on a floating screen. Next to him, Benny's eyes blinked alternately in team colors.

"Nuke," I said abruptly, and his head and neck swung to take me in. "Sorry to interrupt. But where's a good place to get rid of a, uh…" I scratched my head. "It's a difficult… I…"

"Illegal substance?" he asked.

I nodded quickly. "How'd you guess so quickly?"

"I tend to see the worst, I suppose." He put his game on pause and settled back to ponder the problem. "The Tunnels," he finally decided. "You have access to them. I bet–"

"Ah. Maybe someplace else? Someplace permanently lost?"

"Right. Might point back to you." He thought some more and then asked, "How hot?"

"Hot. Real hot. Like, ah…"

"Brite hot."

"You didn't hear that from me. How does one get rid of it… permanently? Without affecting anything else? Can't dump it in the water supply, that's for sure."

"No. That wouldn't be advisable."

"Can't research ways of destroying it or an alert will go off somewhere."

"Yes." More minutes of perusal. Finally he shrugged with both sets of shoulders. "Let me think on it a day or so. You've got time?"

I sighed. "Yeah. It'll keep for a little while. I just want rid of it, forever."

"I have my own research methods," Nuke said.

Nuke and I sat on the porch the next afternoon, eating take-out I'd brought from Sonny's and watching the latest about Limbus. There'd been another attack, this time on Noh-sull, which was five systems away from Nik-a-Dell. This time they'd released the cinderu'um near a dormant volcano.

Near a historic doil city, full of life and culture and joy.

Now it lay in ruins, half of it obliterated. The weapon had struck fast, without warning. The caldera gaped open, oozing glowing lava while what we could see of the area lay black around it. Our television broadcast the pungent smell of sulfur and death to us on our clean, peaceful porch.

"They must be stopped," Nuke rumbled. "People cannot allow this to go on."

From the scenes of destruction and pain the program switched to a retrospective of Limbus and how they had failed in their local war, then grown to such a terrifying threat to the galactic sector. We watched the generations-long war on their home world, saw that there had been legitimate faults on both sides, but peace should have started putting things to rights.

Everything except losers' pride and wish for power.

An anchor reported from an industrial district near the outskirts of the attack area. Brick buildings very much like ones I recalled from Earth composed her backdrop. Noh-sull had used mega-cold projectors to counteract the cinderu'um. Snow tucked in nooks and crannies of the architecture; a frost lay at the reporter's feet. It looked so odd, so far away from my new home that knew no cold.

"This is how Limbus supports itself," she told us as she held up something so awful it made me draw back.

It was a silver bag that shifted as she moved it, shifted as if there were liquid inside.

"Brite," the reporter told us. "Sales of the drug support not only Limbus' research into improving the cinderu'um, but in helping them transport it, even bribe their way across the spaceways."

"Brite. Just brite?" I whispered.

Nuke said, "You haven't heard that before? Limbus' home world, Rom-i-yon, was where brite was developed in the first place. They've got the manufacture down to a fine art now." He hissed. "Damned brite. Damned poison."

He gave me a meaningful look and I nodded.

The announcer went on about brite and Limbus and cinderu'um and death. I watched it all as if from a distance, numb and cold and hot all over.

The next day at SSS HQ, our watch chief directed us to see to the dozens of situations springing up due to the HVAC systems backing up overnight: short or severed circuits here and there, and even vehicular difficulties as ice had formed as a result on some surfaces up on 19. Bree breathed a sigh of relief that the temp problem was on 19 and not 18, the Hatching Grounds. Eggs needed to be kept dry and warm.

The situation had caused a momentary burp in the station's rotation systems, just enough to screw up minor systems across all levels. Safeties had called a mandatory Port-wide four-hour lockdown, everyone to stay indoors in order to give various teams room to move, so if we saw non-service personnel out on the streets we were supposed to alert the cops.

Hydroponics units in the back forty on Level 24 had completely sloshed over their barricades and lucky me got to wade, about thirty pounds heavier than I should have been, through the muck to unclog drains and release the clean-up ag-drones.

"Better you than me," Bree told me when I returned from that one. In addition to heavier grav, she hated being covered in the liquid fertilizer that somehow managed to seep through my coveralls, making a stink that it took three showers to get rid of.

As it was, I discovered her face and scales were stained a rather sickly shade of gray. She'd been working in hazmat and thus had been sealed inside her uniform. Hazmat suit material was impervious to anything– it was practically Kryptonian– or so it was advertised. What had happened?

"It was the damn chemical shower afterward," she grumbled as she checked herself in a mirror. "Maybe I'm allergic." She stuck her great tongue out at herself and seemed satisfied that it was still its usual bright purple. She pulled down the bags below each of her eyes, and those checked out well, too.

"It'll fade," she decided as she settled back in her chair. We were in the lunchroom, with the comm room just beyond, at the West Side sub-station. Slowing radio chatter from Safeties comm monitors told us things were cooling down to normal.

Lots of personnel were using the Tunnels today. I thought of the brite sitting in mine. I couldn't put off dealing with it any longer.

The thought made me pause as I reached into the snack pouch I kept inside my kit. Despite those showers I still felt dirty. I didn't want to be part of any of it. I let Bree and Griggs discuss game scores as I extracted what I'd saved to be my reward for the day: therapy.

Its magic was the same as every time I ate it. I was back on Earth in the kitchen. The pie was baking and Mom and I were talking at the table. I'd never realized how much she looked like me. Same dark hair, slightly frizzed. Same widow's peak. Brown eyes that no longer matched my new blue ones. She was slender. Tough, but soft to hug.

The oven timer went off with a harsh buzz.

"Randi made me hide some drugs," I blurted to her as she drew out the pie.

She nearly dropped it before managing to transfer it safely to the cooling rack. She didn't often use it, but now turned her Baleful Stare in my direction. "What kind of men are you hanging around? 'Made' you?"

"Okay, I had a choice. But the malac here would get in trouble if I didn't take it."

"Or not."

"I don't think Randi would have given it to me if there wasn't a good chance of it. The guy who originally had it has kids. They shouldn't be punished for what he did."

"Hardened criminals will say anything to make themselves feel better. They'll draw anyone else into it, if it can deflect punishment." She drew off her oven mitts, set them on the breakfast table, and then propped herself against a counter to study me. "Why is he handling drugs?"

Good question. "I don't know. They're Randi's friends, the ones with the drugs. Dian–I think he's the main dealer."

"Do they just sell to humans?"

"I don't know." The aroma of cherries and slightly burned baked sugar was almost overwhelming. I inhaled deeply and then heaved a frustrated breath. "I don't think there's that much of a human market for the stuff. Someone's selling to the saurs."

"Mm hm. And where do you stand in all this?" she asked as she reached into the fridge for tea.

"I don't want *any* illegal drugs on the station, Mom. I don't want anyone hurt. They say brite can hurt saurs real bad. Sometimes it kills them; sometimes it just cripples them for life or makes them puppets for people who want to control them."

She sat down, the pitcher between the two of us. She looked at it. The table. Me. She tweaked her necklace. In my own space somewhere else where it lay on my neck, I tweaked it as well. "You're human. You're already one of these malac, though you haven't had time or the opportunity to make all the friend-ships and connections that others in the community have. That will come, honey. Give yourself time."

"Time. I hope to be home, given time."

"Until then you're on Port Malabar. Deal with the hand you've been dealt–but stay true to who you are."

"In other words, stick to my ethics. Turn him in."

Her chin tilted to the right as she shrugged. I realized that I did the same thing when I was thinking. "There might be alternatives to that. *Might*. Okay, I agree:

you need to investigate. Is this man really worth the risk? Make sure you can trust whomever you ask. But you end your active part in this crime– yesterday."

I closed my eyes. "Yeah. I'll tell him what he can do with the brite. Never again."

"Good. I love having such a wonderful daughter."

"Love you, Mom."

I let the breeze sweep over me, let Mom's and the station's voices become a soothing drone in the background as I sat silently, rolling it back and forth in my mind.

What would Randi do with the brite? Realize the error of his ways and destroy it, or would he hand it off to someone else? I didn't think Randi particularly thought a lot about consequences, much less civil order.

How many lives could that brite destroy?

What Nuke and I finally decided on was my idea with a tad of Nuke sneakiness. It was simple, really. The next time I went on outer shell training, which involves magnetic boots and swollen ankles and clomping around outside the station on its surface, laying down new barrier fabric to replace a theoretically damaged section…

Well, you just made sure a silver bag of brite was attached to your silver pressure suit's belt and then, when no one was looking, you unhooked that bag and gave it a little shove out into the Great Unknown. Someone three kazillion years from now might find it, but I bet it wouldn't be in any shape to hurt anyone.

So now the dirty business was over, thank god. I shook all over just thinking about it, and lost my grip on the ladder coming out of the Tunnels behind my place. I fell a couple rungs, cracking my knees hard against the metal. It took more than a moment to catch my breath. Finally I looked up.

A doil stood there, silhouetted against the light. A reddish-bronze, beaked face peered down at me. He stared at me accusingly.

His scales were highly polished, his teeth sharp-looking– that and the large jaw scales made him definitely a male– around the long dragon-like tongue that flicked out of his mouth for a moment. He let out an "Awp."

"Authorized personnel only," I brazened.

He backed up as I came out of the tunnel. "Of course," he said and his head twisted this way and that on top of his skinny neck as he considered me. "Sorry to have startled you." Even as I climbed to the surface he still towered over me. He must be over thirteen feet tall. He wore a stylish blue suit as if he were ready for business, topped with a half-cloak in muted violet. "Could you be Tam, malac?" he asked.

He wasn't Derra's almost-son-in-law, Dibi; I was certain about that. Dibi was neither a smart dresser nor quite that tall. Maybe Liv's ex, the would-be baby-carrier? "Rilf?" I ventured.

"Rilf? Rilf sehawnie koko!" He let forth a chortle that shook the buildings around us. Then he clapped me around the shoulders. I hoped my bones could survive. "I am Noon. Derra's zio, cousin. She has told you of me?" he asked. "I have been delayed, but now I am here."

"Oh. Noon-zio, yes," I said as I made sure the tunnel entrance was secured. "Uh… Pleased to meet you. Derra speaks very highly of you. Everyone at her place does."

Again with the shoulder-clap. "Tam-zio!" he bellowed. "You are friend of the family. You will help us, no?"

"I haven't seen Dibi lately," I said quickly. So this was Derra's mobster cousin. I didn't know if he was packing for poor, cowardly Dibi or not. Besides, it was true: I'd been looking these past weeks and hadn't seen him beyond that once and a couple vague possibilities.

"Dibi!" Cousin Noon's long, skinny tongue darted out of his mouth and then back with a clack of teeth that might very well have resulted in a dragon-like spark if the evening had been dark enough. "He not fit for family," he declared darkly. "I tell Derra-zio, I tell Liv-zio, no Dibi. No!"

"Liv loves him."

"Love." Again with the tongue-flick. "When a baby is on the way, you don't need love. You need responsibility. Dibi– Not responsible."

I led him around to the front of the house. Nuke was just coming out his door, a familiar, small pack tucked under his left lower armpit. He was on the way to one of his outdoor meditations and gave us a double-take– but not as big as the one Cousin Noon gave him. Noon-zio may have been tall and stylish, but Nuke was… Nuke. A medium-sized mountain of arms and muscle and blue.

I introduced them and they eyed each other warily. Both stood well above me. Cousin Noon was extra bottom-heavy in the way that all doils are, though he had brawny arms as well. Nuke was muscle all over, and always stood as if he were prepared for a gladiator fight. Nuke grunted low at Noon-zio and Noon-zio showed his teeth in a friendly smile that implied future decimation.

"We go in to Tam-zio's place," Noon-zio explained to Nuke, who was obviously posturing for my benefit. "We talk."

I nodded to Nuke. "It's okay," I told him. "I think."

But he waited at alert position on the porch. I kept the door open.

Cousin Noon watched through it. "Good neighbor," he said as Nuke finally stalked off. "He watches out for you."

"The best."

I set up Noon-zio with some tea and a bagel with protein schmear before I pulled out a privacy screen to hide behind, using the excuse that I had to get ready for my shift at Sonny's in order to gather my wits. Mobster! And yes, Noon-zio might be an alien but I'd still feel funny parading in my birthday suit in front of him. He finished his bagel and then as I made a few more adjustments, chattered about how he'd known Derra as kids back on the ol' home planet.

When I was through, he drew up a chair for me. It couldn't have been easy since he was barely balancing on his own. My chairs were for child saurs. "We make deal," he announced.

I reached for a bagel of my own. Nothing. I lifted the cloth on my little bagel basket, but nothing hid under the corner. After all the craziness I could use some fuel. With a resigned sigh I settled back with tea. "What kind of deal?" I asked.

"You are in Safeties Services," he said. The flat of his hand lay on my little table, taking up a full quarter of its surface. "You have access to… things."

I thought of the brite I'd just spaced because of my access privileges, and why I'd been given it in the first place. "Yes," I said slowly.

"You can get to surveillance." He held up a flat, shining crystal sliver of magline. "I have identify program. We'll find Dibi in two shakes." As he twisted the crystal this way and that, making the light flash upon its surface, he said, "Computer scans foot traffic, compares key spots on faces. Even in disguise, Dibi can't hide."

I considered. It wasn't illegal, just a tiny stretch of my access jurisdiction. "There are a lot of doils on Port Malabar. It might take more than two shakes."

That made him laugh out of the side of his mouth. "So it might. Dibi may not be as stupid as I think. For Liv's sake, I so hope. I am prepared for long stay. This is acceptable to you, Tam-zio, honorary cousin of my family?"

A stretch, but not so bad. Maybe I could ask Bree about it before I did it. "I would be happy to help Derra and Liv. As long as that–" I pointed to the chip– "is legal."

He cocked his head toward his right shoulder in consideration. A horizontal line of scales rippled above his left eye. "More legal than not," he concluded. "Larger problem might come in who exactly owns rights to original program. People copy all the time. Might be patent infringement, might not. Interstellar law–" his shrug meant that his right eye peered sharply at me– "get hazy in these cases."

It was a lot more legal than drugs. Why had I let Randi talk me into that? Why, why, why?

First things first. "And you won't kill Dibi?"

He reared back at that. "Kill father of my cousin's child? Malac have strange ideas."

"Injure him?"

"We want him well enough to accept his part in this."

"And he has to be healthy for that, right? Really healthy?" Darn it, I hadn't checked the details of doil physiology yet.

With a chuckle, he said, "Correct."

"I think he's confused. Scared. I told him you might be coming."

"When this?"

"A couple weeks ago. He's young, right? He's having to grow up fast with a baby on the way."

"Should have thought of that before conception."

"We agree on that. Okay then," I decided. "I need to do this, well, as right as I can. I have to ask my Safeties partner."

"No. No."

"She's good. She'll understand. Besides, she'll probably know how to use this."

With a "hm," he finally nodded. "Good malac. Derra-zio right about you." He handed me the crystalline chip. "Just follow what it says for install." Another chip. "This is personal data for Dibi. Chip scans surveillance and matches faces." This time the line of facial scales included the ones above his other eye as they laid down flat with disapproval. "Let us hope Liv-zio did not alter this. She tricky, that one. Smart." He chuckled. "That very good in a cousin. Bad in an enemy."

I turned the crystals over in my fingers as if I could read the data there. This was cunning alien technology. At least this was semi-legal.

With his business over, Noon-zio leaned dangerously back in my tiny chair and held his arms out. "Now," he said, "I am businessman. You do me favor, I do you favor. Name it."

I shook my head. "This is for Derra and Liv. That baby needs a father."

He crossed his arms over his chest. "Then consider this a favor for family. What can I do for you, Tam-zio?"

Unless the chair gave away, which amazingly it did not, Cousin Noon wasn't going anywhere until I told him something. I tried to think fast and the first thing that came to mind was the drugs, how to stop them from coming to the station. There was no telling what Cousin Noon would do if he knew I'd had brite. Or what he'd do if he had brite in his possession. I shoved that thought out of my head and what stood there revealed was–

"Noon," I began.

"Noon-zio. We are family."

I couldn't help it. I was touched. Family. A warm wave of pleasure washed through me and I smiled. "Noon-zio. I'm trying to track someone of my own, as it is. I was wondering if you could…"

"Put out feelers?" His fingers traced wavy radio signals or something, fanning out through the atmosphere.

"Yes, feelers for a malac. Male. Just a little taller than me. Yellow hair, though he seems to like to wear dark wigs."

He came up from his lounge then and bent forward with concentration. "A malac who uses disguise. Interesting."

"Yes. Yes, a disguise." I told Cousin Noon every physical particular about Britguy I could remember.

"He's slippery," I explained. "But he's my only ticket home." Well, plus Leslie. Find Max and Leslie had to be near. Max's blond hair would be easy for a saur to notice.

"Umm." The thoughtful sound growled deep within Noon-zio. "Malac. There are many on this station."

"Just under a thousand. This one isn't a resident."

"Even more interesting." Noon-zio perked up before he settled back. "But still… malac. Very difficult to tell your kind apart."

"I understand. Well, it was just a thought."

He bent forward across the table. "I said difficult. Not impossible. I will tell my people, on and off-station."

"Thank you, Noon… zio. If they could keep this, well, on the down-low, I'd appreciate it. I think this guy is a spy or something. On the good side, but dealing with bad guys. Maybe. I don't want whatever he has going on to sour."

"Ahh…" The sound came from deep within him as he blinked at me.

"I appreciate the thought, even if nothing ever comes of it. Really. What's important here is finding Liv's child's father. You're really not going to hurt him, are you?"

Cousin Noon clacked his talons together. "That is something he will decide for himself. If he makes the right decision, no one gets hurt." As he started to roll out of the chair, he asked, "Do you know this Rilf?"

"Just what I've heard from Liv and Derra and the others."

"Good man?"

I couldn't hide the pause before I said, "You know Derra. She has high standards. Liv has standards of her own, and she split up with him some time ago. He'd be acceptable as a substitute, if you're not picky. I heard he's agreed to the plan, but I have to wonder about that. Maybe he follows orders too easily. Then again, maybe he's in love with Liv. Maybe he's too young to stand on his own opinions?"

Noon-zio sighed heavily as he made his way to the front door. I hurried past him to open it wider. "I was afraid of that," he said. "Dibi also, not mature. Thought he was and now he runs away. Now Liv-zio, she wasn't most sensible girl on the block when she was a child. Everyone babied her. Smart, but not sensible. You know the difference?"

"Oh yes."

He nodded. "Maybe she hasn't grown up either, hasn't learned to choose a good mate." His shoulders drooped as he stood on my front porch. "Family. Family responsibilities."

For the merest moment I felt sorry for the giant dragon of a saur.

"If you need more help, call on me," I assured him. "I'll see what I can do, but I can't guarantee that Bree will agree to this. I'm glad you're looking after Liv and Derra too, Noon-zio. Derra is good people. So is Liv."

That made him straighten. "That they are." He clapped me on both shoulders in the way all the saurs seemed to have. "And remember that you are family as well. Goodbye, Tam-zio. You will contact me through Derra-zio. Have a very nice day."

I was up on Level 15. One of my coworkers at Sonny's, Jimeek, was taking part in a performance art event and I wanted to cheer him on. He seemed to be having fun bouncing around in the low grav. He was with a troupe who'd painted themselves with liquid colored material– okay, paint– that stuck but didn't dry. Then they hopped around, using trampolines that propelled them through the air, to bound down upon various canvases and papers.

Imagine baby elephants flying just above your head.

They left massive imprints. Sometimes they stopped to add extra color with their tails or hands, or even a brush. Part of the fun was to watch them sail over the crowd, dripping just a bit on us and threatening to plow into us to make us their personal canvas. Jimeek made sure his two kids– they were middle-schoolers, that age– got thoroughly sloshed with gold and blue, at which they squealed in barks. I got a couple of aimed drops that I couldn't duck away from, even though he grinned at me before he did it.

I'd prefer not to be plowed into by a gimigol, thank you. Even so I kept near the front to get a good view. There were professional acrobats– mostly kalids, who liked lower grav– as part of the troupe who cartwheeled through the air and performed tricks, sometimes in twos and threes. They spattered their paint but never made an impression on the various canvases.

I spotted Kem, a malac friend, and her two kids in the crowd and waved them up front with me. We rallied the troupe along in their efforts with yells, whistles and hoots. Occasionally one of the watchers would use the participants as a volleyball and then– watch out! The danger added to the general fun.

Surprisingly, a few of the finished canvases were handsome compositions! If the artists liked it, they ran it under a light that solidified the paint. Otherwise it was all washable.

After it was over, I cleaned up and then walked around the area to see what I could see. I liked to explore as long as the gravity's fine, and there was a lot of Port Malabar that I'd never seen. Instead I spotted Leslie a block away. She was with a couple of saurs, acting real friendly-like, talking at close quarters with her buddies. When a cop strolled into the area, they nonchalantly turned and ambled away. Hunh.

I followed her down to level 18. As we headed north and the heat and humidity began to rise, my skin started to itch. She'd better not. She wouldn't. The two gimigols with her even seemed to hang back as if they didn't want to encroach.

Level 18, sector 33N: the Hatching Grounds. A lot of the species on the station, gimigols very much included, laid eggs. When they did they usually did so in the hatcheries. There were six of them, all programmed to optimum temperatures and scrupulously auto-monitored 24/7.

The hatcheries held lines of cubicles layered with hot sand. Some cubicles held just one large egg; others in other hatcheries went in for several much smaller ones. Of these kind, only one or two made it all the way to hatching.

Parents were always free to come by and visit their eggs. They decorated their cubicles with family pictures, as if their infants could see through their shells.

Sometimes the visitors arranged for soothing music to be piped in to assure their babies' sweet gestating dreams.

I'd visited one of Kreeger's grandkids-to-be in a hatchery with her and some of her kids– the grandkid's uncles and/or aunts as well as the parents– and they all decorated the egg with ribbons and glitter. Kreeger told me that eventually the heat would melt the glitter and the egg would absorb it. It was dietetic/nutritional frou-frou that would please both the family and the fetus.

I was damned if I was going to let whoever these gimigols were get near those unborn kids. The three entered Hatchery Number Two and went down one of the back aisles, one that would be used after the station put on a few more levels and we got more immigrants needing the space. Now I could see one of them was holding two silver bags that had an oozing motion to them. I kept my comm ready to hit the alarm button that would have these guys behind bars within minutes.

But they never went near any of the working cubicles. Instead Leslie led them to the farthest section and then disappeared from my view. Because I was trying to hide I didn't see what she did.

I breathed a sigh of relief when they left the hatchery. Without the bags.

16

Randi stared at me. "You what?"

"I said, I'm not giving you back the brite."

"And I think you're wrong," Dian growled. He flexed his fist as they both faced me.

We were just off Broad Street, in a park on Level 22. The thick growth in this section hid us from anyone who might have been strolling nearby. Randi had finally called me while I was between jobs. I told him where I was, and he'd showed up– with Dian.

"She's just playing," Randi assured him. "Come on, Tam, stop playing around. We want it back. I need it."

I shrugged. "Sorry. Possessing brite is a felony. I won't have either of you saddled with that." I pointed at Dian. "You have a family to think about."

Dian shouldered Randi aside, a neat trick considering Randi had more bulk. "So you think you can keep it?"

"Nope. It's gone."

"Gone!" "Gone?" The confusion in Randi's face was nothing next to the fury of Dian's.

"What the fuck do you mean, 'It's gone'?"

"I asked around. How does one get rid of an illegal substance? At first I thought the acid vats down on 24 would do the trick, and no harm done. But really, it might have shown up somewhere."

"You didn't," Randi said as he kept turning to take in Dian, then me, then Dian. "She didn't. Come on, Tam. Give it to us. Now."

"Brite doesn't produce a buzz in malac," I told him. "It's all in people's imaginations. They're doing something naughty, so they think it'll make them drunk. Brite isn't for malac at all." I turned to Dian. "Is it? Is it, Dian?"

"Give it to me."

I stared down Randi. "See? He doesn't deny it. He's trafficking it for the saurs. The really, really bad ones. What does that make him?"

"Give it. To. Me!"

Bless his heart, Randi actually stepped in front of Dian as he advanced on me.

I shrugged at Dian. "I don't have it. Nobody has it."

"You do!"

"It's gone."

"Liar! Bitch!"

"Hey, hey," Randi said.

Dian tried to push him aside. "She's going to keep the profits for herself. The money's mine! Ours!"

"It's nobody's now. The stuff was dumped on me and I didn't want it. I said so. It's lethal. Randi, it's financing Limbus."

"Limbus?" He looked confused, like maybe the meaning of what he'd been doing was actually sinking in.

"Limbus," I repeated. "They produce it, they take the profit back so they can make more cinderu'um. So they can kill more innocent saurs."

"What the fuck do we care about saurs?" Dian sneered. "You are in trouble, bitch. You too, Randi. You got yourself a smart-ass girlfriend here, and now she's done the wrong thing. You don't have any idea of who you've angered, sis."

"I don't think I've angered you. I think you're frightened. You working with Limbus, Dian?"

"Of course not. But you've got to cough up some money now to make up for what you've done."

"Nope, I don't think so."

"And you, Randi." Dian swung to grab Randi by his shawl. "You're the one who gave it to her."

As Randi blanched, I said, "It was probably your idea to have him do that. Who's the Safeties employee? Who has access to the Tunnels?" God, I hoped they didn't notice that I was recording this conversation on my comm. Just in case…

Dian shook his head. "I didn't have nothing to–"

"You're not going to slip out of the blame that way," I told him. "I've been talking to the cops."

Dian paled at least five shades at my lie. Randi only managed three. "Cops!?"

"I haven't named names. Yet. They said that if you all cooperate, if we can get rid of every last trace of Limbus and brite on Port Malabar, that they'd be inclined to forget anything happened. As long as nothing happens again. Ever." Well, it sounded good to me, maybe even likely. I bet I could swing the deal.

Dian reared back. "Cooperate? With saurs? Saur cops?"

"That's the plan."

He breathed heavily, looking at the floor, then at Randi, then me, then the wall. "I think you still got the stuff," he finally said. "You're not stupid. You're not like Randi. You've got the stuff and you're just holding out for money."

"I have an aversion to blood money."

He pointed accusation at me. "You'll give it back. I know people who'll have you begging me to take it back." He stepped backwards two paces. "You'll see. You'll regret this." The finger swung to Randi. "You make her get it, bring it back, or you'll be sorry, too!"

With that he trotted off. After a few rows of garden plots, the trot turned into a dead-out run.

"Shit," Randi said. His mouth worked without any sound coming out. Then he managed, "You destroyed it. It's gone. Isn't it?"

"That's what I said."

He gave me a fish-eye.

"No getting it back," I confirmed. "Goodbye."

"Shit," he repeated and closed his eyes. "How could you do that?"

"How could you give contraband to me? To me? Not only because I was your girlfriend, but because you knew I was training for Safeties Systems. If I'd gotten caught, I would be out of a profession. I'd have had to start again from the bottom when I got out of jail. If they ever let me out."

He started to say something but I poked him in the chest. "You're a coward. You weren't brave enough to do your own dirty work, so you pawned it off on a weak woman. Isn't that what you thought? Isn't it?"

"I am no coward!"

"And women are not weak. I am not weak. I'm stronger than you in so many ways, Randi. Unlike you, I have a spine."

"Now you're just being–"

"Go away. Now."

"What?"

"Get out of my life. Consider any shade of a relationship between us dissolved."

"It's that stranger malac. I saw you with him. He's been telling you lies."

"Not nearly as bad as the lies you've told me, Randi. Or the things you had me do for you because I wanted to please you. I don't want that any more. I want to please myself. I want to associate with people who make me feel good. Who love me and wish me well."

"Aw, baby–"

"You don't. It was just a fling for you. Well, it was for me as well. I tried fooling myself a few times, but I always knew. I deserve better."

"Better? Than me?" He tried to puff himself up, make a last stand, but I pointed the way back down the pathway.

"Goodbye, Randi. Watch out for Dian and whatever goons he comes up with."

And without one more word, Randi walked away.

I met Bree up in the Starglow district's personal gardens after dinner time. I'd asked if Brindle could join us.

Half of Bree's plot consisted of a lattice gazebo surrounding tables with potted bonsai, under which were empty pots as well as potting mix and other equipment. She had the current work of foliar art on a little turntable so she could turn it this way and that to frown at it. She'd quickly clip the tip of a branch, then the branch next to it. After that it was turn. Turn. Frown. Turn. Clip.

Believe me, with her large green gimigol lips, Bree could frown up a storm. She was always fascinating to watch when she did her bonsai thing. Well, for about four minutes. After that it got boring. I mean: plants.

Her husband didn't seem bored. Instead he rearranged some pots and peered into some particularly large ones that didn't contain plants, only to reach in to pull out tools. He settled to sharpen the edges of some clippers with a flat instrument. Like Bree, he'd peer at the result of each swipe and then re-angle the clippers to swipe again.

I didn't know how to begin the conversation I really wanted to have. I started by thanking Bree for installing that chip for Noon-zio.

"No one's triggered it so far."

"It hasn't had enough time to do its job?" I asked.

"No one can hide from all our sensors that long on this station. You said this Noon guy thought that the girl might have given a false description," Bree said. "If it were me, if someone were out threatening my man…" She gave her husband a cool look. "Well, I'd do more than just a fake description."

Brindle grinned at her, knocked her on her shoulder, before asking, "Is there a reason why I'm supposed to be here?"

"Ah, well…" I'd thought this through, but now all my speeches disintegrated from my brain. Instead I did a poor job relating what I'd been through with Max, and that he was somehow involved with Limbus, though too many times at the receiving end of their wrath.

"Limbus?" Brindle crossed his brawny arms over his chest and frowned at me like I was bonsai, too. "Are you sure? Limbus out here?"

"That's who Max said they were." I had brought Mother's necklace with me. Now I held it up to show him. "Most of the goons were wearing one of these."

Brindle's massive tail fidgeted as he gave it a good look.

"They kept finding us that day," I said. "I figured either they were following Max or they had some kind of tracking device on the necklace. Or both." I gave him the tiny chip I'd found on the back of the necklace, now held in an evidence bag from my work kit. I'd clipped an e/m nullifier onto it to cut any possible signal. Ever since that day, I'd made sure never to wear that necklace outside my clothing.

Bree looked up. She glanced at the bag, focused in on the nullifier, then at me. "What are you doing getting involved in Limbus?"

"Believe me, it wasn't my idea."

Brindle's upper lip made a wave across his face, exposing some sharp teeth. Then he reached into his back pocket. His hand emerged with an official Police Department padd, which he flipped open to record. "Who is this malac again?" he asked.

"Max… Uh, he doesn't live here. Do I have to give you his full name?"

I did after he assured me that he'd do his own preliminary investigation before turning the information over to higher-ups. He asked me all about Max and I tried not to be vague, but what else could I do? I didn't know what Max was, not for sure. Brindle grunted in frustration.

I said, "I want to know, too. You'll tell me what you find out?"

"I'm getting more than curious, myself," Bree said as she turned her plant once more. "So you were chased by these people, and then you mated with him at the core?"

"It was a really small hotel room," I explained, and she snorted at me.

I was still holding the necklace in mid-air but now Brindle stretched out his palm for it. "Mind if I–?"

"No!" I snatched it away from him and clasped it to my chest.

I should give it to him. I held it out, then drew away. Held it out. Drew it back. It took all the effort I could summon to bring it up again and drop it into his palm. My hand was shaking.

Slowly he wrapped his fingers around it. "I'll keep it for now," he said. "I'll do a full scan on it tonight. You'll have it back soon."

"Don't break it," I almost blubbered. "It– It was my mother's. It's all that I have–"

"Good as new."

"The tsunamis," I began and didn't know where to go from there.

Brindle ruffled his brow scales at me in inquiry.

"Well, people say that they're the result of smugglers. I think they're these Limbus guys."

"I can't see where Limbus would want the attention tsunamis bring," Brindle said.

"Did Max the Bastard show up after one of them?" Bree asked.

I tried to recall. "Once definitely. Maybe twice. Yes, twice for sure, and a big maybe on a couple other times. Not sure about the others, but isn't that enough of a coincidence?"

Bree shrugged. "It's not good that we're getting so many of these things that you're having problems recalling one from another. Maybe he's just a smuggler." She harrumphed. "'Just.'"

"I heard Limbus is smuggling brite here," I said slowly. "They say that's how they're financing their group, smuggling brite. I think Max is following them. Undercover."

"Maybe he's one of them," Brindle said. "He got in trouble and is now on the outs with them. They'll want to silence him."

A cold like a dagger pierced my heart. I couldn't imagine Max dead. He'd been more than warm the last time we'd met, and just for a moment there… Several moments… He and I had made some kind of connection.

Nope, I decided, if someone were going to kill Max it would have to be me. He was mine.

"There's something else," I said slowly. "Something big."

Bree stopped her clippers a millimeter from a leaf to look at me. "Bigger than smugglers and Limbus?"

"Brite." I tried to read both their expressions before slowly pulling two mylar bags from under my tunic.

I handed them to Brindle.

"I spotted Max's cousin with some Limbus gimigols and a doil this afternoon. None of them saw me following them. They hid these there, up on the Hatching Grounds."

"The Hatching Grounds!" Brindle exclaimed. Bree came to his side to glare at the bags.

"It was back in the sections that haven't been finished yet," I reassured them. "I was ready to call for help the minute they got too close to the eggs, but they never did."

"Hatching Grounds," Bree murmured. Both gimigols' tails vibrated against the ground.

I told them that I had returned to the grounds after they'd left and searched for the bags, then hidden them up on Level 16 amid the general chaos there until just before I came to this meeting. Brindle examined the bags as he fired questions at me. Instead of answering them I told them about the malac party and tried to explain how brite didn't affect us.

"Then why do they have it?"

I couldn't answer that other than, "I… I guess they're dealing with saurs."

"Malac," Brindle growled. "No wonder we haven't been able to find how it's being distributed."

"Not all malac!" I insisted. "Just a couple. Maybe a few. But not more than that, for sure."

Brindle nodded. "Their names."

I'd gone through this part in my head ever since Randi'd passed that first bag to me. "What if I can get them to turn themselves in?" I asked. "Will the courts go easier on them?"

"Someone close to you?" Bree asked. She glanced at Brindle before returning her stare to me.

"The malac community here is a close one. Except for me. They're suspicious of outsiders. I've had a hard time trying to fit in the way I want to. If I rat out some of them…"

"Ah," Bree whispered.

Now it was time for Brindle to glance at her. They exchanged facial twitches, shrugs. Finally Brindle nodded.

"I give you two days," he told me.

"A week. Give me a week. No, two. More. I know I can get at least one guy to do it but it'll take–" I groaned. This was Randi. "A month. He's mad at me. Scared more than mad." Then I told them about the bags Randi had asked me to hide.

Bree gave me the side-eye when I told her of disposing of the one bag while on duty.

Brindle recorded everything before giving me a nod. "One local lead will lead us to everyone. Get me that one, Tam. In… a month. The wait better be worth it."

I closed my eyes to blow out the breath in which I'd been holding so much tension for so long. "If he doesn't do this in in that time, I'll give you his name. Two names, the ones I know. But he'll do this. He's respected in the community. He has standards, a position to live up to. I'll make him remember that."

Brindle began to say something but Bree put her taloned hand on his chest. "She will," she told him.

Brindle's jaw worked side to side, but he stayed silent.

This time there'd been no tsunami. Max had sent me a message at work to join him. Cousin Leslie came from wherever she'd been to join us. I didn't want either to know how keen I was to figure out exactly what they were up to.

We sat at a crowded sports café table down in Foggybog Square. Though I liked to sit outside, Max insisted we go in though it was pretty much elbow-to-elbow. When saurs are elbow-to-elbow, there's really not a lot of room left in which to breathe. Large 3-D video screens populated the walls, all tuned to the same channel. We arrived to see the last of the wallow game from Bar-Tok. Amid various howls of anguish and victory at the end, most of the crowd dispersed.

"Thought so." Max stretched his legs, enjoying the space.

Since I had duty later I ordered tea, but Max ordered a good-sized drink and Leslie matched him. We managed to go through a medium tray of snacks, which for tiny humans was a huge amount of food. We talked of anything but what Max and Leslie might really be up to. Instead they pumped me for innocent station gossip. At least, I thought it was innocent enough. How could I get info out of *them?*

The TVs switched to news and the name "Limbus" caught our attention. As one, we swung our gaze to the central screen though we could have called it up at our table.

Another city about twenty systems over had been decimated by that cinderu'um stuff. Limbus had bragged their responsibility for it.

Diagrams and animations showed exactly what cinderu'um could do. Not only did it sink down through a planet's mantle until it reached magma, but it spread out like it could move on its own. Eventually it reached a limit but only after an unimaginable amount of area had been destroyed.

This particular time it hadn't gone down so much as out. Max sat at absolute attention, as if he were absorbing every new detail. Leslie's mouth formed a sour snarl at the screen.

The cinderu'um had crawled up buildings and melted them in a slow, unyielding flow. People fled before it with no time to collect their valuables other than their lives. Too many times they couldn't even manage that. We saw Planetary Safeties Systems try chemicals on it, sonics… Only flash-freezing seemed to tame it.

And by flash-freezing I don't mean ice cubes; I mean a hundred degrees below zero Celsius. That's not very practical in a planetary environment; it tends to kill things over even a larger area than what the Limbus covered. Eventually the landscape would recover. What was left of the cinderu'um after freezing was a thin, rubbery substance. The news showed a guy holding up a piece of it for the camera. Officials were studying it.

I shivered. This attack had been targeted to take the entire city, which seemed to me to be about the size of LA. Luckily, I guess, it had only done about a Pittsburgh's worth of damage.

"Wayley," Leslie murmured and looked at Max. "That's only ten parsecs away."

"From here?" I blurted.

Max waved me down. "From Earth," he said. He rubbed his upper lip as Leslie opened her personal screen. A starry map appeared on it.

She pointed out previous Limbus attacks that had been on a much smaller scale, as if they'd been testing their weapon as opposed to the accident on Earth. "Here, here and here," she said.

"They're aiming for Trik-Kin," Max surmised.

"Would they be that obvious? It's got to be misdirection. They'll be after Nik-a-Dell." The Confederation's capital.

Max agreed. "And they'll target Trik-Kin to keep the attention away from their end target."

"Um, shouldn't we tell anyone?" I ventured.

Leslie regarded me coolly. "They have their own people on this case. Let them figure it out by themselves."

"But the people on Trik-Kin–"

"It's a doil world."

"Yes. What about them? Shouldn't they be warned?"

She snapped her screen shut and secured it in her pocket. Max said, "We only have the one priority, Tam. Making sure Limbus never gets back to Earth, not ever. We cut them off, whatever it takes."

"But what if they, I dunno, stored some of that stuff here, in this station?" A horrible suspicion had come to me. I wanted to know his answer to this. "What if this is a transfer point?"

Max shrugged. "Then we'd have to destroy Port Malabar. If they were using the station they had to have a network of supporters here. This way we'd get everyone."

Leslie added, "We'd clear the humans off first, of course. We have ways of doing that quietly."

"But– what about the innocent beings? There are families here!"

She shrugged. "Casualties of war."

"Our only duty is to keep humans safe."

I couldn't believe it. I couldn't believe Max would believe that. I wanted to throttle him until he saw what he was actually saying– what he was standing for– but instead I just sat there with my mouth flapping like a fish out of water.

Max looked hard at me. "Earth. That's our priority. You got a problem with that?"

Again Leslie looked like she'd just sucked on a lemon. "She's got a thing for aliens."

"No she doesn't. She realizes what's what. What has to be done."

"You'd kill everyone." No one could actually do that, could they?

"The few to protect the many. This is war, Tam."

I pressed my palms against my cheeks before taking a deep breath. He was right about the war thing. What did I know of real war? I didn't want to know anything about it.

Limbus itself would never come to Port Malabar. Some few supporters might be here, peddling that awful brite for Limbus' benefit, but the main guys would stay away. They'd never bring cinderu'um here.

Right?

That was strange. The lights didn't come on after I got home from work when I stepped through the door into my apartment. They always did.

"Lights," I said. Nothing.

As I bumped against a table in the late-night dark I plotted a path to my emergency flashlight. Did I need to flip a circuit breaker? Replace a fuse? Let's see, the desk would have schematics…

I hit my big blue chair even though I knew it was there. I reached down to steady myself.

And a hand clapped over my mouth.

It was brawny. Human, I thought once I could spare a few milliseconds apart from sudden panic to notice.

Oh my god, Dian had come for me. Did he have a weapon?

Another hand– a match to the one over my mouth– grabbed me around the waist and pulled me back against someone's body.

Back in college I'd been taught to use an attacker's momentum against them. But whoever this was, they weren't momentuming.

"You're not as dangerous now, are you?" a male voice whispered, dead against my ear. The voice held a British accent.

I stomped on his feet and bit a finger.

He cursed and gave a jerk of surprise. That gave me enough room to punch backwards, right in that ultimate vulnerable area.

But he sidestepped me so I only slugged his thigh. I tried for a foot again, missed, and then used my other leg. Got him! I gave him a good knee.

He let out a heaving groan. Now I turned to face my attacker.

Even semi-immobilized, he knew a few moves of his own. He popped me behind my own knees and I went down. Through his sheer weight he pinned me to the ground.

"Where are they?" he demanded once he caught his breath.

What? "They who?"

Why did he bother with the lights when his damned British accent was such a giveaway?

"You know who. Your accomplices."

"My–"

Something in the room jangled and I knew exactly what it was: Mom's necklace. I'd stored it in my underwear drawer this morning after Brindle had had someone deliver it to me. Its elements clicked hollowly against each other as he rattled it again. I tried to free my hand to wrest the thing from him.

"Just tell me where they are. Plans would also be appreciated."

"You'll break it!"

"Boo hoo. Tell me now. I know people who would be happy to arrest you for this and throw you in the darkest, coldest, least pressurized cell they have for the rest of your unnatural life."

I managed to grab the hand that held the necklace and squeezed as hard as I could. That didn't do any good, so I bit him. I heard the necklace drop to the floor.

"That was my mother's!"

Fury gave me strength. I knocked him far enough that I could roll out from under him. I reached blindly for the necklace, desperate for Mom. He tackled me. Even as I kicked back I ran my hands across the floor.

"Don't try to blame this on–"

I gave him my full attention with a kick. I think it connected to his chin because this grunt was more an "Ook!" and I was free. I scrambled to my feet but kept a crouch. Searching… searching…

There. As my fingers fastened on it, his hand closed over mine.

"Mine!" I cried. I let him have it with my elbow–

But he twisted away and managed to cage me in his arms at the same time. He knocked me backward into my chair so that my back was on the seat and my butt hanging in the air. Not a position from which to launch an attack.

"You better not have broken it, you creep."

Silence. Then he said, "It isn't yours."

"It is now. Do you honestly think I have no idea who you are? Why the lights?"

He cursed three Lingua curses and managed to twist them with his damned accent.

"I'll track you through surveillance tapes if I have to," I said through gritted teeth.

"Is that why you joined Safeties?" he countered. "Are you the inside man?"

"Inside man for what? Are you always loony tunes?"

Silence again. "The necklace." He said it as if he expected me to continue his sentence. So I did.

"It's my mother's. You can't have it. I swear you will not leave here with a single bone intact if you try to steal it."

He was quiet.

"It's all I have left of her. All I have left of anything, thanks to you."

I could almost hear his jaw creak as he opened it to speak. "You're welcome."

"Yes, you saved my life. Thanks. And thanks so much for leaving me an explanation of what had happened. Why I'm... here."

"I left you a Lingua tape."

"Oh yeah," I snarled. "That helped so much."

"What, you wanted flowers? Maybe a box of chocolates and a 'Get Well Soon' card?"

"It was four months before I could listen to it. Six months before I saw another human being."

His grip lessened. My bottom sank to the floor.

"Lights," he said. For *him* they came on.

He was staring at me and yet not. His brown eyes focused on something far away.

He was dressed as a normal city dweller, a civilian jumpsuit in grayish blues that would have made him blend in with any crowd. Except that he was malac. Very. He'd switched to a reasonable-looking black wig, this one with longish, coarse hair like most of the human men here wore theirs. But they didn't wear goatees, probably because they wouldn't look good on them as his didn't look good on him. It made him look a lot older than I remembered. Sinister.

"So the necklace was your mother's?" he asked.

"You catch on quick."

He pulled at his goatee thoughtfully. It didn't pull off a bit; good glue. "That might explain a lot of things."

"Like what? Like why you insist on skulking about this station? How were you involved in that explosives cache on Level 26 about six months ago?"

He looked at me sharply. "How did you know about that?"

"Chemical leak. I saw the surveillance tapes."

He tipped his head to the side and scrutinized me. "You identified me?"

I didn't want to give him the satisfaction of the truth, so I remained silent. Instead he gave me the most satisfied smirk I've ever seen.

That made me angry. "If you try to harm a living soul on this station, I swear I'll pull your gonads out through your throat and then force you to eat them!"

The threat didn't impress him. He merely rubbed his mouth with the flat of his hand.

"This necklace was really your mother's?"

"You'd better not have scratched it." I examined the turquoise pendant with its strange markings. "She was a cop. A hero."

"Hero, hell. She was a bloody traitor to the human race!"

17

I walloped him across the mouth.

I must not know my own strength, for I slammed him into the floor even while clutching the necklace in my other hand. My mind went white-angry, and I pummeled his face, kicking what parts of his body I could.

"You take that back!" I screamed. "You filthy bastard! My mother was a hero!"

It wasn't until I realized that I was using the fist that held the necklace that I paused. I blinked at it and then tucked it quickly under the chair.

But that had given him enough time to roll out of my reach. He cursed at me, cradling his chin in one hand and then dabbing to check if the blood on his face truly was from his nose. He cursed again.

"Get out of my house," I growled.

"You're fucking mental." He backed away, sliding on his butt.

"You're the one who doesn't know what he's talking about. My mother was an official hero. Decorated twice. My dad was, too, only he couldn't get out of his hospital bed long enough to receive his own medals."

I hauled myself to my feet and a second rush of adrenaline, or the sudden lack of same, made me sway and catch myself on the arms of the chair. "Now get out. Isn't it enough that you abandoned me out here in the middle of nowhere? You destroyed my world. Now you're trying to destroy my mother's name. Get out!" Then I proceeded to call him a few choice names of my own choosing.

After that we just shouted incoherently at each other. His were muffled as he tried to stanch the blood. We took hunched positions across from each other as if we were about to embark in a pro wrestling match.

Somewhere around then it occurred to me that without the element of surprise, he could probably beat the hell out of me.

I didn't care. I told him what I thought of him and everything he was responsible for: my kidnapping, my long convalescence, the bombing back at Greene's Tavern, the illegal chemicals down on Level 26.

"I won't let you hurt anyone here!" I screamed at him before I realized that he had stopped shouting.

"Wait," he said. He took one blooded hand and waved me down. "Wait a minute. You still think *I* set off the weapon on Earth?"

It took me a couple of tries to speak rationally. "You were there. You knew all about it." Righteous anger took hold of me again. "How could you do something like that? There must have been people killed! Lots!"

He waved me down again, but this time he didn't look at me; he gazed past my side wall as if he were considering something. "So you claim you don't know about cinderu'um? Or grebelchay?" he finally asked.

I had to ask, "What's grebelchay?"

He snorted at that. "And you don't have any idea about loeser ren? Or koritzo? Brite running?"

I stiffened at that last one and he saw it. "Brite doesn't hurt humans," I said quickly. "I, ah, may have seen some, but it was being used for human consumption, not alien." Remembering the taste of the stuff, I couldn't stop my nose from wrinkling. "I'll pass on it."

Max sat down on the floor with a thud. "Bloody, effing hell," he grunted. "I've been chasing the wrong person."

"We think you're in the brite smuggling business." I tried to make myself sound, I don't know, haughty or something but somewhere deep inside I knew that I was missing an important piece of the puzzle, and without that things were falling apart.

"Of course I'm not!" Max tried waving his arms with effrontery but had to clap his hands back to his bloody nose. Then he asked, "Who's 'we'?"

"Officer Brindle of Station Police."

"You didn't," Max groaned. "You blew my cover."

"He's checking into my necklace, too. So you see, we have it all in hand. You aren't needed here. Go away."

He waved off the comment. "What did he find?"

"*I* found a chip on it. Brindle's using it to detect if others are on the station. They haven't made any arrests yet. Will you be the first?"

"Dammit, I'm supposed to be undercover."

For some reason that made, well, sense. Or maybe I wanted it to, not only for him but for Mom. That would be something she'd do, right? She'd have been perfect undercover. Would Earth cops be aware of alien conspiracies? Was that why she'd owned a Limbus necklace– to investigate them undercover?

I grabbed a washcloth out of my closet and tossed it to him.

He acknowledged it with a nod as he wadded it in place. "You and your damned uppercuts." His voice was muffled behind the cloth.

"Explain," I snapped.

He looked up at me and frowned around his makeshift bandage. "You *will* take me to hospital if I pass out or anything?"

"Maybe I'll throw you in the nearest gutter, like you did me."

"I also threw you into the best human medicine hospital in the galaxy. I saved your life, you thankless shrew."

"I suppose. Explain."

"About…?"

He had a lot of subjects to explain. I sat there with an eyebrow raised at him and waited for him to choose one.

"Undercover investigations," he finally decided upon.

"Go on."

"My family's always been in the business. A long time ago we joined with some others to expand our venue. We cover the galactic threats to Earth."

"A long time ago. Using the family spaceship, I suppose."

"As a matter of fact, yes. We keep them camouflaged in the parkland adjacent to the manor house."

"Right."

"Well, we do. Earth's lucky that it's such an insignificant blip on the cosmic map, at least so far. Galactic interception has been sporadic, accidental for the most part." He added as if to himself, "Although these few past generations have been seeing more and more of it." He shook the idea away from himself, but his hand on his nose made it look like he was using his proboscis as a handle to do the shaking.

"Be that as it may. The Guardians of Earth– that's us– prides itself on countering galactic threats before they can touch Earth. There hasn't been much to it before now. Like I said, Earth is a backwater. No one notices it, except by accident.

"Perhaps that's why Limbus decided to use it to develop and test a cinderu'um weapon," he mused. "No one except Terrans would have noticed their tests. You saw how it works."

I sucked in air, recalling glowing sewers and dissolving air. "I've also seen it on the news."

"The one on Earth must have been a prototype, a mini-version. It left quite an impact on that town you're from, but nothing larger than that."

"What–"

"Within hours the corrosives had eaten through the mantle. Your old home is now a small volcano. Probably a tourist spot by now."

I couldn't imagine it. And yet I could. I'd seen the ground sink, seen the molten fury of whatever it had been. Even rock couldn't have stood up to that. "How many people died?"

"Not as many as there could have been. Like I told you back then, there were safeties in place, at least a few."

"Safeties? But you said– A volcano–"

He dabbed at his nose, checking the material. "A cinderu'um weapon– the version we think they have now– in full-out, unfettered mode would have disintegrated maybe a sixth of the planet. Not all at once, but with the chain-effect events resulting from the initial blast. I didn't have to hear the details at our briefings. The important thing is that it be stopped. That Limbus be stopped."

"Bastards." The word came out as a hiss, a warning to all those responsible if I ever got my hands on them. Never again would they do anything like this! "They've been using it on other worlds. They aren't testing it anymore."

"Indeed." Max leaned on one hand and pointed with the other, bloody-rag-holding one, before returning it to his nose. He pointed at the medallions on my mother's necklace.

"That," he said, "is an identification badge for Limbus agents and accomplices."

"No." He was absolutely wrong, of course.

"I'm afraid so."

"Maybe Mom was undercover, too. Maybe she just found it somewhere. Maybe… Maybe it's just a coincidence."

"It's a rather cunning design, isn't it? Unique."

It was. Its pendants were trapezoids with silver metal wrapping in broad curlicues around them. It was so much more retro op art than the delicate jewelry my mother usually liked. I mean, come to think of it.

"You lived in the town the cinderu'um was being developed in." His gaze slid sideways to examine my face. "Your mother was not a member of the Guardians. Not associated with us in any way."

"No," I whispered.

"Limbus needed human assistance to do it. Rent the buildings, deal with the inhabitants. Cover energy surges, source supplies."

I balled my hand into a fist around the pendants. "My mother was a hero. Do you hear? She saved lives, she didn't take them. She protected. 'To serve and protect'– that was written on the side of her car. Hell," I declared, "that was written in her heart. It's what she taught me."

He sat there and met my eyes. "It may be that she was a noble woman. But every person has their breaking point. Maybe she was being blackmailed."

"Blackmailed?" I let out a harsh laugh. "We had no money. No one would blackmail us. They wouldn't get a penny!"

Then it hit me. Dad's medical bills.

"What is it?" Max asked.

"None of your business."

"Actually, it is precisely my business."

I stayed silent, but Max kept on. "Maybe it was the lack of money that gave them an in? Does the American police pay so little? I thought you people had a welfare system that kept everyone on–"

"My father," I blurted. "He died from injuries incurred in the line of duty. He was a firefighter, too." Pride blazed through me; here I was, following in my father's footsteps. "But his medical bills were enormous. He was hospitalized for two years; lingered for almost a year in intensive care. We were always broke. I can't… I can't imagine what the bills must have been. Mom had to work two jobs, and once she tried for three. She couldn't take it. But we got by. Barely. And I helped, I got small jobs everywhere I could."

"Yes?"

I fingered the medallion. "Until it was time for me to go to community college. I got a little scholarship and I was working, but Mom came up with some money from somewhere so I could quit my job and study full time. She–" A pain stabbed through my heart. "She died right after that, not even a full semester in."

"And you don't know where she got the money."

I could only shake my head. Dealing with her finances after her death… "The lawyer had someone check all the figures from her estate," I said. "Wouldn't they have noticed? Wouldn't they have said something?"

"Not if they were on the wrong team," Max said. "So your mother did this for money."

I shook my head. But when had Mom first showed me the necklace? I'd found it in one of her drawers, and she said she couldn't resist taking a little of our money to buy it. We'd both admired its design. Every time I'd seen her wearing it she had remarked on how much she loved it. Therefore, I loved it as well. "No, she wouldn't have done anything like this. Not endangering people. My mother was the gentlest, the most courageous–"

I couldn't move. I was in shock. Numb. I knew none of it was true. I suspected it all was.

Mom– a traitor. Responsible for how many deaths?

I could still smell the sulfur in the air that day, still feel the heat from the ground, the stinging as my own skin dissolved on me.

I remembered the video of all those doils running for their lives on that one world. The doils– how long had they had to suffer before they'd died?

But Mom was a hero.

I don't know how long he let me sit there and absorb it all. Mom knew what her personal ethical boundaries were. She never overstepped anything– anything!– of importance. She taught me what was right and wrong.

Then I thought of the brite I'd hidden. Where were *my* boundaries?

He frowned at the length of my silence. "So you don't know who she got the necklace from."

I shook my head. "It was a few years ago. She said it was just something she'd been looking at for a long time and," I swallowed, "now that we had a little extra money, she'd bought it. But everything else was going toward my college."

I stared at it. Wondered what moment it had become That Thing instead of a memory of my mother.

I decided to blame it, not her. At that moment I would have given it to Max for him to destroy, whatever… but I also knew that I wasn't in a very logical place right now. I'd make decisions when I could think straight.

"Where's Giggler?" I asked him. "Leslie."

He shrugged. "You don't have to be concerned with her. She does what she needs to."

"But you'll tell her about my mother. About the necklace."

"When we re-establish contact. She's on another leg of this operation right now. She's the right-hand man" he gave a slight smile at the noun "on my team."

"So you have a team?"

"Humanity is my team." His eyes lit with ferocity. "You must be on it as well."

"When did I ever leave? I mean, other than when you kidnapped me–"

"I did not–" He frowned again and stood. Dried blood made a blotchy pattern on his cheek, chin and upper lip. He paced the room twice before turning back to me. He pointed. "Earth and all humanity is at stake here. You have to know what side you're going to be on."

"Well, duh."

"I'm serious," he snapped. "This is not a game."

"And yet you're talking teams."

"I'm talking covert operations," he said and squatted down to be on my eye level as I sat on the floor. "This is the most important work you'll do in your life. That anyone in your family–" he glanced at the necklace. "Sorry, but you get the gist– that anyone in your family for generation upon generation has done. People on my team, we protect the planet and when we do that we protect the human race. We can make no mistakes. It's too easy for a Galactic to destroy our world. It all actually boils down to a button. One of many possible buttons."

Then he stood up, his feet planted apart as he stared down at me. "This is my sacred duty. I lead my team and we root out those buttons. We destroy them and then we destroy those who'd think of using them."

As I got up I began pulling up a sofa as well as my main comm unit, just to put my nervous energy to use. "And how long have you and your family been doing this? Have they always been the team captains, or have they been lackeys?" I sat heavily onto that sofa. It didn't seem like I could stand on my own.

"We've always led the pursuit in some way," he said. "We report to a headquarters, a central clearing commission, but otherwise we operate on our own.

"At least we now know that you're not playing for the other side." He sat next to me and put an arm around my shoulders. "I was afraid you were," he said. He gave a little shrug, which vibrated over to me because we were so close. "Would have been a blot on the record to have saved a terrorist from certain death, you know. Well, without interrogating them first, I suppose. You certainly played the part of the harpy well enough there. I was never sure. And then the necklace… But we don't have to worry about that now, do we?"

I was sitting there in shock, but when he turned my chin so I faced him and then came in for a kiss, the numbness evaporated, beginning with my lips.

"Hey!" I said against him. "Excuse me!"

He reared back. "What?"

"What were you trying to do?"

"Well…" He eased away from me as his eyebrows came together. "I thought I was kissing you."

"You just told me my mother was a traitor! To the entire human race!" I scooted away from him. "What makes you think that would make me horny?"

"Not so horny as more…" He stared at me, then looked at the blank wall for a second before turning back. "I thought we shared a moment there."

"Yeah. A really bad moment." I glared at him. "Sheesh!" I spread my arms to the room and maybe Heaven itself to invoke witness. "Is this just stupidity or testosterone run amuck? Men!"

With that I twisted to point an accusing arm at him. "My mother. Was not a traitor!"

He held out his hands in surrender. "I'll be investigating that necklace. Maybe I can clear her name."

"Her name doesn't need to be cleared!"

He chewed on that a while. "So I suppose this means we won't have sex?"

"Out!" I shouted. I jumped up, opened the door for him and pointed in the direction I wanted him to go. "Get out! Now!"

He took the hint but turned back to me on the porch. "Do *not* get the local police involved in this," he ordered. "Find a way to explain it away. Leave them out of this. The Guardians have it under control."

I was about to retort that I'd tell anyone I wanted– though that wasn't the case; this was a touchy area– when one side of Max's mouth quirked and a challenging spark came into his eyes. "As for you– we'll see how you feel later."

"Nothing personal, but don't come back," I told him as I slammed the door in his face.

Three minutes later came a knock at the door. I peeked before opening.

"Everything okay?" Nuke asked me. He made no pretense of stretching his neck, trying to see around me into the apartment.

He must have been next door all along. "You heard."

"It sounded like something I shouldn't interrupt."

I sighed. "Sorry for the noise. It won't happen again."

"Sometimes noise is needed." Now he peered at me, his head moving from side to side. I wondered what he saw when he looked at a human. "You all right?"

"I will be." I started to say something to him and decided against it. I had to straighten things out for myself first.

He gave a nod at my silence. "When you are ready, I'll be here."

"You really are the best, Nuke. Thanks. Thanks just for being here."

He lumbered not back to his front door, but to the rocking chair on his side of the porch. There he seated himself and watched the street with the chained vibrancy of a guard dog, Benny the skeleton by his side.

18

Bree yelled at me that day and I took it without complaint, possibly because she'd had good reason. I'd been sloppy. In my misery I just didn't care. Still, I tried to rise above it at least to do my job. People's lives depended on me.

We had all kinds of odd disasters to prepare for. What to do if the lifts stopped. What to do if the bogs on Level 27 began to dry up. If oxygen levels dropped. Pressure drops. If absolute disaster struck and a section of the station had to be ejected. Or even worse: if our spin increased– or decreased.

Today we concentrated on section ejection. The drill involved forty-nine million check-offs, of which I screwed up forty-eight. The final grade was not good. Bree gave a grunt that only gimigols can make, echoing deep from their intestines, and told me, "Clock off. You're no good today."

I slunk to the locker room and she called behind me, "You'd better be snapped out of this tomorrow."

"I will," I promised and tried to believe it.

But how did one snap out of life flipping upside-down? I tried to sort through it all on the way home. There was no trying to excuse it: Mom had dealt with terrorists, and she had to have known at least partially what they truly were. Mom had been the smartest person I'd known. But she'd had a hand in the destruction of my city. Maybe more.

This was the Mom who had raised me, whose smiling face I'd looked forward to seeing every evening and morning. She'd held me and counseled me when I was down. Promised that things would get better when they were bleak as could be. She'd stayed up all night to help that time my orrery had fallen apart the evening before final science projects were due.

She was Mom.

And Mom was a traitor.

"Zup, Tam?" Derra asked as I slunk into the deli. Even through the misery my stomach growled. I hadn't eaten since before Max's thunderbolt had struck.

Just to punish myself I ordered minimum rations, tasteless stuff. Derra frowned at my choices. "Wanna talk?" she asked.

I shook my head.

"Whenever you want," she offered. She went to the pickle jar, lifted the lid and handed me one. "Good for what ails you."

"No. Thanks, but no. Not today." Just the sight of the brown thing in her hand made me ill.

She didn't like that. "What up?" she asked. "You've never turned down tcher-riepi before. I thought this reminded you of mother? You sick?"

And then her right eye tightened on me. I could see it bulge as she focused in. "Oh," she said. "Mother problem. Your mother dead, right?" She didn't wait for me to respond. "Worst kind of mother problem, ghost mother. Been there. Tough times. You sure you don't want to talk?"

I secured my take-home box, shaking my head.

"Okay, Tam-zio. But you only get one day to mope about this. No good to fight with ghosts. They unreasonable. They can lie. You can't beat up ghost to get truth."

When I turned silently toward the door, she called, "You come back tomorrow night. Liv will handle things. We talk. Okay?"

I tried to smile and nodded my head, silently vowing to go somewhere else for dinner tomorrow. Or maybe skip eating entirely. For the rest of my life.

My stomach growled.

"I send someone if you don't come by," Derra said and I glanced up sharply at her. Had she read my mind?

"Told you," she said with a quiet chirrup. "Been there. I can help."

The smile I gave her might be lopsided but it was genuine this time. "Okay, Derra. I'll try to get by tomorrow."

"You will."

"Hsst! Malac!"

I stopped dead in my tracks as my heart leaped into my throat. I was in uniform with some PK tubing coiled around my right shoulder, walking back to the Tunnels through a deserted alley in the west-side industrial district on Level 24. I whirled to see who it was. A Limbus agent? No, it was a doil in an orange-striped jacket over a workingman's jumpsuit. He wore a bright green polka-dotted toboggan cap. His neck had a brownish-reddish cast to it, clashing with his normal green-bronze doil coloring, and his left nostril was slightly higher than his right. His triangular tab of a tail quivered.

"Dibi," I said, fairly sure of myself.

"Malac," he said. "I forget your name."

"Tam. Derra calls me Tam-zio."

He grunted.

"Her cousin Noon calls me that, too." I remarked casually. "He was on the station the other day, looking for you. Don't know if he's still here or not." He wasn't. Business had called him back home, but he'd told everyone he'd be back soon.

Two layers of reddish scales on the back of his neck stood on end at the name I'd dropped.

"Am I Tam-zio to you, Dibi?" I asked. "Are you coming back to your family?"

He gave me a sickly turn of his beak. "There are no malac in my family, Tammalac."

"Then apparently there are no cowardly males in mine, Dibi-doil. No babies crying for their fathers, either. Liv's baby will have Rilf."

"Rilf! Still?"

"Baby's got to have somebody. Wasn't that what you were thinking when you made it?"

He poked a talon against my shoulder, the shoulder saurs usually butted a fist against. "You tell Liv that she can't have that *gradant* Rilf."

"Rilf has other ideas. Rilf likes the idea of a baby with Liv." I hoped the fact that I had never talked that much with Liv or Derra about Rilf didn't come through. I was a lousy liar, but was betting saurs couldn't read humans that well.

"He had better stay away from my child! You tell Liv–"

"*You* tell Liv. She's so emotional these days. She's not listening to reason." This time I poked him. "She's listening to Rilf. And Derra."

Dibi pounded one fist into his other palm and then pointed at me. "She can't. She has to give me time. I'm not ready for this."

"But you made a baby. No mistake there."

"I changed my mind!"

"Too bad the baby can't change theirs."

"It's too soon. Too fast!"

"There's time before the fetus, well, ripens." What did you call it when a fetus switched whose body they went in? I still hadn't researched doil childbearing. "You might change your mind when you're carrying your own child. It would be a bad thing if it took Noon-zio to do that for you. How would you explain it to your kid?"

He touched his belly protectively. "I'm not– I'm…" His cheeks puffed like melons and then he blew air out in a blast of a whistle. I'd heard lesser ones from positively apoplectic doils.

"Well," I said, "Liv mucked up the program on this search thing Noon was doing. At least that's the only reason I can think of why Noon hasn't been able to find you."

Dibi was trying to control his fear. He paced back and forth, his hands forming fists and then relaxing, forming fists again. "You tell Noon to stay away from me! If he wants me to have the child I have to be healthy!"

"Do you want to have the child?"

"I don't know. I don't know! But if I'm dead I can't make up my mind!"

If he didn't make up his mind the correct way, he might well be dead. Seemed to me a pretty clear-cut decision. But there were deeper, more personal questions he had to answer first for himself.

"Do you have a family, Dibi?" I asked. "Are Liv and Derra and even Noon your people now? What does your side of the family make of all this?"

He slammed his fist into a wall before sinking back against it. "My family is back on Harlek," he said. "I broke away to come out here."

"An adventurer?"

He shook his head. "I just wanted to get away from them. They were driving me crazy."

I stood on tiptoe to pat his upper arm, the way I'd seen Derra do to others. "You made your way here, right? And you found Liv."

"Liv." He seemed to ease at the name.

I shrugged. "I know some people think she's, um, a little irresponsible–"

He shot to full attention. "She is not! Who said that?"

"Maybe I got it wrong," I hedged. He towered over me, an exclamation point of sudden rage. "But everyone loves Liv. Everyone wants what's best for her."

"Yes! You remind them of that."

"And what's best for her might just be you, Dibi. Maybe you're what's best for the baby, too. And just maybe," I touched his upper arm again. "The baby and Liv are what's best for you."

My door chimed. When I opened it, there stood Max.

He had one hand behind his back and a smile I could only describe as "tentative" on his face.

"Icomebearinggifts!" he blurted before I could trigger the door to close.

Well. Gifts. I waited, not saying anything. He brought his hidden hand around in an abrupt move, pushing a bag– plastic with a logo that read "Selfridges." A large something had been bundled inside.

"Well?"

Silently I looked at him.

His mouth worked side to side. "I apologize," he finally said.

I wondered if he knew what he was apologizing for, but couldn't stop my curiosity. It was clearly a bag from Earth. I took it and then, despite all common sense, stepped aside so he could enter.

I peeked inside the bag.

I screamed.

"Jeans! Real jeans!" There were over a half-dozen of them.

"I didn't know what size you were, so I guessed," he said as he glanced around. He took a seat at my desk.

For this I triggered the big, comfortable sofa and it rose from the floor. "Stay," I ordered him and trotted off to the bathroom for some privacy to change in.

British sizing is different from American. Plus I had no idea what size I might be any more. Whatever, I thought as I madly tried on first one, then another. Second one was a win, and there were two more, slightly different styles, in the same size.

I had jeans!

I stuck my head out from the bathroom. "What do I owe you for this?" Evil Max. He had said awful things about Mom. He'd made me think awful things about her.

No, I wasn't going to think about that. Not now.

I was shallow. I was shocked.

What would he want? A variety of bribes occurred to me. A very wide variety.

He placed a hand over his heart. "I am merely being chivalrous," he said. "No payback required."

"Hm." Still. Jeans! Jeans!

I doubled over the fabric I had hanging on the wall for a sarong and used it as a halter top. Then I actually modeled for him, the louse.

He seemed pleased. More than that, I thought he took note of what my size had turned out to be. With a nod he stood up.

"Are you hungry?"

"I could use a meal. Think I'll go out for it." I turned my back on him and made for the door. I was in jeans! I wanted everyone to see!

"Excellent. I'm starved."

I stopped to give him a punishing glare. "You're coming along?"

"Sweetheart, I'm buying your dinner. Make it someplace dark. I don't have my wig with me, and I don't want to play the game tonight."

"No game?" So that's what it was to him?

"Not tonight."

He slid his arm around my waist and eased me down the front walk. I let him.

I wanted to walk a bit before sitting next to this guy, so I chose the long way, past our neighborhood park. Now that the surprise was wearing off, my mind was returning.

He didn't seem to mind the walk. "Last time I was a bit wretched to you. Awful, really," he said.

"Yeah."

"I had good reasons. You can see that."

I let the silence sit between us for a while before I said, "Maybe. You couldn't trust me, past tense. But how am I supposed to trust you?"

"I can't tell you everything. Or frankly, much about anything."

I remained silent.

"So maybe we could start again?"

That required me to glance at him. "A fresh start. That might be good."

"Ahh…"

"A start to you turning over a new leaf." I faced him down. "You could become more dependable. Nicer. More forthcoming. You could tell me when you might be in town and not use a tsunami as an announcement. Now every time there's a disaster I expect to see your sorry face somewhere."

"Is it that sorry?"

I tried to make a horrible face at him. Damn my hormones anyway. He looked like a puppy left out in the rain.

"You are such a faker," I told him. "I can't trust you. Not in anything."

He reached to my jaw, and I leaned away, then allowed the touch. His thumb and forefinger rubbed my chin. "Not anything? I'll admit, I'm not the most reliable man as to my schedule, but I'm rather constant in many other things. Faithful."

"You don't give a damn about others. About their feelings."

"Some people, no. Others I care a lot about. About their feelings and other things."

His face was getting entirely too close to mine. His mouth was altogether too fascinating to watch as he spoke, as he paused, as he breathed.

"Where's your cousin?" I blurted.

He gave me a lazy grin at that and leaned back to prop himself against some fencing. "She's working undercover. Silly of her to let you see her here at all. I'll have to tease her next time I talk to her."

"Undercover. Oh."

"Oh." He gave me a dark, sultry and slightly mocking look that sent a shiver up my spine. He caused his own personal tsunamis.

Derra's Diner was close, it was well-lit, and I knew if I got into trouble there'd be a flock of defenders to rush to my rescue. From the look of him, Max was examining every millimeter of the place for trouble as I tried to look coordinated while climbing into a chair.

Max took the seat across from me and I didn't feel so bad about what I'd likely looked like. It would have been nice if our feet had reached the floor.

"Damned chairs," Max muttered. "And I should have gotten yours for you. I've developed bad habits out here, so far from home."

"How far are we?" I asked. "And what direction? Where are we? Where do I find a map?"

"I have a computerized map in my ship," Max said. "It's not really a map; it's directions on how to pilot my way back. Cosmological coordinates. Numbers only, plus string programs."

"So you can't point and say, 'Thar she blows.'"

He gave a small smile and shook his head. He was about to say something when Liv strolled up to us. Her apron was tight, apparently to show off the slight bulge of her belly.

"Tam-zio!" she exclaimed. She gave Max a thorough look, stretching her neck and peering at him in a way that would have done her mother proud.

"Uh, this is Max," I told her. "A, uh, friend." Or something.

She gave a chirpy laugh. "Hello, Tam's uh-friend," she told Max. "Can I get you a drink?"

"Ah, what do you have here?"

"Tam-zio, what will your uh-friend have to drink?" She wagged her tail at me, the doil version of a wicked wink.

"Oh shut up," I told her. "You still have that lynchi wine?"

"Sure thing," she said, and made a croaking kind of sound from back in her throat. A doil raspberry.

Max looked at me and then her, confused. I gave him an innocent look. When Moezu came to take our order, I ordered for the two of us, to Max's consternation. When Moezu turned away, he frowned at me.

"I am not your slave or pet. I do get to order my own food. I'm paying for it."

"Don't work yourself into such a snit. You don't know what they have here."

"So they should get me a menu."

"No menus other than that." I motioned to the daily boards with Derra's scratched scrawls on them.

Max squinted at them. "I thought that was some kind of saur art. Bad saur art. Instead I see someone hasn't taken basic penmanship. Why doesn't the owner at least use a print scrawl?"

"Because then she wouldn't be Derra. This is all her baby, including the writing."

He peered at the buffet, which was not at an easy viewing angle. "I hope the food is better than the penmanship. What is that stuff?"

"See? I told you you wouldn't recognize anything. I know what's good and what's not." A thought occurred to me. "You're not allergic to crocker yeast, are you? Or split?"

"I have no idea what crocker yeast is."

"How about koeber?"

"I don't think so."

"Well, I can call Emergency if you start swelling up," I told him cheerily. Really, I should have ordered something disgusting for him.

He managed some small talk as we waited. I didn't know if I was mad at him or not. What I did know for sure was that I didn't know so much about him. How the heck his family had gotten into Galactic matters. How many brothers and sisters he had. What in the world he really did, and who he had to work with.

All I really knew was that he was British. Let's see… London. Princess Diana. Scrooge. Beatles. Stonehenge. "Clean yor chimbley, guv'nor?" Shakespeare. King Arthur. The Empire. History class had taught us that England had always had a big problem with–

"What religion are you?" I began.

He kind of sputtered around his wine. Don't know why he hadn't read my mind to see the question coming. Men can be so dense.

"What brought this on?"

"Just wondering. Didn't see you say grace before you started eating."

"Neither did you." He tried to saw at his mushroom steak, but it was fork-tender and fell apart under his blade. "I suppose you could say Church of England."

I rolled my eyes. "Why did I even have to ask?"

"I can't help it. That's just what my family is. Moderately." He took a forkful of "meat," with the fork upside-down– typically British. "Mum has the picture of me in the white christening gown. Then I had to go through all the Confirmation training." He looked up at me from his plate. "Is that what you're after?"

"How about Christmas?"

"Huge Christmas tree. I'll bring some mistletoe next time I come through." He gave me that wicked grin and then it faded. "Don't tell me you've gone and joined the heathen malac. What gods do they go after?"

"A lot of them seem to be upstanding Muslims."

"Ah. Right, then. You as upstanding as they?"

"As far as I can recall, my father wasn't the most devout Muslim. I'm Jewish on my mother's side."

His fork paused, though he never put down his knife. "I believe that's the side that matters, no?"

"Yes. Moderately, as you say. I'm not allergic to Christmas trees. Our Hanukkah bushes were rather tall things. We kept kosher and halal… mostly."

He resumed eating. "All right then. All things in moderation and all that."

"So you're not up on converting anyone?"

"They don't pay me to do that. I save worlds, not souls."

I didn't know how I felt about this difference between Randi and Max. Religion was a way of unifying people not only in beliefs but in traditions. And yet religion could be used to rigidly control the way otherwise-sensible people thought.

I shrugged to myself. With Max now here but mostly off there, this was one relationship that wasn't aiming for permanency. No need to worry about an issue that would never arise. Right?

"Waiter." Max snapped his fingers at a doil passing by, who ignored us. Max muttered under his breath.

"That's not our waiter," I told him. "There." I pointed. Moezu looked up and nodded at me. He set down a pitcher and ambled attentively to our table.

Max asked for more bread and then eyed Moezu when he departed to comply. "How'd you know which one it was?" he asked me.

"That's strange coming from someone who has to deal with so many saurs."

"Mine aren't usually wearing uniforms. If they are," he gave me an apologetic grimace, "I have to guess. Unless I've marked them with a bug. Not only can I keep tabs on them, but I get a signal as to who's who."

Ah, the life of a spy. "What happens if they find the bug?"

His nose wrinkled. "I dissolve the things when they've done their job. Haven't gotten caught yet."

"Hm." As he leaned back into his chair I did the same, and let my gaze roam the room. "There are differences, but you have to look. You have to understand them."

"Understand? Just to tell them apart?"

"Take the doils." I leaned in the general direction of a nearer couple, nodding my chin toward them. "Neck flanges are a real tell-tale."

"Go on."

I told him the things I'd learned from Sonny, Nuke and Derra, watching him squint back and forth to compare Moezu and his cousins. I waved a "Don't mind us" gesture at them with an apologetic shrug. Saurs knew shrugs.

"And that's just the flanges." Max tilted his head as he took it all in.

I taught him about the facial differences I'd noticed, the way doils would differ in how they spoke. Derra talked out of the left side of her mouth, and many of her cousins followed suit. There was flaring of nostrils, chin (such as it was) tilting, a preponderance of expressive eyebrow scales, mouth width compared to neck width–that sort of thing.

"I'm impressed. You've made a study of them," Max concluded.

"I need to live among them. Some are my friends and I don't want to accidentally insult them."

"You actually like them."

"I said, they're my friends. Why, don't you have saur friends?"

"Saurs are my business, not my recreation."

I chewed that over with my dinner. "You're missing out," I decided. "Most of them are really nice. They've shown me so much that's new. They've opened their hearts to me."

"Whereas I didn't do that when I dumped you here."

"I didn't say that."

"But you were thinking it."

"Oh, so you're telepathic now?" Damn it, why did he have to remind me of his kidnapping ways? "You might want to learn about hospitality from the saurs. It might help you work with them if you got to know them better."

"Believe me, I don't want to know the saurs I have to work with better. They're scum, Tam. They deserve to be hanged and quartered, all of them."

Something in his shawl pocket bleeped and he pulled out a phone comm. He tried talking to it but frowned. "Sync me," he told whoever was on the other end. "You're coming in garbled. That's better." He listened closely.

After a few minutes he set it on the table so we could both see: a news report. Though Limbus had been targeting just doils to test and show off their cinderu'um, they had now staged their first attack against a colony of lampeys.

A colony that included lots of kids.

What is it about terrorism that is so much worse when children are involved? Adults are kids grown up, but deep inside they're still kids.

It's the absolute innocence and vulnerability that childhood stands for that we hate to see wounded. Anyone who deliberately hurts a kid should roast an eternity in Hell. My personal opinion, but I hope God shares it. I mean, if there is a Hell.

I wished someone would take out those Limbus goons soon. Hunt 'em all down and space 'em, toss 'em out into the vacuum and let 'em pop.

That's not evil of me. There are just some people who shouldn't be taking up space in the universe with the rest of us.

I glanced up at Max's face. His expression was beyond grim. "Saurs," he told me. "They're not getting to Earth again, not so long as I live."

19

Max walked me home in the station's twilight, which was almost always lavender-tinged. As we neared my block, the Vee-Pers' garden perfumed the air with sweet floral scent and we heard a band playing in the plaza that marked the edge of the public recreation area.

I felt a touch on my forearm, then seeking fingers until Max found my hand and clasped it in his. I tilted my head to him and began to say something, but he gave me an intimate smile. His eyes crinkled just a bit as he tilted his chin back at me.

Okay, I decided. Maybe I'll allow this. So I let him hold my hand as we joined the small gathering.

Night grew deeper and the streetlamps turned on. Saurs swayed to the slow music. A singer took over for one selection and then the band played a snappier tune.

"May I?" Max bowed to me and swept an arm toward an open area of grass.

I've never been that much of a dancer but I can get around at a wedding reception. We box-stepped in time to the music, no toes trodden upon. As the music changed to a faster beat Max whirled me around and I laughed, breathless.

"Malac are so graceful," I heard a comment from the crowd.

"Just like fairies," someone else said.

When the music stopped the crowd clapped for us. Max bowed to them and I curtseyed and then we joined hands and eased back to watch everyone else dance.

When we finally got to my place, it was full dark. Nuke was rocking on the porch. If I hadn't heard the *critch-cronk* of his rocker I wouldn't have noticed him. I gave him a nod and he said, "Evening."

Max jumped nine full inches. He peered into the dusk. "What the bloody hell– That's a mutie monster!" he blurted.

"That is my neighbor and you will be civil," I told him.

But Max stared. And stared. Up and down.

Nuke's mouth set in a hard line. His upper left hand closed into a fist.

Male confrontation imminent, I said, "Max is new to these parts."

"Too new to be polite?" Nuke growled.

I pulled at Max's arm, but he didn't notice. "You're a construct," he accused. "An artificial mutie, genetically engineered for war." He turned to me. "A pit bull." For Nuke's benefit he said in Lingua, "A trained animal of war."

Nuke stood up. And up. He stretched out his four arms the way a cat will assume the largest position it can to cow its opponents. Except that this cat was all muscle with hard intelligence behind it.

"Max!" I barked. "You will not bother Nuke. You will apologize."

"Apologize? For what?"

"For calling Nuke an animal."

"He is."

Max took a wide-legged stance in front of Nuke. Standoff at the OK Corral. Why did this happen so much? I grabbed his shoulder and as hard as I could twisted him around while I made a "stop" signal to Nuke with the other hand.

"Nuke is my neighbor," I said evenly and tried not to grit my teeth. "He is a very good neighbor and I do not like to see him upset. So stop upsetting him."

"He's a–"

"Very good singer," I finished for him. Nuke grunted, whether to laugh at me or warn off Max, I didn't know. "He helps me with my comm system. On occasion he brings food over. We discuss the weather and music. He is my good friend."

Max glowered at me. "He's a bloody mutie construct who should never have been allowed to live. There's no controlling him. You don't know what kind of damage–"

"He waters my begonias when I forget," I said.

I could see Max's teeth bared. "He's a regular pussy cat," he said tightly. "We should get him a leash."

Nuke might not know what a pussy cat was, but he got the gist. "I could kill you as you stand looking at me," he said quietly. "You'd never see death coming. They would never find a trace of you afterward."

With that he sat down slowly and actually looked away from Max. He seemed perfectly relaxed. Too perfectly. He directed his words at me next. "Why are you hanging out with this drebbik, Tam? Even that Randi malac is better than this, and that's not saying much."

"Drebbik?" Max snarled.

"Five times by now you would be dead if I wished," Nuke told him. "And that would be with me unarmed, not even trying."

"You don't know who you're talking to."

"Without getting out of this chair. I recognize an amateur when I see one."

My hair was practically standing on end. Why did testosterone do this to men? They couldn't even drop trou for the quick conclusion of this pissing game, because Nuke, like most of the aliens on station, probably wore his genitalia on the inside.

And speaking of genitalia I was suddenly not in the mood to flash mine at anyone.

"I think it's time to call it a night, Max."

That brought him around! All of a sudden he forgot Nuke and turned to me. "What?"

"I," I said with all the coolness I could summon, "have a headache."

Nuke guffawed. I scowled at him. "That was not for your benefit."

"I enjoyed it nonetheless," he said and leaned back in his chair, fully at ease. Next to him, Benny the skeleton hee-hawed with his bony jaw. His eyes flashed twice, deep red, and his left upper arm made an impolite gesture.

Max stepped back at the sight. "What the bloody– Have you gone insane?"

"That's Benny," I said. "Benny says goodnight, too."

"But–"

I palmed my door and slipped inside. "Let's try this again sometime when your civilized brain is functioning," I said as I shut the door behind me. "Thanks for the jeans," I called from inside.

I could hear Nuke's loud laughs through the walls.

A week later Max returned, this time bearing shoes. Real shoes with real soles and real arch supports, and real sneakers! Out of the Santa bag he'd lugged in, six pair fit well, including the sexy red pumps.

Okay, he could come in. He even sat quietly near the open front door as I studied. Nuke was sitting outside eating sandwiches and watching the world while Max tried to ignore him as he read a novel I'd downloaded from Ali. We'd agreed to another attempt at a date… in a while.

But the silence didn't last long.

Tam!" Derra's bark made me jump. "Here you are. Where you been? You make me come to find you!"

I eased back from the desk and peered out at her. I couldn't recall Derra ever visiting in person. "Things have been happening. Now I'm studying for finals," I told her. "What's up?"

Derra gave a glance to her left and right at the mutant and the stranger malac just inside. Then she lifted her beak, ruffled her neck scales, twitched her tail in dismissal, and waddled in the door. She was carrying a basket, which, after a moment's perusal of the mostly bare room, she dropped on my computer desk.

"You should get out more. Not good for you to be cooped up like this."

"What's this?"

"We worry about you. You probably not eat." Derra lowered her head so she could whisper next to my ear. "Is that the bastard?"

"Yes."

Before I could say anything else, Derra had whirled around and peeked– no, stared– at Max.

"Uh… You want something?" I heard Max say as he put down his reader.

I got up to follow Derra as she stood before Max. Her neck worked like a snake so she could view him from all angles.

He didn't look pleased at the perusal. He wore his funky wig, but that probably wasn't the reason for Derra's sour look.

"What it like?" she demanded of him. She poked him in the shoulder.

Max jumped right out of his chair away from her. "What the hell–"

"You a bastard," Derra said.

I choked. Max snarled.

"Right?" Derra persisted. "That what Tam say."

Max looked at me, fire in his eyes. I ducked behind Derra's bulk as Nuke snorted between bites.

"I'm–"

Derra poked in Max's general direction. "What it like? What it like to be a bastard? You got good job, good family?"

"Bastard?"

I pulled at Derra's apron. "It's not a literal thing, Derra. An expression, just an expression."

Derra turned to stare at me. "He not a bastard?"

"Only in the figurative sense." Then I cocked her head at Max. "I think. I've never really asked."

"I am not a bastard," Max declared.

Derra seemed to deflate. "Oh," she said, and took a few steps to turn away from Max. She looked lost.

"Why did you need to know?" I asked quietly. "What's this about bastards? Did something happen to Liv?"

With a plop, Derra sat down hard on the porch's top step and let out a series of squawking wails. "Everything wrong! Everything!" She honked and bleated and people on the street stopped to look our way.

It took all three of us to pry Derra loose from her position and shuffle her into the house. "I'll make tea," Max offered as I steadied Derra and Nuke pulled up chairs for us all. Apparently he'd invited himself to join us.

An "Ah!" told us that Max had peeked inside Derra's basket. He pulled out its food containers and laid out a snack tray to go along with the drinks. By the time he was finished, Derra was over the worst of the racket. Her hands were shaking so badly I had to hold the mug to Derra's beak to get her to drink.

"There, there," I soothed.

"My grandchild," Derra moaned. "It will be bastard!"

"No it won't," I purred. "No it won't. One way or another it'll get a father."

At last Derra could hold her own cup. I knelt beside her, just in case. "Liv wants Dibi," Derra groaned. "Rilf won't do for her, not for after it born. She is stubborn, stubborn girl!" She took an angry swig of her tea and then shook her head violently, sending a few drops here and there.

"Stubborn like her mother." I patted Derra's upper arm.

Derra snorted. "Maybe. But I had better taste in men. I chose mate for his standing in community, for paternal instincts, for… integrity."

"Not for his sexy good looks?"

Derra actually gave me a little grin. "Didn't hurt."

Nuke bellowed a laugh.

Max chuckled as he picked through the snacks. "What's all this about bastards? And who else have you been talking about me like that to, Tam? And what the hell are these?" He twirled a cherry pickle slowly as he examined it.

"Try it," I told him and explained the situation in Derra's family.

"Cherry. Cherry pie," Max said in amazement. "Yow, sour." As Nuke reached for a pickle Max snatched the plate away from him. "Mine!"

"Tam's," Derra corrected. "It a bribe to get her back to the deli. We miss her."

I shrugged. "I've been too busy for your therapy."

Which garnered another snort from Derra. "We need to talk more about you and your ghost. In private."

"No, about you now." I didn't feel like talking about my mother yet. Every time I thought about Mom it seemed my thoughts came from a new angle. Had she been duped? Was she in on the plan? Or was it something between those two stances? "I saw Dibi the other day and he sounds like he's really torn in his decision."

Derra growled.

"I asked Brindle– you know, Bree's husband– to see what he could find out about Dibi, but so far…" I shrugged. Yet part of me was glad that even the professionals had come up with nothing. Really, *really* glad that Noon-zio hadn't either.

"So the kid won't have a father," Max started, but Derra let out such a squawk that he had to clap his hands to his ears.

"He has to have a father! He has to have his blood father!"

"He'll have a father of sorts," Nuke told her. She turned to him as if she'd just realized he was there. "Isn't that good enough?"

"No. Not for my family. Not for community." Derra sighed. "And not for Liv."

"Will he be loved?" Nuke asked. "Even without a blood father, will your family accept him? Love him?"

Derra sputtered, which involved a great deal of saliva. She ended with, "Bastard!"

"Bastards are people, too," I offered.

"That's not what you say."

"Figurative, Derra. Figuratively. It's a leftover from an ancient time, I guess."

Max nodded. "Way back when people had to know parentage for sure. It involved inheritances, knowing bloodlines for titles and such."

"Plus it cast aspersions on the mother," I said. "Call a kid a bastard, and that means that the mother was promiscuous."

"Not the father, too?" Derra asked.

"Malac don't reproduce the way doils do," I assured her. "A mother carries the child all the way to birth."

Derra considered. "Ow," she finally decided.

Max and I both laughed. "'Ow' is correct," I told her. "So I've heard."

Derra shook her head. "The stronger male should carry the heavy fetus."

Max said, "The stronger male goes out and works hard to provide for the mother and child."

"If he has integrity," I added quickly. "If not, he skips off and– bastard child."

Derra mused at that, but Nuke was the one who spoke. "Derra," he asked, "what happens when a doil gets the blood father to carry the child, but he doesn't want it afterward?"

Derra gasped. "Not want–"

"You know it must have happened at some time."

"Never! Never in my family! Never for as long as memory in my family!" Her hackles rose. Her face darkened.

Nuke waved her down. "What about in someone else's family? Parents who didn't want their child?"

Derra was too incoherent to speak, but I patted Nuke's lower arm. "I'm sure there must have been someone to love them, to raise them as their own."

"Sometimes there is no one," he said darkly.

"That's the worst sin there is," I whispered. "Every child deserves love."

Nuke gave me a little nod but said nothing more.

"Of course this child will be loved." I turned back to Derra. "It's got you. And his mother. No one will say a word against it. " I smacked my right fist into my left palm. "At least they won't if I'm within hearing distance."

"Or in mine," Nuke rumbled. Derra turned to him in surprise. "No one puts down an innocent baby for something it didn't have any say in."

Derra eyed him, then did the same to me before she turned to Max, who had a mouthful of food and stopped chewing immediately.

"So malac males do not carry babies? Only female? Does that make malac females more masculine? Or males more feminine?"

"Mexcuse muh?" Max said around his food. "Um, um, Were you insinuating that I was a wuss just because–"

"It's the cootie factor," I explained to Derra and Nuke. "Malac males are afraid of–"

"I am not afraid–"

"–Of being compared to females. They have to be macho." I puffed herself up and struck a muscle pose to get the meaning of the word across. When I resumed my normal posture, I said, "Women can be anything they want."

Derra shook her head and clucked. "Poor malac males."

"Now, see here," Max began. "It's not like that at all. I–"

"Was your mother masculine?" Derra asked me.

I tried to see it from Derra's point of view. "After my dad died she had to try to fill in what he'd contributed to the family."

"Which was?"

"Well, she couldn't very well be macho, but she started bringing her coworkers– mostly men– home like she was trying to get some masculine vibe into my life. Father figures. They started showing up at the sports games I was involved in. It was kind of obvious, what she was trying to do." I gave a little laugh. "And it was sweet of them to try to help like that. Mom would have done anything for me.

"And then there was Dad's lost income, of course. We'd been left with a lot of medical bills. They'd wiped out most of what they'd saved for my education. Mom had to take on some extra jobs… Extra jobs…"

Like betraying the Earth.

I shoved that thought out of my head and knelt by Derra. "I've spoken with Dibi; I told you. He's confused. He's young right? Really young."

"Yes," she admitted. "So is Liv."

"How young were you when you had Liv?" Nuke asked.

Derra looked at him, her eyes holding surprise. "About her age," she admitted. "Maybe just a bit older. You forget how dumb kids can be. Think they're grown up."

"They think they're ready for kids."

Derra stared me down. "I was ready. So is Liv."

"So give Dibi a little more time to grow up," I told her. "He knows he has a deadline. I think he'll come around. If Liv chose him–"

"But it won't be long now. Not long at all. Liv a stupid kid," Derra growled, but I knew her heart wasn't in the sentiment.

"Liv is a wonderful kid who's going to go far. She's going to be a great mother, too."

Derra patted my shoulder and I tried not to wince. "You come to deli more, Tam-zio. Talk to Liv."

"We are family," I assured her. "We stand together, whatever happens."

A great tear fell from Derra's eye as she nodded.

20

I was handing a gallon of Sonny's Best to Jimeek when the shockwave hit. Cold brew splattered every which way as I fell against him even as he toppled off his stepladder.

"What the–" Jimeek sputtered, and then growled, "Tsunami! Damned idiot–"

But I lost the rest of his opinion as to interstellar hotshot pilots with no respect for others. "Sonny!" I yelled across to the bar even as I made for the back of the brewery.

"Get going!" he waved me to my duty, as if that would have made a difference.

"Everyone, remember your safety drills!" I reminded the crowd as I ran past. I must have been going the speed of light as I jumped off the loading dock out back, rounded the corner, and tore down two blocks to the nearest Tunnel entrance.

Yet I checked in no quicker than anyone else. Everyone was out of breath. Bree had assumed command of our section, but no emotion played on her face. She was the ultimate professional.

"Tunnel systems are out in the outer two rings, north sectors D through S," she told us. I made a note on my comm because I wanted the equipment to remind me if I forgot during the heat of things. I didn't want to think how close the gravity wave must have been to do that kind of damage.

But our job was to see to the safety of the station, not worry about what had happened. Stop-gap was the order of the afternoon. Later we'd go back and make it pretty and permanent.

It was going to be a long night.

Half the station was under fluctuating power outage. That didn't mean just lights; it meant heat as well. I'm not talking about a few degrees here. I'm talking about the possibility of getting down to Absolute Zero.

Exterior teams were working on a few holes in the structure. We couldn't afford to lose more than a tenth of our atmosphere.

Since I was still in training, Bree put me in charge of evacuation of a ten-mile section of Level 26. We were herding everyone up to Levels 22 and 24. High-grav types could take the change in stride; for me, keeping pace on Level 26 was not fun.

I did it because there were people there. Frightened ones, all of 'em, even if some of them tried to hide it. I had a squad of civilian volunteers to command and we gridded our territory.

Some of the folks wanted to go back for their stuff. You'd be surprised how many didn't do it because of possessiveness. It was more a *if my stuff's safe, so am I* thing. I instructed them firmly (had to shake two people around a bit, not fun in high grav) to remote their place on safety lockdown and everything should sit well enough. I sent four vacuum-suited volunteers with armfuls of pet masks to round up the various pets left behind.

Then I coordinated with a ranch far out on level 26. I heaved a hefty sigh of relief when I learned that they'd escaped the damage. We wouldn't have to evacuate the swamp livestock that thrived in that grav. The station encourages livestock that produces high-quality fertilizer, not meat, but some of the things were uber-slimy and others seemed only to produce unbearably foul farts.

We loaded the refugees into what lifts were still working. A surprising number of them were not. Even a slight warpage in the station was enough to derail the system. But everyone went up, store owners and farmers and anxious parents with wide eyes but calming arms for their kids. Some had their pets with them already. I had to secure a snakey thing with six flappy, webbed feet so that it wouldn't wander off, but my tether harness worked and the snake sullenly slithered away with its mebban family.

Once evac was done, J-Mall– he's Bree's chief– directed me to the farm sectors within damaged territory. There might be some farmer still out trying to protect something. Those farmers were real stubborn, independent types sometimes; that's why they were here on Port Malabar. They were like Kreeger. They might be digging in their heels to keep watch over their lands. Or they could just be out of earshot and didn't hear the alarms. It happens.

For this I commandeered a taxi, as all our Bugs were in use or stranded in damaged Tunnels. Within two minutes, top speed (there was no one left to be careful of), I came to the ag air lock, which separated agricultural lands from the metropolitan ones. Systems were iffy so I had to get out to manually release it, go through in the taxi, and then get out again to put the barrier back. Within minutes I was joined by Bree herself. She'd been in this section for a while, but not on this level. She might not be happy to be this heavy, but she didn't show it. Whirlpool and aspirin for us both tomorrow, I promised myself.

Together we searched the vat-fields. It wasn't like we could look across a section and spot any stragglers, because the vats were layered so that walls of greenery lined the east-west roadways and paths, blocking our long view. Besides, most of the farmers down here were probably short guys. High grav favors people built with low profiles. So we zipped up and down the ag-paths on an endless mission, keeping running chatter through our radios.

When we got bored we added a second channel, coming from three sectors over, to listen in on repairs outside. It was either that or have Bree complain about all these tsunamis. In older days she said the station could expect one, maybe two, tops, a year. If she were in charge… Her description of just punishment was grisly, but it fit well with my own ideas.

Seems as if that gravity wave had done quite a job on one of the sections of outer hull. I wanted to see them catch whoever it was who'd been responsible. I wasn't sure if I was for or against a lynching in this case. Guess we'd have to wait and see how it all turned out.

Sure enough, we found three workers who hadn't evac'd. I found two and Bree rounded up the third they mentioned. Nope, they hadn't had their comms with them. Why, was that required? They seemed shocked to discover that it was.

With only a few complaints they let us ferry them to the nearest lift. Then it was back to running the ag-mazes for a few more hours. We collected two more stragglers and one escaped (but mellow) buffie the size of a stunted hippopotamus before we could call the job done.

Back at HQ I listened with half an ear to various reports of the cleanup. I caught my breath when I heard someone say "malac," and turned to find out more.

"Green Level?" I asked, afraid that the malac community had been hit.

Kakura shook his head at me. "Level 22," he said. "Some malac got caught in a scuffle down there."

"A malac fighting?"

"No, just caught in someone else's fight." Helpfully, Kak called up a surveillance tape. A half-dozen short-version gimigols pummeled on each other. Someone's personal vehicle was parked nearby. It looked like the red light district. Probably the fight had been with some drunks trying to relax after work.

"Was the malac hurt?"

"I don't know." The surveillance zoomed in on the slender, smaller being at the edge of the crowd.

Max.

Someone's elbow caught him and he tumbled backward. Then he disappeared under two bolinks roly-poly'ing through the crowd, a tornado of tiny fists. Then Kreeger came rolling behind them. She gathered them up in the air, one to each side of her, and shook them but good. I could see her yelling at them, though any area speakers hadn't picked it up. Good for her.

But where was Max?

"I guess he wasn't hurt that badly," Kakura concluded. "No ambulance was called for anyone."

Less than two days later I stumbled home from training and final tsunami cleanup. Bree had become quite creative at combining the two and working me three times as hard as everyone else. But now I was nearing home. All it needed was a sunset behind the house to make it the perfect picture of domestic tranquility. I could see Nuke sit up in his rocking chair when he saw me coming down the street.

"Tam!" he called and I managed an exhausted wave. Wouldn't it be nice if he had extra supper so I didn't have to prepare anything?

Instead he turned and dashed inside his place. I blinked a moment: what was wrong with this picture? and then decided I was too tired to worry. I had a full eight hours of sleep coming that I planned to turn into twelve if I could.

But by the time I got to the porch and was reaching to trigger my door, Nuke stepped back out. This time he had a fully-grown, wriggling human in each upper hand. Both had been tied stem to stern with strips of material and hung upside-down, like mummy bats. He'd left their nostrils and eyes uncovered. Judging from the wig that stuck out between seams, one was Max. It must be glued on. On the other one a tattoo peeked between lines of tape. I'd bet three paychecks it was Randi.

"These malac came by, " Nuke informed me gravely. "They looked to me like they wanted trouble. They were loud. I don't like loud."

The wheeze that came out of me sounded like it had been aged ten years. "I'll take 'em off your hands," I assured Nuke.

"They won't make noise?"

"I'll make sure they don't."

"You aren't planning to mate with them tonight, are you? I was going to meditate in a while."

"Not tonight, Nuke. Things will be nice and quiet. Could you please–?" I motioned for the squirming bundles to be dropped on my living room floor and Nuke obliged. He didn't offer to remove the tape and I didn't ask him to.

"You are seriously weird," I whispered to him as I shut my door. I heard his snort through it.

Two sets of eyes bulged at me out of their tape masks. "Mmf!" one bundle cried. "Rr! Mowrws!" the other one countered.

I stood there in a small puddle of oil I must have brought home from the last installation I'd crawled through. "I am taking a shower," I announced. "When I come out, I'll see what I have in the fridge. For me. So relax a while."

Even so I made sure they were both breathing well. Guess I'm just a sucker for the helpless.

I took care using my dryer before I returned– not a speck of damp hair remained. Then I set about the serious business of making a sandwich. Okay, I started to feel a bit guilty, or maybe it was all the glaring I was getting from the audience, so I stuffed half a yeast loaf sandwich as far as I could into my mouth and chewed as I sawed through tapes.

I did Max's hands first even as I wondered, *does this priority mean anything?* With his arms freed I gave him an extra set of clippers and set to work on Randi until he could handle his own liberation too. Then I finished my sandwich and started on some soup as I watched them grimace and hiss through their self-liberation. That tape wasn't exactly a clean-release kind.

They had bands of stickum left on their clothes and skin, and Randi's hair stood on end. Max's wig didn't survive the process. Randi stickily stomped past me, reached into the fridge and pulled out a beer. Max must have seen it despite scowling at me, for he did the same… and grabbed a nexer fruit to one-up Randi.

They both pulled chairs up from the floor and plunked themselves into them.

"I'm calling a cop," Randi finally announced. "I hope they lose the key for wherever they throw that mutie neighbor of yours."

"He's very protective," I said. "Besides, I hope they're saving their deep-freeze cell for whoever caused that tsunami." Subtly– I hoped– I glanced side-long at Max. "It caused a helluva lot of damage. People were hurt. Could have been more people hurt worse if," I gave a modest shrug, "Safeties Systems weren't so damn well trained. We ought to space the perps."

He frowned at me. A bit guiltily, I thought. Not so much that he'd caused the wreckage, but that he knew who had. Maybe. You can only read so much into frowns, you know.

We mostly sat with the guys staring at each other the way guys do. They spoke in grunts to my innocuous questions and deigned to accept more food I finally scrounged together for them.

"Sparkling conversationalists," I said as I settled in my lounger and turned on some music.

"Who is he? The yellow-hair. Why is he here?" Randi snarled.

Max squinted at him over his beer. "I was just going to ask the same question."

"What am I, a mind-reader? Max, Randi. Randi, Max. Wait, I know. You both want something." I pointed at Randi. "No. Not again."

"Good," Max said.

"You don't even know what it is he wants," I started and then saw the scowl he was giving Randi. "Oh hell, it's not that." I stopped. Randi was never one who didn't constantly think about sex. "Unless it was. In addition. You took your time getting here."

Randi shook his head. "Oh no, I'm getting it. You've been calling me. Leaving me lots of messages. I know what you want." He gave Max a triumphant expression.

"I didn't want to get too specific with those," I explained. "The cops know about you, about what you've been doing. I didn't give your name."

Randi sputtered, his face going violet.

"They said that if you turned yourself in, they might go easy on you. There was a time limit involved. Only five days left. You need to get on the ball."

He opened and closed his mouth a few times while Max watched, his head cocked to the side. Finally Randi said, "You wouldn't do that. Not to me. You're bluffing to get me back."

"You've now been officially warned," I told him. "It's all on your head. You might want to tell your… friend… the same. As I have said so many times about the other thing, we are through. Done. Now as for you…" I swung my head to view Max. Scruffy and tape-smeared, dammit, he still looked real good— for someone who might be a fink. "I'm never sure what you're after, though I know you're always trouble."

"I thought it was the other way around." He gave me the slightest of smiles on the side of his mouth that was away from Randi. "You're trouble with a capital T."

Then he gave Randi a very strange, considering look. To make it worse, he said in English, "I can't trust him, can I? He's not on our team."

"Hey!" Randi said. "In Lingua. Who the hell *is* this?"

I regarded him coolly. "He's my husband."

Randi's shock kept him from seeing the surprise on Max's face, which I'd made sure I had in my view. By the time Max turned back to me I had constructed a scowl just for him. After a moment he scowled back, and I relaxed.

"Randi's one of the malac here," I said. "Max is fresh out of Earth, just passing through."

"Married! To him!" Randi raised up in his chair as if he would jump out of it. "He's got yellow hair!"

"And you're wearing a skirt," Max observed. He had to keep "skirt" in English since Lingua had no word for it, but his gesture got the object across and his tone, his derision of Randi's lack of manliness.

"Pity no good Scotsman heard you say that," I said and took a swig of Sonny's Best.

It took a final scoonch to position himself, but Randi jumped out of the chair. He aimed an accusing finger at Max. "I have never seen you before. I know everyone who passes through this station. You're not married to Tam. She would have mentioned you."

Max shrugged. "Maybe not. Maybe so. Depends on who you ask, I suppose."

"You have to choose," Randi told me. "Now."

"Choose what?"

"You don't have any male relative to choose for you," Randi said, but Max waved his hand.

"Hello, husband here."

"I make my own choices," I said.

"I don't like your choices if this man is who he says he is," Randi growled. He stomped over to stand knee-to-hip with the sitting Max. "Maybe I'll make the choice. I am her man, Earthman. She lives here. She lives with us."

"I live with myself, last I checked," I told him calmly. "If we're talking any kind of relationship–" I patted down the air between me and the men placatingly. "Heaven forbid I should use that term. But I thought we were just in a 'with benefits' situation, Randi. In the past. We were handy– past tense– for each other. You've never treated me otherwise, except worse, and frankly I don't think I've treated you otherwise either."

Randi sulked. "So you love this man. Your husband."

Max turned to me expectantly.

"I still haven't seen the marriage certificate," I said. "Never got a ring. Not even a proposal."

"I took you to dinner," Max said. "And a couple times–" He gave me an evil leer that quite unfortunately made my toes curl.

"Max and I have, well, sort of collided through the past months," I finally decided to say.

"Collided." Randi stared at Max, obviously wondering what that entailed.

"Pretty much literally. Due to business."

"Monkey business," Max grinned at Randi. "I bought her clothes. Sexy clothes. She looked real hot in them."

"Randi, I was surprised as you are about the marriage, but Mr. Max here produced some paperwork to someone that said we were indeed married. I have no memory of that happening or reason why it should. I think it was…" I gave Max another side-eye, "some kind of trick Max was playing on someone. Not necessarily me."

Randi fumed in Max's general direction. Then he scowled his patented tattoo scowl at me before stomping out the door.

It was a bit of a relief to turn to Max and say, "Okay, now you owe me. Tell me why Leslie was lugging a bunch of brite around with some gimigol goons a few weeks ago."

Max's eyebrows raised.

21

There'd been a flood down on Level 27, our most favorite of levels– not. Just to make things more enjoyable, contaminants had gotten in the waters and then seeped into the agricultural areas. It had taken two full shifts of work to set things right.

To top it off, we were finishing our reports when the call came in: a doil death, Level 22. Cause:

Brite.

I could feel Bree's eyes on me as I growled, but I filed my report, checked off my duties for the day, and signed out of the system.

The two of us were still in the department whirlpool when everyone else had departed wearily for their own beds. We had muscles that were screaming at us. Good thing I'd rigged a chair for me for the thing, or I'd have drowned in it. Happily.

Bree passed me a tiny glass of a liquid that made my eyes sting when I sniffed it.

"All at once," she instructed, and up-ended her own glass, which was much larger than mine.

I did the same.

When I could breathe again and my eyes rolled back into their proper place, I discovered that all my aches were pleasantly over across the room and not actually residing in my body.

"Good stuff," I said.

"Mm-hm. I keep a stash here for difficult days."

We let those kind of days float over there with our aches, leaving us in an in-between, okay kind of state.

After a while of deep meditation I asked, "Is it legal?"

She let the question sink in slowly. Probably had to take a few minutes to register it. "That depends on how you read the law," she finally decided.

"How would a court read it?"

She shrugged. "Depends on what level court. Let's just call it borderline."

"I'm not sure I like doing borderline," I told her. I sniffed the remains in my glass and decided I shouldn't ask for more. The fumes alone made me dizzy.

"Yeah? What have you done borderline lately? I mean, that's new?"

There was just a thread of proper neural synapses flitting across some deep part of my brain. "Nothing new," I said and she nodded. "Thank god. But I did get an explanation about Leslie."

"Leslie?"

"She's the Bastard's cousin, the one I saw up near the Hatching Grounds."

With that she straightened up. "Where you found that–" she glanced around the empty room– "stuff."

"Yeah. She told Max that she's closing in on them. She's gone undercover to join… their inner group."

Bree nodded as she leaned back, her lids half-closed. "Inner group."

"She said nobody was ever in danger, that the… stuff… would never be used."

Bree's head rocked at the water's edge, creating small waves. "Yet she didn't keep track of it. Didn't know you'd found it."

"Yeah." I'd thought of that. "Every time I get more info, I find I have more questions. Maybe it makes sense somewhere down the line."

"And maybe it doesn't, though Brindle says he's willing to work with your Bastard." She poured herself another and offered it to me. I shook my head. She upended her glass and then kind of vibrated there as she sat in the oscillating water. Finally she let out a shuddering groan, leaned her head back on the rim of the tub, and heaved out a breath with a burped afterthought.

For a while I assumed she was asleep. I didn't say anything not because I didn't want to disturb her, but because I was quite incapable of thinking of anything to say.

Her brain must have had some functioning left. "If you don't like doing borderline, why do you do it?" Her left eye opened, stared at me, and then closed.

"You mean, why'd I take the brite from Randi in the first place?" I thought. Hard. It was difficult to think, but this would have been hard anyway. "I'm… convenient," I finally surmised.

She grunted but said nothing else.

"I'm the easiest person they can find to do some things. And I have… access to places."

"Say no if you don't want to. What can they say to that?"

"That I won't ever fit in here. They won't like me. That's why I did it that first time."

"Why, you never had people not like you before?"

I must have said it out loud for her to answer me. "But I like people to like me," I protested. "I like them to say, 'Good job,' and 'Aren't you nice.'" Then for some reason, "And 'You're the sweetest girl around,'" slipped out of my mindless mouth.

Why would I think of something that Randi said? "'You're the best, babe,'" I recalled him saying after I'd done him a favor.

"Ah," Bree mumbled in her sleep. "That'll do it."

I went on with the litany. "'There's nobody like you.'"

And suddenly I heard myself say, "'Here's a little something for your work, Miz Yussuf.'"

My mouth flapped open; I'd surprised myself. It was as if someone else had control of my body. When had I heard that?

It was so faint, but somehow whatever Bree had given me illuminated the memory with sharp edges over faded colors. Mom, in uniform, standing at the back door. Somebody outside. A man in a dark outfit. Someone who had come around before but Mom had never introduced me to. She'd always shooed me out of the room when he'd come. When he'd left, she'd had to open the living room blinds, which she must have closed while he was here.

Why didn't she want anyone to see him?

"Your mother was a traitor," Max's voice whispered to me. I pressed the heels of my hands against my ears, though the speech came from within me.

There was Mom. There was the man. He had money– a lot of it. Cash. He pressed it into her hand.

"Go away," she hissed at him and spared me a quick glance. A guilty glance. "Not here," she said. "Not now." She tried to give the money back, but he was gone.

Bree burped again.

"Oh, Moooooommmmm," I groaned.

"Are you like your mother, Tam?" Bree asked.

"No." Mom. Cherry pie. Commendations. Lullabies and midnight talks. "Yes," I groaned. "Just like my Mom."

When I woke up four hours later, still at the station but on a rest area cot, my head informed me that I'd imbibed in some heavy-duty spirits. I slapped a saur-sized pain patch behind my ear and went back on duty, this time thankfully on Level 16 with its low gravity. It seemed the problems down below had begun with the construction up there. Everything on Port Malabar was connected in some devious way. Now Bree worked in a different sector with more specialized work while I was assigned the "Hold that while I do something important" detail.

I ran out of small stuff to hold for the techs, so they found some civilian gimigols to work while the tiny malac was instructed to wedge her aching self into tiny fissures in the station's structure and knit wiring that was only partially solid into a webbing that would... Uh...

"It would be nice to know what the heck I'm doing," I called to the tech overseeing my work via a micromonitor.

"Not necessary," he assured me as my fingers tingled to numbness from the voltage that hummed along the field.

I caught a few mini-meals as I could as I shimmied through a dozen acres worth of infrastructure. "I am a lineman for the counteeee," I sang, and wondered if somewhere five miles from where I was, the non-wires had carried my voice. From Glen Campbell I switched to Roger whatshisname (if I'd had access to

Google I could have looked it up) to sing of how I was king of the road, and somehow that road took me through Dolly Parton and her 9 to 5 job. My coworkers groaned, but they gave me a little chuckle each time they pulled me out of whatever dark, tight hole they'd stuck me in.

"At least we know you're breathing in there," one told me, and I gave him an air-punch.

Somewhere around "You gotta put in work, work, work, work," which I was managing to translate fairly well (okay, that one wasn't so difficult) as I sang, the chief called an end to my shift, and those who had had the luxury of a few hours sleep more than I had last night were left to carry on without me. Raggedly the shifts began to return to normal.

The full month minus one day had passed since Brindle's ultimatum and though I'd continued leaving message after message, I didn't hear anything more from Randi. I'd also left a message a few days before for Randi's drug friend, Dian, to contact me as well. Didn't like doing that. I didn't trust Dian. Didn't really know him, or what he might– or could– do. But I had to give him a chance, didn't I? Even so, I'd kept looking over my shoulder any time I went out.

Instead, it was Max who showed up at my door that evening. This time he brought blouses. And bras.

"Leslie picked those out." He rolled his eyes as he handed me the smaller bag, trying not to blush. He didn't quite make it.

I checked it. Along with bras there were a few panties. Not the kind guys get for their women, but basic everyday stuff. These were more items I could give to the local tailors to copy. I now had a closet of jeans they'd made, and Ali and Arti were curiously wearing their own copies of what were to them weird but very functional clothes.

I was pleased with Max's offerings. Very pleased. Within a short amount of time he became very pleased as well. A couple hours later, he again was very, very pleased.

I hoped that made up for Brindle coming by for breakfast. I'd invited him over without consulting Max. I left for work with the two of them quietly discussing all kinds of things around my dining table. I heard Max say "coordinate." Maybe that would gain Randi a day or two to wise up and turn himself in.

The next day, I walked the last blocks home after class, absorbed in my own thoughts, automatically raising my hand in a half-wave to neighbors who were still out and about. I turned onto the walkway that led to the porch and looked up from the pavement.

There was something in front of my door, a long lump on the front porch, dark in the deep twilight.

After the initial halt of surprise, I ran to it. This was no gift from Max. Something in my gut warned me…

The lump was human-sized, draped in a tarp. I lifted up a corner.

Randi.

He lay unconscious or worse. His face was blackened with bruises, his nose was half-gone. Deliberately sliced. A thick tracery of blood added to the design of his tats.

I checked for a pulse in his neck even as I saw his chest move. There. Breathing shallowly, but breathing. Still alive. I hit the comm button on my uniform.

It didn't take five minutes for Emergency Services to arrive. A human specialist soon followed, and he took over from me. "He'll live," he kindly informed me as they placed Randi in a stasis capsule.

I was about to take off after them when the police came. One of the officers was Brindle– it's a small station– and they had all kinds of questions.

"Can you hurry this up?" I asked after I'd called Randi's mother. "I want to be there when he wakes."

Brindle was remarkably sensitive to the situation but efficient. While he talked to me and took notes, his partner recorded the area and found a note left in my door.

"Get the brite," was all it said.

Brindle read it. His tail switched as he passed it to me. I swallowed hard.

"Your friend Max left this?" he asked me.

"No. If he'd left this note it would have been in English. Our native language. Besides, he wouldn't have done this."

"This was your ex-lover. I didn't get the impression Max was that docile a malac."

I gave him the ghost of a smile. "Not where business is concerned. Randi… Randi's the guy you gave me a month to find."

"Ah."

"He's been hiding from me. It seems someone else found him."

Brindle growled softly. "One of the malac, or someone higher up in the Limbus organization."

"Limbus?" Brindle's partner butted in.

But Brindle waved him back. "Later," he promised. Turning back to me he said, "You're sure."

"That's what it has to be. Maybe they think I've got the brite I gave to you. Maybe they think Randi gave it to me. Or that I still have that other pack."

"That sounds like they're getting desperate. There was another malac involved who knew about you, right?"

Only one other. "Dian. He seemed to be in charge of the brite business, at least when it came to malac. But he wasn't with Leslie and the gimigols that time."

The partner mouthed "brite" to himself and peered more closely at me, then questioningly at Brindle.

"Do I have to come down to the station?" I asked, wringing my hands. "I need to get to the hospital. I need to contact Randi's cousins. His friends."

"Some of his friends don't appear to be very good ones," Brindle said. He and his partner held a quiet conversation I couldn't make out. Then he said, "You go ahead, Tam. We'll see you in a while at the hospital."

"Thanks," I said, already running off.

They put lots of patches on Randi and then consulted with his family while he still slept. Dr. Tube peered at their faces and made extensive photographic and scan notes about their noses. He'd be doing Randi's reconstruction. Dr. Tube had been on the team that had worked on me, so I assured Randi's family that they were getting the best. I mean, I'd turned out well.

When Randi woke up the third time, the doctors let Brindle and another saur in to talk with him in private. After that, a saur was stationed outside Randi's room. I let her explain to the family why.

I took that as meaning that I could go home. Or *should* go home. Randi's mother and uncle stayed there. I was running on fumes by then and hit my bed hard. Even so, when my alarm went off, I obeyed it. Too much work to do. The morning's quiet lasted only a little while. I had the front door open so the slight breeze and street sounds could keep me awake as I studied for finals.

Not only did I have to perfect my Lingua but there were also the intricacies of my Safeties work that I had to know backward and forward if I was to become certified. Already this morning I'd jumped up twice to run to the Tunnels and check out a Systems cloaca, just to be sure I could feel my way through various processes in case lights had been cut. I'd heard rumors that that was on the final exam.

I shook my head at my mistakes. People's lives would be in danger. I couldn't screw up anything!

Speaking of "screw," Max sat on the porch where I'd exiled him. (Too many "Where do you keep the beer?" and "Do you have an extra filbish?" as well as "What else can you tell me about Randi and the brite?"-es kept interrupting my studies.) Yes, he'd shown up again. Turned out he'd been roaming the station for the past few days, seeing what he could find. I think he'd checked in with Brindle a couple times along the way.

Now he sat on the opposite side of the porch from Nuke. Nuke liked to eat outside. He was finishing his breakfast, which involved a small mountain of food, and Max kept searching for various info and communicating with his team via his phone comm. I hoped he wasn't illegally tapping into Station Systems, but was afraid to ask.

The only reason I took a break was to go to work. I said goodbye to both Max and Nuke. After seven hours I returned home. Someone human was sitting in my porch chair, rocking, and I couldn't help but flinch, thinking of the tarp, before I recognized him.

"I feel quite suburban," Max's voice told me. "All I need is a cat to share some tea with. Your neighbor is not here."

"It's his mudbath night," I said as the door recognized me and clicked unlock. "He treats himself to one every other week."

Max got up and moved to the door.

"Excuse me. Did someone invite you in?"

He paused. The streetlight caught a look of surprise on his face. "I, ah… May I come in?"

"I don't see why you should." All these drains of my time were beginning to get to me. A person can take only so much stress, can't they? I held the door open in front of me only a few inches, blocking it with my body. "Are you injured? Dying of hunger or thirst? I could call Emergency."

"I am a little parched," he admitted. "A glass of water?"

"I'll bring you one." I made a move to slip inside alone, but he touched me on the shoulder.

"Please," he said.

22

Someone was pounding on the front door. I rolled over, encountered a lump behind me that I recalled quite fondly was Max. So it wasn't him doing the pounding. In fact, it might be because of him that I was feeling a little… relaxed, that was the word.

Ignore the door. But the pounding continued. Okay, okay!

"Who is it?" I called. A glance at the clock showed me it was the middle of the night.

"Dibi!" came a hoarse, loud whisper, as if he didn't want anyone else to hear. "Let me in!"

Two snorts penetrated the wall from Nuke's apartment. He didn't sound pleased. And a grunt behind me told me that Max wasn't as well.

I wrapped a robe around myself and lurched to the door. It practically flung itself open in my face and there indeed was Dibi.

He was all flushed, half of his scales unevenly raised in various states. His eyes were wild, his breathing labored. "It's time," he gasped. "It's time! I don't know what to do!"

I pulled a fistful of my hair as I took in the situation. "Hoo boy," I said. "Okay. Dibi. You haven't made up your mind yet? Have you been afraid of the decision or just too lazy to think?" Aw, that wouldn't solve anything. "Sorry," I said. Stress. "Do you love Liv? Do you want to be a father?"

"Yes! No!" He wrung his hands. "Yes to the first thing. No… Yes to the… Oh, I don't know!" He howled that final word. "All I know is that I have to see Liv again!"

There were other doils on the sidewalk, watching us. Young. Male. I kept my attention on Dibi. "Rilf has volunteered–"

Nuke's door erupted as he jumped out onto the porch, looking for all the world like he was ready to devour all interlopers. Dibi shrieked as only a doil could: high frequency blasts that made me slap my hands to my ears. His gang drew back, practically to the street. But they didn't run farther than that from their friend.

"You. Are. Idiots!" Nuke roared. Their scales seemed to blow back in the storm of his anger.

He eyed them individually until their necks shrank, their shoulders hunched forward.

"Here you are," Nuke declared, "pampered young Malabar males. Doing as little as you can and thinking you're better than everyone else for having done so. Yet you have families– hard-working families– you can rely on. You've not been cast adrift. Some of us cannot claim that."

He looked at me and I, at him. Of the two of us, Nuke was the more adrift.

He returned his attention to the males. To Dibi, who sat sprawled on our porch beneath his gaze. "Do you have a community? Do you have families? Why aren't you standing with them? They should be your pride, and you, theirs. In this universe, who will claim you? Whose honor will you join with? Whose future will you build toward?

"Who raised you when you were helpless? Who saw to your education, both as students and as doils? As citizens of the port?"

The males began to look at each other before turning back to Nuke.

"You have siblings you love," he reminded them. "Mothers. Fathers. Aunts, uncles, and grandparents. Cousins, most likely. If they aren't here on the station, they are out there someplace. Even dead, they remain in your hearts."

Now he bent down over Dibi so they were practically nose to beak. "Does being loved mean nothing to you? Do you think so little of your mate? Where is she– the one who will stand beside you through the years to come?

"Where. Is. Your. Child?!"

Dibi took three great gulps of air before he began to crabwalk backward, leaving a trail of scales behind himself. He hopped up to a crouch before stretching out in a confused standing position. Another two breaths and his stance firmed. He glanced at Nuke but then took in his compadres. "Rilf be damned!" he bellowed at them. "I'm the father! That baby is mine! Liv is my mate!"

"Yeah!" "Yeah!" Let's go get her!" The gang closed ranks, babbling to each other and making fists in the direction of downtown.

The door of the house on my right opened even as its porch light turned on. "What's going on out there?" Burdt called.

"We'll be out of here soon!" I assured him. "It's an emergency. Sorry about the noise."

Then Dibi put both hands high in the air. "Wait!" he called. "Wait!"

He turned back to us on the porch. "Noon's men will never let me through. I've seen them. I've seen *him*," he explained, though he kept a glancing nervously at Nuke and the open door on my side. Max, putting on his shoes at the edge of my bed, caught his eye for a half-second. "They want Rilf for this. I need someone to vouch for me. Get me to her before it's too late."

"How much time do you have?" I asked.

"Huh?"

"Will this baby process take a few minutes, a few hours, a few days?"

Dibi's beak slacked open. "How the hell should I know? This is my first time!"

Nuke started forward at this, but I waved him back. "Get dressed," I told him even as I pushed Dibi toward Nuke's porch chair. "Everyone get dressed! Get cleaned up!"

The ever-alert agent in my bed was still blinking awake. "Dressed," I ordered him as well as two of Dibi's buddies headed for my bathroom. "Sit," I told Dibi. "We'll just be a few minutes." Then I explained to Max, "Dibi and Liv– you've met her; she's Derra's daughter– Remember? The baby who won't be a bastard."

But Dibi paced, tearing at his chin scales, as Max and I pulled on whatever we could grab. Dibi pushed us outside even as we were doing up the final fasteners.

"Hurry, hurry!"

"I'll talk to Noon-zio," I assured him. "I'll get him to see reason. He won't hurt you."

Nuke stood ready, clad in his heavy-duty worksuit, the one with the huge boots… and two gunbelts slung across his chest. He patted his left lower arm against his pocket as a signal to me that he was definitely armed with something that needed that ammo. I nodded.

"We go in peace," I instructed the mob as I collapsed my crowd-control baton and secured it to my belt. "But we are prepared to fight our way through. No one will get hurt, on either side. Not badly."

"Liiiiiiv!" Dibi howled as we ran through the midnight street. Lights flickered on as we passed.

"So these are your friends," Max muttered as he trotted beside me.

"Yes. You'd better get used to them."

Though Liv lived the next neighborhood over, Derra was just around the corner. I rang at her door; no answer. Station Systems Info told us that she was at a temple about a mile away. Very late for such visits.

"It's begun!" Dibi shrieked. "I'm too late!"

"You are not!" I pulled him to get him to come with us, but he stayed rooted to the spot, howling in frustration.

Nuke stepped forward ready to grab and I supposed carry, but Max moved between them. He slapped Dibi hard on the jaw. It was a difficult shot, since Dibi was so much taller than he, and just then was kind of arched backward, but he managed it neatly. "Get a hold of yourself, man! You have a job to do!"

The slap stopped Dibi's yowl in mid-breath and he just stood there for a moment blinking at Max. Then he was off, running down the street at a speed I didn't think doils could manage.

"Let's go," Nuke said, and grabbed both our hands, pulling us after him as he barreled in pursuit. I think both our feet left the ground.

We may not have done a four-minute mile, but it was close. The temple was easy enough to find. It was lit up like Christmas. There was the outskirts of an overflow crowd milling around the open double doors. Or at least they milled until Dibi let out a howl that brought up apartment lights all along the street.

I saw at least three of the crowd draw weapons, and I threw my arms up in the air.

"No guns! No guns!" I cried. "Someone get Noon-zio out here! Tell him Tam-zio is here with a very willing father-to-be!"

Dibi's buds fanned out in defensive formation. Some of them looked armed as well.

"Liiiiiiiv!" Dibi keened. His heart was in his cry.

The crowd surged toward us. They were angry. But Nuke shifted so he was in front of our troops. He stretched out, all arms making a barricade. "Let them through!" he ordered the crowd.

He used his massive arms to sweep two doils to the left, some more to the right. "Back!" he shouted. "Back!"

Reluctantly everyone eased away from his wrath, helping those he'd man-handled up off the ground. Nuke bared his fangs to all, and they shrank back farther. The temple doors opened. Cousin Noon stepped forth to take in the scene. The crowd quieted. Then behind him, Liv waddled out. Her eyes were ringed with dark ridges, but they brightened at the sight of–

"Dibi?"

"Liv! I've been an idiot. I've been crazy." Dibi ducked around Nuke to run up to her, take her hands. Then he looked down her swollen body. "Are you all right?"

"Ohh, Dibi!" She flung her arms around him.

Noon-zio stood with his hands on his hips, listening to Dibi babble about being a fool and wanting to be with Liv for the rest of his life, how he'd be a good father once he learned how. Noon-zio's gaze settled on Nuke, and his beak twisted in a scowl. Then he saw me standing there with my baton out, pressed his beak together in a straight line, and nodded. He raised his hands to click his talons in the air, sounding like high-volume castanets.

"Quickly!" he ordered. His people, dressed in solemn, off-station-style suits, appeared from the mob to shuffle both impending parents in. I pulled Max close beside me and looked around for Nuke to find that he, like us, was surrounded by doils herding us inside as well.

It was definitely a chapel in here. Beautiful transparent colors flooded the hall and soft windchimes tinkled nearby.

"Dibi!"

I turned to see Derra trotting toward us, along with a couple of cousins behind her.

"Dibi, thank the old gods!" Derra said as she hugged him and by extension, her daughter who clung to him. Through his hysteria and hormones, Dibi looked shocked at his reception.

"Someone call Dibi's parents," Derra ordered. "They're back on Mixi-Tar. Get them a video feed." Doils scrambled to obey.

Beyond the crowd stood Rilf. I swear, I don't know how to read every type of alien body language, but by the slump of his neck and droop of his lower beak I thought he looked like a mighty relieved doil there in his empty corner. He also looked a bit puffy. Oh well, the extra hormones would wear off in time.

The reunited couple were escorted off and Dibi soon reappeared in much more dignified state, wearing a ceremonial shawl over a black jumpsuit, much as his mate wore. Their hands were clasped tightly. The crowd urged them into an inner chamber where the doors closed behind them, leaving them alone. Everyone went down onto their knees.

"What now?" I asked Max. The floor was rather hard under my jeans.

"I thought you knew."

I looked to Nuke but he shrugged with all four shoulders.

So I inched my way on hands and knees to Derra, who was kneeling on the floor along with everyone else. They were chanting something that was not Lingua.

"What's happening?" I hissed to her.

"We pray for safe demi-delivery of the baby," Derra whispered back. "We pray for health, happiness and prosperity."

"I can do that." I crawled back to my group and repeated the news. We all prayed silently, or at least I *think* Max and Nuke were praying. At least they were silent. I prayed hard enough for all three of us.

We were witnessing the birth of a family.

As time went on I cracked my eyes and saw that doil medics with full kits had positioned themselves in front of the inner sanctum doors. They looked expectant but didn't go inside. I crawled back to Derra.

"The demi-birth consists of, ah, special kind of hug at climax," she whispered to me. "Experienced couple can do it no problem, most of time. A prepped male can do it easy, more often than not. We pray it goes well, but just in case…"

After a while someone on the inside opened the door an inch or so. One of the medics spoke to whoever was on the other side. The door opened just enough to let her slide in as her teammate handed her their bag, and the crowd seemed to breathe a sigh of relief. An excited buzz now filled the hall.

Now Derra was the one who came to us, this time on her feet as everyone rose. "Only one medic means it was success," she said. "There's just the cleaning up, and then–"

The doors opened wide. Liv stepped out, supporting a very wobbly Dibi, who suddenly sported quite a potted lower girth. His beak tilted sheepishly but then broke into a silly grin as he met Liv's eyes. She beamed with joy.

The crowd cheered and someone brought a chair for the suddenly-pregnant Dibi to rest in and adjust to his new state. "It's a boy," he announced.

"A fine and healthy-looking boy!" Liv added proudly.

"Already a point on his beak," Dibi told us, which was followed by some very ribald jokes which I didn't really get unless I tried to correlate beak point to penis size.

We all hugged each other, and there were exclamations after Nuke's hugs. Though he's gentle when he wants to be, getting a double-hug can be an experience.

Then the party began, shoulder-deep in doils and in the middle of the night. I recognized many of the invitees, as well as Dibi's gang. Somehow Kreeger was there as well– Kreeger knew everything that went on on-station. She was letting some kids roll her around while she kept her ever-present valise snugged in one hand and a glass of bubbly upright in another.

The pregnant couple did a slow, formal dance as we gathered into a circle around them. "They both have new centers of gravity," Derra reminded us, but the two did pretty well. They were so cute. When the dance ended, they stood together and rubbed necks, to the delight of the crowd.

Then the real dancing began and everyone joined in. Max and I danced to show them some new steps, and Nuke danced with me and surprised me at how lightly he could prance. I danced with doil after doil, and even with Noon-zio.

"You come through for us, Tam-zio," he chortled. "I am proud you are family!"

We both watched Nuke as female doils came up to him to dance. At one point he threw back his head and laughed as a crowd around him, drinks in hand, laughed with him.

"Good times," I told Max when he came with our refills.

"You'd like my family better." Max had to lean close for me to hear.

"Hm. Would I?" I trailed my finger along his collar bone. "Do they really own a castle?"

"Manor. It's the summer place. Winter in Fiji."

"And your family? Are they all operatives?"

"My sister opted out of the family business," Max said. "She's too busy raising all those little hellions of hers." A far-off look came into his eye. "Future operatives."

"So the universe is safe." I smiled at him and he smiled back.

In that bubble of our own and the party flowing around us, my shoulder beeped.

It took a moment for me to register anything other than Max's eyes. I hit the com with my jaw.

"Level 22 section 8-32," the Systems voice told me. "Fire in compartment 48W6."

"On my way," I responded and broke away from Max's embrace. "Gotta go." I waved to the happy couple across the room. "Mazel tov!" Dibi saw me and returned the gesture.

With that I was off. I was out of my regular territory, but the nearest Tunnel access should be right around the corner, along the main north-south artery. There– the marker was straight ahead. I made a beeline for it and triggered the door with my passchip.

And another hand covered mine. Human. Male. I looked up to see Dian— Randi's friend with the brite.

23

"Just wanted to get you out of there, doil-lover," he said.

Two gimigols came up behind him. I may have met one of them. Maybe not. It was dark.

"I have an emergency–"

Dian shook his head. "We hacked into Systems' comm frequency. Like I said–"

The shock of the forbidden shot through me. "That's a felony," I gasped. "You can't–"

"You won't tell on us. We just want the brite."

I stared at him. He'd risk a felony for that? "What? It– Hell, I don't have it. I got rid of it a while ago."

"Rid?"

"I spaced it."

The guy behind him must not have had great comprehension. "She doesn't have it?"

"Of course she does." Dian turned back to me. "She never lets others down. Do you, babe?"

"I–" I began, but then I saw it.

A medallion, just like Mom's. The other gimigol was wearing it.

I pushed past Dian and grabbed it. "Where'd you get this?" I demanded.

He swatted me away. Dian, bless his black heart, stepped between us. "Hey!"

The big gimigol with the medallion stared bullets at Dian. "She's got the stuff, right?" He turned to me. "Get it. Now."

I sneered at him, angry that he should dare to wear something my mother had worn. "I don't work with Limbus," I said.

He hissed and drew back. I grabbed Dian's sleeve and swung him around. "Are you with these scum? Do you know who they are? What they do?"

"You're crazy. He's not Limbus," he told me and then the others: "She's crazy. But she can get the stuff."

"Do you owe them money?" I asked. "Is this part of some kind of drug deal? Do you know what that money buys? Do you know who it hurts?"

I guess our voices had carried through the still air because the next thing I heard was Noon-zio's bass behind me. "Is there a problem here?" More shuffling came from behind me, the sound of several doils.

The big guy with the medallion looked past me with wide eyes that became squints. "No problem," he said and produced a ghastly smile. "The lady just has some property of ours. We need it." He turned to try to stare me down. "In two hours. At your place." The smile he gave me was nasty with a meaning of *we know where you live* all over it.

The two gimigols trotted away, leaving me and Dian and the doils. Dian glanced nervously at Noon-zio and whispered to me, "You do have it, don't you?"

"Even if I still had it, I wouldn't give it to you or those creeps. They're involved with murderers. Mass murderers. Limbus destroyed my old town."

Dian shrugged. "That was back then. They're harmless enough here. C'mon, babe, it's just a bag." His eyes sharpened on me. "I really need that bag. Please."

Good lord, what would get him to believe me? "They aren't going to get it. It's not anywhere to be got. It. Is. Gone." I considered calling Brindle, but dawn was still hours away. Let him sleep a while more.

I turned to Dian. "You know what happened to Randi. If I were you, I'd find a good hidey-hole. Or give myself up to the cops. Safer in jail. They've promised to go easy if you turn yourself in."

He was three shades paler than normal. His eyes flicked all around, taking in the streets, the doils, the shadows where people could ambush him. "I'm gone," he told me. "I'm off this station. Tell them– when they come for you!"

Like the Flash, he was off in the direction opposite what the gimigols had taken.

"An interesting conversation." Cousin Noon's low tones were behind me. "Trouble. Two hours, they said?"

I nodded as I faced him and his cohorts. "Have you ever made an idiot mistake that ballooned out of control?"

He gave a reminiscent sigh. "Too many times. Tell me about it, Tam-zio."

I looked at the others doubtfully.

"They are family also. Your secrets are ours."

"You may not like my secrets, Noon-zio," I said.

And I told him of the drug, of the party and how the stuff didn't affect humans. I didn't tell him about the medallion. I told him how Randi had given me brite to hide.

The doils behind Noon-zio nodded and spoke among themselves. Noon-zio bent his long neck to hear and nodded. "Corrosives are our best bet," he told me. "The drug can break down completely, and there is the plus of getting rid of evidence. Heat will not do it well, and it takes too long to render it inert with other chemicals."

"We don't have any on our ship," the female behind Noon-zio volunteered, "but we could find some."

I shook my head. It struck me just how much they were offering, and my eyes got watery. "Thank you, Noon-zio, and you, too," I told the lady behind him, "but there's no need. I spaced the stuff. And I told the cops about it, cops whom we can trust to keep our station safe."

Noon-zio sucked in a breath before he nodded. "Sometimes that's the right thing to do."

"I'll call them about this two-hour business."

"That will only protect you in two hours," he said. "What about afterward? And what about this malac fellow?"

"He said he was leaving."

"His mouth was moving. Some people, if their beaks move, you know they're lying."

I blew out a breath at that. Cousin Noon was likely right.

By then Max was trotting up to see what was going on, and then had to be briefed.

"I think I'll call Brindle after all," I said.

"Good. Get yourself put in protective custody, at least for a few days."

"Maybe they can catch those Limbus creeps when they try to come for me."

Noon-zio asked, "What about this Dian malac? Does he have associates?"

"I don't know. I've only seen Dian. And Randi."

Max frowned. "I don't think Randi's smart enough to be allowed into the operation farther than the outskirts. There have to be others. Malac, maybe. Gimigols for sure."

"The gimigols Leslie was with?" I asked him in English, and he pursed his lips.

Noon-zio butted in, almost literally as he craned his great neck toward us. "I will put out the feelers. See what I can find on the black market shipping routes." His beak rolled in a nasty wave. "I can make any… problems… harmless if they threaten me or one of mine."

"Harmless? Does this involve–" I choked on the next word.

"Harmless," Noon-zio repeated and the cohorts behind him nodded. "There are ways. You give them something bigger to worry about." He ran his thumb along the length of his neck, landing at where it connected to the rest of his body. "They never know if you will actually fulfill your threats. Many times it requires a mere show of force so that they believe that the possibility of their imminent demise exists. Which it does."

"Are you sure you want to take this on?" I asked.

He patted my hand. "Family," he said and smiled.

"Family," I replied. "You know that if there is ever anything–"

"Tut-tut," he clucked. "You have returned Dibi-zio to us, and soon there will be another cousin to add to the family record. That is two lives you have given us."

"Not that we're keeping score or anything," I insisted. "Family doesn't keep score."

"Malac are wiser than I thought." Noon-zio chuckled once for me and then once, a deep, threatening choke of a chuckle, for the threat he was about to lay out.

I had to go back and whisper to Nuke that there might be some problems at the house when he got back. Noon-zio saw me and assured Nuke that there would be no problem.

"No, there won't," Nuke told him. "Just the two gimigols? I'll take care of it if it comes to that."

"The police will be there as well," I assured Nuke. "You might want to find somewhere else to stay for a day or so. We don't want you to get hurt."

"Very good," Noon-zio rumbled. His head stretched higher than I'd seen him do before as he looked back toward the party. Someone down the street was motioning to him. Cousin Noon touched his ear as if he'd had a bud there, and nodded. "I go now," he told us. "There is indeed chatter in the area. I'll look into it."

Now I woke up Brindle through my radio. We made fast arrangements for me to use the Tunnels to go to his home station, where he'd arrange protective custody.

Max spoke into my mike. "I'll be going with Tam."

"Good idea," Brindle told him. He signed off to arrange a proper police greeting for those Limbus goons.

Max hooked his hand around my upper arm and propelled me through the Tunnel entrance. Normally I would have objected to him coming along, but felt a lot better with him there. On the way in the Bug he contacted Leslie, telling her what was going on.

"On my way," she responded. "I'll stake out Tam's house."

"We will have reinforcements there of the civilian and police variety."

"Oh no."

"Oh yes. Be prepared."

"What's that mean?" I asked when he got off the line.

"We don't need civilians messing up our operations. Amateurs."

I made sure to use a hard acceleration. Max slammed back in his seat. "I think you'll be surprised at how efficient we amateurs can be," I purred.

No one showed at my house.

Surveillance tapes showed Dian buying a ticket for off-station and then boarding a shuttle that sent him to a rinky-dink brane gig heading out of system. Police would be waiting at the other end of his trip.

The two gimigols took longer to find. They knew how to evade the systems. Eventually they were tracked to another shuttle and ship, this one private. Registration was recorded and the suitable authorities were notified.

It took two days to make sure all three were off-station. You would not believe the sigh of relief I gave when the all-clear was called.

Brindle was ecstatic. This was a real break in the war against Limbus. His entire department was involved with interstellar conferences with other agencies. They were putting the pieces together, making serious headway.

Things were looking up!

It had been a few days, but I was still looking over my shoulder. Once I spotted Nuke tailing me, and he and I had a little talk about safety. I appreciated it, but he shouldn't change his life to keep tabs on me.

Twice I thought I saw some of Noon-zio's people in the background, but didn't know them well enough to have the same chat with them. Besides, I felt safer with them around.

Now they didn't have anything to protect me from, I breathed *so* much easier.

That is, until the tsunami.

It was a slight one, just a slight jiggle that we managed quickly. The next day I was working my shift at Sonny's (Cousin Noon had talked to him so he was also on guard) so it came as no great surprise that two of Sonny's customers looked familiar: Max and Leslie. I relaxed, as I'd been jumping every time someone new had entered the place.

He was in The Wig and slouched over the bar, while she sat in a booth behind a large tablet.

I sidled over to Max. "Real subtle," I said. "Two human customers in Sonny's. What do you think are the odds of that happening? It's a regular convention."

"Can't be helped."

"Why don't you guys have any saurs on your team?" I asked.

He caught me by the shoulder and drew me near to whisper in my ear, as if we were two lovers. Come to think of it, we were, kinda. "I've sent in that suggestion."

I had my argument all set up, but he beat me to the resolution. "Really?"

"First we protect Earth. Then we protect this station."

"For the humans here."

He rolled his eyes at me and heaved a theatrical sigh. "Saurs are people, too," he said.

"I am amazed," I told him. "I think in your language, that's 'gobsmacked.' For a bastard kidnapper, you are full of surprises. Wonderful ones."

He shrugged. He was adorable, trying to make it seem like not so big a thing.

He said, "It's more efficient to combine our forces, make the galaxy a safer place and all that."

"I'll have to buy you a cape."

That made him laugh.

"And you can hire a better navigator or engineer or whatever it is. Can't you guys come in at normal speeds? You shook the station again. Really, it's danger–"

"Wasn't us."

"No?"

"Nope." Now he swung about to give me a face-to-face gaze. "Tsunami? When was this?"

"Yesterday. You didn't feel it?"

"We got here today."

"Hunh." The implications of that weren't good.

"Keep your eyes peeled, love. I can't guarantee I can keep watch over you."

It was me who grunted this time. *Love?* That might be a British thing. Yet it sounded kind of wonderful.

The side of his mouth quirked as he watched my expression. "This evening?" he asked.

"Maybe. Stop over and see if I'm in the mood."

Half of me had leapt into that mood as soon as he mentioned it, but the other half was cowering, wondering just who'd triggered the quake yesterday. If Max hadn't, who was he trailing?

To my astonishment, he rose and gave me a real kiss. "Stay safe until then," he said.

Well. That was nice. There was a spring to my step as I moved around the dining room, gathering and distributing orders. I could hear Sonny singing in the back of the brewery as he watched over his equipment.

Following Max's hint, I treated Leslie like any other customer who had zero relation to him. I chatted her up like I'd do almost anyone, but she, being a Space Spy, wanted information. Neither seemed to be staying in the shadows today. Maybe they wanted to be a little obvious in case anyone came after me.

"So," Leslie said. "You and Max. Getting serious, eh?"

"When he bothers to come around," I replied. "You guys couldn't let me in on your travel schedule, could you?"

She gave a little laugh that wasn't a giggle. "I wish I knew what our schedule was. We go when we're needed." She perused the menu on the wall screen but said, "Max says you got rid of the brite. I said you've got it stashed somewhere. We have a rather sizeable bet on it."

"Max gets the payout."

Her eyebrows raised at me. "Really? Do you know how much that stuff goes for?" Then she shook her head. "No. You've got it secured. I bet it's in the Tunnels."

"Fine," I said, getting a bit cross. "You go look for it. It's yours if you find it."

"All I'm saying is that somebody else wants to find it. They might get upset if you don't turn it over without a fuss."

I shrugged and tried to look cool, though the thought made me sweat buckets. "If they come looking they're going to be disappointed. Nothing to find."

She nodded and ordered a sandwich.

Max eventually wandered out of the grill, giving me a wave as he departed. It wasn't ten minutes afterward that my shoulder buzzer sounded.

"Tam." It was Bree. I asked her what was up. "Is Kreeger there?"

"Yeah." She was in her usual spot, looking all zen-like over her drink like only Kreeger can.

"There's a problem at her farm. We've got sensors doing strange things. Can you bring her to her main gate? Eco-Systems wants to check with her."

"Sure." I went in the back to notify Sonny and he shooed me off. Then I went up to Kreeger.

"There might be a problem at your farm," I told her.

Most of her arms jerked. She began to roll up but straightened herself out quickly. "Easy," I told her, remembering her age. "Tell you what, we'll take a Bug through the Tunnels and be there in a flash. Okay?"

It took only a moment for her to gather up her things, which of course included her valise. I helped her unroll into a standing position, though she could make two of me. As we hurried out of the grill, Leslie came up behind me.

"Something wrong?"

"Problem at Kreeger's property," I told her.

"I don't like this," Leslie said. "Let me come along. Just in case."

So we stuffed Leslie in the back of the Bug, behind the two main seats. I didn't think Leslie would have much room to breathe back there. I told both my passengers to hang on as I gave the Bug some gas. We zipped down-level and then out south along the main line until we came to Kreeger's bogs.

Three Systems people I didn't know were there to meet us. Another Bug drew up, and Kakura, a coworker, climbed out. The Systems people showed Kreeger some scans: energy usage had a little blip on it, but atmospherics showed some abnormal gases.

"That's not right," she muttered, and then rolled off into her farm. We all trotted to keep up, but the gimigols and one doil didn't function as well as malac did in the heavier gravity here.

Kreeger was fast when she rolled. I kept her in sight as she took the main road and then veered off onto paths that were about a Kreeger wide, certainly wide enough for me. Leslie was right behind, puffing away.

The swampy fields stretched out around us. They were a humid forest whose trees never got larger than gimigol size. The trunks were wide and limbs twined between the trees like they were embracing each other. Along those limbs hung thick carpets of lichenish moss. It was all shades of green with threads that made it look like tangled fishing netting. I knew the greens and pink kind were good to eat, and cooks used the red variety as a spice. Don't eat it in large quantities, though, or you'd burn your tongue off.

Ahead and slightly above us on the curve of the station we could see saurs along one pathway. An Eco-Systems mini-Bug raced by us, aiming for that. I could see a female gimigol at the controls. The minis were used for situations like this, where they had to travel narrow surface routes instead of streets.

We were making good time, but the mini made better. She reached the saurs well before us. We watched her get out of her mini to address the saurs.

"Do you know those guys?" I huffed at Kreeger.

"Only my family should be in the fields," she told me– and then came to a complete halt.

I ran into her, and Leslie skidded to a stop behind us. Ahead on the slope: the distinct, linear glowing red of laser fire.

"This is not good," I surmised. I used my jaw to click on my comm unit and advised them.

"Retreat," came the order from HQ. I could definitely agree with it. I put a hand on Kreeger. "Let's go," I told her. She stood there, staring, so I pulled her back. "Let's go *now*," I urged. "We'll let the cops deal with these guys. Now, Kreeger."

Reluctantly she turned and we trotted back the way we came, looking back to see we were keeping a safe distance from whoever that was. I couldn't see the Eco-Systems officer. She could be hiding; she could be down. I wasn't equipped with armor or training to check the situation.

Almost immediately a pair of minis marked "Police" zipped toward us and we made way. Kreeger cursed at the intrusion but I patted her upper shoulder and told her things would be okay. We had to get the old gal out of there.

And then…

A *hoo,* like some giant had inhaled.

I felt a breeze kick up. My hair began flying in the general direction of the strangers.

"Vacuum leak!" I shouted. "Kreeger, where's your nearest Safeties shed?"

I saw it before she could tell me. I sped up to pure adrenaline speed and reached it well before the others. I grabbed a mask for myself and put it on, informing HQ, then took others for Kreeger and Leslie. Outside, I helped them with the fit even as we aimed for our Bug.

Other people had gathered where we'd parked. Two gimigol and one doil Systems officers, plus Kakura, all with masks on. They were waving at us to come quickly.

We threw ourselves into our Bug and as soon as we were off toward the section wall, the others were zipping ahead of us.

My shoulder comm had cross-conversation in it. People shouting. The buzz of laser fire.

Kreeger began to keen. "What are they doing on my land? My land?"

In my rearview monitor I could see a red glow. It was more than laser fire.

It looked familiar.

It had purple polka-dots dancing around it.

My phone comm buzzed and I answered. "Tell me you're not in there," Max's voice demanded.

"Me and Leslie and Kreeger are almost out," I reassured him. "I hope some-one–" The alarms began to peal, almost drowning me out. "Someone should be standing by the doors. I think we have cinderu'um on the station!"

24

Central's comm had picked up my comment. Bree interrupted. "Quiet! Quiet! Tam, repeat that."

"Cinderu'um," I said. "Repeat, cinderu'um has been released in this section. Somebody check the scanners to confirm."

I heard cursing from both sources. Lots of "What do we do?" coming from Central, as HQ streamed data readouts.

"All right, Tam," Bree told me. "I have a preliminary confirmation."

"What about the officers in the field?"

"Dead bodies as far as we can tell. Confirmation on that. Two gimigols traveling west– repeat that–" she was also directing Police systems, it seemed– "heading toward the section doors there."

Her voice lowered. "Get the hell out of there, Tam. You and whoever else you're with."

"Initiate deck ejection," I told her. "As soon as we're out."

"Deck eject–?"

"Confirmation," someone's voice was in the background. "Cinderu'um. Definite confirmation, cinderu'um! It's spreading!"

"Only intense cold will stop it," I insisted. "Start outer decks ejection *now*."

We were three decks up from the port's skin. Other decks could be safely sealed, the heat kept on, even if they were ejected. But they had to eject before we did.

Even with a million items on the checklists, the process was a quick one. Pity anyone walking between sections. They'd have to jump fast to safety, even with the slow section airlocks.

I could feel the station shudder.

"Station section skin ejection, check," someone's voice said on my shoulder. Already?

We were almost at the section wall. The air sucking away from us was slowing our speed. I could see the large, industrial doors that separated this station's section from the next. Everyone ahead of us had arrived, but there were other people there as well.

The shuddering increased. The siren's wail was deafening. The wind was rising to storm proportions, pulling at us. We were on the main road and another Eco-Systems Bug that must have just begun its investigation screamed past us from right angles toward the door, though I had ours going at maximum.

I could see them now: More Safeties officers. Police. There was Brindle. From behind him stepped Max. And Noon-zio.

I could see the gigantic bulk of Nuke running up behind them. He began passing around ropes to secure to.

The alarm went silent. "Prepare for section ejection," a loud voice declared. "Clear the section doors."

"Not yet! Not yet!" I shouted. "We're not there!"

"Holding for you," Bree's voice told me. "Hurry up!"

We squealed to a stop and everyone piled out. I shoved Leslie toward the door, where rescuing arms met her to pull her through, despite the storm trying to suck her away. Kreeger took some work, though. She got tangled in the Bug's door. Then–

"My valise!" she shrieked. "My valise!"

She'd dropped it. It slid down a pathway paralleling the section's wall, bumping against vegetation, trying to break through to follow the wind.

"You go," I told her. "I'll get it!" I had a half-moment to reach inside the Bug for a Safeties emergency bag, and as I ran, keeping low to present less surface area, I jerked a protecto-jacket out of it. After all my practice, I could put it on in one smooth motion. It was way too big for me, but it would do if things went even sourer.

Not if. *When.*

I looked back over my shoulder to see the shocked people standing there, watching me run. I waved them off. "Close the door!" I shouted. "I'll get the a sub-Tunnel door." It was ahead on the left and I pointed wildly to it, in case they couldn't hear me over the increasing roar. It would be just a lift and would shoot me up a level, though in the same section. They wouldn't be ejecting that level.

I heard the big door *hunk-aaah!* close behind me and dared a glance to see all had evacuated. Now there was just that valise to catch. The wind was making it carom across the decking crazily, toward the conflagration.

But I caught it, brought it to my chest. *This storm is not going to stop me!* I knew I could reach that wall. That door. That safety. I could! I could!

The cinderu'um was an inferno now, eating its way across the section like lightning. It was maybe a hundred yards from me.

But there was my lift door. Got to it, slammed my palm on the latch, and it opened. I literally jumped through. "Go! Go!" I screamed. "I'm out!" I shouted into my comm.

The entire lift wall behind me vibrated like a hurricane was behind it. I lay on the floor, catching my breath. "Is it?" I asked my comm. "Did you–"

"Ejection complete," Safeties HQ droned as if they did this every day. The lift was shuddering so hard I didn't know if it was still operating correctly. At the least it was solid enough to keep me from the vacuum. I told the wall monitor to tie into Systems to give me a view of what was going on.

Four slices of the station were arcing away from us. You could tell which one the skin was, because it was so very thin. Two other slices were moving away, ever so slightly separated from each other. I could see engine units firing on both, steering them.

And then came Kreeger's section. It was glowing red Swiss cheese. In the moments it had taken me to get to safety, the cinderu'um had cut through everything: farm, swamps, structure… leaving just scraps that had been disintegrating but now froze in the absolute zero of space.

I lay there staring. I thought of Kreeger. All her work. All her family's work. Gone.

And then a cold hatred bloomed in my gut. They'd brought this here. Limbus. To my home.

Death was too good for them.

The lift doors opened and I rose before the scene registered:

Two gimigols, pointing blasters down at me. One of them was wearing a necklace like Mom's.

The necklace guy noticed Kreeger's valise.

"Is it in there?" he demanded to know.

"Is what– Good god, you guys still think I have brite? I dumped it weeks ago."

They looked at each other before the other shook the gun at me. "Like it wasn't worth a small fortune."

"I dumped it. Told the cops." I shrugged. "They might have a record of it, since all EVAs are monitored. You might be able to find it if you know a physicist who's good at mapping trajectories."

"You spaced it?"

"I doubt if it's any good now, being subjected to all that cold and cosmic radiation and stuff."

The necklace guy grabbed the valise and tried to open it. "Locked," he said.

The other changed the setting on his gun and shot the bag's lock. The gun's beam was needle-like. Even so, the lock popped open. They both peered in.

I leapt to my feet and–

The one guy put out an arm, blocking me from escape.

"What is this?" the other asked, motioning to the valise.

"Seeds. Just some experimental seeds they're trying on the lower levels."

He dumped the contents all over the floor of the lift. Most were in containers, but some busted open and there was seed-dust all over the place. Was that what spores looked like?

Kreeger would be able to retrieve them, a part of my brain thought. Once I'm dead, at least she'll still have something to begin again with.

Instead I found myself being marched out of the lift. We were still in the ag sections, just on a lighter level, so there weren't people around.

That gun was a sharp poke in my back.

"Keep walking, malac," the grating gimigol voice told me.

I did as instructed. I knew before he prodded me again that we were heading for the nearest Safeties Tunnel. Sure enough, when we arrived he said, "In. And as soon as an alarm sounds, you're dead."

"There's only room for two saurs in a Bug," I told him. "Not two saurs and a malac."

A brief discussion left the guy without the necklace behind. I made sure the sensors cleared the one with the Limbus pendant as well as me. We got into the Bug.

I didn't strap in. I turned off all alarms. That, of course, would light up an alarm at HQ.

Then I floored it.

The Bug took off through the narrow tunnels at what felt like light speed. I thrust my strapping into place before I grabbed for his weapon.

He tried to hold on to it as his entire body flattened against his seat. I hit the "turn corner" button and we made ninety degrees in a second. He sprawled across the cabin, across me.

A few more turns and he was out of it. I pried the gun out of his hand. It took a few moments to figure out the safeties on it, but I soon had it secured in my right hip pocket.

He groaned and I reached for the first aid kit to find something to knock him out. Yeah, ruumer would do it. I gave him a double dose.

That left me time to sit there in a side-tunnel to get my brain back in working order. I nudged my shoulder comm, got hold of Bree and told her the story so far.

"I'll get things started," she assured me.

I made sure she knew where Kreeger's seeds were.

With that I Bugged over to Police HQ, where they gleefully took my passenger.

"Where are you?" my phone asked. It was Max.

I gave the phone comm a shake. "No video," I told him. "You sound fuzzy."

"I'm surprised it works at all. I got in a fight right after we got separated."

I told him my coordinates and he said they were getting ready to board a shuttle. He and some other people on his team I'd never met were all in place now; they could finally bust the entire gang.

"Level 1?" I asked, and he confirmed. "Which gate? What ship?"

"No matter what," he demanded, "you are not to go there!"

Yeah, right. "You've given Brindle the info, right?" He'd bring a small army with him.

I was *pissed off.* Damn Limbus and everyone in it. I wanted to bust some heads, but I'd be quite satisfied to watch some cops and Max do the busting instead, as long as none of them got hurt.

"You're going after them, aren't you?" Leslie's voice came on my phone.

"Close enough," I replied. Max must have given her my number.

"Don't be an idiot. Wait for me to arrive. I have weapons." She gave me the number of a gate near to where the Limbuses would be, and I agreed. It would be good to have a little defense on my side from the get-go. "We'll act as reinforcements if it comes down to it. We'll wait unless Limbus is quicker than they are."

Sounded good.

The gates were far out in the boonies, some five miles or so from the more populated areas of the core. I got out of the Bug, exited the Tunnel, and floated with a few touch-downs to the access door for this sector. I clicked the monitor that would give me the outside view.

Technical difficulties, it told me. My Aunt Fanny's big toe, technical difficulties.

From around a corner Leslie appeared, and I breathed a sigh of relief.

"Thank goodness," I told her. "Where're the cops? Is Max with you? He said you had–"

The largest doil I'd ever seen came up behind her. He was dragging a bloody and unconscious– or worse– Max in mid-air behind him.

"I'm afraid Max's phone hasn't been working for some time now." Leslie leveled a blaster at me.

25

ax was awake– and still bleeding. Breathing awkwardly, as blood trickled from his mouth. His eyes darted this way and that, taking in our situation, but they'd trussed up his hands and feet. Me, they hadn't worried about. I was just dumped on the floor.

"Sorry about all this, cuz." Leslie shook her head at Max and took one last, quick glance at me. "But you've started to get in the way of all this. Both of you."

We had been transferred from the station to a shuttle, to Limbus' ship. That Max was conscious made me breathe easier. But judging from where we were, that wouldn't last long.

We were in one of the ship's main airlocks.

Leslie stood in the open doorway to the interior, her gun still aimed at us. Two gimigols flanked her. "I'll give the family the usual story," she told Max. "Killed in the line of duty, all glory to the Guardian Network." One hand held Max's phone. "I may send them one last, heartbreaking voicemail from you. I might take time to add video to it, too: you trying to keep the tears from coming. So brave. Just for best effect."

"What…" he gasped around whatever injury he had, "Tam too? Don't… Don't…"

"She got on my nerves. All that lovey-dovey stuff with the saurs." She used the English word that the guys next to her wouldn't understand. "We don't need that. She'll get the blame for this. Your voicemail will pin it on her. Her mother's in our records as a traitor, after all. You still leave the spare keys to the cruiser in the same place, right, Max?"

"You're working with them," I said, trying not to look like I was looking for a way out.

She switched to English again. "I'm looking forward to a very easy retirement, moneywise. Spying is difficult. These idiots are making money hand over fist, and they're lazy bastards, every one of them. A smart girl doesn't let something like that go to waste."

She slapped Max's phone comm against the door release. "Toodle-pip," she called as the inner lock door slammed down, leaving us alone in the airlock.

Max cursed as he tried to get up off the floor. A click came through the door. "They've neutralized the lock. No getting back in." He squirmed. "I've got a knife in my boot. Help me."

As I rushed to do so, I looked all around to assess the cargo space. It was for industrial use, large enough to hold a semi if needed. Limbus was not an orderly organization. The area was filled with junk equipment and mechanical repair paraphernalia. Some of it was secured by regulation strapping. Other stuff had been tied down haphazardly.

Bingo.

"Safeties locker!" I pointed and ran even as Max turned. "Do you see any loose rope? Can you walk?" I asked as I clicked through the standard locks on it. I knew the codes; they opened right away.

I tossed a mask to Max, who was half-crawling as fast as he could toward me. He caught it, put it on. I pulled up the mask that had been dangling from my neck since being on Kreeger's property.

"This won't–" he began.

"Shut up and get over here." I tossed him the end of some strapping.

He grabbed it and pulled himself up even as I started to secure it to the decking.

The outer wall began to rise slowly, and all hell erupted as every loose item on deck was sucked towards the opening. Oxygen created a maelstrom as the vacuum tugged at it. The door *eek*ed as if on unoiled hinges. Thank goodness for that sound, though; in a few moments when the air was gone there'd be no sound.

In space no one can hear you scream, and all.

"You ever see *2001*?" I asked as I rummaged through the locker, trying to hold down any loose items. Messy people had come before me. Unthinking people… There!

"The, um…? Got some!" His voice came thinly, due to injuries or deteriorating air pressure, I didn't know. I mimed holding my breath.

Max waved the rope at me triumphantly and I nodded, trying to disregard the rip current of wind. My feet were dragging toward the outside. Within moments it was all I could to do hang on to the locker. I pulled out a suit.

"Secure yourself!" I yelled, wasting air. "Close your eyes hard. Hold your breath. You can last extra seconds that way, even without the mask."

It was a suit for a gimigol, acres larger than me. There was space for a thick tail. Space enough for two? I doubted it even as I climbed in.

I looked back at Max. He was half-out the door, hanging in mid-air– or what was left of it.

"Maaaax!" It was the last of my air. I didn't care.

He'd managed to tie one end of his rope to a hitch and now he was trying to wrap the other end around his midsection. He motioned to me: something I couldn't catch.

I mimed the squeeze-shut eyes even as I waded into the suit. It was hard to do in this hurricane, but I'd trained hard over the years. We had to be able to suit up quickly in all kinds of conditions. On a good day I could get it done in less than four seconds. Today I made it in three.

The hurricane diminished all too quickly. I tried to clamp both lungs and eyes shut as I felt my way around the suit. A hundred safety lectures came back to me, but I'd always used the suits tailored to my human needs. Still, there was a basic standard… There!

The suit's helmet was too big, but it sealed all the same, thank the Lord for universal connectors.

I began to slide towards the gaping nothingness, still secured by my tether. I wasn't ready yet! I pulled on some nearby tethers to return to the Safeties chest. A coil of industrial rope went over my shoulder, and at the last moment inside I managed to snag some magnetic overboots and snapped them to the wall.

Air hissed as the last connection sealed and the suit seemed to breathe around me.

Max was still in the doorway. He'd curled into a ball. How many seconds had it been?

Nope, no way there was enough room in here for both of us. Without the hurricane I could use both hands to rummage through the locker, tossing out what was in my way, searching for another suit. Any kind of suit. Maybe we could connect them in tandem and get enough–

A stasis box sat on the back shelf. I reached for it and some last breath of air popped it off its shelf right into my hands. *Thank you, God!*

The locker had rope of its own, already secured inside. I grabbed the boots, which latched on to the stasis box. Then I cast off into the gravity-free space toward Max. He looked blue, but that could have been the weird light inside here. Realistically: probably not.

The stasis box was built to unfold in a trice, gravity or no gravity, air or no air. I prayed like I'd never prayed before. I could feel the sides pop into real dimensional space as they appeared: length, breadth, depth. Big enough for a good-sized gimigol.

Max didn't respond as I shoved him into the box. I secured the lid, making sure I got all sides.

We were outside the ship now. Just me, a bunch of rope and strapping, and the box. I watched the outer door of the airlock come down. It snapped the end of the strapping attached to me.

But I'd seen it coming. Using the suit's jets I'd aimed for the safety railing that allowed workers to operate on their ships' skins. With Max's box under my arm and some rope around it tightly wound around me, I grabbed the railing.

An emergency equipment bag hung off my belt, part of Safeties requirements. It had a laser knife. I used it as quickly as I could to cut lengths of rope. We were both, box and I, as secure as I could manage, tied a dozen ways to the railing. I pulled on the boots over my suit's, adding to our adhesion. I hoped.

Just in time.

The hair on every part of my body stood up as one. My stomach did a 180.

Then it *really* hit: a crush of gravity that seemed to roll from the very skin of the ship, though I knew it came from the projector network. For a moment I thought it alone would squash us like bugs, but it passed through without doing more damage than making me ralf my guts out.

The suit cleaned itself up nicely.

I hung on like I'd never hung on to anything before. If I let Max's box escape, he'd float out here in limbo for eternity, neither alive or quite dead. If I fell off, I'd float for a while before becoming quite dead.

A blue glow– maybe it was a black glow– rose from the sides of the ship, distorting the panorama of stars. Something to my left cracked a spark off into nothingness. Something below me did the same, then to the right and above.

The very blackness of space distorted. Color ran up through the spectrum, but not the pure colors: muted pastels pulsed around. Stars blazed suddenly black, others all colors, but those were the pure hues.

I could swear that a wind roared around us. My bones and skin throbbed with a vibration that didn't seem to come from the ship, though I couldn't hear anything beside my heart pounding.

We slipped outside the cosmos.

After that I wasn't aware of any acceleration or gravity. We just sort of floated, maybe. I was surprised that there was light around us, but it was patterns of translucent, technicolor bubbles that were either exercise ball-sized and just out of arm's reach or half an eternity away and enormous beyond imagination. Now and then a streak like a falling star would run across the expanse. Behind it all wasn't black, but rather a shifting neutral color.

I hoped my suit had enough air to handle all the curses I directed at Leslie and her Limbus buddies. After I got that out of my system– though really, a lifetime wouldn't be long enough for that– I thought about our options.

They would certainly check the airlock we'd come from. No going back there. Still, I wanted some kind of shelter. No telling what kind of radiation was out here. Had I already gotten too much, or was my suit protecting me?

I'd checked bunches of ships and knew the pattern of airlocks because the airlocks were where one found the main Safeties lockers. There'd be one up there and down and over there. I peered around over the bulk of my spacesuit and sure enough, saw the doors. There were usually gimigol-sized manual doors nearby.

From where we'd been I did my best impression of Frankenstein, slowly lifting each foot in its turn to move forward, turn on magnets, clamp down. Other foot: magnets off, forward and down. We were strapped together well, but I added a few more loops. I made sure that I had triple tethers looped over the railing. There were no clips, so the setup had to be continually tied and untied as we moved around the rail's anchor points. The gargantuan suit didn't help things.

I tried to turn off my brain when it came to worrying about Max. Either I'd retrieved him in time or I hadn't. Right now I had to see to our continued safety.

I slogged forward slowly when all of a sudden: a clamp. Some slob had left a tether and clamp hanging from the railing. I borrowed it and it increased our pace by at least a third.

We finally reached the manual entrance. Per safety regs, it was kept open in case of emergencies. I slung Max inside, then carefully rearranged our strapping so I could enter as well. Inside I again strapped us in, and used a loop of strapping not only to close the outer door, but to block it from shutting all the way. Closing it would have lit a light or two up on the command deck, but I wanted it shut enough to offer some shelter from any radiation coming through.

This manual entrance was actually a minor airlock. I checked a screen on the wall. The airlock just beyond us was full of vacuum as well, not any better than our present surroundings, but any curious crew wandering around inside could only see into the main airlock and not into ours. All righty, this would be home for as long as it took. Our door to the outside had a window on it, so there was my entertainment: the non-cosmos.

How long did riding cosmic branes take? Surely the universe would not like intense little disruptions breaking out on its skin and probably had some kind of logical whatever to stop whatever parasite was messing with it, to slap it down if it went on too long. I had no idea how long it had taken Max to reach Port Malabar from Earth, but he seemed to do it regularly. I'd listened to pilots and passengers. Their trips had lasted anywhere from days to a few weeks. But not months.

I settled myself into a comfortable pose behind the safety of the outer door, easy to do with no gravity. At first my situation was terrifying, but there's only so long your adrenaline can occupy your full attention. Then it was puzzling as I tried to work out the physics of what I saw outside the window. I came to the mind-blowing conclusion that it was different from the usual starry sky, but pretty in its own way. Then I was thirsty. I drank from the suit's supplies. I slept a while. I ate. I pooped.

Good suit. I hoped Max was enjoying the blank advantages of his stasis just as much.

The suit was big enough that I could duck down and disappear into it. I had lots of water, food and air, enough to keep a good-sized gimigol alive for at least a week. For me, maybe two, two and a half. Maybe more if I rationed.

I checked my Safeties jacket, the one I'd pulled from the Bug back on station. That also contained a couple bags of drinks and a sandwich. It also held a handful of tcherripies.

The curtains breathed in spring at the the open kitchen window. Mom puttered away, wiping down the counters and then starting to fill the sink for dishes. The smile she wore seemed forced for my sake. She looked tired.

"Mom," I finally asked, "why'd you do it? For real?"

"Why'd I do what, hon? Here, earn your keep." She tossed me a dish towel and I stood from my chair at the table and joined her as she placed cleaned dishes in the drainer.

"Why did you betray Earth?" I asked. "Why did you want to destroy it?"

In the midst of wiping a plate, she turned to stare at me incredulously. "What? What have you been watching on TV? Did you sneak into one of those horror pictures?"

"I've seen the horror, Mom. I was a part of it. It almost *killed* me. Twice!"

She snorted. "How we do blow things out of proportion. Don't put that away like that. The bottom's still wet."

I attended to the plate before putting it into its proper cabinet. "You made a deal with those guys. They were building a weapon."

Silently she scrubbed and set another plate in the drainer. Then another. And another. If it weren't for the breeze carrying the smell of the pie strong and then weak, strong, then weak, I would have thought that time stood still.

"It's not easy being a single mother," Mom whispered when I wasn't concentrating.

"No," I said.

"You have to scrimp and save for everything. Emergencies wipe you out completely. It's so easy to go into debt."

"So it was the money."

"It was all a disaster," she groaned. "Your dad's medical bills… I was always fighting with the hospital, with the insurance. For years there was no letup. The calls, the constant calls… We were about to lose everything. They were even going to take our home. I hadn't thought they could do that. People were telling me to put you in foster care. Then came… a solution."

"Yeah?"

She crossed her arms, wet hands and all, over her chest and turned away from me. "It was just for little things. They didn't seem all that illegal to me. All I had to do for most of them was look the other way. I ran a few computer searches for them."

I wondered what else she could have done in her position, things that she could still come home at night after doing and look me straight in the eye.

"I used police records to investigate them on my own. They came up clean. They shouldn't have. That bothered me. But… But…" She gripped the counter edge and leaned into it. "I didn't have the strength left for any of it. They say God never gives you so much you can't handle it. He made a mistake that time. I couldn't. I was beyond my rope's end. I'd gone through every resource. Every. Last. Thing.

"And here all I had to do was look the other way.

"I didn't have any idea what they were doing, only that what they were doing was surely illegal. Betray Earth? That's movies, honey. What they were doing was…

"Was…

"Just destroying me and everything I stood for."

Finally she turned. Her expression had been twisted, but now it smoothed out as if asking for forgiveness as she gazed at me. "Whatever it was, it was worth it. I protected you. That was the one thing left to me that I was able to do."

A single mother with few resources and a young daughter. If it were me, I'd stretch myself pretty damn far afield of the law and still be able to smile at my kid. Family was more important than legalities– as long as no one got hurt.

"No." She put a hand on my shoulder. "I wouldn't have sold out Earth. That's where you lived, darling. I would never have harmed you."

"Yeah." I looked up at her. "Thanks, Mom."

Even though she'd helped them, even though she'd aided the enemy in making a doomsday weapon, she'd done it for me. That was the only answer possible. She hadn't known the extent of what she was doing; she'd just been stretched to her own extremes and had been fighting to survive– to make sure I survived– each day.

"It was harmless, what I did," she insisted. "Mostly harmless."

"I love you, Mom," I said and she hugged me hard.

I had some more talks with Mom, most of them a lot happier, recalling the good times we'd had. It was nice. Now and then I'd come out of it to check Max's box. It looked okay to me. How would I know if it wasn't working right?

Max.

One of the last things he'd done was to call me "love." Did he mean it, or was it just a figure of speech?

And what did I feel about him?

He'd gone way out of his way to save me, a nobody. We'd taken turns saving each other from Limbus, and now… Well, I didn't know if I'd saved him or not. I had. I sat there making my hands into fists. I had! He'd be fine if I could get him back to Port Malabar and the doctors there.

Time passed while I recalled the times we'd been together. Talking. Making love. I might have rolled through those scenes more often than I did the talking ones. And he'd brought me clothes. Who travels light-years, parsecs… just to deliver some jeans?

Somebody who cared for me, that's who. Maybe even somebody who loved me.

He was sweet. He was hot. He was dear to me.

He lived an exciting life, protecting Earth. Kind of like I did, protecting Port Malabar. Yeah, I was a hero, too, one hundred percent. We were two of a kind.

And damn it, I wanted us to go on being two of a kind for a long time to come. I wanted him in my life. I wanted him to argue with and to explore in my bed. He was even coming around to liking saurs. He might be a dope at times, but he was *my* dope.

"I really like him, too," Mom told me.

I wasn't going to let him die, not if it was in my power!

What would my friends say when they were told I was gone? Would Bree be angry at me for ever getting involved with brite? Would Ali and Arti target their attentions on someone else? Would anyone say the Salat al-Janazah for me? Who'd replace me in Safeties? Would they take good care of the station? Who'd listen to Derra when she went crazy? Who'd water my begonias? Who'd help Kreeger replant her fields? Who would take care of Nuke?

Blue. They'd painted the airlock a slightly greenish shade of blue. It was soothing. It was infinite. It was… blue. Blue… Bl–

A hard swipe of nausea awakened me from my daze. I had just enough time to blink and wonder where the hell I was before another wave of gravity crashed against me. I smashed into the outer door, the stasis box next to me. Thank goodness Max and I were still roped in!

On Level 27 back home I weighed about three times what I should. This was more like a fictional Level 50 would be. It was hard to breathe because my lungs couldn't operate against the strain. I felt like some giant was crushing me in his hand. My vision blacked out for a few seconds until it let up. Blessed weightlessness–

And stars. We'd come out of the gravity bubble. All that was left of the barrier was a few almost reassuring rocks back and forth before the ship steadied.

Couldn't see any station around, but that didn't mean much as I had only a narrow slice of sky available out my window. It might be right next door, or we might have a ways more to go. More Limbus traitors might be joining our happy crew, and I didn't want to encounter them.

So I took a moment– okay, I took three– to catch my breath and resituate myself in my lovely suit for real movement. In however long I'd been in this airlock, I'd made Plans.

I climbed outside and made my way down the side of the ship to the next airlock, away from Max. There I found another open manual door, but from there I went into the larger neighboring airlock. Likely entering set off an alarm, but I hid and hoped that this old ship sometimes bleeped when it shouldn't.

After a while I got up. There was a window in the inner door. Every now and then somebody would walk down the corridor outside. One peeked in once and moved on. It was dark in here. They didn't see me. There was no reason for them to expect me.

I explored the more hidden parts of the airlock and found a weapons cache. Among the various items were some rifles. If they were stored here, they could take vacuum. I examined one that was just my size. It looked simple enough.

To make sure there were no surprises, I fired it outside the manual airlock's door. Oops. Nothing. Some kind of safety? I hit some switches, tried, and then tried again. There. It fired. It looked like it would fire quite a lot, too.

We were drifting toward a station that looked like an early version of Port Malabar. It was still skeleton over more than half its bulk. I'd heard of a station being built out somewhere. Port... Tchumki, something like that. They often advertised for zero-grav construction workers. This station would be like the early days Kreeger so often spoke of. Lawlessness pervading it, but there would also be law there to counter it. Harsh law. Just my type, right now.

I eased back inside the main airlock.

A group of five gimigols appeared down the hallway. They were lugging a large crate by means of ropes and arguing as the crate bounced from wall to wall, ceiling to floor, back and forth in zero G. That's when I punched the airlock's emergency manual release.

The door hesitated as if it tried to counter its programming. I had been a diligent Safeties student, and after a moment the door shot up into the ceiling at my overriding command.

I stepped aside to allow the guys down the hall as well as their little crate to fly through the doorway and out into space. Such a shame.

Once the hurricane dissipated, I released my tethers and swam into the ship, helped by my suit jets. A computer panel showed me the layout and the shortest way to the bridge.

I tried to be quick.

Along the way I set off the Hazardous Materials Leak alarms on every section of deck. Sure, that might alert the crew, but it also sent out a signal to the nearest legitimate HazMat facility. That station out there would be sending a team to investigate. I didn't think that the people on this ship really wanted any kind of investigation. I just had to keep them from blasting out of the universe first.

All this killing was nothing to them. But to me, it was as personal as it got.

I passed a door with a good-sized window and fancy door. This must be the place. Inside, a group of gimigols were excitedly gathered around control boards as navigation screens and shipboard schematics played upon the walls. I saw a screen showing me in the hallway, but no one was looking at it.

Leslie was standing with them, pointing helpfully to some alarm or another. For some reason she turned to face me. Her gaze came to the window I was at and I gave her a finger wave with a smile.

Her face twisted into a look of hatred and shock as I shot right through the window.

It wasn't like I had to have good aim. I stood back so debris didn't hit me, and I couldn't hear the bodies inside as they slammed against the door as the room decompressed. I thought they wouldn't have had time to send out a distress signal. No time to delete computer files or communications records.

After a good fifteen minutes and a thorough squint inside, I released the door to go in. From here I froze computer memory systems and ran ship records. There were only a few cabins with crew, few ways for them to get into the systems from there. I locked them out of the computers just to be sure. Then I locked them into their rooms. They'd be needed alive for questioning.

After that I plugged into comm and got a response from the station. We had a lovely talk, their law enforcement team and I. They switched me over to the Hazmat folks and I let them see ship's records and just what was in this ship's hold.

Then I settled back to track down whatever galley this joint might have. I could damn well use a drink.

26

Interstellar newslines clamored for the story and accompanying video.

I insisted that all interviews be done at touristy areas on Port Malabar. Therefore, all pictures of me showed me waving in my Safe-Shell (TM) suit in front of Port Malabar's decadent mud flats, the flower fields, performance art events, et al with a crowd behind me, many lifting their bottles of Sonny's Best. Sometimes I'd allow an interview and photo at Sonny's or Derra's. A girl's got to eat and drink sometime, you know. It got so packed 24/7 at the brewery that Sonny began talking about opening two more places and maybe exporting his brew.

The entire station concentrated on setting Kreeger's farm, and others that had been disturbed, to rights. She was allocated new space on Level 26, and within weeks the structures for new beds were set up. Some rich saur somewhere saw her story and donated saplings over and above what insurance provided. In a few weeks she and her family would begin to dust them with her spores. Prices for good moss and fungus would go up on the station for a while, but in time her crops would be in full production again.

As for me, the money that Safe-Shell gave me to retell my story with emphasis on how well their suit held up at the very edge of space/time even though it hadn't been custom-fitted for me– well, that was some nice cash indeed. I had more than enough to buy a place up on Green Hill.

But I liked the place I had. I liked my neighbors and my neighborhood. From there it wasn't all that far to walk to get a weekly treat of cherry pie and a chance to talk with Mom. Even if I had to stand in line sometimes to eat at Derra's.

I'd dropped Max off at High Spokes Hospital and had to stick around for two days while I got the most thorough examination of my life, as well as a tune-up. The docs were surprised I didn't have much radiation damage. As it was, I had a couple broken ribs and pinky toe. If I'd been one of a larger species I wouldn't have survived.

I wanted to stick around and see Max uncorked, hear what the prognosis was– they kept him in stasis until they were completely prepared to quickly treat his most egregious injuries– but Dr. Tube assured me that they got these kinds of cases in maybe twice, three times a year and could probably pull him through. Even if he was a malac.

Despite all the travel downtime I fell asleep for two full days at my place. My own, wonderful home with its lovely bed and all the smells that were just so right. Bree let me sleep, but it was still the buzz of her presence at my door that finally woke me. She couldn't stop chirruping at me and slamming her talons against my shoulder.

"Brought the whole movement down!" she bellowed as we rocked in the chairs on my porch at my place. Mine, mine. Nuke leaned against the wall behind her, two arms crossed diagonally across his chest as he allowed her access on his property, an amused smile on his face. The neighbors wandered over to see what the commotion was about and see where I'd been.

"Saved Nik-a-Dell. The entire planet. They were going to poison it and melt most of the upper crust of the world as a side effect." Bree gave another cascading round of chortles. "But you– You led us to every agent they had! Malac! You never know what they can do. You saved the lot of us, you did."

Even with being a hero it was still up to me to feed the crowds that now came to congratulate me. Derra saw the problem and brought over drinks and noshes that I doled out to people I didn't know. They avoided Nuke until they forgot about him and ate and ate and then nodded their various-shaped heads and said,

"Malac!" and even "Muties!" approvingly. When they were done, they remembered where the good food had come from. Hence Derra's lines. I didn't mind… much.

Of course the entire malac population trooped over. They had to inspect my living quarters and some returned with little knick-knacks for it. They shook Nuke's hands. They spoke to any saurs that were visiting, and sometimes ate with them. Mawar from up on High Spokes brought a cake that almost tasted chocolate. Bliss!

Even my next-door neighbors, Burdt and Shkarb, trundled up one day to get the story from me. Nuke was sitting in his chair and they gave him the side-eye, but then Burdt extended his hand to introduce himself. The next day Nuke had his own begonia on his railing.

A couple weeks went by. The hospital assured me that Max would end up fine, but that his general condition right then might upset me. Brindle whispered that they'd had to take his skin off, it had been in such bad shape.

I gulped. I liked Max's skin. I bet he liked it even more than I did.

So I left him voice messages, which was what everyone recommended since he had few touch receptors at the moment on the surface of his body and his eyes were being replaced. I wasn't sure if he could hear them right now, but there'd come a time when he would.

The wait made me antsy and spurred me to use that extra energy to double up on my studies. The entire Safeties network now didn't mind taking the time to accompany me on the various drills the system demanded.

In another month they swore me in as a full-fledged Port Malabar Safeties Tech. I got a sizeable raise. After much soul-searching, Nuke told me he was going to move due to all the noise my additional traffic was making.

"This was your home before it was mine," I told him. He shrugged.

We both turned at the sound of more people approaching. Derra and a few of her cousins were all bearing armloads of containers that I guessed was deli food.

But she didn't come to my door. She gave me a half-nod as the parade came up to Nuke. He gave a bewildered expression before he masked it down. "Hello," he said and darned if there wasn't the slightest hint of a question at the end.

Derra squared her shoulders and pushed the food toward Nuke. "You don't eat enough," she declared. "Now you eat well."

Nuke fumbled to retrieve the containers she held. It took all four hands to take what she'd piled in her arms. "Ah," he began.

Now that she had her hands free, she could point accusingly at him. "You must come down to deli more often," she said. "Every night. Well?" That last was a barking cluck directed at her cousins. They jumped to step forward and press their offerings into Nuke's arms.

"We'll be expecting you, Nuke-zio," Derra ordered. "No excuses. No dark corners. You eat in our front window, you hear me?"

Nuke juggled the containers as the cousins kept handing over more. "Um," he said. "Ah…"

"Everyone will see that Nuke is part of our family," Derra said. "I tell them that they have to be polite to you. You'll see."

"Ah, I have too much food here to come to your place," Nuke decided. "This will take me months to go through."

"I've seen you eat," I interrupted. "This might last two days, tops."

He ruffled his mouth at me.

"Nuke-ZIO," I added with a smirk.

Apparently he hadn't caught it the first time. His eyes widened for a half-second. The left side of his mouth did another ruffle-thing I almost missed.

"Nuke-zio, you come!" one of the cousins said.

The others chimed in, "Yes, Nuke-zio. Nuke-zio!" as Derra put her fists on her hips.

Nuke's eyes went from one to the other and on to the next, maybe judging their sincerity. Finally his gaze settled on Derra. "Family discount," he said.

She let out a squawk and then clucked in consternation.

"Derra-ZIO," Nuke drawled. He watched her closely. I realized that he wanted to know just how sincere she was in this. Was he trying to guard his heart?

She clucked. And clucked. And paced the porch. Finally she stopped, eye to eye with Benny the skeleton. "Family discount," she announced to the crowd. Then she poked her finger at Benny. "But *he* not family. You not bring him!"

With a nod, she turned and marched away, the cousins scrambling to take their places behind her. One turned to wave goodbye.

So Nuke had his own crowds he couldn't escape. It seemed to me he took it with more than good humor, and our porch gained more rocking chairs.

I accepted the reward money and bought my side of the house. Otherwise, since it was subsidized housing, I would have been kicked out for making too much. Instead, I made a deal with Central and half-bought a place down on Level 25, where they needed more cheap housing, and donated my portion to the station, which bought the rest.

I installed soundproofing panels between my apartment and Nuke's.

Since I now owned the ground surrounding my place, Nuke and I consulted with Burdt and Shkarb to fashion a pretty flower garden out front. Nuke claimed a plot of our neighborhood's communal garden in which to grow vegetables. He liked to ask for advice from the people there. Apparently a mutie monster isn't quite so fearsome when he's patiently hoeing weeds.

Finally I got the go-ahead for visiting hours at the hospital. I couldn't decide what to wear: sex kitten (too soon)? Uniform (impersonal but impressive)? So I went with the jeans and blouses Max had brought me.

I tried to tone down my expectations. He'd have brand-new skin. It might be completely unsensitive or maybe over-sensitive to touch. Maybe they'd have him sealed away so as not to catch any germs. Could he see yet? Could he hear me? Had his brain been damaged so he might not even remember me?

They made me go through a chemical bath so I wound up going in in a disposable robe instead of the jeans. I could barely walk, my heart was beating so hard as the door to his room opened and I entered.

There he was in bed watching TV. He turned as the door opened.

His head was fairly bald, but it held a blondish down to it, all over the places that were supposed to have hair, including his chin. From what I could see where all the bandages allowed, his skin was extremely red but didn't look dried out. Just new. He was gaunt. But he was alert.

His eyes widened on me and the corners of his mouth lifted in what I could see must be a painful movement. "Tam." His voice rattled. He lifted his right hand toward me.

I ran to the bed.

One day Dibi wandered up from a lower level of the hospital. He wore a wrap-gown– hospital standard issue– and carried his newborn son. I oohed and ahhed once more (I'd seen him the night before when Derra was showing him off behind nursery glass to friends and cousins). Dibi held the babe down where Max could get a good look.

"Good… boy," he managed.

That made Dibi grin like a fool. Which was something he'd been doing often since giving birth.

Max's arm trembled as he tried to reach up. Finally he touched Dibi's arm. "Good… man," he said. "Good. P-proud."

It took four more months before I dragged some luggage into Max's custom Brane-rider and settled into the front passenger seat. He took the controls and I didn't throw up when we left normal space.

We were heading to Earth. Max told me that he'd signed me up for a subdivision of the Guardians before all hell had broken loose, and I had back pay coming. I planned to use it buying clothes. And books. And movies. Max assured me they could be transferred to Galactic media, which suited me fine.

I didn't ask for a map… yet. Right now I was content to be going back. Max had looked up what far-off members of my family might still be around, and none were that close to drop in on, tell them I was still alive.

But I was meeting Max's family.

Max was also transferring to some new section that would cooperate with Galactic law enforcement, while keeping Earth as far out of the picture as modern conditions could allow. For that he'd be stationed permanently some place he could set up as an off-planet headquarters.

I had an idea of a place that might be very well situated.

I didn't know quite how long we'd be on Earth, but I suspected that it would be a bit too long. Soon enough, I'd be eager to return home.

Illustration by Strick.

ABOUT THE AUTHOR

When you think of strong women and strange worlds, think Carol A. Strickland.

Although born in a small town in Illinois noted for its Nineteenth Century demonic possession cases, Carol claims that all those voices inside her head are a result of having stories to tell and books to write. Even so, her strange devotion to and study of Wonder Woman would seem to indicate an abby-normal brain.

A one-time comics letterhack and outspoken member of various comics message boards, Carol has found herself the basis for two comic book villains (at times her opinions have not been taken well by the books' creators) (both villains were soundly thrashed) (and both, for some perverse reason, were male) and had one superhero wear her costume design. (Light Lass!)

Carol has also become an award-winning painter. Along with her writing, she exercises this skill in her secondary hours (both of them) as she waits for the lottery to free her 9-to-5 time to more fulfilling pursuits.

Applesauce and Moonbeams

by Carol A. Strickland

No other site in this world could rival Sin City's seductions. Along the Strip, evening disguised itself as a false dawn. Ribbons of colorful hellfire directed the eye this way and that, inviting ordinary tourists to indulge in extraordinary debauchery. Gambling? That was the merest tip of Perdition's iceberg.

David Lumen couldn't hide his delight in watching the city's visitors hurry to their doom. Even in this new century, Vegas still advertised that what happened here stayed here. Whatever flashy personas tourists chose to adopt they could leave behind when they returned to their normal lives.

But David knew that was a lie.

He could pick out the ones who were ending their stay. With their inhibitions still loosed, they headed back to the ordered lives that society required. For many of them that reentry could turn into frustration or rebellion.

What a heaven-sent opportunity for healing breakthroughs!

"My card," he offered one man. "I can help." The man paused to read it and then nodded, offering his wrist and its info-band. David tapped it with his card, bowed his head in thanks, and moved on.

It was an unorthodox way of getting patients. David abhorred the unorthodox, but he had an unorthodox talent. In his life he allowed this one exception to conformity. The ends justified the means.

Dr. David Lumen, psychotherapist, his card read. *Licensed telepath. Helping you fit comfortably into your world.*

Out here in the crowd he could catch the ones who might otherwise slip off to wither away their lives, not knowing that another path was available to lead them to suitable contentment.

"I can help," he told another, and another info-band registered his name.

Far beyond the fakery and razzle-dazzle, the gibbous disk of Luna hovered halfway above the horizon. In a time before West Coast smog had spread in earnest to this desert city, perhaps its glow had matched that of Vegas. Now it hung muted behind a thick, sour curtain of dusty red. Still, David found it comforting to see the familiar face in the sky.

He squinted to make sure it was unchanged. Someone was building one of those Lunar complexes up there, up on the Man in the Moon's left cheek. Of course the law forbad marring the side of Luna that forever faced Earth. The might-have-been mole on the Man's face was neatly camouflaged, hidden even from a low-power telescope.

Luna was David's private joke. Humanity needed its heavens pristine and beautiful. To fulfill that purpose, Luna hid its true self like everyone else. Even the Man in the Moon had to conform to the Fashion Police's rules.

A crowd of young rowdies with alcohol breaths hustled by him on the way to an inhibition-free night. David smiled at them. They were still so malleable. In his heart of hearts he fancied himself a sculptor. He could form well-adjusted adults out of them.

Two Fashion Police officers in full, sequined Vegas display patrolled on foot just ahead. The drunks paused to tape the spectacular duo. Both women were top-make Oughts: willow-slender builds with faces (and other features) cosmetically enhanced. They looked alike enough to be twins. The air-filtered warmth of the walkways had the FeePs in minimal uniform– and Vegas "minimal" was very minimal indeed. They wore their identification pins as necklace pendants.

Having Oughts on fashion duty was a spark of city marketing genius. They contrasted so well to all the voluptuous Sixty-makes who were usually employed in the Strip's entertainment venues. When more tourists gathered to admire, one of the FeePs wrote up a drooling teenager for having an untreated zit. The kid didn't seem to mind his ticket. He even continued to grin stupidly at the pastied officer even as she turned away.

David couldn't blame him. The FeePs looked spectacular coming and going. Beauty might be only scalpel-deep, but they'd obviously benefited from some truly fine modern medicine.

One tipped her brimmed hat to David. "Evening, Dr. Lumen."

"Evening, Officer Dora," he returned, then nodded to the other. "Officer Elise. You're both on top of your form tonight. Officer Dora, the surgery looks great."

She pirouetted for him and he tried not to ogle. After all, he was a professional. He had an image to maintain, despite what his instincts told him to do.

"Doesn't it? I'm a perfect Ought now. Applied for my perfection pin this morning. Thanks for the recommendation, Doc."

"Dr. Haggerty's method of shaving bones is legendary. Glad I could help. But that wouldn't have gotten you perfection if you hadn't–"

Dora grinned at him. "Focused on my goals," she said, parroting her mantra. "Diet, exercise and resolve."

"That's the ticket."

Dora wiggled her now-svelte butt at him. "I not only fit into my world, but into size double-zero über-fashion. I'm recommending you to all my friends."

David laughed. "Then I'll have to see about giving you a cut of my business, won't I?" He shook his head at the FeePs. "You two should be on Vegas's advertising. Magnificent!"

They beamed at the compliment and continued on their way, scanning the crowds to maintain beauty and conformity.

David had nothing to fear from their judgment. He might be an ordinary mid-make Thirty, neither burly nor skinny, but he was a conscientious one. He kept his outrageous red hair muted under brown dye and owned this season's complete line of Jakob Gallindor superior-grade suits. Not the perfection-grade, of course. He purposefully positioned himself only in the upper-eightieth percentile of the population when it came to fashion.

Sure, he could have hit mid- or even upper nineties if he'd wanted. He could afford the surgeries to up his make as well, but being more impressive might intimidate his patients. He'd splurged on a top-line chin implant when he was sixteen. Before that he'd had only a trainer chin to disguise his weak real one. A few nips and tucks beside that were all he had needed to produce a pleasant but average appearance for his inborn body type: a mid-make.

David passed a woman whose shoulders hunched ever so slightly, which caused her chest to concave. The posture unflatteringly exaggerated her pear-shaped Eighty body make. She never looked up to meet another human being in the face. Body language told him she was protecting her core being, and her thoughts skittered scared in typical victim mode. David didn't search deeper; people deserved their privacy. Instead he pressed a hard copy of his business card into her hand and then continued on his way.

Her thoughts broadcast her rebellion at the thought of therapy. Of course she'd react that way. Many did at first. But as David continued his brisk walk toward his office building, he felt confident that she'd be calling for an appointment within the next few days. Excellent!

The warm flush of success snapped cold as that *something* brushed him again. In the warm Vegas night it felt as if someone swept an arctic fan across him, just enough to bring every hair on his skin to shocked awareness. Then it was gone.

Twice this week he'd felt that icy darkness, a bitter taste in his mind. It was so quick he would normally have dismissed it as a wild thought from the crowd, but this third time was too often to be random.

Was this someone new to the neighborhood? Las Vegas still thrived on thrill-seeking tourists, but its permanent population grew faster than most cities in North America. The city drew all types. Baser personalities in particular seemed to target the area as they responded to the historic Vegas reputation.

He threw up a simple thought-deflection shield to protect himself from another intrusion. If it happened again, he'd try to pinpoint it so he could report the culprit. Rogue telepaths could be dangerous.

When David arrived at his office building he waited patiently for one for the public vanity stations in the lobby. Mustn't run the chance of a client seeing him in slight disarray from the street. They must always know that David was in control of his world.

Everyone should fit into their role in society as well as he. How glad he was to have the skills and abilities to accomplish what he loved most: helping people. If he swaggered as he walked because of his accomplishments, it was only just enough to let people see his self-confidence so they might emulate it.

The work he did upstairs literally saved lives. He taught his clients how to live with society's rules. As the cosmetic surgeons shaped them physically, he shaped them psychically, blunting their square pegs to fit into the round holes that the world demanded of them.

Unyielding egos clashing with conformity pressures were his specialty. David reached the mirror and adjusted his clothing. His tie was the tiniest bit wider than fashion norm this month, a hint to his clients that they could still push the envelope of life's constrictions and not feel claustrophobic. Then again, that tie was ever so slightly longer than normal too. That was to remind his clients about who was in charge.

He adjusted with planned irony two small, color-coordinated, triangular snake bites to bring out the barest beginnings of friendly smile creases at the edges of his brown eyes. As usual, they stung for a half-second as they released a dose of tox over the newly-covered skin before that skin went pleasantly numb. They cemented his image as an average, friendly joe.

When he was alone at home he placed the snake bites correctly so they'd do their job and reduce the signs of aging. Out here in the world, though, he was ever conscious of the image he made. Appearance was everything.

Now he was ready to smooth some more of the world's rough edges and face the day... or night, as it were, as his office hours were Vegas ones. A final glance at the moon outside the lobby windows: *Don't ever change, Old Man*, and he went upstairs.

David's "morning" passed quickly as he dealt by direct video with clients who were close to completing their therapy. The satisfaction of a job well done returned to him. Instead of futilely straining at society's bindings, he'd shown them how they could reshape themselves, their goals and the things they thought important, to be what others needed them to be.

Trenton Thomas was a shining example. He was more than halfway through his make, a Seventies as compared to David's mid-Thirty, which meant he had the lean, angular features over a solid body that should signify the ideal aggressive executive. When he'd first come to David– the first cycle of sessions were conducted in person as much as possible– he'd kept twisting in his seat, and he'd had a habit of rapping his fingertips against any surface he could reach. He would screw his mouth around as if he'd just sucked on a lemon when he didn't think he was giving the answer that David wanted to hear. He did that a lot.

Now he sat up straight. His arms lay loose on his chair, and he even crossed his legs occasionally, as David had taught him, to include the person to whom he was speaking into a more direct connection.

His expression was calm, though David thought there was a blank look to his features as well as his mind. Well, that was a final step to work on at the next appointment. David made a note to that effect after Trenton signed off. Trenton had managed to snag a prime job at NaniTech in northern Bostington. It wouldn't be long before the crisply-attired Seventy rose in their ranks.

If Trenton was a success story, Ragnar was another matter entirely.

"Good morning, Ragnar," David greeted the last patient before midnight "lunch," Ragnar Sveinsson. Because he was just beginning therapy, Ragnar came in person. He could afford the weekly trips from Reykjavik, and arranged his business so that he could accomplish other things while in the Vegas/San-San area.

It was a mark of distinction to David to have such a famous name on his list of clientele, even if the man were the *capo* of *l'Ögre*, the notorious international crime syndicate. David tried to repeat that accolade to himself every time he met with Ragnar, but the truth of the matter was that Ragnar bothered him.

Ragnar had been coming to him for a month now. He was a referral, and again David tried to keep in mind that this was a reflection on his own good name. Two very respected European therapists had thought enough of his work to send Ragnar to him.

Ragnar greeted David with a sullen nod. David returned it with a professional smile. Ragnar liked a businesslike demeanor. He required strict obedience in all his underlings, which his previous therapist hadn't been able to provide.

Here was another Seventy, but Ragnar placed at the top of the make. Perhaps his surgeons had gone too far. Perhaps Ragnar had planned to create the unnerving effect. The same facial angles that had given Trenton executive appeal seemed feral and wolfish on this man.

His large hands clenched on his chair arms. As he crossed his legs, one impeccably-shined shoe bobbed up and down at a heartbeat pace. Obviously he had no time to be sitting idle for so long. His keen eyes switched this way and that, taking in everything– or keeping watch out for danger that could come from any direction.

Two hulking Ninety-make bodyguards waited in the lobby.

David knew precisely how far he could push Ragnar. He'd studied the man and his infamous career carefully. He'd consulted with Ragnar's three former therapists.

That, and David considered himself a good telepath. Normally he allowed mental impressions to come to him without seeking them out, but Ragnar kept his mind clenched closed. At first David had had to delve into Ragnar's mind lightly to lead the therapy and ease Ragnar's barriers.

But those barriers were thick. Ragnar had unconsciously kept them strong for years, over a century if the impressions David got were correct. *L'Ögre*'s history went back almost that far. It was likely that Ragnar started with the bloody business as it was born.

In David's opinion Ragnar was one of those people– too many in the world– who had no conscience. He truly had no sense of right or wrong, but was only interested in what he could get away with. He distrusted the entire world and every living soul within it. David wondered just how much Ragnar distrusted himself.

David settled deeper in his chair and hoped that Ragnar hadn't noticed that he'd angled his "Comfort in Conformity" motto plaque so that his client could see it more easily from his favorite position on the couch.

Ragnar was going to be a tough nut to crack. Already David dreaded the job ahead, and yet they had barely begun these sessions. Usually the beginnings of molding a new, acceptable personality excited David. This time he wasn't sure he could accomplish the task.

Ragnar didn't want to change. He wasn't under any kind of pressure from the law (a situation David didn't want to question closely), life was comfortable, and Ragnar saw no reason not to continue doing what he'd always done. It was only Ragnar's wife of three years who had hounded him into therapy. She was a full-make Sixty and Ragnar worshipped her. Otherwise, Ragnar wasn't ready to make the commitment.

They began as usual by discussing Ragnar's week and the situations that had set him over the edge of rage. There was always something. Ragnar knew he had a problem with anger management. That plus guns, plus the ability to hire other unscrupulous men with guns, made for the occasional body popping up here and there.

David had to consciously unclench his jaw at the revelations. He knew that even with this much, Ragnar was holding back. He reminded Ragnar of the sanctity of patient-therapist conversations. After pausing to acknowledge that, Ragnar tried to excuse his anger over a cousin who'd botched bribing a pair of customs inspectors.

A sudden picture came very clear in Ragnar's mind, his barriers cracking enough to let David see. Usually the most David sensed at such a basic level was emotions, perhaps a quick visual impression, but this time he got full color and complete sensory surround-sound. The blood was real enough to smell.

"Your punishment was excessive," he commented in the flattest, most unjudgmental voice he could summon. "Your anger went off the scale. Can you tell me why?"

Ragnar talked his way around it. How typical of him to avoid responsibility. The cousin was a good-for-nothing, a pain to have around. Another pocket eating up the organization's money without good result. It was best that he not take up space in this world.

"Come on, Ragnar," David urged. "Trust me."

The man squirmed in his seat. Another man might have sweated profusely in his position; his face was red enough. Instead he sat there smelling faintly of MaxCompoz body bar and not a sweat gland rose to the occasion.

"He was scum," Ragnar finally confessed. "He said some very nasty things about my late father." He clasped his hands tightly in his lap. First he stared at them, and then glanced quickly about the room, as if some invisible demon might be recording. "And my mother." The hands became fists. He began to slam them against his thighs. "Nobody says anything about my mother! I'll kill 'em! Kill 'em!"

David had triggered an undetectable dose of tranqui-spray when he sensed Ragnar about to erupt. By the time he got to his third "Kill 'em!" Ragnar was winding down, sinking back into the couch.

"Insulting parents is a terrible thing," David purred. "It hits us all hard, but you especially. You had such a difficult childhood."

"My mother was a saint," Ragnar whispered, a wild glaze on his eyes even as his pupils dilated.

"People know they can get you angry by disparaging your mother," David said. "It's predictable. Your reason stops and raw emotion takes over. They can slip things by you then. They think this gives them power over you."

"Power? Over me." Ragnar considered it. He shook his head almost as if trying to throw off the trank. "No one has power over me."

"Exactly. Let's see if we can lessen the negative emotional grip your childhood has on you," David suggested. He swiveled to check his neuro-hypnotics. "I'd like to try acupuncture along with directed subliminals. I think you'll find the rest of this session a relaxing one."

"Can you feel it, David?" Ragnar asked. "You're a teep. Can you feel what I'm feeling? See what I've seen?"

David looked up from his control board with its muted displays. "Sometimes I can," he said. "It's part of my job to pinpoint sessions by focusing your thoughts precisely where you'll get the most benefit."

"Do your patients' problems ever bother you?" Ragnar asked. "Since you get–" He tapped on the side of his skull.

David smiled at the familiar question. "Of course they do," he said. "Some of my patients are quite troubled. But telepathy is an invaluable tool in my work. I went through a lot of training to learn to use– as well as not to misuse– it."

Ragnar grunted.

"The privacy of the mind is a sacred thing," David said with a firmness he rarely used. For some reason Ragnar's comfort level had plummeted. Suspicion rose to take its place. "So are doctor/patient confidences," he repeated.

"Sometimes I think I tell you too much."

"My notes are triple-secured behind logarithmic password encoding," David reassured him. "Even if the police should seize my records, there's no way that they could ever access these private conversations."

Another grunt.

"I'm going to adjust your meds, Ragnar," David said as he crosschecked his patient's records. "The anxiocedin might be interacting with your omega-3 supplements." A paper fed out of the slot in David's desk. He glanced at it before handing it to Ragnar, who frowned as he read it.

"This will still keep me in clear mind?"

"Of course. I don't believe in fuzzing up people's heads," David said. "You will still be able to think quite clearly. That's what these sessions are all about, to help you recognize when and why you make poor decisions, and to give yourself the tools to make good ones."

The left side of Ragnar's mouth turned up. "And a little telepathic push always helps."

David let him see his recoil. "That hurt. I've never used telepathy to manipulate anyone. It's unethical. And just to set your mind at ease, I'd have no idea how to begin to do it."

Ragnar nodded. "Good," he said, and then more definitely, "Good."

David rose to get his equipment. "Glad you agree. Let me explain the acupuncture procedure as I set up."

David wasn't the kind of man to rely solely on flexochairs for good muscle tone. After midnight lunch he liked to power-walk the air-filtered streets of Vegas, taking in the dazzle that still made downtown a world landmark. Fresh air– well, as fresh as air ever got these days– he sucked it in and exhaled his troubles. No thoughts about work now. He tried to be one with the world and regain his control upon it at the same time as his power-walk controlled his body.

Sometimes when he got tired outside thoughts scratched at the boundaries of his mind. It had been a problem in his youth as his telepathic ability had sharpened, but now he could keep the thoughts at bay as long as he allowed himself to rest after tough telepathic sessions.

Tonight he couldn't retrieve a calm meditative state. He pushed away his problems once more, but some nagging depression remained.

For a few moments it disappeared as he admired another set of Fashion Police patrolling the Strip, these two coed. Impeccable. Sexy. Stylish. Vegas had the best FeePs in the world. It was comforting to see people fitting into their niche and enjoying it.

Just as he was turning back to his meditation, the thought came: *Somebody's watching you.*

Everyone had a little voice, sometimes a whole slew of voices, in their heads. David's voices usually gave him good advice, but they rarely interrupted his meditations.

The realization shocked him out of his after-lunch haze. Who would be watching him? Not the Fashion Police; he was perfectly within bounds. But there– he could feel it now. That now-familiar icy darkness was nearby, for it had a Vegas feel to it. Strobing lights seemed to echo around it, just like the ones that surrounded him.

Maybe Ragnar's paranoia was rubbing off?

No, there was a focus to this that pulled back as soon as David reached for it. A dark mind with violence rippling behind it.

A laughing couple passed him and made him realize he had frozen on the sidewalk. What to do? His mind seemed paralyzed as well, his control over the world shattered.

He fought himself into rationality. He couldn't call the police. What would he tell them? He couldn't pinpoint this when it deliberately hid. Maybe this was just a telepathic punk out for a joy ride.

Maybe it was something more.

He made sure he kept to the crowded sections of the Strip as he strode the midnight bustle. He knew where all the civil police call-points were, where the officers usually posted themselves, and he adjusted his return route from post to post.

Every time he searched, he could sense it. It fell back before his seeking mind, but still it focused on not just any mind, but him– Dr. David Lumen.

This wasn't right. Life wasn't supposed to be interrupted by the unexpected. David returned to his office, determined to reestablish his rhythm, but he merely half-listened to his first after-midnight patient. He would have apologized, but the presence– or was it merely the memory of that presence?– obsessed him.

The situation finally forced him to admit that tonight he was doing his patients no good. He canceled the rest of his appointments. He gave his auto-receptionist a hazy apology to transmit with a request to reschedule, and then on a whim used a public, anonymous phone in the lobby to call a taxi.

The familiarity of his condo should have reassured him, but he paced the spacious apartment. A wall of windows overlooked downtown and its never-ending festival. Somewhere out there someone was tracking him.

It had to come from Ragnar Sveinsson. Only he was still in the entry-level process of a major social rehab. Only he would have the motivation to send someone out to get David.

David mulled their session. Then he checked his previous notes. Yes, Ragnar had voiced consistent concern over David's telepathy. David now possessed knowledge about ghastly crimes that Ragnar had never admitted out loud. But David would never betray the doctor-patient confidence.

Didn't Ragnar realize that?

In the east, the sky lightened. Still David paced. How many murders could he himself trace to Ragnar? How many could he guess at? And how many more would he never know about, murders ordered through layers of *l'Ögre*'s organization and never directly touched by the *capo* himself?

He replayed memories of that icy mental touch. How much of it had he exaggerated through his own fear? Not much. It was real. The mind behind it was a cruel one, clearly capable of murder or worse.

Who would hire a rogue telepath? David kept coming up with one answer. That naturally led to the big question:

Had Ragnar ordered David's murder because of what he knew?

Though such betrayal went against all codes of ethics, David finally admitted to himself that Ragnar would not trust him. Ragnar was riddled with trust issues that stemmed from his dysfunctional childhood.

And Ragnar had vast international criminal resources at his command: ordinary citizens kept on the payroll just in case. Politicians. Police. Hit men. Rogue telepaths.

With a start, David realized that he'd begun gathering clothing in a pile on his bed. He stared at it and then retrieved his suitcase from the closet. No, make it a gym duffel. Mustn't look like he was doing anything odd. He could arrange– somehow– for his possessions to follow him later.

Carefully he arranged his clothing into the rounded pack so as to avoid wrinkling. Only minimal moisturizers, snake bites and toiletries made the cut. His passport card was the single thing he took from his small safe. The hard copy of his will he left inside.

As a final step, he checked his financial passcodes. Good, they hadn't been tampered with. Yet. He triple-sealed them with new passwords, and on a whim added a retinal scan requirement with EEG. Letting out a vindictive chuckle as a thought came to him, he then sent a request to Identity Theft Central, indicating that he had suspicions that someone was tapping into his accounts, and could they keep an eye on them for–

How long? How long would he run from this? He needed to check into police protection on an international scale. He set his jaw, considered a worst scenario, and gave it a three-month window. If the situation turned out not to be what he suspected, or if Ragnar called off his telepathic dog, he could always rescind the request.

Then he placed an "In case of my untimely death" code over his notes, to be routed to authorities if and when. It was a bit unethical, but if Ragnar were the one to so grievously disregard the doctor-patient relationship, then by God he'd pay for it.

After David died.

David snatched up his bag, checked that his hair was presentable and his tie straight, and then slipped out of his apartment.

You can pick the format and store you want to buy from here:
http://www.carolastrickland.com/fiction/applesauce.html

Sign up for my newsletter and get a free book!
www.CarolAStrickland.com

An author's bread and butter (maybe with a little jam in there) is… are… whatever… Anyway, PLEASE LEAVE AN HONEST REVIEW somewhere: Amazon or Goodreads or with your second cousin twice removed. It can be just one sentence. Thanks!

Carol Strick

Other books by Carol A. Strickland

Touch of Danger– vol. 1 of the Three Worlds Saga

Lost in the Stars– vol. 2 of the Three Worlds Saga

Stalemate– vol. 3 of the Three Worlds Saga

Worlds Apart– vol. 4 of the Three Worlds Saga

Applesauce and Moonbeams– wacky soft sci fi

Burgundy and Lies– sweet historical romance

www.ingramcontent.com/pod-product-compliance
Lightning Source LLC
Chambersburg PA
CBHW060758210726
48292CB00013B/700